TREACHEROUS TRAPS

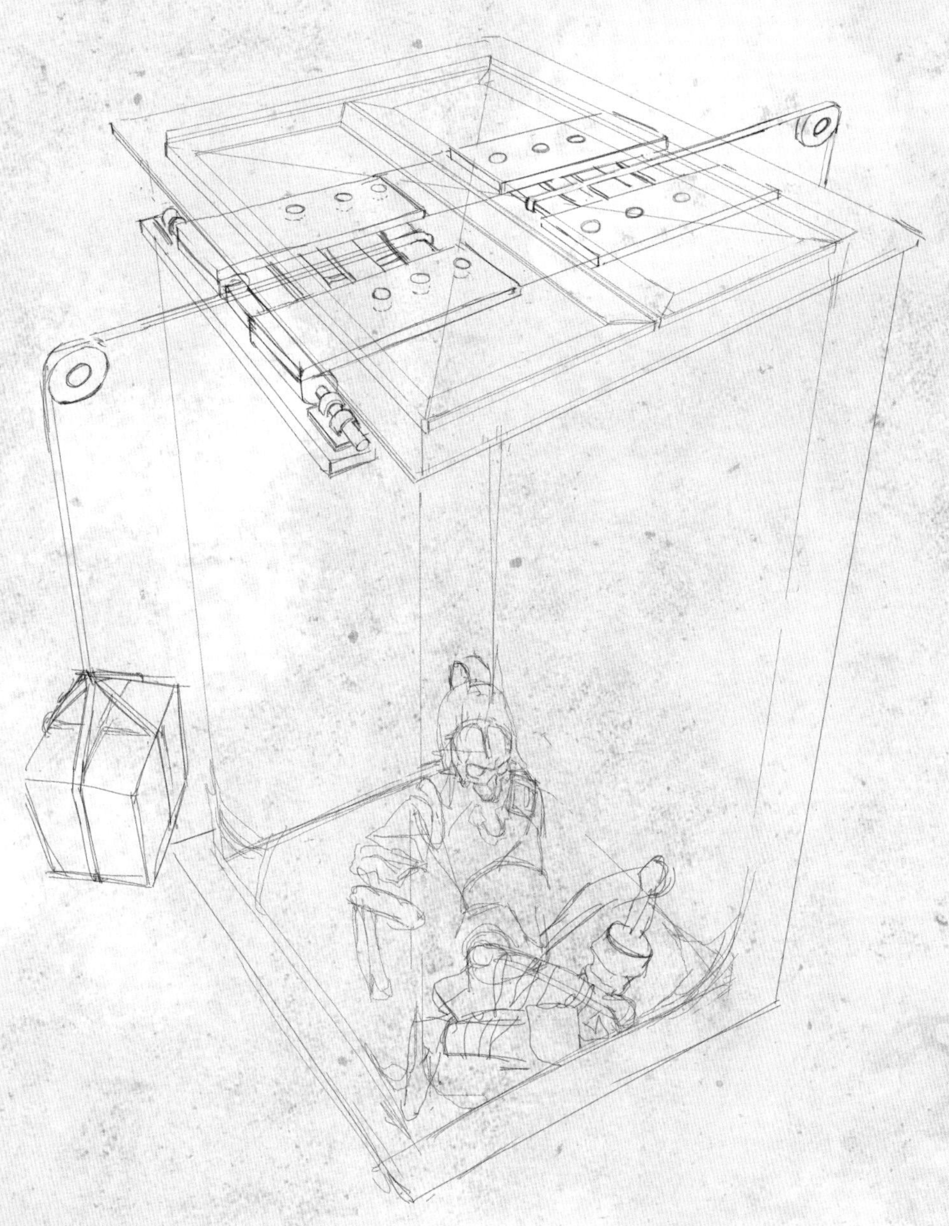

FOREWORD

A common misconception regarding traps is that their purpose is solely to inflict damage on characters. This is a very limited view. A trap that is blundered into, goes off, injures a few characters, and then is forgotten can be a wasted opportunity. The best traps are the ones that characters find and then spend time and brainpower trying to overcome in interesting ways, asking questions like: Can it be disabled? If not, can it be circumvented? Can its effect be minimized?

One of our primary goals as storytellers is engagement, and traps can be an *excellent* tool for this! An adventuring party is made up of players who all have fun in different ways. As diverse as our players can be, so too are their characters, with different skills, proficiencies, and areas of expertise. Traps, when used well, can add to everyone's experience. A trap can allow a player to flex their roleplaying muscles or it can highlight a meticulously optimized character build. This book has hundreds of examples of ways to challenge players. When using them, consider the things your players enjoy, and what their characters can do, and use obstacles that play to these things. Be conscious of where they get invested, when they are having fun, and how they react. Give everyone opportunities to contribute and to overcome the challenges laid before them. This creates a satisfying experience for everyone.

This book is the culmination of thousands of hours of combined game-mastering experience and the wisdom that those contributors have imparted to us. The traps and puzzles found herein are designed to fit many situations, but you will certainly find some you enjoy more than others. Some may be perfect for your campaigns, while some will almost certainly not be. Investigate, delve, and seek out those that are just the right fit for you. It is also our hope that as you read, you will be inspired to create your own. Use this book as a guide and as a companion on the hazard-strewn path that is the craft of trap-and-puzzle-making.

It is with those words that we send you forth into the cobwebbed corridors, neglected crypts, and warrens of the dark unknown to find many hours of fun, tension, and excitement.

Warmest Regards and Happy Gaming,

The Writers

LEGAL

CREDITS

Authors: Andrew Geertsen, Chris Haskins, JVC Parry, Megan Roy
Lead Designer: Chris Haskins
Proofing and Editing: James Vacca
Art Director: Ralph Stickley
Layout and Typesetting: Chris van der Linden, Ralph Stickley
Illustrators: Shen Fei, Joel Holtzman, Konrad Krogull, Evgeny Maloshenkov
Additional Contributors: Spike Murphy-Rose, Steve Winter
Project Management: Chris Haskins, Greg Peterson
Brand and Marketing: Chris Haskins, Megan Roy

Table of Contents

Introduction

Welcome to Treacherous Traps! If you're a GM (Game Master) looking to spice up your games with some unique, intriguing, and downright diabolical obstacles, you're in the right place.

This book is a resource meant to aid you when creating traps, puzzles, riddles, and other exciting challenges for your players. Follow our charts, guidelines and tips to create your own, or drop any of our hundreds of pre-made traps and puzzles into your game at a moment's notice.

How to Use This Book

Treacherous Traps is intended to be something you consult regularly, as opposed to something you read "cover-to-cover" (though you certainly could). It's very unlikely that you will need all the information in this book at once. Read this chapter first. Then, to help you maximize your time and efforts when accomplishing your goals, you can cherry-pick through the book's sections as needed. Here is a breakdown of what you can expect in each chapter:

- **Chapter 1: Introduction and How to Use Traps.** This chapter breaks down the general philosophy of how to think about traps and other related subject matter. Detailed breakdowns of the topics in this chapter are found elsewhere in the book.
- **Chapter 2-6: Simple Traps.** These chapters are filled with pre-made simple traps. These are ready to be dropped into your game as they are, or with very little adaptation. Each chapter has 50 traps split into 5 levels of lethality (setback, moderate, dangerous, perilous, deadly), organized by level range (1-4, 5-8, 9-12, 13-16, 17-20).
- **Chapter 7: Complex Traps.** This chapter has 25 traps designed to be more elaborate than the simple traps. They feature multiple elements that trigger in stages and present a range of obstacles for character to overcome. There are 5 complex traps per level range (1-4, 5-8, 9-12, 13-16, 17-20), one for each level of lethality (setback, moderate, dangerous, perilous, deadly).
- **Chapter 8: Designing Traps.** This is the perfect place to start when making your own traps. In it there are general guidelines and best practices for trap design, tables that cover different variable elements of a trap, and suggested experience rewards if you choose to award experience for overcoming traps.
- **Chapter 9: Random Trap Generator.** This chapter contains a table to help you create a simple randomized trap that you can adjust and implement to fit your needs. Below the random table are sections that cover each of the 50 triggers and 50 effects in detail.
- **Chapter 10: Trap-Centric Dungeons.** This chapter contains some general thoughts about designing dungeons focused on or built primarily around traps, as well as a few examples of how to accommodate traps of different types within certain spaces or corridors.
- **Chapter 11: Perplexing Puzzles.** This chapter contains brief guidelines on implementing puzzles and their solutions into your game. There are also 30 pre-made puzzles you can use in a variety of situations and settings. Almost all include tweaks and suggestions to alter their difficulty or customize them for your campaign.
- **Chapter 12: Subtle Secrets.** This brief chapter contains a selection of story, quest, and environmental secrets that can be used in your campaign.
- **Chapter 13: Ridiculous Riddles.** This brief chapter contains general guidelines regarding the creation of riddles, as well as some example riddles.
- **Chapter 14: Trapsmith Legends.** This brief chapter introduces a new player background, the Trapsmith, who begins their journey with a new kind of tool: trapsmith tools. The chapter also includes 3 NPCs with the Trapsmith background who specialize in creating and disarming traps. These Trapsmith Legends can be hired to accompany characters on their journey and come complete with stats for easy reference.

How To Use Traps

In either case, before you charge over and begin perusing the vast selection of ways in which you can hamper, harangue, and otherwise haze the poor characters about to encounter them, it is a good idea to understand the very basics of how and why traps work as they do.

Trap Entries

The traps in the following chapters will always contain the following elements:

- The type of trap (mechanical, magic, or hybrid)
- The trap's level range, lethality, and any purpose keywords.
- A description of the trap, providing its general layout and position.
- ***Trigger (Random Table Entry)***. This is what triggers the trap. We've also noted what entry from Chapter 9 was used to make this trap, to give you an idea of how to use the triggers from that chapter.
- ***Effect (Random Table Entry)***. This is what happens when the trigger conditions are met. Again, there's a reference to the table in Chapter 9. Most of the time, trap effects require a saving throw or make an attack roll and have instantaneous results. But if there are lingering effects that characters can deal with, information about that is listed here.
- ***Countermeasures (Trait).*** Options for what characters can do to find, notice, or disarm the trap are provided in this section. If the trap has any traits (like **difficult** or **sensitive**) those are noted here.

Trap Types

In the following chapters, you will find traps in 3 categories:

- **Mechanical.** These are traps where the trigger and effect are both mundane.
- **Magic.** These are traps where the trigger and effect are both magic, and are usually spell traps.
- **Hybrid.** These are traps where the either the trigger is magic and the effect is mundane, or vice versa.

Spell Traps

Many of the magic and hybrid traps described in this book could be a *glyph of warding (spell trap)* or the *symbol* spell. These spells each have their own specific rules for detection and disarming. A *glyph of warding* or *symbol* can only be found with an Intelligence (Investigation) check, using the caster's spell save DC, and can only be disabled with *dispel magic*. You can use the DC determined by the trap's lethality, or if you know that an NPC wizard cast the spell you can use their spell save DC.

As an optional rule you can allow a character to use a successful Intelligence (Arcana) check to disable a *glyph of warding* or *symbol* as well as *dispel magic*. When we present these kinds of traps throughout this book, we assume that this optional rule is in effect.

Whether or not creatures can use Investigation passively is up to you; if you decide to allow for passive Investigation to discover a *glyph of warding* that can make them less threatening. However, if a glyph can only be found with an active check, you might consider allowing for a Wisdom (Perception) check or leaving some clues in the trapped area to let the characters know that something might be hidden.

Hybrid Traps

These kinds of traps combine mundane triggers and magic effects, or magic triggers and mundane effects, and this can lead to some interesting combinations. Hybrid traps can usually be detected with Wisdom (Perception) or Intelligence (Arcana), and they can also be found with *detect magic*.

When a mundane trigger activates a magic effect, the trapped area or object is enchanted with a spell effect but just waiting for input from the trigger to complete the arcane circuit. When activated, the trap targets the creature that triggered it with the effect. If the trap affects an area, the area is centered on that creature. If the trap summons hostile creatures or creates harmful objects, they appear as close as possible to the triggering and attack it. If the effect requires concentration, it lasts until the end of its full duration.

When viewed with *detect magic*, this kind of hybrid traps usually have an aura that reflects the school of magic for the effect. A trap that creates a blast of fire usually shows up with an evocation aura when looked at with *detect magic*.

If a magic trigger activates a mechanical effect, the trap usually has some sort of rune or sigil that acts as a detector. When activated, the rune creates a Tiny, invisible, mindless, shapeless force that only lasts long enough to interact with the mechanical elements of the trap, setting off the mundane effect. If you'd like, you can add the following spell to your game to provide a way for spellcasters (usually sorcerers and wizards, or clerics of deities devoted to protection) to make these sorts of detectors.

Rune of Detecting

2nd-level abjuration (ritual)

Casting Time: 1 hour

Range: Touch

Components: V, S, M (incense and powdered precious metals worth at least 50 gp, which the spell consumes)

Duration: Until dispelled or triggered

When you cast this spell, you inscribe a rune upon a surface (such as a table or a section of floor or wall), or on an object. If you choose a surface, the rune can cover an area of the surface no larger than 10 feet in diameter. If you choose an object, that object must remain in its place; if the object is moved more than 10 feet from where you cast this spell, the rune burns away, and the spell ends without being triggered.

You can hide the rune in a larger design, but the rune is visible and can be spotted with a successful Wisdom (Perception) check. With a successful Intelligence (Arcana) check, a creature that spots the rune can erase a portion of it, ending the spell without triggering it. The DC for both these checks is your spell save DC.

You decide what triggers the rune when you cast the spell. For rune inscribed on a surface, the most typical triggers include touching or standing on the rune , removing another object covering the rune, approaching within a certain distance of the rune, or manipulating the object on which the runeis inscribed. For glyphs inscribed on an object, the most common triggers include approaching within a certain distance of the object, or seeing or reading the rune.

You can further refine the trigger so the rune activates only under certain circumstances or according to physical characteristics (such as height or weight), creature kind (for example, the ward could be set to affect aberrations or drow), or alignment. You can also set conditions for creatures that don't trigger the rune, such as those who say a certain password.

When the rune is triggered, it creates a Tiny, invisible, mindless, shapeless force that only lasts long enough to interact with a nearby mechanical element, such as the workings of a trap, a lever, or a button. The mechanical element must be within 10 feet of the rune. Once the force interacts in this way, the spell ends and the rune fades away.

Trap Level & Lethality

The pre-made traps in this book are arranged by level and lethality. These are used together to determine things such as the variables of the trap, such as appropriate damage output, spell level, duration of effects, and (if needed) appropriate experience reward.

Level. A trap's level is expressed as one of five ranges: 1-4, 5-8, 9-12, 13-16, and 17-20. An appropriate trap will be in the range that includes the average level of your characters.

Lethality. Variable statistics of a given trap, such as attack bonus, the DC for a saving throw to resist its effects or an ability check to overcome it, and the damage it deals all depend on the trap's lethality. A trap intended to be a **setback** is unlikely to seriously harm characters of the indicated levels, but a **moderate** trap likely will. A **dangerous** trap is likely to seriously injure (and potentially kill) characters of the indicated levels and a **perilous** trap almost definitely will. A **deadly** trap is likely to kill characters of the indicated levels.

Trap Purpose

A trap's purpose keyword describes its primary usage in the area, including the reasoning behind its placement and the overall goal of the trap. Some traps may do more than one of the following, but their primary purpose is reflected in the keyword.

- **Alert.** These traps notify someone or something to the presence intruders. The alert need not only in the form of a sound.
- **Block.** These traps impede creatures from proceeding in a particular direction. The trap could stand in the way of multiple avenues, not only one. It could also prevent retreat.
- **Harm.** Traps intended to cause damage or possibly kill creatures have this keyword.
- **Hinder.** These kinds of traps disable or hamper creatures, damaging their senses or imposing conditions.
- **Subdue.** A trap that captures creatures alive, either by containing them physically or with magic, has this keyword.

Trigger and Effect

A trap is easily thought of as an "if/then" statement: "If this happens, then that happens." This means that the most basic components of a trap are its trigger and its effect. Every trap has at least one of each.

Triggers come in all shapes and sizes. They can be as basic as a tripwire strung across a path, but they can be more complex, such as a weight-sensitive floor which only activates when a certain amount of weight, or more, is placed on it. Triggers come in three varieties:

- **Mundane.** The trigger has some sort of mechanical apparatus or it relies on things like gravity and momentum.
- **Ambiguous.** The trigger could be created using mundane or magical means and functions respectively (i.e., a "wrong key" trap could detect a wrong key using internal pins and mechanisms, or simply with an arcane enchantment).
- **Magic.** The trigger functions purely by magical means.

No matter the type, all triggers share a common trait: if their requirements are met, they activate.

Effects come in the same three varieties that triggers do:

- **Mundane.** The effect functions via mechanical means, or relies on things such as gravity or momentum. No part of the effect is magical (fire comes from a natural source, real rocks fall down, etc).
- **Ambiguous.** The effect could be created using mundane or magical means and functions respectively (i.e., poison gas could start filling the room, but the gas could be created with either chemicals or magic).
- **Magic.** The effect is created purely with magic.

No matter the type, all effects share a common trait, if their trigger is activated, the effect occurs.

Countermeasures

No one likes being hit with something they had no chance to see coming. When it comes to traps, it is important to always know what the characters can do to detect elements of the trap. Each trap entry will provide options like:

- Ability checks to notice elements of the trap.
- If necessary, ability checks to understand how the trap works and how to disable it.
- Different ways in which the creatures involved can slow, stop, or otherwise interfere with the trigger or effect.

Not all trap triggers can be detected in the same ways, and some can be more difficult to detect than others. A trigger housed within the doorjamb of a closed door is very difficult to find, but a pressure plate might be much easier to spot.

Detecting Triggers

The following are some concepts to consider when it comes to how characters detect traps in your game.

Alternative Skill Usage. There may be times when using a skill with an unorthodox ability may be appropriate, depending on the task. Consider the situation and your players' levels of creativity to determine whether doing something like this would be appropriate. Some tables also allow for something called the "Rule of Cool"; the the GM will allow something that the system typically does not, simply because it makes the game more fun or adds to the situation in a way that makes for a better experience.

Immersion. Have players describe what senses their characters are using to detect traps, instead of simply listing the skills they have on their character sheet. This can help engage the players and paint a more vivid picture of the scene in their mind's eye. Try to be aware of each creature's passive Perception. If a character or creature has a passive Perception high enough to notice certain elements of the trap, be sure to let them know without forcing them to roll. More information about this is in Chapter 9.

Timing. Think about how much time is passing as the characters find and deal with traps. Even though it may only take a few minutes of real-world time, it may have been hours or even days in game time (or vice versa).

Too Many Rolls. Don't just let every player roll dice until someone detects and/or disarms the trap. Have the players describe, with some specifics, how they are attempting to detect or disarm the trap. This can slow things down just enough to add a bit of tension and get the players thinking, instead of just rolling until they win. Also consider that it rarely makes sense for every character to take turns attempting to disarm a trap. This is especially true if someone particularly suited to the task has already failed. Instead, characters can use things like the Help action, class features like Bardic Inspiration, or spells like *guidance*. This will allow most everyone to participate, even if there is a specialist.

Trap Clues. If you're designing or including traps that relate to the overall story of your campaign, such as a ritual or important location within the dungeon, make sure to leave clues sprinkled throughout the rest of your adventure. If the players get their characters to this important spot and have no idea how to prevent a deadly trap, then it's not going to be very fun springing it on them unexpectedly. However, if they arrive armed with at least *some* information about the trap (how to detect it, or at least how to survive it) the experience will be far more memorable for all involved. You can also throw out subtle clues to trap triggers or effects, such as an odd smell, things out of place, or marks on the walls. How much information you put in your clue will impact what your players immediately decide to do.

Trap Lore. In some cases a trap's trigger or effect may be extremely difficult to detect. It may be appropriate to use an Intelligence (History, Nature, or Religion) check in order to reveal lore about the trap and its location within the surrounding area.

Disarming Triggers

Once a trigger has been detected, it usually needs to be disarmed (unless it can simply be avoided, such as a tripwire). Depending on the type of trap, disarming tends to work in different ways.

Mundane. Mundane triggers, or ambiguous triggers that are being used as mundane, are usually disarmed with a successful Dexterity check while using thieves' tools or trapsmiths' tools. The main objective when disarming a trap is to do so without accidentally setting it off.

Magic. Magic triggers, or ambiguous triggers used as magic ones, are usually disarmed with *dispel magic*. In the following chapters, if a trap can be disabled this way and the spell effect would be 4th level or higher, the DC for the *dispel magic* ability check is noted. If there is no DC provided, the spell effect is 3rd level or lower.

Sometimes a magic trigger can be disarmed by erasing a rune on the wall or otherwise disrupting the magic of the trap. A successful Intelligence (Arcana or Religion) check can disable a magic trap in this way, or reveal how it might be done. Optionally, another method could be allowing a spellcaster to make a spellcasting ability check to disarm a magic trap with intuitive knowledge of a small burst of magic.

Encourage players to be creative when dealing with traps. They may come up with a way of disabling or circumventing a trap that is not listed in the trap's entry. It's up to you to determine if this method could work, and what rolls or actions are required.

When players think outside the box to disarm or avoid a trap, consider rewarding them with something they can use later. This will help encourage players to bring their creativity to the table. Granting Inspiration or advantage on the character's next trap-related roll can be great motivation.

Some traps are rigged to activate on a failed attempt to disarm them, no matter the result of the ability check, while other traps are only triggered if the final result is particularly low. A critical failure (rolling a natural 1) when disarming a trap may result in additional hardships, at your discretion.

If a character has encountered a particular type of trap before, then they may gain advantage when it comes to dealing with that kind of trap. If they have been successful in dealing with a particular trap (or type of trap) in meaningful ways, they could slowly move toward gaining a bonus to disarming traps of that type. This is something that the player would need to keep track of on their character sheet, but it could be a realistic way to mechanically represent expertise. Characters that have dealt with a kind of trap many times could get advantage or a bonus die (such as a d4 or d6) to roll when making ability checks to detect or disarm that kind of trap.

Detecting Effects

Sometimes a trap's effect stands out more than its trigger. In any case, detection still often uses the same skills as when detecting triggers, though a few more skills become relevant. Wisdom (Perception) accounts for the five senses and can be used actively or passively. Depending on the effect, other applicable skills are Intelligence (Arcana, History, and Religion). And for magic effects, there is always *detect magic*.

Not all trap effects are hidden. Sometimes a nasty wall of spikes or a pendulum blade hanging from the ceiling in plain sight is enough to stop intruders in their tracks.

Disabling Effects

Sometimes the only option to deal with a trap is to disable or negate its effects. Wedging climbing pitons between the cracks of a trapdoor, packing dart holes with wooden dowels, or affixing a bag of holding to the water inlet of a flooding chamber are all ways to negate a trap's effects instead of disarming it's trigger.

Reset

When designing or placing a trap, it is important to consider whether the trap would be able to reset itself or not.

Mechanical traps may or may not reset, depending on the elements of the trap itself. Very basic traps, such as a tripwire or a leaf-covered pit break or fall apart when activated. On the other hand, something like swinging blades attached to a pressure plate may reset, depending on how well-engineered its internal mechanisms are.

Magic traps may reset depending on the parameters of the trap. A *glyph of warding* spell trap only casts a spell once, but a room enchanted to consistently affect a type of creature does so until dispelled or disarmed.

Hybrid traps factor in mechanical and magic elements, so may or may not reset based on the design of their component elements.

Complex traps usually reset automatically after a period of time, whether with magic or by mechanical means.

Traps as Templates

The pre-generated traps in the following chapters are designed to be as usable in multiple settings and situations, but there is no reason that you cannot make changes to them to suit your needs. Some of the traps may have slight bits of flavor, mentions of certain detection criteria, or other elements that are specific about one thing or another. These can be easily changed. For example, a trap could describe a room decorated with tapestries of dwarven war victories, with a magic trigger that activates whenever an elf walks into the room. Instead, you could change this trap to be set in a forest clearing with trees carved to depict elven war victories, with a magic trigger that activates whenever a dwarf enters the clearing.

Level 1-4 Traps

We were heading to a centuries-old abandoned temple deep in the jungle. The whole place has been swallowed up by vines, lichen, and saplings. The trail we chose was well used, but as we got deeper into the jungle, it got uncomfortably narrow. Scattered throughout the undergrowth were vestiges of strange shrines and crudely constructed altars made of stone, wood, and animal parts.

It bears mentioning that, given the unnerving nature of all this, — not to mention the admonishments from the locals that went something like "don't visit the temple," and "you could be taken captive by ancient sorceries," and "you'll surely perish,"— we were a bit on edge. Our ranger, keenly interested by the shrines and altars, inspected them but could not discern their purpose. That doesn't mean they didn't have one.

Of course, per usual, our big barbarian took the lead because should an axe, spear, or wave of arrows fly at us, it's better to have someone up front who can take it. Myself and the ranger were behind him and the cleric and wizard were at the back, discussing the artifact we were looking for, thoughts about the temple, and what challenges might lie inside.

So there we were, walking down this dense, green, throat of a path through the jungle when I noticed something. A little play of light near the ground caught my eye, and there before my eyes was a tripwire. And sure enough, just as I realized what I was seeing, the big man's foot ran right into it...

Who needs a rogue when you've got a barbarian that "detects traps"?

The traps in this chapter are designed to challenge characters who are levels 1-4 and are grouped by their lethality. Any of these traps can be dropped right into a dungeon or similar adventure and shouldn' t require any preparation. For more information on customizing traps, go to **Chapter 8: Designing Traps**, or for a completely random and unexpected trap, go to **Chapter 9: Random Trap Generator**.

Level 1-4 Traps Table

Roll a d100 on the table below to choose a random trap appropriate for 1-4 characters, or select a desired lethality and roll a d10.

	d100	d10	Trap	Page
Setback	1-2	1	Aging Offerings	12
	3-4	2	Rune of *Acid Splash*	12
	5-6	3	Rune of *Fire Bolt*	12
	7-8	4	Hidden Crossbow	12
	9-10	5	Falling Net	13
	11-12	6	Fossil Fingers	13
	13-14	7	Poison Spray Statue	13
	15-16	8	Sinister Seal	13
	17-18	9	Swinging Stones	14
	19-20	10	Trapdoor Pitfall, Minor	14
Moderate	21-22	1	Blinding Crystal	14
	23-24	2	Covert Counteraction	14
	25-26	3	Extinguish Flame	15
	27-28	4	Oath of Pacifism	15
	29-30	5	Silent Guardians	15
	31-32	6	Rogue's Bane, Minor	15
	33-34	7	Spear Strike, Minor	16
	35-36	8	Stair Slide	16
	37-38	9	Swinging Stars	16
	39-40	10	Uprising Underfoot	16
Dangerous	41-42	1	Choking Vapors	17
	43-44	2	Circle of Bewitchment	17
	45-46	3	Fire Jug	18
	47-48	4	Glyph of Sleep	18
	49-50	5	Hidden Hellion	18
	51-52	6	Liability Lamp	18
	53-54	7	Missile Orb	19
	55-56	8	Pain Threshold	19
	57-58	9	Poison Darts, Minor	19
	59-60	10	Trapestry	19
Perilous	61-62	1	Glyph of Burning Hands	20
	63-64	2	Falling Rocks	20
	65-66	3	Intruder Grab	20
	67-68	4	Night Terrors	20
	69-70	5	Restraining Chains	21
	71-72	6	Rotating Tunnel	21
	73-74	7	Speak Sand, Don't Enter	21
	75-76	8	Stony Glare	22
	77-78	9	Swinging Log	22
	79-80	10	Whirling Blades	22
Deadly	81-82	1	Blazing Ring, Minor	22
	83-84	2	Exploding Chest	22
	85-86	3	Flaming Tome	23
	87-88	4	Glyph of Force	23
	89-90	5	Lightning Gem	23
	91-92	6	Mysterious Relic	23
	93-94	7	The Other Other White Meat	24
	95-96	8	Shrinking Chamber	24
	97-98	9	Symbol of Congealing	24
	99-100	10	Tipping Floor	24

Level 1-4 Setback

These traps should present a minor inconvenience to characters of this level range.

Aging Offerings

Magic trap (level 1-4, setback, hinder)

Atop a shrine rests a copper bowl filled with gemstones.

Trigger (Offering). A creature that removes the offerings from the bowl triggers the trap.

Effect (Aging). A pulse of necromantic energy emanates from the bowl, aging the thief. The triggering creature must succeed on a DC 10 Constitution saving throw or be magically aged 1d10 years. If the roll is even, the creature is made younger; if odd, it becomes older. This forced aging can be undone with *remove curse* or more powerful magic.

Countermeasures. A creature can infer the importance of the offerings with a successful DC 10 Intelligence (Religion) check, and *detect magic* reveals an aura of necromancy on the bowl. Casting *dispel magic* on the bowl disables the trap.

Rune of Acid Splash

Hybrid trap (level 1-4, setback, harm)

A *rune of detection* is inscribed on the wall, floor, or ceiling.

Trigger (Creature Detector). A creature that gets within 20 feet of the rune triggers the trap.

Effect (Acid/Slime Blast). When triggered, the rune activates a hidden nozzle which sprays a jet of acid, making a ranged attack against the triggering creature, and 1 additional creature within 5 feet of the triggering creature. The attack has a +5 attack bonus and deals 3 (1d6) acid damage. This attack can't gain advantage or disadvantage.

Countermeasures. A successful DC 10 Wisdom (Perception) check reveals the rune, and a creature that succeeds on a DC 10 Intelligence (Arcana) check knows how the rune works.

A creature next to the rune can disable it with a successful Intelligence (Arcana) check, but getting that close would set off the trap. Casting *dispel magic* on the rune makes it fade away, disarming the trap.

Rune of Fire Bolt

Hybrid trap (level 1-4, setback, harm)

A magic rune is inscribed on the wall, floor, or ceiling.

Trigger (Creature Detector). A creature that gets within 20 feet of the rune triggers the trap.

Effect (Elemental Blast). When triggered, the rune activates a hidden nozzle that emits a blast of fire, making a ranged attack against the triggering creature. The attack has a +5 attack bonus and deals 5 (1d10) fire damage. This attack can't gain advantage or disadvantage.

Countermeasures. A successful DC 10 Wisdom (Perception) check reveals the rune, and a creature that succeeds on a DC 10 Intelligence (Arcana) check knows how the rune works.

A creature next to the rune can disable it with a successful Intelligence (Arcana) check, but getting that close would set off the trap. Casting *dispel magic* on the rune makes it fade away, disarming the trap.

Hidden Crossbow

Mechanical trap (level 1-4, setback, harm)

A surface such as a wall or ceiling has visible openings on it, such as cracks or another form of small space.

Trigger (Pressure Plate). A creature that gets within 10 feet of the opening steps on a hidden pressure plate and triggers the trap.

Effect (Bolt). The trap makes a ranged attack against the triggering creature. The attack has a +5 attack bonus and deals 4 (1d8) piercing damage. This attack can't gain advantage or disadvantage.

Countermeasures (Sensitive). A successful DC 10 Wisdom (Perception) check reveals the pressure plate. The pressure plate can be disabled with a successful DC 10 Dexterity check using thieves' tools, but a check with a total of 5 or lower triggers the trap.

NOOKS AND CRANNIES

Someone with experience in dungeons or ancient ruins might become all too familiar with what hidden dangers can be housed within cracks or small gaps.

Falling Net

Mechanical trap (level 1-4, setback, subdue)

An interesting object in the area, such as a chest or a large gem, is bait for this trap. A large net of thick hempen ropes is hidden above the object, waiting to drop.

Trigger (Tension Cable). The object is attached to a tension cable; moving the object triggers the trap.

Effect (Net). The trap releases a net onto all creatures in a 10-foot radius, centered on the object. Creatures in the area must make a DC 10 Dexterity saving throw. A creature that fails the saving throw is trapped under the net and restrained, while creatures that succeed avoid the net. A creature restrained by the net can use its action to make a DC 10 Strength check, freeing itself or another creature within its reach on a success.

The net has AC 10 and 20 hit points. Dealing 5 slashing damage to the net (AC 10) destroys a 5-foot-square section of it, freeing any creature trapped in that section. A glass bottle is tied to the net, and it breaks when the net drops, alerting nearby creatures when the net hits the floor.

Countermeasures. A successful DC 10 Wisdom (Perception) check reveals the tension cable or hidden net. A successful DC 10 Dexterity check using thieves' tools disables the cable, but a check with a total of 5 or lower triggers the trap

Fossil Fingers

Mechanical trap (level 1-4, setback, hinder)

A finely crafted lock protects a door, chest, or other container. The lock has a unique maker's mark and appears to be more complex than most.

Trigger (Pick Lock). A creature that succeeds at picking the lock, or opens the container without its key, triggers the trap.

Effect (Needle). A hidden needle springs out, attacking the triggering creature with a +5 attack bonus. If it hits, the needle deals no damage but delivers a dose of stone hands poison. This attack can't gain advantage or disadvantage.

A creature exposed to stone hands poison must make a DC 10 Constitution saving throw. On a failed save, it takes 3 (1d6) poison damage and is poisoned for 1 hour. While poisoned in this way, the creature automatically fails any ability checks using Dexterity. On a successful save, the creature takes half damage and isn't poisoned.

Countermeasures. A successful DC 10 Wisdom (Perception) check lets a creature spot the mechanism attached to the lock, and a creature that succeeds on a DC 10 Intelligence (History) check recognizes the maker's mark on the lock and knows about trap. A successful DC 10 Dexterity check using thieves' tools disables the trap.

Poison Spray Statue

Hybrid trap (level 1-4, setback, harm)

A small, alluring statue with glittering gems beckons adventurers to inspect it. The statue could be a snake with emerald eyes, a monkey with diamonds for teeth, or a dragon with a ruby in its mouth. A *rune of detecting* is inscribed somewhere on the statue.

Trigger (Creature Detector). A creature gets within 5 feet of the statue triggers the trap.

Effect (Elemental Blast). A noxious gas suddenly erupts from somewhere on the statue (mouth, nose, ears, etc). The triggering creature must make a DC 10 Constitution saving throw, taking 6 (1d12) poison damage on a failed save, or half as much on a successful one.

Countermeasures. A successful DC 10 Wisdom (Perception) check lets a creature spot the rune. A creature that succeeds on a DC 10 Intelligence (History) check recognizes the statue and knows about the trap. A successful DC 10 Intelligence (Arcana) check or casting *dispel magic* on the statue disables the trap.

Sinister Seal

Hybrid trap (level 1-4, setback, block)

A unique and ornate seal is carved into the floor of this room; a *rune of detection* is hidden in the design of the seal.

Trigger (Pass Area). A creature that walks over the seal activates the rune, which activates a timed mechanism. After 1 minute, the trap effect occurs. The GM can set specific criteria for what activates the rune.

Effect (Barrier). A heavy stone slab or metal portcullis slams down in the entrance to the room.

Countermeasures. A successful DC 10 Wisdom (Perception) check lets a creature spot the rune, and a creature that succeeds on a DC 10 Intelligence (History or Religion) check recognizes the seal and knows about the trap. A successful DC 10 Intelligence (Arcana) check or casting *dispel magic* on the rune disables the trap.

Swinging Stones

Mechanical trap (level 1-4, setback, harm)

Two large stones are tied to the ceiling with hempen ropes, clearly visible to all. A thin tripwire is stretched across the room, underneath the stones. This trap is often used in narrow corridors, making the stones harder to avoid.

Trigger (Tripwire). A creature that walks through the tripwire triggers the trap.

Effect (Swinging Object). The stones tied to the ceiling swing toward the triggering creature, who must make a DC 10 Dexterity saving throw. A creature has disadvantage on this saving throw if the trapped area is only 5 feet wide or smaller. The creature takes 7 (2d6) bludgeoning damage on a failed save, or half as much on a successful one.

Countermeasures (Sensitive). A successful DC 10 Wisdom (Perception) check reveals the tripwire. A successful DC 10 Dexterity check using thieves' tools disables the tripwire, but a check with a total of 5 or lower triggers the trap.

Trapdoor Pitfall, Minor

Mechanical trap (level 1-4, setback, harm)

A 20-foot deep vertical shaft is hidden under a trapdoor disguised to look like the rest of the floor. The trapdoor covers a 5-foot square space and has a pressure plate embedded in it.

Trigger (Pressure Plate). A creature that steps on the trapdoor activates the pressure plate, making the trap door swing open.

Effect (Drop Into Empty Pit). The triggering creature must make a DC 10 dexterity saving throw. On a successful save, the creature is able to grab onto the edge of the pit. On a failed save, the creature falls into the pit and takes 7 (2d6) bludgeoning damage.

Countermeasures. A successful DC 10 Wisdom (Perception) check reveals the pressure plate and a successful DC 10 Dexterity check using thieves' tools disables the trap.

Level 1-4 Moderate

These traps will probably harm characters of this level.

Blinding Crystal

Hybrid trap (level 1-4, moderate, hinder)

A small crystal sits on a pedestal; a *rune of detection* is inscribed on the crystal.

Trigger (Touch Object). A creature that touches the crystal triggers the trap.

Effect (Blindness). When triggered, the rune opens a small hatch under the crystal which releases a beam of light that hits the crystal, creating a blinding flash. All creatures within 30 feet must succeed on a DC 12 Constitution saving throw or be blinded for 1 minute, or for 2 minutes if the creature has darkvision.

At the end of each of their turns, a creature blinded in this way can attempt a DC 12 Constitution saving throw. On a success, the creature is no longer blind.

Countermeasures. A creature can spot the rune with a successful DC 12 Wisdom (Perception) check and *detect magic* reveals an aura of abjuration magic on the crystal. Once discovered, a successful DC 12 Intelligence (Arcana) check or *dispel magic* can disable the rune.

Covert Counteraction

Hybrid trap (level 1-4, moderate, hinder)

The chamber has many columns around its edge and a single source of light near its center. This combination casts dark and solid shadows along the walls. A *rune of detection* is inscribed near the light source, and bags of flour or a similar substance are concealed on the ceiling of the shadowed areas, ready to drop.

Trigger (Step Into Light/Darkness). A creature that enters an area in shadow triggers the trap.

Effect (Falling Object). When activated, the rune releases a bag of flour over the triggering creature, who must make a DC 12 Dexterity saving throw. On a failure, the creature is covered in flour for 1 minute. Any attack roll against a creature doused in flour has advantage if the attacker can see it, and the affected creature automatically fails Stealth checks. An affected creature can remove the flour as an action on their turn.

Countermeasures. A creature can spot the rune with a successful DC 12 Wisdom (Perception) check; if a creature makes this check with disadvantage and succeeds, they can spot the bags of flour. A creature that can reach the rune can disable it with a successful DC 12 Intelligence (Arcana) check, and a creature that can reach the bags without entering the shadows can remove them easily. Casting *dispel magic* on the rune also disables the trap, and increasing the light in the room is a way to bypass the trap.

Extinguish Flame

Magic trap (level 1-4, moderate, hinder)

Within the area, etchings on the floor, a lone crystal, or something is the locus of this magic trap.

Trigger (Produce Flame). If any non-magical source of light such as a candle, torch, or oil lamp is created or brought into the area, the trap triggers.

Effect (Spell Effect). The trap casts *prestidigitation* and with a loud *woosh*, the triggering flame is extinguished by a strong and localized magical wind.

Countermeasures. *Detect magic* reveals an aura of transmutation magic on the etchings. A creature that succeeds on a DC 12 Intelligence (Arcana) check understands the etchings and knows about the trap.

A spellcaster can disable the trap with a successful DC 12 ability check using their spellcasting ability; casting *dispel magic* on the area will also disable the trap

Oath of Pacifism

Magic trap (level 1-4, moderate, block)

This chamber's floor is covered with pictographs, and the walls are painted to resemble armored warriors standing behind shields.

Trigger (Mortal Sacrifice). Any creature killed in this area triggers the trap.

Effect (Suggestion). The pictographs on the floor glow with a soft light, and the trap attempts to implant a suggestion in the mind of creatures in the chamber. All creatures in the chamber must make a DC 12 Wisdom saving throw. On a failed save, a creature puts their weapons away and doesn't engage in combat for 1 minute. Creatures that can't be charmed are immune to this effect.

Casting *dispel magic* on a creature affected by the trap ends the effect for that creature.

Countermeasures. A successful DC 15 Intelligence (Arcana, History, or Religion) check lets a creature identify the pictographs on the walls, alerting them to the trap. The pictographs also have an aura of enchantment magic when viewed with *detect magic*.

The trap can be disabled with *dispel magic* or by a spellcaster that succeeds on a DC 12 spellcasting ability check.

Silent Guardians

Mechanical trap (level 1-4, moderate, harm)

2 suits of armor, made of boiled leather and chainmail, stand in various locations in the area. A creature that approaches a suit of armor quietly can hear the soft clicking of clockwork gears emanating from within.

Trigger (Musical/Auditory). Creatures who move or perform actions within 20 feet of a suit of armor must make a successful DC 12 Dexterity (Stealth) check each round to avoid triggering the trap.

Effect (Animate Object). When triggered, the suits of armor animate and attack all other creatures in the area. The suits of armor use the game statistics for animated object, armor with the following changes:

- The armor's hit points are 18 (4d8).
- The armor's AC is 15.
- The armor's Constitution is 12 (+0)
- The armor doesn't have the Antimagic Susceptibility trait.
- The armor doesn't have the Multiattack action.

Countermeasures (Difficult). A successful DC 12 Wisdom (Perception) check alerts a creature to the clockwork and gears inside the armor, and a successful DC 12 Intelligence (Investigation) check lets a creature figure out that the armor could animate if activated with vibrations from sound.

A creature next to a suit of armor can attempt a DC 12 Dexterity check using thieves' tools, deactivating their mechanisms on a success. A check that totals 5 or less triggers the trap. Using a spell like *silence* to muffle sound can also work, but spellcasting within 20 feet of the armor will trigger the trap.

Rogue's Bane, Minor

Mechanical trap (level 1-4, moderate)

A poorly disguised tripwire is easily detected, but it is a facade. The true trap is well hidden and set to go off if the decoy is tampered with.

Trigger (False Trigger). Disarming, or attempting to disarm, the false trigger triggers the real trap.

Effect (Random Trap). Randomly select another mechanical trap of the same or lower lethality and use its effect.

Countermeasures. A successful DC 12 Wisdom (Perception) check reveals the false and real triggers. A successful DC 12 Intelligence (Investigation) check reveals the nature of the trap and allows a creature to make a DC 12 Dexterity check using thieves' tools to disable the real trigger. On a success, the real trap is disabled.

Spear Strike, Minor

Mechanical trap (level 1-4, moderate, harm)

Three spears are hidden within the walls, floor, or ceiling of this area. A thin, almost invisible tripwire is strung across the area, under the spears. This trap is usually used in narrow corridors, doorways, or other passages that are frequently traversed.

Trigger (Tripwire). A creature that walks through the tripwire triggers the trap.

Effect (Spears). Spears thrust toward the triggering creature, who must make a DC 12 Dexterity saving throw. The creature takes 10 (3d6) piercing damage on a failed save, or half as much on a successful one.

Countermeasures (Sensitive). A successful DC 12 Wisdom (Perception) check reveals the false and real triggers. A successful DC 12 Intelligence (Investigation) check reveals the nature of the trap and allows a creature to make a DC 12 Dexterity check using thieves' tools to disable the real trigger. On a success, the real trap is disabled.

Stair Slide

Mechanical trap (level 1-4, moderate, harm)

At the bottom of a steep flight of stairs is a 30-foot deep pit under a trap door. A pressure plate is disguised as part of one of the steps, halfway up the stairs.

Trigger (Pressure Plate). A creature that steps on the pressure plate triggers the trap.

Effect (Drop Into Empty Pit). The trap door at the bottom of the stairs opens and the stairs themselves flatten into a slide, sending any creature on the stairs down to the bottom and into the pit. All creatures on the stairs must make a DC 12 Dexterity saving throw. On a successful save a creature is able to grab onto the edge of the pit. On a failed save, the creature falls into the pit and takes 10 (3d6) bludgeoning damage.

The trap door doesn't close, and climbing out of the pit doesn't require a Strength check, but the stairs do not reset. Travelling up the stair slide requires a DC 12 Dexterity (Acrobatics) check or a DC 12 Strength (Athletics) check to climb the walls. A creature that fails either check falls onto the slide and might fall in the pit again.

Countermeasures. A successful DC 12 Wisdom (Perception) check reveals the pressure plate. A successful DC 12 Dexterity check using thieves' tools disables the pressure plate, and a check with a total of 5 or lower triggers the trap.

Swinging Stars

Mechanical trap (level 1-4, moderate, harm)

A pair of double doors engraved with a scene of the night sky blocks the path. These doors pull open easily, but a tension cable is attached to them on the side opposite the engraving.

Trigger (Tension Cable). A creature that opens the doors triggers the trap.

Effect (Swinging Object). A spiked ball on a chain swings down at the triggering creature. They trap attacks the triggering creature with a +6 attack bonus, dealing 5 (1d10) bludgeoning damage and 5 (1d10) piercing damage if it hits. This attack can't gain advantage or disadvantage.

Countermeasures. A successful DC 12 Wisdom (Perception) check lets a creature spot the cable through some gaps around the hinges, and a successful DC 12 Dexterity check while using thieves' tools disables the trap.

Uprising Underfoot

Hybrid trap (level 1-4, moderate, harm)

This corridor is entirely unlit. There are sconces along the length of the corridor, and a basket of torches at one end. The basket has enough torches for all of the sconces. In the middle of the corridor, a *rune of detection* is inscribed on the wall.

Trigger (Bring Object). A creature that brings a lit torch 30 feet into the corridor triggers the trap.

Effect (Spikes). When activated, the rune engages the mechanisms below the floor and spikes shoot up along the corridor. Each creature in the corridor must make a DC 12 Dexterity saving throw, taking 7 (2d6) piercing damage on a failed save or half as much on a success.

Countermeasures. A successful DC 12 Wisdom (Perception) check lets a creature spot the rune and the holes in the floor for the spikes, although this check has disadvantage if the creature has no other source of light and cannot see in the dark. A creature can disable the rune with a successful Intelligence (Arcana) check or *dispel magic*.

Level 1-4 Dangerous

These traps are likely to seriously injure (and potentially kill) characters of these levels.

Choking Vapors

Mechanical trap (level 1-4, dangerous, harm)

The floor of the empty tunnel is paved with uneven flagstones.

Trigger (Weight Sensitive Surface). When 20 or more pounds of weight are placed on the central flagstone, it depresses and cracks a glass vial filled with liquid.

Effect (Poison Gas). The liquid quickly becomes a 20-foot-radius sphere of poisonous, yellow-green fog centered on the triggering creature. The fog spreads around corners. It lasts for 10 minutes or until strong wind disperses the fog. Its area is heavily obscured.

When a creature enters the fog's area for the first time on a turn or starts its turn there, that creature must make a DC 15 Constitution saving throw. The creature takes 16 (3d10) poison damage on a failed save, or half as much damage on a successful one.

Countermeasures. A successful DC 15 Wisdom (Perception) check reveals the hidden vial, and a successful DC 15 Dexterity check while using thieves' tools disables the trap.

Circle of Bewitchment

Magic trap (level 1-4, dangerous, hinder)

This circle of runes covers a 10-foot radius sphere and emits a thick, green smoke that smells of sulphur.

Trigger (Command Word). Using a wand, rod, ring, orb, or similar item that requires a command word activates the trigger.

Effect (Bewitchment). The triggering creature must succeed on a DC 15 Charisma saving throw or be cursed by bad luck. When a cursed creature enters a new situation or starts a new encounter, roll a d20 and reference the table below.

This poor luck does not extend to dice rolls, inflict status effects, confer advantage or disadvantage, or impact combat in any way. It is intended to impact circumstances, such as extra guards or a poor first impression with an important NPC.

d20	Bad Luck
1-2	**Catastrophic.** The circumstance is as bad as it could be. Important NPC's are hostile or the city watch is on high alert for some reason. A serious, time-consuming, or difficult impediment crops up.
3-9	**Terrible.** The circumstance is much worse than it might otherwise be. There are a few additional guards, a moderately difficult complication, or an unfriendly NPC.
10-19	**Unfortunate.** The circumstance is slightly worse than it might otherwise be. There's only 1 or two guards, an indifferent NPC, or a complication that's easy to overcome.
20	**Lifted.** The cloud of bad luck lifts and the creature is no longer cursed.

At the end of each day, a bewitched creature can make a DC 15 Charisma saving throw. If it succeeds, this effect ends for that creature. *Remove curse* or more powerful magic can also end the bewitchment.

Countermeasures. A successful DC 15 Intelligence (Arcana) check or casting *detect magic* reveals the nature of the runic circle. Another successful DC 15 Intelligence (Arcana) check, or *dispel magic* cast on the runes disables them.

Fire Jug

Mechanical trap (level 1-4, dangerous, harm)

A large, oil-filled ceramic jug hangs from the ceiling by an old hempen rope, subtly connected to a tripwire stretched across the room. Its lid has a sparking mechanism that will set the oil ablaze if the jug falls and breaks.

Trigger (Tripwire). A creature that walks through the tripwire triggers the trap.

Effect (Falling Object). The jug falls and breaks on the floor, spreading flaming oil in a 15-foot-radius sphere centered on the triggering creature. The triggering creature can try to catch the falling jug with a successful DC 15 Dexterity (Athletics) check. Otherwise, each creature in the area must make a DC 15 Dexterity saving throw, taking 10 (3d6) fire damage on a failed save, or half as much on a successful one.

Countermeasures (Sensitive). A successful DC 15 Wisdom (Perception) check reveals the tripwire. A successful DC 15 Dexterity check using thieves' tools disables the trap, but a check with a total of 10 or lower triggers it.

Glyph of Sleep

Magic trap (level 1-4, dangerous, block)

Carved into the wooden statue is a *glyph of warding (sleep)* which looks like a wreath of flowers and leaves. Soft, ambient forest noises fill the air around it.

Trigger (Creature Detector). A creature that approaches within 5 feet of the glyph triggers the trap.

Effect (Sleep). When triggered, the trap casts *sleep*, sending creatures into a magical slumber. Roll 5d8; the total is how many hit points of creatures this spell can affect. Creatures within 20 feet of a point next to the triggering creature range are affected in ascending order of their current hit points (ignoring unconscious creatures).

Starting with the creature that has the lowest current hit points, each creature affected by this spell falls unconscious for 1 minute. If a sleeper takes damage, or someone uses an action to shake or slap them, they wake up.Subtract each creature's hit points from the total before moving on to the creature with the next lowest hit points. A creature's hit points must be equal to or less than the remaining total for that creature to be affected.

Countermeasures. A successful DC 15 Intelligence (Investigation) check reveals the trigger, but usually a creature would need to be within 5 feet of the glyph to make this check. *Detect magic* can also reveal the trigger. A creature adjacent to the glyph can disable it with a successful DC 15 Intelligence (Arcana) check. *Dispel magic* also disables the glyph.

Hidden Hellion

Magic trap (level 1-4, dangerous, harm)

A sprawling passage of demon script, written in Infernal, spreads across the pages of a dusty tome. It glows like the embers of a dying fire.

Trigger (Read Writing). Any creature can read the writing, even if they don't speak Infernal. Reading the writing aloud triggers the trap.

Effect (Summon Creature). When triggered, the trap summons **2 dretches**, or other fiends of CR ¼ or lower. The dretches attack all other creatures in the room and will not leave the area. After 1 minute, or if reduced to 0 hit points, the dretches vanish into a puff of brimstone.

Countermeasures. A successful DC 15 Intelligence (Religion) check lets a creature understand the danger of the text. The tome has an aura of conjuration magic when viewed with *detect magic.*

A spellcaster can disrupt the enchantment on the tome with a successful DC 15 spellcasting ability check; *dispel magic* cast on the tome also disables the trap.

Liability Lamp

Mechanical trap (level 1-4, dangerous, harm)

Darkness fills the chamber. Hanging on the doorframe is an extinguished oil lamp.

Trigger (Activate Light Fixture). A fine thread concealed within the lamp snaps when exposed to the heat, activating the trap.

Effect (Scything Blades). A curved blade concealed in the wall slashes at the triggering creature, which must make a DC 15 Dexterity saving throw. The creature takes 16 (3d10) slashing damage on a failed save, or half as much on a successful one. On a failed save, the creature is also restrained as they are pinned against the opposite wall by the blades.

A creature restrained by the blades can free themselves with a successful DC 15 Constitution (Athletics) check or another creature can free them with a successful DC 15Strength (Medicine) check.

Countermeasures. A successful DC 15 Wisdom (Perception) check reveals the thread, and a successful DC 15 Dexterity check using thieves' tools disables the trap.

Missile Orb

Magic trap (level 1-4, dangerous, harm)

A brilliant blue glass orb floats at a 4 feet off the ground. The light within it appears to dim and brighten in gentle pulses. A *glyph of warding (magic missile)* is inscribed on the top of the orb.

Trigger (Creature Detector). A creature of a particular type, race, or alignment that gets within 60 feet of the orb triggers the trap. The specific criteria are up to the DM, but should fit into the themes or overall nature of the area where this trap is placed.

Effect (Spell Effect). The glyph casts *magic missile* at the triggering creature. The creature takes 10 (3d4 +3) force damage and the orb stops glowing.

Countermeasures. A creature adjacent to the orb can detect the glyph with a successful DC 15 Intelligence (Investigation) check, or with *detect magic*. The glyph can be disabled with a successful DC 15 Intelligence (Arcana) check or with *dispel magic.*

Pain Threshold

Mechanical trap (level 1-4, dangerous, harm)

The floor in front of a closed door is perforated with small holes. Hidden beneath the surface of that floor is a collection of tall, rusty spikes, triggered by a mechanism in the door frame.

Trigger (Open/Close Door). A creature that opens the door triggers the trap.

Effect (Spiked Floor). Spikes shoot up from the floor and pierce the feet and/or legs of any creature standing in the two 5-foot squares in front of the door. The triggering creatures must make a DC 15 Dexterity saving throw, taking 15 (6d4) piercing damage on a failed save or half as much on a success.

Countermeasures. A successful DC 15 Wisdom (Perception) check reveals the holes in the floor, and a successful DC 15 Dexterity check using thieves' tools disables the trap.

Poison Darts, Minor

Mechanical trap (level 1-4, dangerous, harm)

Several holes along the walls of the chamber are disguised with relief carvings of snakes, gargoyles, or other menacing creatures. A pressure plate is hidden near the center of the chamber.

Trigger (Pressure Plate). A Small size or larger creature that steps on the pressure plate triggers the trap.

Effect (Darts). The trap makes three ranged attacks against the triggering creature. Each attack has a +8 attack bonus and deals 2 (1d4) piercing plus 3 (1d6) poison damage. These attacks can't gain advantage or disadvantage.

Countermeasures (Sensitive). A successful DC 15 Wisdom (Perception) check reveals the pressure plate. A successful DC 15 Dexterity check using thieves' tools disables, but a check with a total of 10 or lower triggers the trap.

Trapestry

Hybrid trap (level 1-4, dangerous, block)

Woven from sparkling threads, this tapestry depicts a dwarven army being defeated by a horde of undead. It is made of two parts, and can easily be separated to pass through. A *rune of detection* is hidden in the design of the tapestry.

Trigger (Pass Area). If a dwarf moves through the tapestry the trap is triggered.

Effect (Barrier). A creature passing through the tapestry when the trap is triggered must make a DC 15 Strength saving throw. On a failed save, the creature takes 16 (3d10) piercing damage as a falling portcullis crushes them. Additionally, they are trapped beneath the portcullis and restrained. Freeing a creature from beneath the portcullis requires a successful DC 15 Strength check.

On a successful save, the creature dodges the portcullis, and can choose which side of the barrier to be on.

Countermeasures. A creature can detect the rune with a successful DC 15 Wisdom (Perception) check or with *detect magic*. A successful DC 15 Intelligence (Arcana) check or *dispel magic* disables the trap.

Level 1-4 Perilous

These traps may kill characters of these levels, and will definitely injure them severely.

Glyph of Burning Hands

Magic trap (level 1-4, perilous, harm)

A *glyph of warding (burning hands)* is written in ash on the wall, floor, or ceiling of this area.

Trigger (Creature Detector). A creature that gets within 10 feet of the rune triggers the trap.

Effect (Elemental Blast). The glyph casts *burning hands*. Each creature in a 15-foot cone centered on the triggering creature must make a DC 17 Dexterity saving throw. A creature takes 3d6 fire damage on a failed save, or half as much damage on a successful one.

The fire ignites any flammable objects in the area that aren't being worn or carried.

Countermeasures. A creature can discover the glyph with a successful DC 17 Intelligence (Investigation) check, but to do so they would have to be within 10 feet of the glyph. *Detect magic* can also reveal the glyph. With a successful DC 17 Intelligence (Arcana) check, a creature adjacent to the glyph can disable it; *dispel magic* can also disable the glyph.

Falling Rocks

Mechanical trap (level 1-4, perilous, harm)

The ceiling is lined with large rocks held up by unseen mechanisms. The way forward is blocked by a door, portcullis, or other non-magical obstruction which can be opened by a lever on the wall. However, there are three levers, and pulling the wrong one sets off the trap.

Trigger (Move Lever/Press Button). Pulling the wrong lever triggers the trap.

Effect (Falling Objects). All creatures within the chamber or passageway must make a DC 20 Dexterity saving throw, taking 14 (4d6) bludgeoning damage on a failed save, or half as much on a successful one. The area is difficult terrain unless the rocks are moved.

Countermeasures (Difficult). A successful DC 17 Wisdom (Perception) check reveals the hidden mechanisms that hold up the rocks, and a creature that succeeds on a DC 17 Intelligence (Investigation) check can deduce the correct lever from the amount of wear on each. A successful DC 17 Dexterity check using thieves' tools disables the trap.

Intruder Grab

Hybrid trap (level 1-4, perilous, harm)

Shadowed archways line the walls of this chamber. The floor is a crumbling mosaic of a giant skull with flames in its eyes and a gaping mouth. A *rune of detection* is hidden in the mosaic

Trigger (Fail to Speak Password). A creature that walks atop the skull mosaic and doesn't speak the password triggers the trap.

Effect (Net). When activated, the rune releases a large rope from the ceiling. Each creature in a 10-foot radius centered on the triggering creature must succeed on a DC 17 Dexterity saving throw or be restrained by the net until freed. The net is covered with a sticky acid that burns on contact. A creature that touches the net for the first time on a turn, or who ends its turn touching the net, takes 14 (4d6) acid damage.

A creature restrained by the net can use its action to make a DC 17 Strength check, freeing itself or another creature within its reach on a success. The net has AC 10 and 20 hit points. Dealing 5 slashing damage to the net (AC 10) destroys a 5-foot-square section of it, freeing any creature trapped in that section.

Countermeasures. A creature can spot the rune with a successful DC 17 Wisdom (Perception) check or with *detect magic*. A creature that succeeds on a DC 17 Intelligence (Investigation) check can find the password hidden in the mosaic.

Speaking the password, a successful DC 17 Intelligence (Arcana) check, or *dispel magic* cast on the rune disables it.

Night Terrors

Magic trap (level 1-4, perilous, harm)

Tiny sigils line the walls of this chamber, difficult to notice, but ready to activate once a creature falls asleep.

Trigger (Unconsciousness). A creature that goes unconscious within the area triggers the trap.

Effect (Summon Creature). The runes glow with an eerie light and summons fey spirits that take the form of 4 swarms of bats that appear in unoccupied spaces within the chamber. The bats are hostile and attack, targeting unconscious creatures first. The bats disappear after 5 minutes or if reduced to 0 hit points, and will not leave the chamber. The trap could summon other creatures of an appropriate theme for the environment, as long as they are CR ¼.

Countermeasures. A creature can discover the runes with a successful DC 17 Wisdom (Perception) or Intelligence (Arcana) check, or with *detect magic*. The runes can be disabled with a successful DC 17 Intelligence (Arcana) check or with *dispel magic*.

Restraining Chains

Magic trap (level 1-4, perilous, block)

A pile of chains lies on the floor of this chamber. They are rusted with age but have symbols of enchantment chiselled on their surface.

Trigger (Pass Area). A good-aligned creature passing within 10 feet of the chains triggers the trap.

Effect (Restraint). The chains animate and attempt to bind the characters. All creatures within 10 feet the area must succeed on a DC 17 Wisdom saving throw or be restrained. A creature can free itself from the restraints with a successful DC 17 Strength check.

Countermeasures. A creature can discern the nature of the symbols on the chains with a successful DC 17 Intelligence (Arcana) check, and *detect magic* reveals an aura of enchantment magic around the chains. A creature can disable the trap with another successful DC 17 Intelligence (Arcana) check, or *dispel magic*.

Rotating Tunnel

Mechanical trap (level 1-4, perilous, harm)

The interior of this short tubular passageway is lined with conical spikes and grooves in a spiral pattern.

Trigger (Pressure Plate). At one end of the tunnel there is a pressure plate. A Medium or larger creature that steps on the pressure plate triggers the trap.

Effect (Spiked Walls). Once activated, the passageway spins slowly. Creatures within the tunnel while it is rotating must make a DC 17 Dexterity saving throw, taking 14 (4d6) piercing damage on a failed save, or half as much on a successful one.

Countermeasures (Sensitive). A successful DC 17 Wisdom (Perception) check reveals the pressure plate and a successful DC 17 Dexterity check using thieves' tools disables it. A check with a total of 10 or lower triggers the trap.

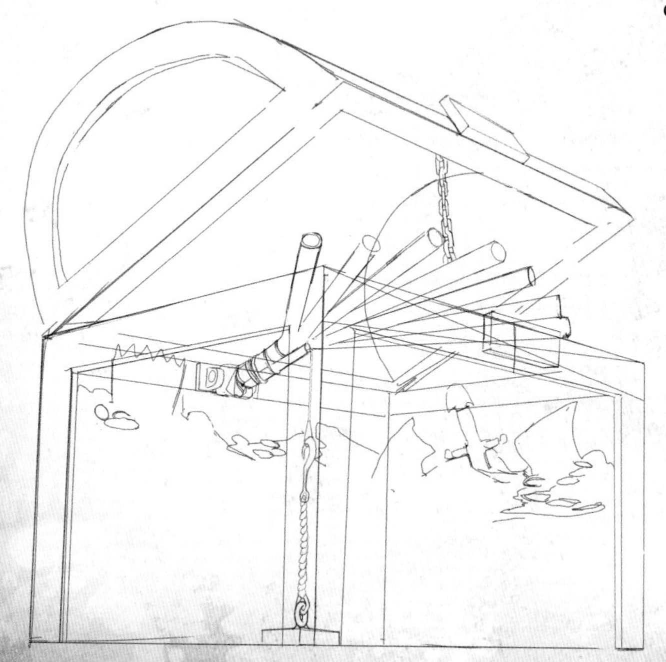

Speak Sand, Don't Enter

Hybrid trap (level 1-4, perilous, block)

A wide stone archway adorns the way out of this room. Chiselled into the adjacent wall is a short sentence; 'Only the small may pass, like sand through an hourglass'. A *rune of detection* is inscribed on the apex of the archway.

Trigger (Speak Trigger Word). A creature that says the word 'sand' in Common or one other language appropriate to the area triggers the trap.

Effect (Falling Sand). When activated, the rune releases blocking mechanisms in the room's ceiling and sand starts to pour in. A creature in the room must make a successful DC 17 Dexterity saving throw at the beginning of its turn to stay atop the sand. The save DC increases by 2 each round.

A creature that fails one saving throw is buried up to their knees and restrained. On their next saving throw, if the creature succeeds they dig themselves out and are no longer restrained; if they fail they are buried waist-deep and remain restrained.

A creature buried waist-deep must make a DC 17 Strength saving throw at the beginning of their turn; if they succeed they dig themselves free of the sand and if they fail they are buried to the neck and immobilized. On their next turn, the creature is completely buried and starts suffocating.

As an action, a creature can dig out another creature with a successful Strength (Athletics) check against the current save DC of the trap. Spells like *freedom of movement* or movement modes like burrow can also allow creatures to freely move through the sand.

Countermeasures. A creature that succeeds on a DC 17 Wisdom (Perception) check finds the rune and the hidden holes in the ceiling. *Detect magic* can also reveal the rune. If a creature makes a successful DC 17 Wisdom (Insight) check, they deduce the trigger word.

A successful DC 17 Intelligence (Arcana) check or *dispel magic* disables the trap.

Stony Glare

Magic trap (level 1-4, perilous, hinder)

The gnome statue is partially shrouded in shadow, though it is clear that the eyes are made from gemstones.

Trigger (Look Into). A creature that looks directly into the eyes of the statue triggers the trap.

Effect (Paralysis). The triggering creature must succeed on a DC 17 Wisdom saving throw or be paralyzed. At the end of each of its turns, a creature paralyzed by this effect can make another Wisdom saving throw. On a success, this effect ends for that creature.

This effect ends if dispelled, either with *dispel magic* or *lesser restoration*, or after 1 minute.

Countermeasures. A successful DC 17 Wisdom (Perception) or Intelligence (Arcana) check reveals the tiny symbols embedded in the statue's eyes, the trigger for the trap. With *detect magic*, a creature sees an aura of transmutation magic around the statue.

A successful DC 17 Intelligence (Arcana) check or *dispel magic* disables the trap.

Swinging Log

Mechanical trap (level 1-4, perilous, harm)

A 5-foot wide, 30-foot long corridor stands between the entrance and destination. A thin, barely visible wire stretches across the corridor at the 20 foot mark.

Trigger (Tripwire). A creature that trips the wire triggers the trap.

Effect (Swinging Object). When the trap is triggered, a 5-foot wide log swings down in a 15-foot long line. Each creature in that line must make a DC 17 Dexterity saving throw, taking 14 (4d6) bludgeoning damage on a failure or half as much on a success.

Countermeasures. A successful DC 17 Wisdom (Perception) check reveals the tripwire, and a successful DC 17 Dexterity check while using thieves' tools disables it.

Whirling Blades

Mechanical trap (level 1-4, perilous, harm)

This 20-foot wide corridor has scratch marks all over the walls, and is splattered throughout by blood. At the end of the corridor is a plinth, atop which is a silver decanter.

Trigger (Weight Sensitive Surface). Removing the decanter from the plinth triggers the trap.

Effect (Scything Blades). Posts affixed with curved blades pop up from the floor and spin rapidly, slicing anything within range. Each creature in the corridor must succeed on a DC 17 Dexterity saving throw or take 15 (6d4) slashing damage.

Countermeasures. A successful DC 17 Wisdom (Perception) check reveals the hidden mechanism in the plinth, and a successful DC 17 Dexterity check while using thieves' tools disables the trigger.

Level 1-4 Deadly

These traps will almost certainly kill characters of these levels.

Blazing Ring, Minor

Mechanical trap (level 1-4, deadly, harm)

A 1-foot thick ring of decorative stonework surrounds a 25-foot diameter circle area in the center of the room. The ceiling directly above the ring is blackened with soot. In the 5-foot square at the circle's center is something intriguing.

Trigger (Weight Sensitive Floor). When a Small or larger creature steps onto a space adjacent to the 5-foot square at the center of the area within the ring, they activate a pressure plate. Parts of the stonework slide away, revealing spouts which pour flaming oil onto the floor from the ring's inner edge.

Effect (Wall of Fire). The flaming oil creates a ringed wall of flames 25 feet in diameter, 20 feet high, and 1 foot thick. The wall is opaque and lasts for 1 minute. When the wall appears, each creature within its area must make a DC 20 Dexterity saving throw. On a failed save, a creature takes 17 (5d6) fire damage, or half as much damage on a successful save.

The side of the wall facing inwards deals the trap's fire damage to each creature that ends its turn within 10 feet of that side or inside the wall. A creature takes the same damage when it enters the wall for the first time on a turn or ends its turn there. The other side of the wall deals no damage.

A creature that is adjacent to the wall can make a DC 20 Constitution check using thieves' tools to end this effect.

Countermeasures. A successful DC 20 Wisdom (Perception) check reveals the pressure plate, and a successful DC 20 Dexterity check while using thieves' tools disables it.

Exploding Chest

Mechanical trap (level 1-4, deadly, harm)

A nondescript, locked chest is filled with explosives and several hundred tiny ball bearings. The chest may contain valuables, or it might be a decoy.

Trigger (Open/Close Object). The lock on the chest is relatively easy to open; it can be picked with a successful DC 10 Dexterity check using thieve's tools.

Effect (Elemental Blast). When the trap is activated, the explosives go off and the ball bearings are sent up to 120 feet in all directions. Any creature within range who is not behind cover must make a DC 20 Dexterity saving throw, taking 17 (5d6) damage on a failed save, or half as much on a successful one. Half of this damage is fire and half is piercing.

Countermeasures. A creature that opens the chest triggers the trap. A successful DC 20 Wisdom (Perception) check reveals the mechanisms hidden in the lid that will trigger the explosives. A successful DC 20 Dexterity check using thieves' tools disables the trap.

Flaming Tome

Mechanical trap (level 1-4, deadly, harm)

A large tome lays open on a lectern in the middle of the chamber.

Trigger (Tension Cable). A tension cable is attached to the book's cover. The trap activates when the book is closed.

Effect (Elemental Blast). A sheet of flame erupts from the lectern. Each creature within 5 feet of the book when the trap is triggered must make a DC 20 Dexterity saving throw, taking 17 (5d6) fire damage on a failed save, or half as much on a successful one.

Countermeasures. A successful DC 20 Wisdom (Perception) check reveals the tension cable and the small nozzle in the lectern. A successful DC 20 Dexterity check while using thieves' tools disables the trap.

Glyph of Force

Magic trap (level 1-4, deadly, harm)

The walls of this 15-foot square chamber are covered in large metal spikes. In the centre of the room is a stone monolith, into which a glowing, blue *glyph of warding (thunderwave)* has been carved.

Trigger (Creature Detector). Creatures that come within 10 feet of the monolith trigger the trap.

Effect (Elemental Blast). The glyph casts *thunderwave*. Each creature in a 15-foot cube centered on the triggering creature must make a DC 20 Constitution saving throw. On a failed save, a creature takes 9 (2d8) thunder damage and is pushed 10 feet away from the triggering creature. On a successful save, the creature takes half as much damage and isn't pushed.

A creature that is pushed hits the spikes on the walls of the room, suffering another 9 (2d8) piercing damage.

In addition, unsecured objects that are completely within the area of effect are automatically pushed 10 feet away from the triggering creature, and the spell emits a thunderous boom audible out to 300 feet.

Countermeasures. A successful DC 20 Intelligence (Investigation) check or casting *detect magic* reveals the glyph. A successful DC 20 Intelligence (Arcana) check, or *dispel magic* cast on the glyph disables it. However, in most cases a creature would need to be within 10 feet of the monolith to detect or disable the glyph with an ability check.

Lightning Gem

Hybrid trap (level 1-4, deadly, harm)

A brilliant, sparkling white gem is prominently displayed on a pedestal or set into a statue. When the gem is picked up, the pedestal or statue unleashes a blast of lightning.

Trigger (Pick Up/Shift Object). A creature that picks up the gem triggers the trap.

Effect (Elemental Blast). The rune creates an explosion of lightning in a 20-foot-radius. Each creature in the area must make a DC 20 Dexterity saving throw, taking 17 (5d6) lightning damage on a failed save, or half as much on a successful one.

Countermeasures. A successful DC 20 Wisdom (Perception) check reveals the trigger, and a successful DC 20 Dexterity check using thieves' tools disables it.

To bypass the trigger, a creature can attempt to replace the object with one of equal weight. The creature must succeed on a DC 20 Intelligence (Perception) check to accurately estimate the weight of the object and a successful DC 20 Dexterity (Sleight of Hand) check to switch the objects. Failure on either roll activates the trap.

Mysterious Relic

Hybrid trap (level 1-4, deadly, harm)

A wondrous item sits on display in the center of the chamber, with a *rune of detection* inscribed on it. The floor of the chamber is comprised of several sections connected by obscured hinges.

Trigger (Touch Object). Touching the relic, even with a spell, activates the trap.

Effect (Drop Into Monster Lair). When the trap activates, the room's floor falls away, swinging down on hinges connected to the walls. All creatures within the chamber must make a DC 20 Dexterity saving throw. On a successful save a creature is able to jump to safety or cling to the floor as it goes vertical. On a failed save, the creature falls into the pit and takes 17 (5d6) bludgeoning damage.

The pit is the lair of 2 rust monsters, or some other appropriate creatures of CR ½ or lower.

Countermeasures (Difficult). A successful DC 20 Wisdom (Perception) check reveals the rune on the object and the small gaps between each section of the floor. A successful DC 20 Intelligence (Investigation) check reveals the nature of the trap and allows a creature to attempt a DC 20 Intelligence (Arcana) check to disable the rune.

The rune can also be found with *detect magic*, and *dispel magic* will disable the rune.

The Other Other White Meat

Mechanical trap (level 1-4, deadly, harm)

Nailed to the walls of this subterranean tunnel are dozens of pointed ears. The trap designer enchanted the area with an *alarm* spell, set to alert a creature that lairs nearby.

Trigger (Creature Detector). A good elf that enters the tunnel triggers the trap.

Effect (Release Creatures). The sound of a hand bell fills the tunnel for 10 seconds, audible out to 60 feet. The sound wakes up a creature. Roll on the table below to determine what creature is roused.

d8	Creature
1	1 brown bear
2	**4 constrictor snakes**
3	**4 giant badgers**
4	**4 giant centipedes**
5	**4 giant poisonous snakes**
6	**1 giant scorpion**
7	**1 giant spider**
8	**2 swarms of insects**

Countermeasures. A creature that succeeds on a DC 20 Intelligence (History) check can recall some rumors about the trap; casting *detect magic* reveals an aura of abjuration on the tunnel. A spellcaster can disrupt the enchantment on the tunnel with a successful DC 20 spellcasting ability check; *dispel magic* also disables the trap.

Shrinking Chamber

Mechanical trap (level 1-4, deadly, harm)

At the end of the corridor is a locked iron door, covered with rust. Next to it is a polished metal button.

Trigger (Press Button). A creature that presses the button triggers the trap.

Effect (Crushing Ceiling/Walls). The walls of this corridor start to move slowly inwards, at a rate of 1 foot per round at the end of the initiative order. Once the surface reaches a creature's space, they take 1d10 bludgeoning damage. If the surface is still moving on the next turn, the creature is restrained and takes 2d10 bludgeoning damage. A third round spent being crushed inflicts 4d10 bludgeoning damage, the fourth and every round thereafter inflicts 10d10 bludgeoning damage until the surface retracts. The walls retract after covering 5 feet.

Countermeasures (Difficult). A successful DC 20 Wisdom (Perception) check reveals something about the button. A successful DC 20 Intelligence (Investigation) check reveals the nature of the trigger, and allows a creature to attempt a DC 20 Dexterity check while using thieves' tools to disable it.

Symbol of Congealing

Mechanical trap (level 1-4, deadly, harm)

The floor of this sandstone temple is cut with blood stained gutters that form a complex pattern of sinister design. Statues of half-human half-ooze creatures line the walls.

Trigger (Spill Blood). If a creature that bleeds loses at least 5 hit points in this chamber, the blood fills the gutters and starts to drip down to the oozes below, awakening them.

Effect (Release Creatures). The round after blood starts to reach them, 2 **gray oozes** flow up from beneath the floor of this chamber and attack all creatures within.

Countermeasures. A successful DC 20 Wisdom (Perception) check reveals the tiny holes in the gutters and the gentle pulsing of ooze below. The gutters can be blocked up with sand or mud or something similar, no ability check required.

Tipping Floor

Mechanical trap (level 1-4, deadly, harm)

The floor of the passageway is balanced so that it tips when enough weight gets past the halfway point.

Trigger (Weight Sensitive Surface). When one Medium sized or larger creature passes the halfway point of the passage the trap activates.

Effect (Drop Into Lower Area). When the trap activates, the passage tips, forming a ramp. All creatures in the passageway must make a DC 20 Dexterity saving throw. On a successful save a creature is able to jump to safety or cling to the floor as it tips downward. On a failed save, the creature falls into a lower area of the dungeon or structure and takes 17 (5d6) bludgeoning damage.

Countermeasures. A successful DC 20 Wisdom (Perception) check reveals a gap along the edges of the passageway floor, and a successful DC 20 Dexterity check using thieves' tools locks the hinge in place. A DC 20 Intelligence (Investigation) check reveals a well-hidden lever to deactivate the trap.

Level 5-8 Traps

So, we were finally out of that godsforsaken jungle and into the somewhat cooler interior of the temple. After clearing aside some cobwebs and most certainly disturbing more insects than I care to think about, we sallied forth into the bowels of the temple, ready to get our hands on this artifact we've been hearing so much about.

We head along down a corridor and, in retrospect, I feel like I should have known something was up. Long abandoned temple, tripwires-of-barbarian-murdering hidden in the trees, and here we were with a nice, long, open corridor? Not bloody likely...

I looked around and saw dust motes floating in the air, shimmering in the sunlight coming through the temple entry. It was almost kind of pretty. Then I noticed more dust. Falling dust. From the ceiling. As soon as I opened my mouth to say something, we all felt this deep rumbling coming from around us. Yes, it was pretty clear that things were about to get bad, and quickly.

The left wall started inching toward us and I could sense tiny (or, in some cases, not-so-tiny) bouts of claustrophobia blossoming in all of us. To make matters worse, foot-long spikes erupted from the mouths of the sculptures on the wall to our right. If we didn't do something fast, we were going to be pulped or skewered; a fate I would perhaps wish on my worst enemies but almost certainly not upon myself or my companions.

As the walls got close, our barbarian (gods bless the brute) stretched out his arms and braced against them. Every vein in his face stood out as he strained, his feet wide, his shoulders and back bunching and flexing as the pressure built. A horrendous grinding sound came from a mechanism within the walls as it fought the big man's incredible strength. He started screaming as his bones began cracking, muscle tearing. Our cleric started healing him, mending his body even as it was breaking...

And then there was a sound, like a clank, a clatter, or something falling apart, and the wall stopped. We were alive for the moment, but something told me this isn't the worst this place can do...

The traps in this chapter are designed to challenge characters who are levels 5-8 and are grouped by their lethality. Any of these traps can be dropped right into a dungeon or similar adventure and shouldn't require any preparation. For more information on customizing traps, go to **Chapter 8: Designing Traps**, or for a completely random and unexpected trap, go to **Chapter 9: Random Trap Generator**.

Level 5-8 Traps Table

Roll a d100 on the table below to choose a random trap appropriate for 5-8 characters, or select a desired lethality and roll a d10.

	d100	d10	Trap	Page
Setback	1-2	1	Baffling Barriers	27
	3-4	2	Burning Blade	27
	5-6	3	Chasm of Capturing	27
	7-8	4	Dastardly Darts	27
	9-10	5	Fire Grate	28
	11-12	6	Open & Close	28
	13-14	7	Rune of *Scorching Ray*	28
	15-16	8	Safeguarded Sword	28
	17-18	9	Sticky Situation	28
	19-20	10	Trapdoor Pitfall, Lesser	29
Moderate	21-22	1	Chest of Fumes	29
	23-24	2	Glyph of Blazing Nuisance	29
	25-26	3	Gunge Tank	30
	27-28	4	Peacekeeper	30
	29-30	5	Putrid Slime	30
	31-32	6	Rogue's Bane, Lesser	30
	33-34	7	Separating Slab	30
	35-36	8	Spellcaster's Spirit	31
	37-38	9	Still Water	31
	39-40	10	Urn of Silence	31
Dangerous	41-42	1	All or Nothing	32
	43-44	2	Ambiguous Ascension	32
	45-46	3	Falling Fids	32
	47-48	4	Frozen Tome	32
	49-50	5	Gruesome Decoration	33
	51-52	6	Magical Melting	33
	53-54	7	Sanguine Idol	33
	55-56	8	Shocking Surprise	33
	57-58	9	Step Lightly	33
	59-60	10	Vampiric Shrine	34
Perilous	61-62	1	Blazing Rings, Lesser	34
	63-64	2	Crystal Combination	34
	65-66	3	Drowning Pool	35
	67-68	4	Eye of Madness	35
	69-70	5	Formidable Glare	35
	71-72	6	Illusion Confusion	36
	73-74	7	Knowledge is Dangerous	36
	75-76	8	Life-Giving Light	36
	77-78	9	Pressurized Poison	36
	79-80	10	Wall of Fireball	37
Deadly	81-82	1	Crushing Chamber	37
	83-84	2	Curiosity Petrified the Cat	37
	85-86	3	Dead of Winter	38
	87-88	4	Fiery Feast	38
	89-90	5	Fire Bad	38
	91-92	6	Introspection	38
	93-94	7	Ooze Fault Was That?	39
	95-96	8	Restless Guardians	39
	97-98	9	Sinister Flame	39
	99-100	10	Writhing Embrace	39

Level 5-8 Setback

These traps should present a minor inconvenience to characters of this level range.

Baffling Barriers

Mechanical trap (level 5-8, setback, block)

A sturdy hand crank is affixed to a wall next to a closed portcullis. Turning the crank raises the portcullis, but also makes hidden portcullises drop down and block other exits from the area.

Trigger (Turn Wheel/Crank). Raising the portcullis more than 1 foot triggers the trap.

Effect (Barrier). All other exits to the chamber are blocked by a portcullis which drops into their threshold and locks in place. A portcullis can be unlocked with a successful DC 10 Dexterity check using thieves' tools and then raised with a successful DC 10 Strength check.

Countermeasures (Difficult, Sensitive). The hidden portcullises and the mechanism on the crank can be spotted with a successful DC 10 Wisdom (Perception) check, and successful DC 10 Intelligence (Investigation) check allows a character to understand the mechanism enough to disable it. A successful DC 10 Dexterity check using thieves' tools disables the trap, and a check with a total of 5 or lower triggers the trap.

Burning Blade

Magic trap (level 5-8, setback, harm)

A cresset filled with crackling flames stands in a place of pride at the centre of the chamber. It has been forged to resemble a diabolical face with its mouth open as if in a hideous scream of pain.

Trigger (Draw Weapon). Unsheathing a metal weapon or carrying a drawn metal weapon into the trapped area triggers the trap.

Effect (Heat Metal). The trap makes the drawn or unsheathed weapon glow red-hot. Any creature in physical contact with the object takes 8 (2d8) fire damage from the trap.

If a creature is holding or wearing the object and takes the damage from it, the creature must succeed on a DC 11 Constitution saving throw or drop the object if it can. If it doesn't drop the object, it has disadvantage on attack rolls and ability checks until it does so.

This effect lasts until dispelled or for 1 minute.

Countermeasures. An aura of transmutation magic surrounds the cresset when viewed with *detect magic*, and a creature that succeeds on a DC 10 Wisdom (Perception) check finds some melted remnants of weapons scattered around the area. With a successful DC 10 Intelligence (Arcana) check, a creature knows the melted pieces were affected by a spell of some kind.

A spellcaster that succeeds on a DC 10 spellcasting ability check can channel a little bit of magic into the cresset and disable it. Casting *dispel magic* on the cresset also disables the trap.

Chasm of Capturing

Hybrid trap (level 5-8, setback, subdue)

A rickety rope bridge is the only way to span a chasm, beneath which is a swirling portal.

Trigger (Weight Sensitive Surface). If a creature of size Medium or larger moves across the bridge, they must succeed on a DC 10 Dexterity (Acrobatics) check or the bridge breaks.

Effect (Drop Into Portal). Any creatures on the bridge when it breaks fall into the chasm unless they succeed on a DC 10 Dexterity saving throw. At the bottom of the chasm is a portal that teleports creatures into a large holding cell, deeper into the surrounding area. A successful DC 10 Intelligence (Arcana) check, or *detect magic*, reveals the nature of the portal, but not where it goes.

Countermeasures (Difficult). A creature that succeeds on a DC 10 Wisdom (Perception) check spots the flimsy nature of the bridge. A successful DC 10 Intelligence (Investigation) check reveals that the bridge won't bear much weight, and allows a creature to attempt a DC 10 Dexterity check while using thieves' tools or carpenter's tools to disable the trap.

Dastardly Darts

Hybrid trap (level 5-8, setback, harm)

This chamber has dozens of dart holes along it's walls, but no pressure plates, tripwires, or mechanical triggers of any kind. A *rune of detection* near the floor of the chamber lights up when creatures of a certain type reach the middle of the area, filling the room with poisoned darts.

Trigger (Creature Detector). When a creature of the chosen type reaches the middle of the trapped room the trap activates.

Effect (Darts). The trap fires two darts at each creature in the room. Each ranged attack has a +5 attack bonus and deals 1 piercing damage and 3 (1d6) poison damage.

Countermeasures. A creature that succeeds on a DC 10 Wisdom (Perception) check can find small darts scattered around the outside of the room, as well as the rune near the floor. The rune can also be found with *detect magic*.

With a successful DC 10 Intelligence (Arcana) check, a creature can disrupt the rune; *dispel magic* also disables the trap.

Fire Grate

Mechanical trap (level 5-8, setback, harm

This bare chamber is featureless except for the large, ornate fireplace against the far wall. The mantle and hearth are made of marble sculpted into the form of a twisting dragon. A dim light emits from the back of the fireplace, but it is otherwise cold.

Trigger (Pressure Plate). The fireplace is large enough for one Medium creature to investigate, but if they do they step on a pressure plate and trigger the trap.

Effect (Barrier). The triggering creature must succeed on a DC 10 Dexterity saving throw or be trapped as metal bars shoot up from the floor behind them, sealing them in the fireplace. The cage bars can be pushed down with a successful DC 10 Strength check.

Countermeasures. The pressure plate can be spotted with a successful DC 10 Wisdom (Perception) check, and a successful DC 10 Dexterity check using thieves' tools disables the trap.

Open & Close

Mechanical trap (level 5-8, setback, block)

The circular steel door leading out of a tunnel has a metal wheel attached to it, which can open the door but also triggers the trap.

Trigger (Turn Wheel/Crank). Turning the wheel triggers the trap and locks the door.

Effect (Barrier). A portion of the tunnel ceiling 20 feet back from the door opens, and boulders and debris rain down on a 10-foot square area. Any creatures in the area of the rubble must make a DC 10 Dexterity saving throw, taking 7 (2d6) bludgeoning damage on a failure, or half as much on a success.

Clearing the rubble or smashing open the door requires a successful DC 10 Strength check. The door can also be unlocked with a DC 10 Dexterity check using thieves' tools.

Countermeasures. The mechanism on the crank can be spotted with a successful DC 10 Wisdom (Perception) check, and a successful DC 10 Dexterity check using thieves' tools disables the trap.

Rune of Scorching Ray

Hybrid trap (level 5-8, setback, harm)

A *rune of detection* glyph is written on the wall, floor, or ceiling. When a creature gets too close, the rune activates a hidden jet of flame.

Trigger (Creature Detector). A creature that gets within 20 feet of the rune triggers the trap.

Effect (Elemental Blast). When activated, the rune releases a jet of flame from the hidden nozzle. The trap makes a ranged attack against the triggering creature and up to two other targets within 20 feet. These attacks have a +5 bonus and deal 7 (2d6) fire damage each, and these attacks can't gain advantage or disadvantage.

Countermeasures. A creature that succeeds on a DC 10 Wisdom (Perception) check can spot the rune and the hidden nozzle for the flame jet, 5 feet below it. The rune can also be found with *detect magic*.

A creature adjacent to the rune can disable it with a DC 10 Intelligence (Arcana) check, although in most cases getting that close would set off the trap. *Dispel magic* can also disable the rune.

Safeguarded Sword

Hybrid trap (level 5-8, setback, subdue)

Resting atop a stone plinth covered by an embroidered velvet cloth is an immaculate blade. The silvered sword shines with radiance, illuminating a poem engraved upon the blade. A *rune of detection* is worked into the embroidery on the cloth.

Trigger (Read Writing). Reading the script on the blade aloud triggers the trap.

Effect (Drop Into Empty Pit). When activated, the rune opens a trapdoor that creates a pitfall around the plinth. Any creature within 5 feet of the plinth must succeed on a DC 10 Dexterity saving throw or fall into a 20-foot deep pit.

A creature that falls into the pit takes 7 (2d6) bludgeoning damage and is restrained by the thick grease at the bottom of the pit. A creature restrained by the grease can free themselves with a successful DC 10 Strength check.

Countermeasures. A creature that succeeds on a DC 10 Wisdom (Perception) or Intelligence (Arcana) check can spot the rune, and it can also be found with *detect magic*. A successful DC 10 Intelligence (Arcana) check or casting *dispel magic* on the rune disables it.

Sticky Situation

Mechanical trap (level 5-8, setback, hinder)

When a creature steps on a pressure plate, a hidden hatch in the ceiling springs open and several gallons of an extremely sticky slime drop down.

Trigger (sensitive, Pressure Plate). The hatch is 15 feet square, and the pressure plate is a 5-foot square in the middle of that area. Stepping on the pressure plate activates the trap.

Effect (Falling Object). The slimed area is difficult terrain and any creature that enters or starts its turn in the area must succeed on a DC 10 Dexterity saving throw or be restrained. As an action, a creature restrained by the slime can make a DC 10 Strength (Athletics) check; if it succeeds it is no longer restrained.

Countermeasures (Sensitive). A successful DC 10 Wisdom (Perception) check reveals the pressure plate and ceiling hatch and a successful DC 10 Dexterity check using thieves' tools disables the trap. A check with a total of 5 or lower triggers the trap.

Trapdoor Pitfall, Lesser

Mechanical trap (level 5-8, setback, subdue)

A 30-foot deep vertical shaft is hidden under a trapdoor, disguised to look like the rest of the floor. The trapdoor covers a 5-foot square space and has a pressure plate embedded in it.

Trigger (Pressure Plate). A creature that steps on the trapdoor activates the pressure plate, causing the trap door to swing open.

Effect (Drop Into Empty Pit). The triggering creature must make a DC 10 Dexterity saving throw. On a success, the creature is able to grab onto the edge of the pit. On a failure, the creature falls into the pit and takes 11 (3d6) bludgeoning damage.

Countermeasures. A successful DC 10 Wisdom (Perception) check reveals the pressure plate and a successful DC 10 Dexterity check using thieves' tools disables the trap.

Level 5-8 Moderate

These traps will probably harm characters of this level.

Chest of Fumes

Mechanical trap (level 5-8, moderate, harm)

This well-adorned and locked chest contains something of value. A glass vessel containing a noxious concoction is hidden in the lid and breaks open if the chest is unlocked by any means other than with its key.

Trigger (Wrong Key). Using the wrong key (such as a skeleton key), or successfully picking the lock triggers the trap.

Effect (Poison Gas). When triggered, the glass vessel within the lid breaks open and creates a 20-foot-radius sphere of poisonous, yellow-green fog centered on the chest. The fog spreads around corners. It lasts for 1 minute or until strong wind disperses the fog, Its area is heavily obscured.

When a creature enters the fog's area for the first time on a turn or starts its turn there, that creature must make a DC 12 Constitution saving throw. The creature takes 14 (4d6) poison damage on a failed save, or half as much damage on a successful one.

Countermeasures. A successful DC 12 Wisdom (Perception) or Intelligence (Investigation) check reveals the mechanism in the lid that will release the vial. A successful DC 12 Dexterity check using thieves' tools disables the trap.

Glyph of Blazing Nuisance

Magic trap (level 5-8, moderate, harm)

A *glyph of warding (flaming sphere)* is inscribed on the floor of this room. If an open flame is created within or brought into the chamber, it instantly leaps off its torch, escapes from its lantern, or hops out of the campfire and becomes a *flaming sphere.*

Trigger (Produce Light/Darkness). If a creature creates or brings an open flame into the chamber, the trap is triggered.

Effect (Spell Effect). When activated, the glyph casts *flaming sphere*; a 5-foot-diameter sphere of fire appears in an unoccupied space next to the triggering creature. Any creature that ends its turn within 5 feet of the sphere must make a DC 12 Dexterity saving throw. The creature takes 7 (2d6) fire damage from the sphere on a failed save, or half as much damage on a successful one.

Each round, on initiative count 10, the sphere moves up to 30 feet, always trying to stay next to the triggering creature. If the sphere runs into a creature, that creature must make the saving throw against the sphere's damage, and the sphere stops moving this turn.

The sphere can jump over barriers up to 5 feet tall and across pits up to 10 feet wide. The sphere ignites flammable objects not being worn or carried, and it sheds bright light in a 20-foot radius and dim light for an additional 20 feet.

The sphere lasts until dispelled, or for 1 minute.

Countermeasures. A creature can find the glyph with a successful DC 12 Intelligence (Investigation) check or with *detect magic*. A successful DC 12 Intelligence (Arcana) check, or *dispel magic*, disables the glyph.

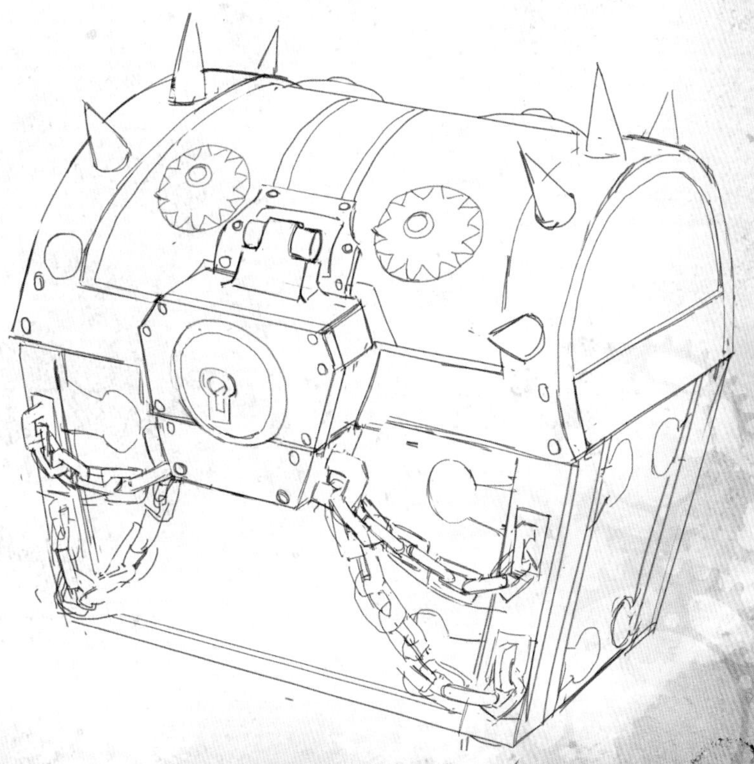

Gunge Tank

Mechanical trap (level 5-8, moderate, harm)

An alcove large enough for a single Medium creature is empty, except for a chain dangling in the middle. Etched into the back of the alcove is a door frame. Pulling the chain doesn't open the door; it drops a barrel of acidic slime onto the triggering creature.

Trigger (Pull Rope/Chain). Pulling on the rope triggers the trap.

Effect (Falling Objects). The barrel falls onto the triggering creature and splashes it with slime. The creature must make a DC 12 Dexterity saving throw, taking 5 (1d10) bludgeoning damage plus 16 (3d10) acid damage on a failed save, or half as much acid damage on a successful one, and no bludgeoning damage.

Countermeasures. A successful DC 12 Wisdom (Perception) check reveals the trigger, and a successful DC 12 Dexterity (Sleight of Hand) check disables the trap.

Peacekeeper

Magic trap (level 5-8, moderate, harm)

A *glyph of warding (shatter)* is hidden in this chamber, destroying drawn weapons. Hopefully, the explosion will let cooler heads prevail.

Trigger (Draw Weapon). The first creature to draw a weapon in the area or bring a drawn weapon into the area sets off the trap.

Effect (Spell Effect). When activated, the glyph casts *shatter*. Each creature in a 10-foot-radius sphere centered on the triggering creature must make a DC 12 Constitution saving throw. A creature takes 13 (3d8) thunder damage on a failed save, or half as much on a successful one. A creature holding an item in their hand must succeed on a DC 12 Dexterity saving throw or drop what they are holding as they cover their ears.

Countermeasures. The glyph can be found with a successful DC 12 Intelligence (Investigation) check or *detect magic. Dispel magic* or a successful DC 12 Intelligence (Arcana) check disables the glyph.

Putrid Slime

Mechanical trap (level 5-8, moderate, hinder)

The faint smell of death and decay comes from this chamber. The corpse of a slain adventurer, monster, or animal is lying on the floor. A putrid slime, giving off a wretched smell, coats the corpse.

Trigger (Interact With Bait). A creature that touches or searches the dead creature inadvertently gets the slime on their hands and clothing.

Effect (Acid/Slime Blast).The slime is especially difficult to remove, and the smell gets worse and worse as the creature moves around. Creatures stained with the slime have disadvantage on Dexterity (Stealth) checks for 1 hour. The slime can be removed with 10 minutes of thorough scrubbing with soap and water.

Countermeasures. A successful DC 13 Wisdom (Perception) check reveals the slime on the corpse, and a successful DC 13 Intelligence (Nature) check reveals the effect of the slime.

Rogue's Bane, Lesser

Mechanical trap (level 5-8, moderate)

A poorly disguised tripwire is easily detected, but it hides the real trap that is set to go off if the decoy is tampered with.

Trigger (False Trigger). Disarming or attempting to disarm the false trigger sets off the real trap.

Effect (Random). Randomly select a mechanical trap of the same or lower lethality and use its effect.

Countermeasures (Difficult). A successful DC 12 Wisdom (Perception) check reveals the false trigger. A successful DC 12 Intelligence (Investigation) check reveals its true nature. A successful DC 12 Dexterity check using thieves' tools disables the real trap.

Separating Slab

Hybrid trap (level 5-8, moderate, block)

A rotting fresco on the walls depicts hundreds of alarmed faces; a *rune of detection* is worked into the fresco. Parts of the plaster have fallen away, revealing the moldy walls beneath.

Trigger (Pass Area). A creature that moves past the center of the room triggers the trap.

Effect (Barrier). A 1-inch wide stone slab drops down across the center of the room with a massive thud, splitting it in two. A creature that succeeds on a DC 12 Dexterity check can slip under the slab as it descends.

Countermeasures. If a creature succeeds on a DC 12 Wisdom (Perception) check, they spot the rune worked into the fresco. The rune can also be found with *detect magic*. A creature can disable the rune with a successful DC 12 Intelligence (Arcana) check or with *dispel magic*.

Spellcaster's Spirit

Magic trap (level 5-8, moderate, hinder)

An enormous glass tube takes up the majority of this arcane workshop. Floating inside it is the corpse of an elderly female human, dressed in robes and wielding a staff.

Trigger (Break Object). If a creature breaks the glass tube, the trap triggers.

Effect (Fear). A ghostly figure that resembles the human in the tube flies out of it, screaming and flailing. All creatures that can see the terrifying figure must succeed on a DC 10 Wisdom saving throw or become frightened. A creature frightened this way must take the Dash action and move away from the tube by the safest available route on each of its turns, unless there is nowhere to move.

If the creature ends its turn in a location where it doesn't have line of sight to the tube, the creature can make a Wisdom saving throw. On a successful save, this effect ends for that creature.

This effect ends for all creatures if dispelled with *dispel magic* or after 1 minute.

Countermeasures (Difficult). The glass tube has an aura of illusion magic when viewed with *detect magic*. A creature that succeeds on a DC 10 Intelligence (Investigation) check finds some scattered notes in the workshop that explain the nature of the trap.

A spellcaster can disrupt the enchantment on the tube with a successful DC 10 spellcasting ability check; *dispel magic* cast on the tube also disables the trap.

Still Water

Mechanical trap (level 5-8, moderate, harm)

A large fountain takes up most of this room. The fountain is 10 feet wide, 20 feet long, and 2 feet deep. Coins and gems litter the bottom of the fountain, but disturbing the water releases 4 ice mephits.

Trigger (Disturb Liquid). Disturbing the water triggers the trap.

Effect (Release Creatures). The ice mephits have made this fountain their home. When the water is disturbed they attack, trying to drive off intruders.

Countermeasures. Due to their False Appearance trait, the mephits are almost impossible to spot under the water; they appear as crystal clear shards of ice. However, they could be detected with *detect evil and good* or with features like the paladin's Divine Sense.

Urn of Silence

Magic trap (level 5-8, moderate, hinder)

A beautifully painted urn depicting monks in silent worship sits in a depression. The urn rests on a plinth that glows with a soft radiance. Lifting the urn reveals a small *glyph of warding (silence)*.

Trigger (Cast Spell). A creature that casts a spell within 20 feet of the urn triggers the trap.

Effect (Spell Effect). When activated, the glyph casts *silence*. For 10 minutes or until dispelled, no sound can be created within or pass through a 20-foot-radius sphere centered on the triggering creature. Any creature or object entirely inside the sphere is immune to thunder damage, and creatures are deafened while entirely inside it. Casting a spell that includes a verbal component is impossible there.

Countermeasures. A successful DC 12 Intelligence (Investigation) check or *detect magic* reveals the glyph. *Dispel magic* or a successful DC 12 Intelligence (Arcana) check disables it.

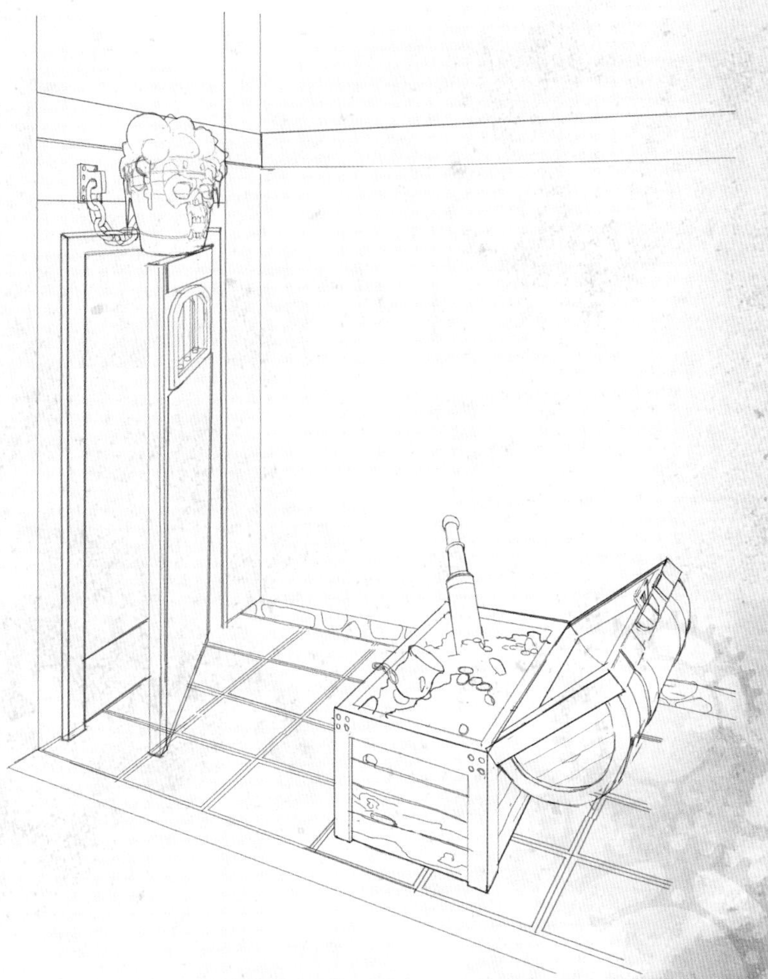

Level 5-8 Dangerous

These traps are likely to seriously injure (and potentially kill) characters of these levels.

All or Nothing

Mechanical trap (level 5-8, dangerous, block)

A series of portcullises blocks the path forward: one every 5 feet. The first one is resting at an angle around 3 feet up as if jarred in place. Creatures could easily get beneath it.

Trigger (Remove Barrier). Removing a portcullis, usually by lifting it up, triggers the trap.

Effect (Barrier). Lifting a portcullis makes the previous one close, forcing creatures to proceed forward.

Countermeasures (Difficult). A successful DC 15 Wisdom (Perception) check reveals the mechanisms hidden in the slots for each portcullis. With a successful DC 15 Intelligence (Investigation) check, a creature understands the trap, and a successful DC 15 Dexterity check while using thieves' tools disables it.

Ambiguous Ascension

Mechanical trap (level 5-8, dangerous, harm)

A thick, knotted rope dangles from the top of this cylindrical shaft. The bottom end of the rope is coiled on the floor of the chamber, and the top end is attached to something out of sight at the top of the shaft.

Trigger (Pull Rope). Pulling on the rope in an attempt to climb it or test its sturdiness triggers the trap.

Effect (Falling Object). When pulled off it's ledge, a 10-gallon ceramic vessel crashes and spreads alchemist's fire and oil in a 15-foot radius centered on the triggering creature. All creatures in the area must make a DC 15 Dexterity saving throw, taking 28 (8d6) fire damage on a failed save, or half as much on a successful one.

Countermeasures (Difficult). A creature that succeeds on a DC 15 Wisdom (Perception) check notices something odd about the rope, and with a successful DC 15 Intelligence (Investigation) check they can spot that the rope is tied to a ceramic jar at the top of the shaft, instead of a firm anchor point. A creature can remove the rope without setting off the trap by succeeding on a DC 15 Dexterity (Sleight of Hand) check.

Falling Fids

Mechanical trap (level 5-8, dangerous, harm)

The lower deck of the pirate ship is poorly lit and filled with hammocks; a large chest is secured here, obscured by tarps.

Trigger (Tension Cable). A thin wire connects the chest lid to the ceiling. If the lid is lifted the wire goes slack, triggering the trap.

Effect (Falling Objects). Conical wooden spikes (called fids) fall from the ceiling. The triggering creature must make a DC 15 Dexterity saving throw, taking 33 (6d10) piercing damage on a failed save, or half as much on a successful save.

Countermeasures (Sensitive). A successful DC 15 Wisdom (Perception) check reveals the trap, and a successful DC 15 Dexterity check while using thieves' tools disables it. If the check to disable the trap totals 10 or less, the trap is triggered.

Frozen Tome

Magic trap (level 5-8, dangerous, harm)

Horrifying wailing sounds burst forth from a tome resting on a plinth made of ice. Swirling ink covers the pages of the tome, throbbing in sync with the screams.

Trigger (Open/Close Object). Closing the tome stops the screams, but triggers the trap.

Effect (Elemental Blast). A blast of cold erupts from the tome, freezing it in a block of ice. All creatures in a 15-foot cone centered on the triggering creature must make a DC 15 Dexterity saving throw, taking 21 (6d6) cold damage on a failure or half as much on a success. The tome can be broken free of the ice with a DC 15 Strength check.

Countermeasures (Difficult). The tome has an aura of evocation magic when viewed with *detect magic*, and a creature that succeeds on a DC 15 Wisdom (Perception) check can spot fragments of shattered ice around the base of the plinth. Examining the tome and succeeding on a DC 15 Intelligence (Arcana) check lets a creature understand how the trap works.

A spellcaster can make a DC 15 spellcasting ability check to try and disrupt the magic around the tome, and *dispel magic* cast on it will disable the trap as well.

Gruesome Decoration

Mechanical trap (level 5-8, dangerous, harm)

The corpse of a slain adventurer is suspended on the wall by four spears jutting out from holes in the wall. Four more spears are hidden in the wall, set to go off when the corpse is disturbed.

Trigger (Interact With Bait). A creature that searches the corpse triggers the trap.

Effect (Spears). Four heavy, poison-tipped spears thrust out of the wall. The triggering creature must make a DC 15 Dexterity saving throw, taking 18 (4d8) piercing damage and 14 (4d6) poison damage on a failed save, or half as much of both on a successful one.

Countermeasures (Sensitive). A successful DC 15 Wisdom (Perception) check reveals the mechanism attached to the corpse. A successful DC 15 Dexterity check using thieves' tools disables the mechanism, and a check with a total of 10 or lower triggers the trap.

Magical Melting

Magic trap (level 5-8, dangerous, hinder)

The door frame before you seems to be made of melted laboratory tools. The majority of the frame is metal of swirling colors, but poking out of it are random spurs and spikes, as well as shards of crystal, glass, and wood. A *glyph of warding (dispel magic)* is hidden in the lintel of the door frame.

Trigger (Fail to Speak Password). A creature that passes through the opening without speaking the password "solidify" triggers the trap.

Effect (Dispel Magic). When activated, the glyph casts *dispel magic*, targeting the triggering creature. Any spell of 3rd level or lower active on the creature ends.

Countermeasures. A successful DC 15 Intelligence (Investigation) check or casting *detect magic* reveals the glyph. The shards of crystal and glass spell out the password in Primordial.

Speaking the password, a successful DC 15 Intelligence (Arcana) check, or *dispel magic* cast on the glyph disables it.

Sanguine Idol

Magic trap (level 5-8, dangerous, harm)

An idol made of flesh and bone smashed together into the mockery of a man, sickening to behold, stands upon a raised dais. Oil paintings of hideous creatures from the depths of the Abyss surround the dais.

Trigger (Insult Idol). A creature that passes through the chamber with the idol must give it a sacrifice of blood. Failure to do so triggers the trap.

Effect (Summon Creatures). The idol summons 2 quasits that attack the triggering creature. The quasits will defend themselves and attack other creatures but their primary target is the creature that failed to provide a sacrifice. The quasits will not leave the chamber with the idol and return to the Abyss if reduced to 0 hit points or after 24 hours.

Countermeasures. A creature that succeeds on DC 15 Intelligence (Religion) check understands the sacrifice required to propitiate the Abyssal idol. The idol also has an aura of conjuration magic when viewed with *detect magic.*

A spellcaster that succeeds on a DC 15 spellcasting ability check can siphon away some of the magic of the idol, disabling the trap. *Dispel magic* cast on the idol also disables it.

Shocking Surprise

Magic trap (level 5-8, dangerous, harm)

An idol, weapon, relic, or door handle is enchanted to blast any creature that touches it with lightning.

Trigger (Touch Object).Touching the object triggers the trap.

Effect (Elemental Blast). The triggering creature is hit with a lightning blast and must make a DC 15 Constitution saving throw, taking 33 (6d10) lightning damage on a failed save, or half as much on a successful one.

Countermeasures (Difficult). With a successful DC 15 Wisdom (Perception) check, a creature can find scorch marks and the remnants of lightning blasts around the item; a creature that spots this and then succeeds on a DC 15 Intelligence (Arcana) check understands the trap. When viewed with *detect magic*, the object has an aura of evocation magic.

A spellcaster that succeeds on a DC 15 spellcasting ability check can disrupt the enchantment on the object, disabling the trap. *Dispel magic* cast on the object also disables the trap.

Step Lightly

Mechanical trap (level 5-8, dangerous, subdue)

A 10-by-10-foot section of the chamber floor is a hidden trapdoor, designed to break away down the middle when it bears enough weight. Under the trap door is a 30-foot pit with spikes at the bottom.

Trigger (Weight Sensitive Surface). When two Medium creatures or three Small creatures occupy the 10-by-10-foot area, the trapdoor opens.

Effect (Drop Into Spiked Pit). The triggering creature(s) must make a DC 15 Dexterity saving throw. On a successful save, the creature is able to grab onto the edge of the pit. On a failed save, the creature falls into the pit and takes 10 (3d6) bludgeoning damage and 10 (3d6) piercing damage.

Countermeasures (Sensitive). A successful DC 15 Wisdom (Perception) check reveals the weight-sensitive floor. A successful DC 15 Dexterity check using thieves' tools disables the trap, and a check with a total of 10 or lower triggers the trap.

Vampiric Shrine

Magic trap (level 5-8, dangerous, harm)

The stench of blood dripping from an altar fills the air. The scarlet liquid seems to ooze from the stone by some magical means, flowing into cracks in the floor in a constant cycle. On either side of the altar are bronze statues of humanoids with open mouths, baring long fangs.

Trigger (Corpse). Bringing a corpse within 20 feet of the altar triggers the trap.

Effect (Reanimate Creatures). The corpse that triggered the trap is animated as a **ghast** that attacks any creatures in the altar room. The ghast will not go farther than 40 feet from the altar. It crumbles to dust if reduced to 0 hit points or after 24 hours.

Countermeasures. A creature that succeeds on a DC 15 Intelligence (Religion) check knows about the altar and understands the trap. The trap also has an aura of necromancy magic when viewed with *detect magic.*

A spellcaster that succeeds on a DC 15 spellcasting ability check can disrupt the enchantment on the altar, disabling the trap. *Dispel magic* can also disable the trap.

Level 5-8 Perilous

These traps may kill characters of these levels, and will definitely injure them severely.

Blazing Ring, Lesser

Mechanical trap (level 5-8, perilous, harm)

A 1-foot thick ring of decorative stonework surrounds a 25-foot diameter circular area in the center of the room. The ceiling directly above the ring is blackened with soot. In the 5-foot square at the circle's center is something intriguing.

Trigger (Weight Sensitive Floor). When a Small or larger creature steps onto a space adjacent to the 5-foot square at the center of the area within the ring, they activate a pressure plate. Parts of the stonework slide away, revealing spouts which pour flaming oil onto the floor from the ring's inner edge.

Effect (Wall of Fire). The flaming oil creates a ringed wall of flames 25 feet in diameter, 20 feet high, and 1 foot thick. The wall is opaque and lasts for 1 minute. When the wall appears, each creature within its area must make a DC 17 Dexterity saving throw. On a failed save, a creature takes 28 (8d6) fire damage, or half as much damage on a successful save.

The side of the wall facing inwards deals the trap's fire damage to each creature that ends its turn within 10 feet of that side or inside the wall. A creature takes the same damage when it enters the wall for the first time on a turn or ends its turn there. The other side of the wall deals no damage.

A creature that is adjacent to the wall can make a DC 17 Constitution check using thieves' tools to end this effect.

Countermeasures. A successful DC 17 Wisdom (Perception) check reveals the pressure plate, and a successful DC 17 Dexterity check while using thieves' tools disables it.

Crystal Combination

Hybrid trap (level 5-8, deadly, harm)

A locked door has 6 colored crystals embedded around the edges and a *rune of detection* inscribed on the front. To unlock the door, the crystals must be arranged in the correct order in a pattern of holes in the center of the door.

Trigger (Wrong Combination). Arranging the crystals in the incorrect order triggers the trap.

Effect (Falling Sand). Small chutes open in the room's ceiling and disgorge sand that quickly fills the room. Creatures in the area must make a successful DC 17 Dexterity saving throw at the beginning of their turns to stay atop the sand. The save DC increases by 2 at the end of each round.

A creature that fails one saving throw is buried up to their knees and restrained. On their next saving throw, if the creature succeeds they dig themselves out and are no longer restrained; if they fail they are buried waist-deep and remain restrained.

A creature buried waist-deep must make a DC 17 Strength saving throw at the beginning of their turn; if they succeed they dig themselves free of the sand and if they fail they are buried to the neck and immobilized. On their next turn, the creature is completely buried and starts suffocating.

As an action, a creature can dig out another creature with a successful Strength (Athletics) check against the current save DC of the trap. Spells like *freedom of movement* or movement modes like burrow can also allow creatures to freely move through the sand.

Countermeasures. A successful DC 17 Wisdom (Perception) check reveals the hidden chutes for the sand. A creature that succeeds on a DC 17 Intelligence (Investigation) check understands that only the correct combination of crystals in the door's center will open the door. Clues for the correct combination might be present in the room or elsewhere in the surrounding area.

The *rune of detection* is plainly visible, and also revealed with *detect magic.* A creature can disable the rune with a successful DC 17 Intelligence (Arcana) check, which disables the trap.

Drowning Pool

Mechanical trap (level 5-8, perilous, block)

This chamber is filled with algae-strewn water that sloshes at ankle-height. Moss has grown on the pillars and walls, as well as the door leading out of the chamber. Affixed to one pillar is a large iron wheel.

Trigger (Turn Wheel/Crank). Turning the wheel clockwise triggers the trap.

Effect (Drop Into Water). Trap doors open beneath the creature turning the wheel, pulling them into a pit filled with water unless they succeed on a DC 17 Strength saving throw. The trap doors close and lock above the triggering creature, sealing them in the water where they begin suffocating. A creature can unlock the trap doors from either side with a successful DC 17 Dexterity check using thieves' tools.

Countermeasures. A successful DC 17 Wisdom (Perception) check reveals the trigger, and a successful DC 17 Dexterity check using thieves' tools disables the trap.

Eye of Madness

Magic trap (level 5-8, perilous, hinder)

A demonic statue sits cold and silent, with two rubies for eyes. One of its eyes glows with an enchanted twinkle, which hides a *glyph of warding (confusion)*. If a creature gets close enough to look at the enchanted ruby they risk being driven mad.

Trigger (Look Into). A creature that gets within 20 feet of the statue and looks into the enchanted ruby triggers the trap. A creature can avoid looking at the ruby, but they have disadvantage on any ability checks made to find or disable the trap.

Effect (Spell Effect). The triggering creature and each creature in a 10-foot radius around them must succeed on a DC 17 Wisdom saving throw or be confused for 1 minute or until dispelled (*dispel magic* DC 14). A confused creature must roll a d10 at the start of each of its turns to determine its behavior for that turn.

d10	Behavior
1	The creature uses all its movement to move in a random direction. To determine the direction, roll a d8 and assign a direction to each die face. The creature doesn't take an action this turn.
2-6	The creature doesn't move or take actions this turn.
7-8	The creature uses its action to make a melee attack against a randomly determined creature within its reach. If there is no creature within its reach, the creature does nothing this turn.
9-10	The creature can act and move normally.

At the end of each of its turns, a confused creature can make another DC 17 Wisdom saving throw. If it succeeds, this effect ends for that creature.

Countermeasures. A creature that succeeds on a DC 17 Intelligence (History or Religion) check recognizes the statue and is aware of the trap. The glyph can be found with a successful DC 17 Intelligence (Investigation) check, or with *detect magic*.

Once found, the glyph can be deactivated with *dispel magic* (DC 14) or with a successful DC 17 Intelligence (Arcana) check.

Formidable Glare

Magic trap (level 5-8, perilous, hinder)

A polished glass dome protects a lifesize statue of a fearsome dragon, somehow sculpted from solidified lava. The dragon's eyes are made of rubies that flare and glow like embers. A *glyph of warding (hold person)* is inscribed on the left eye.

Trigger (Look Into). Looking into the statue's eyes triggers the trap.

Effect (Restraint). When activated, the glyph casts *hold person* on the triggering creature, which must succeed on a DC 17 Wisdom saving throw or be paralyzed for 1 minute. At the end of each of its turns, the creature can make another Wisdom saving throw. On a success, the spell ends. *Dispel magic* can also end the spell.

Countermeasures. A successful DC 17 Intelligence (Investigation) check or *detect magic* reveals the glyph. A successful DC 17 Intelligence (Arcana) check or *dispel magic* disables it.

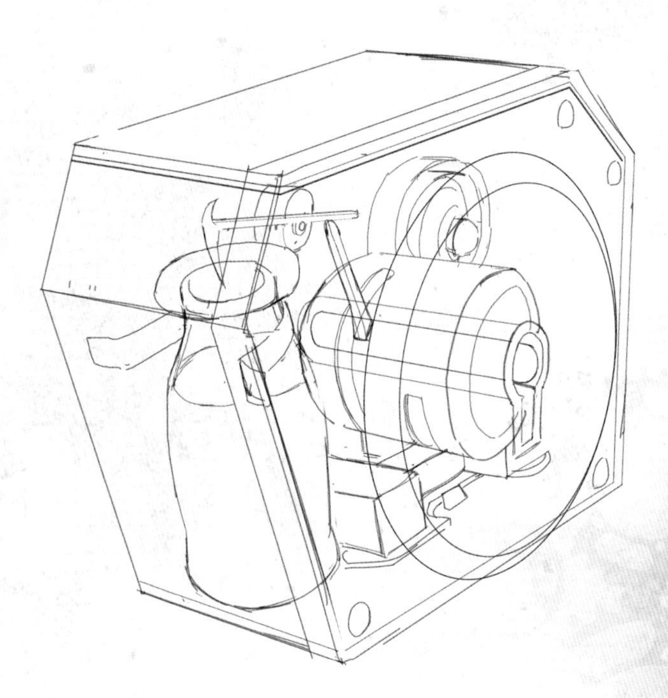

Illusion Confusion

Magic trap (level 5-8, perilous, harm)

The chamber is filled with a strange, lingering ash-like dust. A relief carving on the floor depicts a strange sigil. The same symbol, but in reverse, is on the ceiling directly overhead. A *glyph of warding (phantasmal killer)* is worked into the reversed symbol.

Trigger (Pass Area). A creature that passes over the runic symbol on the floor triggers the trap.

Effect (Spell Effect). When activated, the glyph casts *phantasmal killer*, targeting the triggering creature. The spell taps into the nightmares of the creature and creates an illusory manifestation of its deepest fears, visible only to that creature. The target must make a DC 17 Wisdom saving throw. On a failed save, the target becomes frightened for the duration.

At the end of each of the target's turns before the spell ends, the target must succeed on a DC 17 Wisdom saving throw or take 22 (4d10) psychic damage. On a successful save, the spell ends. The spell also ends if dispelled or after 1 minute.

Countermeasures. If a creature investigates the dust around the room and succeeds on a DC 17 Intelligence (Arcana) check, they can discern the residue of materials used to make the glyph and they know about the trap. This doesn't reveal the location of the glyph, but the creature knows it's in the room somewhere.

A creature can find the glyph with a successful DC 17 Intelligence (Investigation) check or with *detect magic*. Once found, a successful DC Intelligence (Arcana) check or *dispel magic* (DC 14, 4th-level spell) disables the trap.

Knowledge is Dangerous

Mechanical trap (level 5-8, perilous, block)

Floor-to-ceiling bookshelves cover the walls of this room. Although all of the books could be interesting, one with a golden spine catches the eye.

Trigger (Pick Up/Shift Object). Pulling the golden-spined book from the shelf triggers the trap.

Effect (Barrier). Every door leading out of the library slams shut and locks. The doors can be opened with a successful DC 17 Strength check, or a DC 17 Dexterity check using thieves' tools.

Countermeasures. A successful DC 17 Wisdom (Perception) check reveals that the book is trapped, and a successful DC 17 Dexterity check using thieves' tools disables it.

Life-Giving Light

Magic trap (level 5-8, perilous, harm)

The floor of this dark cavern is uneven, and something crunches sickeningly beneath your feet as you enter.

Trigger (Produce Light/Darkness). Bringing or producing light, non-magical or magical, into the cavern triggers the trap.

Effect (Reanimate Creatures). Light reveals the bones in this room and they begin to glow with a sickly hue, animating into 8 **skeletons** that attack all creatures in the cavern. The skeletons will not leave the cavern, and they stay active until reduced to 0 hit points, or until 24 hours pass, at which point they crumble to dust. The skeletons can also be dispelled with *dispel magic*.

Countermeasures (Difficult). A creature that succeeds on DC 17 Wisdom (Perception) finds bone fragments scattered all around the room; with a successful DC 17 Intelligence (Arcana) check, a creature can discern the fragments are remnants of animated creatures. When viewed with *detect magic,* the room has an aura of necromancy magic.

With a successful DC 17 spellcasting ability check, a spellcaster can disrupt the enchantment on this room. *Dispel magic* also disables this trap.

Pressurized Poison

Mechanical trap (level 5-8, perilous, harm)

Wooden floorboards cover the floor of the corridor ahead, in stark contrast to the carpeted floors behind you. The corridor is relatively wide, allowing several creatures to walk side-by-side, and is at least 30 feet long.

Trigger (Weight Sensitive Surface). When a Medium or larger creature steps on the central floorboard, the bottles of poison hidden beneath burst and emit a noxious gas.

Effect (Poison Gas). The trap creates a 20-foot radius sphere of poisonous gas. It lasts for 10 minutes or until strong wind disperses the fog. Its area is heavily obscured. When a creature enters the fog for the first time on a turn or starts its turn there, that creature must make a DC 17 Constitution saving throw. The creature takes 28 (8d6) poison damage on a failed save, or half as much damage on a successful one.

Countermeasures. A successful DC 17 Wisdom (Perception) check reveals the trapped floorboard, and a successful DC 17 Dexterity check using thieves' tools disables it.

Wall of Fireball

Magic trap (level 5-8, perilous, harm)

This charred-black chamber is notably hotter than the rest, and a single stone in one wall glows bright with orange veins of a lava-like substance. A *glyph of warding (burning hands)* is inscribed on the glowing stone.

Trigger (Creature Detector). A creature that gets within 5 feet of the stone triggers the trap.

Effect (Elemental Blast). When activated, the glyph casts *burning hands* as a 5th level spell. Each creature in a 15-foot cone centered on the triggering creature must make a DC 17 Dexterity saving throw. A creature takes 24 (7d6) fire damage on a failed save, or half as much damage on a successful one.

The fire ignites any flammable objects in the area that aren't being worn or carried.

Countermeasures. A creature can spot the rune without activating it with a successful DC 17 Intelligence (Investigation) check; *detect magic* can also reveal the glyph.

With a successful DC 17 Intelligence (Arcana) check a creature can disable the rune, but to do so they would need to be next to the glyph, activating it. *Dispel magic* can also disable the glyph.

Level 5-8 Deadly

These traps will almost certainly kill characters of these levels.

Crushing Chamber

Mechanical trap (level 5-8, deadly, harm)

The exit to the chamber or corridor is blocked by a locked door, portcullis, or other removable barrier. On the wall next to the exit are six small levers inset in the wall. They are all in the down position.

Trigger (Move Lever/Press Button). Moving any of the levers except one to the up position triggers the trap.

Effect (Crushing Ceiling/Walls). Any other exits to the chamber or corridor are suddenly blocked by a door, portcullis, or other barrier. A grinding noise fills the area the ceiling begins to drop down. The ceiling moves at a rate of 1 foot per round at the end of the initiative order. Once the surface reaches a creature's space, they take 5 (1d10) bludgeoning damage. If the surface is still moving on the next turn, the creature is restrained and takes 10 (2d10) bludgeoning damage. A third round spent being crushed inflicts 20 (4d10) bludgeoning damage, the fourth and every round thereafter inflicts 50 (10d10) bludgeoning damage and then the surface retracts.

Countermeasures (Difficult). A successful DC 20 Wisdom (Perception) check reveals the gap between the walls and the ceiling. A successful DC 20 Intelligence (Investigation) check reveals that one of the levers is far more worn than the rest, indicating that it's the correct lever while the rest are decoys. The locked exit can also be opened with a successful DC 20 Dexterity check using thieves' tools.

Curiosity Petrified the Cat

Magic trap (level 5-8, deadly, hinder)

The room is packed full of strange curiosities and trinkets, including a throne made of leather and bone, a suit of armor made of red metal, a flask of silvery liquid, an open book filled with symbols and glyphs, a twisting obsidian candlestick, and dozens of other oddities. Standing out from them all is a prism filled with swirling purple smoke.

Trigger (Detect Magic). A creature that casts *detect magic* within the chamber triggers the trap.

Effect (Petrification). When triggered, the prism shatters and the smoke within surges towards the triggering creature and down their airways. The creature must make a DC 20 Constitution saving throw. On a failed save, the creature is restrained as their flesh begins to harden and change into ivory. On a successful save, the creature isn't affected.

A creature restrained in this way must make a DC 20 Constitution saving throw at the end of each of its turns. If it successfully saves against this effect three times, the effect ends for that creature. If it fails its save three times, it is turned into a statue of ivory and petrified. The successes and failures don't need to be consecutive; keep track of both until the creature collects three of a kind.

The creature remains petrified until the effect is dispelled, either with *dispel magic* or *greater restoration*, or after 1 hour. If a creature is physically broken while petrified, it suffers from similar deformities if it reverts to its original state.

Countermeasures (Difficult). A creature that succeeds on a DC 20 Wisdom (Perception) check can find fragments of stone in odd shapes scattered around the area, remnants of petrified creatures. With a successful DC 20 Intelligence (Arcana) check, a creature understands the danger of the smoke inside the prism and how the trap is activated.

A spellcaster can disrupt the enchantment on the prism with a successful DC 20 spellcasting ability check or with *dispel magic* (DC 15).

Dead of Winter

Magic trap (level 5-8, deadly, harm)

A strange book with an intricate blue leather cover rests in this room, surrounded by chunks of ice. A *glyph of warding (ice storm)* is inscribed inside the book.

Trigger (Creature Detector). The trap is triggered if any non-good creature opens the book.

Effect (Spell Effect). When activated, the glyph casts *ice storm* as a 5th-level spell. A hail of rock-hard ice pounds to the ground in a 20-foot-radius, 40-foot-high cylinder centered on the triggering creature. Each creature in the cylinder must make a Dexterity saving throw. A creature takes 13 (3d8) bludgeoning damage and 14 (4d6) cold damage on a failed save, or half as much damage on a successful one.

Countermeasures. A creature that succeeds on a DC 20 Intelligence (History) check remembers details about this book and understands the trap. The book also has an aura of abjuration magic when viewed with *detect magic*, and the glyph can be found with a successful DC 20 Intelligence (Investigation) check.

Once found, the glyph can be disabled with *dispel magic* or with a successful DC 20 Intelligence (Arcana) check.

Fiery Feast

Mechanical trap (level 5-8, deadly, block)

This chamber is lit by lava which flows in gutters around the top of the walls. The floor is made of hexagonal blocks of obsidian, as are the room's long, central table and the surrounding chairs. The table is covered with roasted meats, ash-covered molten cheeses, and crusty loaves of bread.

Trigger (Weight Sensitive Surface). The six armless chairs are each a single piece of obsidian, including the floor piece. When a Small size or larger creature sits in a chair, the floor below them erupts in a jet of flame. Each chair can be triggered separately, and disabling one chair doesn't disable the others.

Effect (Elemental Blast). The triggering creature must make a DC 20 Dexterity saving throw. They take 55 (10d10) fire damage on a failed save, or half as much on a success.

Countermeasures. A successful DC 20 Wisdom (Perception) check reveals the mechanism connected to each chair, and a successful DC 20 Dexterity check while using thieves' tools disables the trap for that chair.

Fire Bad

Magic trap (level 5-8, deadly, harm)

A *glyph of warding (conjure elemental)* is inscribed on the ceiling of this room. If any kind of open flame - candles, torches, or lanterns - are brought into or ignited in this room, the glyph summons an **air elemental**.

Trigger (Produce Flame). If any open flame is brought into or ignited in the room, the trap is triggered.

Effect (Summon Creature). When activated, the glyph casts *conjure elemental*. An air elemental appears in an unoccupied space within 10 feet of the open flame that triggered the trap. The elemental disappears when it drops to 0 hit points or after 1 hour. The elemental also disappears if targeted with *dispel magic* (DC 15, 5th-level spell).

The elemental is hostile to all creatures in the room and attacks indiscriminately, but it will not leave the room.

Countermeasures. A creature that can see in the dark can find the glyph on the ceiling with a successful DC 20 Intelligence (Investigation) check; *detect magic* can also reveal the glyph. Once found, a creature can disable the glyph with a successful DC 20 Intelligence (Arcana) check or with *dispel magic*.

Introspection

Magic trap (level 5-8, deadly, hinder)

Polished to perfection, the enormous black opal in the centre of this chamber shows a shadowed version of reality in its reflection. Resting on a small plinth, the spherical jewel is at least six feet across and exudes a chilling aura.

Trigger (Look Into). A creature adjacent to the opal can look into it to investigate distorted reflection. Unfortunately, gazing into the opal triggers the trap.

Effect (Invisibility). The creature must succeed on a DC 20 Constitution saving throw or become invisible for 10 minutes, or until this effect is dispelled (*dispel magic* DC 15). Anything the creature is wearing or carrying is invisible as long as it is on their person. A creature rendered invisible by the jewel can be seen in the shadowy version of reality inside it, but is otherwise invisible.

Countermeasures. A creature that succeeds on a DC 20 Intelligence (Arcana or History) check recognizes the jewel and understands the danger of the trap. The jewel has an aura of illusion magic when viewed with *detect magic*.

A spellcaster can disrupt the enchantment on the jewel with a successful DC 20 spellcasting ability check; casting *dispel magic* (DC 15) on the jewel also disables the trap.

Ooze Fault Was That?

Mechanical trap (level 5-8, deadly, harm)

Hundreds of bottles hang from the ceiling on thin pieces of wire, each filled with a strange, ooze-like creature. The miniature oozes slop against their glass prisons as you walk past, as if sensing your presence. By the chamber door is a shelf of bottles filled with different fluids, and a complex device resembling a set of scales. The scales are weighed down completely on one side with one of the fluid-filled bottles.

Trigger (Wrong Combination). Weighing down the other side of the scale completely triggers the trap.

Effect (Falling Objects). The ooze-filled bottles fall from the ceiling. Avoiding a falling bottle requires a successful DC 20 Dexterity saving throw. Creatures who fail to avoid the vessels are covered with mini-oozes. The first time the oozes cover a creature, and at the start of each of their turns when covered with ooze, the creature takes 17 (5d6) acid damage. A creature can scrape an ooze off themselves or another creature as an action.

Countermeasures. A successful DC 20 Wisdom (Perception) check reveals the trigger and a successful DC 20 Dexterity check using thieves' tools disables it.

Restless Guardians

Magic trap (level 5-8, deadly, harm)

The statue of a deity sits atop a well-adorned pedestal with a *glyph of warding (spirit guardians)* inscribed on it. The glyph is keyed to creatures of a particular type or alignment.

Trigger (Creature Detector). A creature of the chosen type approaching within 5 feet of the statue triggers the trap.

Effect (Spell Effect). When activated, the glyph casts *spirit guardians* as a 5th level spell. A sudden swirl of tiny angelic (good deity), fey (neutral deity), or fiendish (evil deity) spirits materialize around the triggering creature. The glyph doesn't specify any creatures to be unaffected by this spell.

The guardians affect an area in a 15-foot radius around the triggering creature. In that area, other creatures' speed is halved and when a creature enters the area for the first time on a turn or starts its turn there, they must make a DC 20 Wisdom saving throw. On a failed save, the creature takes 22 (5d8) radiant damage (if the deity is good or neutral) or 22 (5d8) necrotic damage (if the deity is evil). On a successful save, the creature takes half as much damage.

The guardians last for 10 minutes or until dispelled with *dispel magic* (DC 15, 5th-level spell).

Countermeasures. A creature that succeeds on a DC 20 Intelligence (Religion) check recognizes the statue and understands the trap. The glyph can be found with a DC 20 Intelligence (Investigation) check or with *detect magic*.

Once found, the glyph can be disabled with *dispel magic* or with a successful DC 20 Intelligence (Arcana) check.

Sinister Flame

Magic trap (level 5-8, deadly, harm)

In the center of this room's floor is a broad, low-rimmed stone bowl, with a *glyph of warding (conjure elemental)* inscribed within. A drip of flammable liquid from the ceiling lands in the bowl periodically. If an open flame is brought into or ignited in the area, the flame of the torch or lamp suddenly becomes animated, leaps down to the floor, runs to the bowl and jumps into it, igniting an incredible blaze. From the inferno emerges a **fire elemental**.

Trigger (Produce Flame). Bringing an open flame or igniting one in the room triggers the trap.

Effect (Summon Creature). When activated, the glyph casts *conjure elemental*. A fire elemental appears in an unoccupied space within 10 feet of the bowl and is hostile to all creatures in the room. The elemental disappears after 1 hour, or when it drops to 0 hit points or if dispelled with *dispel magic* (DC 15, 5th-level spell).

Countermeasures. A creature that can see in the dark can find the glyph in the bowl with a successful DC 20 Intelligence (Investigation) check; *detect magic* can also reveal the glyph. Once found, a creature can disable the glyph with a successful DC 20 Intelligence (Arcana) check or with *dispel magic*.

Writhing Embrace

Magic trap (level 5-8, deadly, block)

A small black opal rests alone on the smooth flagstone floor in the middle of a long corridor. A *glyph of warding (black tentacles)* is inscribed on the underside of the opal.

Trigger (Creature Detector). When a creature gets within 5 feet of the opal the trap activates.

Effect (Spell Effect). The glyph casts *black tentacles*; squirming, ebony tentacles fill a 20-foot square on the ground, centered on the triggering creature. For 1 minute or until dispelled, these tentacles turn the ground in the area into difficult terrain.

When a creature enters the affected area for the first time on a turn or starts its turn there, the creature must succeed on a DC 20 Dexterity saving throw or take 10 (3d6) bludgeoning damage and be restrained by the tentacles until the spell ends. A creature that starts its turn in the area and is already restrained by the tentacles takes 10 (3d6) bludgeoning damage.

Countermeasures. A successful DC 20 Intelligence (Investigation) check can find the glyph, but a creature close enough to examine the opal sets off the trap. *Detect magic* also reveals the glyph.

A successful *dispel magic* disables the glyph; a successful DC 20 Intelligence (Arcana) check can also disable the glyph but a creature would need to be close enough to set off the trap to tamper with the glyph in this way.

Level 9-12 Traps

I am a self-aware rogue. I can admit my faults. I know what I am. I say this because, and I know this may surprise some of you, I have a weakness for gold and expensive looking things. With that out of the way...

We got through that godawful corridor, ultimately unscathed thanks to the combined efforts of the cleric and the barbarian. After this harrowing moment, we, of course, chose to continue onward, perhaps because we may not be the best at taking architecturally-based hints that none-too-subtly say "STAY OUT!"

We came to this lovely courtyard surrounded by walls and overgrown greenery. In the center of this courtyard was a pedestal, and on this pedestal sat a wonderfully expensive-looking golden idol of a happy little monkey. I know what you're thinking, and yes, I am not so lacking in humility to admit that I wanted it. Badly.

Something in my head started encouraging me to take the idol. Taking expensive-looking things tends to be my modus operandi anyway, so of course, I strode boldly forth and snatched the little golden rascal. Easy as taking candy from someone incapable of stopping a thief from taking their candy.

Then, before I knew it, as I was staring lovingly at my new favorite thing, I couldn't feel my hand. A blackness started creeping from my fingertips, over my hand, and up my arm! Everyone saw. I started screaming. Then the barbarian started screaming and decides he can solve the problem in his usual way: with his axe! Thankfully, before he turned me into an idol-less amputee, our wizard (bless her) got in his way.

Out of what I can only guess was a sense of self-preservation that overcame my sense of self-enrichment, I dropped the idol back onto the pedestal. Our cleric made it over to me and used some of that wonderful divine magic to get my arm back to its old familiar self again.

I'll never understand the people who build these places, using perfectly good valuables as mere bait for good rogues like myself just trying to get by. What's the world coming to...

The traps in this chapter are designed to challenge characters who are levels 5-8 and are grouped by their lethality. Any of these traps can be dropped right into a dungeon or similar adventure and shouldn't require any preparation. For more information on customizing traps, go to **Chapter 8: Designing Traps**, or for a completely random and unexpected trap, go to **Chapter 9: Random Trap Generator**.

Level 9-12 Traps Table

Roll a d100 on the table below to choose a random trap appropriate for 9-12 characters, or select a desired lethality and roll a d10.

	d100	d10	Trap	Page
Setback	1-2	1	Animal Article	42
	3-4	2	Bad Key	42
	5-6	3	Blinded by Greed	42
	7-8	4	Demonic Bars	43
	9-10	5	Earthen Clearing	43
	11-12	6	Gas Bomb	43
	13-14	7	Hydroblast	44
	15-16	8	Portal Puddle	44
	17-18	9	Sleep Sounds	44
	19-20	10	Trapdoor Pitfall	44
Moderate	21-22	1	Acid Arrow	45
	23-24	2	Bloody Chamber	45
	25-26	3	Dropped into Hell	45
	27-28	4	Green Mist	46
	29-30	5	Manticore Statue	46
	31-32	6	Pilfering Pincushion	46
	33-34	7	Rogue's Bane	46
	35-36	8	Scrap Room	46
	37-38	9	Spirit Skull	47
	39-40	10	Shafted	47
Dangerous	41-42	1	Bewildering Bait	47
	43-44	2	Caustic Drop	48
	45-46	3	Disappearing Tube	48
	47-48	4	Font of Fire	48
	49-50	5	Ice Entice	48
	51-52	6	Magnum Ignis	48
	53-54	7	Murderous Menagerie	49
	55-56	8	No Wizzids Alawd	49
	57-58	9	Popping Rot	49
	59-60	10	Vile Touch	50
Perilous	61-62	1	Bathe the Tiger	50
	63-64	2	Crystal Light	51
	65-66	3	Cube of Encaging	51
	67-68	4	The Forest Walks	51
	69-70	5	Invisible Barricade	51
	71-72	6	Mirrored Flame	52
	73-74	7	Model Disaster	52
	75-76	8	The Old Needle in Lock	52
	77-78	9	A Riveting Read	52
	79-80	10	Rolling Stop	53
Deadly	81-82	1	Back to the Cradle	53
	83-84	2	Blazing Rings	53
	85-86	3	Burning Barricade	54
	87-88	4	Corrosive Pit	54
	89-90	5	Enchanted Armory	54
	91-92	6	Lightning Breath	54
	93-94	7	Scything Blades	55
	95-96	8	Shockingly Secure	55
	97-98	9	Sinister Skulls	55
	99-100	10	Small Folk Only	55

Level 9-12 Setback

These traps should present a minor inconvenience to characters of this level range.

Animal Article

Magic trap (level 9-12, setback, hinder)

A small statuette of an animal is enchanted to transform a creature that picks it up, to prevent thievery. This sort of trap may be used by someone who has a use for such animals, or perhaps just has a strange sense of humor.

Trigger (Pick Up Object). A creature that picks up the statuette triggers the trap.

Effect (Transmutation). The triggering creature makes a DC 10 Wisdom saving throw. If the creature fails, they are transformed into the same beast as the statue for 10 minutes, or until they drop to 0 hit points or die. This effect doesn't work on a shapechanger or a creature with 0 hit points.

A transformed creature's game statistics, including mental ability scores, are replaced by the statistics of the beast it transforms into. It retains its alignment and personality. The creature assumes the hit points of its new form. When it reverts to its normal form, the creature returns to the number of hit points it had before it transformed. If it reverts as a result of dropping to 0 hit points, any excess damage carries over to its normal form. As long as the excess damage doesn't reduce the creature's normal form to 0 hit points, it isn't knocked unconscious.

A transformed creature is limited in the actions it can perform by the nature of its new form, and it can't speak, cast spells, or take any other action that requires hands or speech. The creature's gear melds into the new form. It can't activate, use, wield, or otherwise benefit from any of its equipment.

At the end of each of its turns, a creature transformed by this effect can make another Wisdom saving throw. On a success, this effect ends. This effect also ends for all creatures if dispelled, either with *dispel magic* or *remove curse*.

Countermeasures (Difficult). With a successful DC 10 Wisdom (Perception) check, creatures can find evidence of the animal around the room: things like fur, horns, broken pieces of tack, and the like. Once found, a creature that succeeds on a DC 10 Intelligence (Arcana) check realizes these are from polymorphed creatures and is aware of the trap.

The statuette has an aura of transmutation magic when viewed with *detect magic*. With a successful DC 10 spellcasting ability check, a spellcaster can disrupt the enchantment on the statue, disabling the trap. Casting *dispel magic* on the statuette also disables the trap.

Bad Key

Mechanical trap (level 9-12, setback, harm)

The corridor slopes down towards a single, battered door. The door looks as if it has been battered by something big, but it remains locked. The keyhole is complex, with lots of tiny spurs inside.

Trigger (Use Wrong Key). Picking the lock or using any key but the correct one activates a separate mechanism inside the door.

Effect (Rolling Boulder). The ceiling above the higher end of the corridor opens, releasing a massive circular boulder that rolls toward the bottom of the corridor. All creatures present roll initiative as the sphere is released. The sphere rolls initiative with a +8 bonus. On its turn, it moves 60 feet in a straight line. The sphere can move through creatures' spaces, and creatures can move through its space, treating it as difficult terrain.

Whenever the sphere enters a creature's space or a creature enters its space while it's rolling, that creature must succeed on a DC 10 Dexterity saving throw or take 10 (3d6) bludgeoning damage and be knocked prone. The sphere stops when it hits a wall or similar barrier. It can't go around corners.

As an action, a creature within 5 feet of the sphere can attempt to slow it down with a DC 10 Strength check. On a successful check, the sphere's speed is reduced by 15 feet. If the sphere's speed drops to 0, it stops moving and is no longer a threat.

Countermeasures. A creature can spot the hidden mechanism with a successful DC 10 Wisdom (Perception) check, and a successful DC 10 Dexterity check using thieves' tools disables the trap.

Blinded by Greed

Magic trap (level 9-12, setback, hinder)

An ornately detailed scroll case is mounted into a heavy stone base carved to resemble a humanoid hand.

Trigger (Tension Cable). Lifting the scroll case puts tension on the cable attached to it, triggering the trap.

Effect (Blindness). Magical darkness fills a 15-foot-radius sphere around the scroll case. The darkness spreads around corners. A creature with darkvision can't see through this darkness, and non-magical light can't illuminate it.

The darkness emanates from the scroll case and moves with it. Completely covering the case with an opaque object, such as a bowl or a helm, blocks the darkness. If any of this effect's area overlaps with an area of light created by a spell of 2nd level or lower, the spell that created the light is dispelled.

The darkness lasts for 10 minutes or until dispelled with *dispel magic*.

Countermeasures. A creature that succeeds on a DC 10 Wisdom (Perception) check spots the tension cable, and a successful DC 10 Dexterity check using thieves' tools disables it.

The scroll case has an aura of evocation magic when viewed with *detect magic*, and a creature that succeeds on a DC 10 Intelligence (Arcana) check understands the effect of this trap but not the trigger. With a successful DC 10 spellcasting ability check, a spellcaster can disrupt the enchantment on the scroll case, disabling the trap. *Dispel magic* also disables the trap.

Demonic Bars

Mechanical trap (level 9-12, setback, block)

The long corridor ahead is covered by green, shimmering demon mouths carved from stone. They appear every 10 feet down the 60-foot long corridor in vertical lines on the walls. At each line of demon mouths, a pressure plate is set into the floor.

Trigger (Pressure Plate). A Small or larger creature stepping on a pressure plate triggers the trap.

Effect (Barrier). Iron bars shoot from each line of demon mouths, forming a 6 grates across the corridor. A creature in the 5-foot wide area in front of the demon mouths must make a DC 10 Dexterity check. On a success, the creature can choose which side of the barrier they end up on; otherwise, the creature lands on a random side of the barrier.

Countermeasures (Sensitive). A successful DC 10 Wisdom (Perception) check lets a creature spot a pressure plate, and each one can be disabled with a successful DC 10 Dexterity check using thieves' tools. However, a check that totals 5 or less sets off the trap.

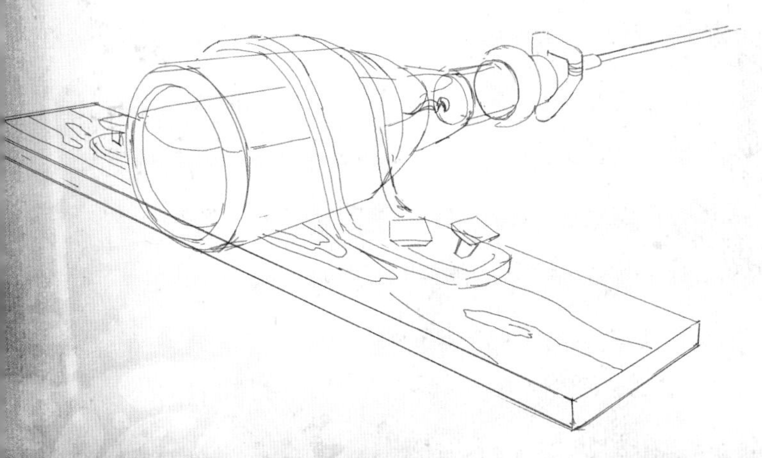

Earthen Clearing

Mechanical trap (level 9-12, setback, harm)

Rune-covered monoliths mark the edges of this clearing. In the center of the clearing is a large spherical stone that sits in the opening of a vertical tunnel shaft, blocking it from being opened. 4 dust mephits are trapped in the shaft.

Trigger (Pick Up/Shift Object). Moving the sphere away from the opening it covers triggers the trap.

There is no ability check to disable this trap because nothing is preventing the stone from being moved.

Effect (Release Creatures). The dust mephits trapped held in the vertical tunnel beneath the stone are released into the area and attack all other creatures. If dropped to half of their hit points or fewer, the mephits flee.

Countermeasures. A creature that succeeds on a DC 10 Wisdom (Perception) check hears the sounds of the mephits scrabbling and chattering in the tunnel. With a successful DC 10 Intelligence (Arcana) check, a creature recognizes the sounds and can identify the mephits.

Gas Bomb

Mechanical trap (level 9-12, setback, harm)

Often used to alert the trap setter of incoming danger, the gas bomb is triggered by a tripwire along the floor connected to the cork of a bottle containing a clever alchemical concoction. As soon as the cork is pulled the bottle explodes in a cloud of gas; the sound of the bottle opening is audible at quite a distance.

Trigger (Tripwire). A creature that walks through the trip wire activates the trap.

Effect (Poison Gas). A 20-foot-radius sphere of poisonous, yellow-green fog erupts from a point next to the triggering creature. The fog spreads around corners. It lasts for 10 minutes or until strong wind disperses the fog, ending the spell. Its area is heavily obscured.

When a creature enters the spell's area for the first time on a turn or starts its turn there, that creature must make a DC 10 Constitution saving throw. The creature takes 10 (3d6) poison damage from the trap on a failed save, or half as much damage on a successful one.

The fog moves 10 feet away from its starting point at the start of each round, rolling along the surface of the ground. The vapors, being heavier than air, sink to the lowest level of the land, even pouring down openings.

Countermeasures (Sensitive). A successful DC 10 Wisdom (Perception) check reveals the trip wire. A successful DC 10 Dexterity check using thieves' tools disables the trip wire, and a check with a total of 5 or lower triggers the trap.

Hydroblast

Hybrid trap (level 9-12, setback, harm)

The alcove ahead is shrouded in darkness and a soft tinkling can be heard from within it, perhaps the sound of coins or gemstones falling into a pile. It's distinctly different from the sounds heard throughout the rest of the area. In the alcove, a *rune of detection* waits to activate a powerful jet of water.

Trigger (Step Into Light/Darkness). A creature moving into the shadowed alcove triggers the trap.

Effect (Elemental Blast). When activated, the rune triggers a hidden mechanism that emits a blast of water. The blast attacks the triggering creature with a +5 ranged attack bonus and deals 16 (3d10) bludgeoning damage if it hits. A creature hit by the blast is knocked prone.

Countermeasures. A creature that succeeds on a DC 10 Wisdom (Perception) check spots the signs of massive water damage outside the shadowed area. A creature that can see in the dark can find the rune with the same check; *detect magic* also reveals the rune.

Once found, the rune can be disabled with a successful DC 10 Intelligence (Arcana) check or with *dispel magic*. Using light sources to remove the darkness can also bypass the triggering conditions for the trap.

Portal Puddle

Magic trap (level 9-12, setback, subdue)

A beautiful pool sparkling with starlight fills the chamber; a tiled walkway leads around its edge to doors at the far end of the chamber. Steps lead down into the waters, and at the bottom of the pool there is a mosaic of marine scene.

Trigger (Disturb Liquid). A creature that enters the pool triggers the trap.

Effect (Teleport). The triggering creature is instantly teleported into a chamber above this one. The chamber could be a holding cell, or the lair of a monster, or a laboratory.

Countermeasures. A creature that succeeds on a DC 10 Intelligence (History) check recognizes the scene in the mosaic and knows the dangers of the trap. When viewed with *detect magic*, the pool has an aura of conjuration magic.

With a successful DC 10 spellcasting ability check, a spellcaster can disrupt the enchantment on the pool; *dispel magic* cast on the pool also disables the trap.

Sleep Sounds

Magic trap (level 9-12, setback, hinder)

A beautiful noise echoes throughout this gemstone-encrusted cavern. It sounds something like a mixture of whalesong, lyre music, and a heavenly choir. A *glyph of warding (sleep)* is inscribed in this cavern, hidden among the gems.

Trigger (Speak Trigger Word). A creature saying the word 'sound', in either Common or a language appropriate for the area, triggers the trap.

Effect (Sleep). When activated, the glyph casts *sleep* as a 2nd-level spell, sending creatures into a magical slumber. Roll 7d8; the total is how many hit points of creatures the glyph can affect. Creatures within 20 feet of a point next to the triggering creature are affected in ascending order of their current hit points (ignoring unconscious creatures).

Starting with the creature that has the lowest current hit points, each creature affected by this spell falls unconscious for 1 minute, the sleeper takes damage, or someone uses an action to shake or slap the sleeper awake. Subtract each creature's hit points from the total before moving on to the creature with the next lowest hit points. A creature's hit points must be equal to or less than the remaining total for that creature to be affected.

Undead and creatures immune to being charmed aren't affected by this spell. The spell can also be dispelled with *dispel magic*.

Countermeasures. With a successful DC 10 Wisdom (Perception) check, a creature can spot remnants of a journal in the cavern. After reading the journal, a creature can make a DC 10 Wisdom (Insight) check; if they succeed, they deduce the trigger word.

The glyph can be found with a successful DC 10 Intelligence (Investigation) check or with *detect magic*. The glyph can be disabled with a successful DC 10 Intelligence (Arcana) check or with *dispel magic*.

Trapdoor Pitfall

Mechanical trap (level 9-12, setback, subdue)

This 50-foot deep vertical shaft is hidden under a trapdoor which has been disguised to look like the rest of the floor. The trapdoor is 5-foot square and has a pressure plate embedded in it.

Trigger (Pressure Plate). A creature that steps on the trapdoor activates the pressure plate, causing the trap door to swing open.

Effect (Drop Into Pit). The triggering creature must make a DC 10 Dexterity saving throw. On a success, the creature is able to grab onto the edge of the pit. On a failure, the creature falls into the pit and takes 17 (5d6) bludgeoning damage.

Countermeasures. A successful DC 10 Wisdom (Perception) check reveals the pressure plate and a successful DC 10 Dexterity check using thieves' tools disables the trap.

Level 9-12 Moderate

These traps will probably harm characters of this level.

Acid Arrow

Magic trap (level 9-12, moderate, harm)

Hanging from the ceiling above is an ornate brass longbow, covered with strange gears and pistons. Beneath the bow is a copper bowl filled with small cogs, springs, screws, and bolts. The items in the bowl cover up a *glyph of warding (acid arrow)*.

Trigger (Offering). If a creature enters this room and then leaves without placing a small piece of metal into the bowl, the trap activates.

Effect (Elemental Blast). When activated, the glyph casts *acid arrow* as a 3rd-level spell, targeting the triggering creature. A shimmering green arrow streaks towards the target and bursts in a spray of acid. The glyph makes a ranged spell attack against the target with a +6 bonus. On a hit, the target takes 5d4 acid damage immediately and 3d4 acid damage at the end of its next turn. On a miss, the arrow splashes the target with acid for half as much of the initial damage and no damage at the end of its next turn.

Countermeasures. A creature that succeeds on a DC 12 Intelligence (History or Religion) check recognizes the bow and understands the trap.

A creature can find the glyph with a successful DC 12 Intelligence (Investigation) check or with *detect magic*. Once found, the glyph can be disabled with a successful DC 12 Intelligence (Arcana) check or with *dispel magic*.

Bloody Chamber

Hybrid trap (level 9-12, moderate, harm)

The walls of this antechamber are covered with obsidian spikes the length of a human finger. On the floor is a dull *rune of detection*.

Trigger (Spill Blood). A creature that spills blood in the antechamber triggers the trap.

Effect (Impaling Spikes). When activated, the rune engages hidden mechanisms that power impaling spikes. The spikes move at a rate of 1 foot per round, always at the end of the initiative order. They start at one end of the chamber and keep moving until the spikes touch the opposite surface, at which point they retract. When the spikes enter a creature's space, it must make a DC 12 Dexterity saving throw. If the creature fails they take 21 (6d6) piercing damage, or half as much on a success. A creature that fails the saving throw is impaled on the spikes and restrained.

A creature impaled by spikes can free themselves with a DC 12 Constitution (Athletics) check but not until there is room equivalent to their size available in front of the spikes. Another creature can free an impaled creature with a successful DC 12 Strength (Medicine) check, as long as there is room. Once the spikes reach the opposite surface, they retract and return to their starting point, releasing any impaled creatures.

Countermeasures. The rune is easily spotted, and a creature can understand what triggers the rune with a successful DC 12 Intelligence (Arcana) check. A creature can disable the rune with *dispel magic* or with another successful DC 12 Intelligence (Arcana) check.

Dropped into Hell

Mechanical trap (level 9-12, moderate, harm)

This chamber has a strangely bouncy floor and is uncomfortably warm. Mounted on the walls are dozens of busts of infernal creatures with sneering smiles and leering eyes.

Trigger (Musical/Auditory). Making a sound in the chamber causes the floor to vibrate and give way. Creatures who move or perform actions in the trapped area must make a successful DC 12 Dexterity (Stealth) check each round to avoid triggering the trap.

Effect (Drop Into Fire). When triggered, the entire floor to give way. Each creature in the room must make a DC 12 Dexterity saving throw. On a success, the creature is able to grab onto the edge of the pit. On a failure, the creature falls into the 20-foot deep pit and takes 7 (2d6) bludgeoning damage. Green flames lick through a grate at the bottom of the pit. A creature that enters the flames for the first time, or starts its turns in the flames, takes 7 (2d6) fire damage.

Countermeasures (Difficult). A successful DC 12 Wisdom (Perception) check reveals sensitive nature of the floor, and allows a creature to make a DC 12 Intelligence (Investigation) check; if they succeed they understand how the trap works.

A creature who understands the trap can a DC 12 Dexterity check using thieves' tools, disabling the trap on a success. Alternatively, casting *silence* can negate this trigger entirely.

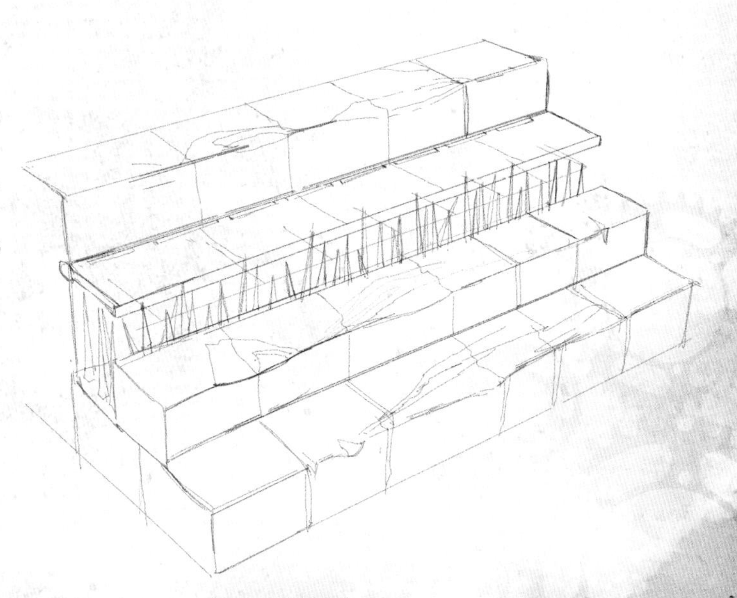

Green Mist

Mechanical trap (level 9-12, moderate, harm)

Atop a stone pedestal sits a shallow copper bowl filled with a clear liquid. A vial of grayish, green liquid is held over the copper bowl, balanced on a thin copper stand. When enough weight is applied to the floor in front of the pedestal, the vial is knocked off of its perch and it drops into the clear liquid. A grayish green mist forms immediately.

Trigger (Weight Sensitive Surface). A creature of Medium size or larger standing in front of the pedestal triggers the trap.

Effect (Poison Gas). A 20-foot-radius sphere of poisonous, grayish-green mist erupts from a point next to the triggering creature. The fog spreads around corners. It lasts for 10 minutes or until strong wind disperses it. Its area is heavily obscured.

When a creature enters the fog's area for the first time on a turn or starts its turn there, that creature must make a DC 12 Constitution saving throw. The creature takes 21 (6d6) poison damage from the trap on a failed save, or half as much damage on a successful one.

The fog moves 10 feet away from its starting point at the start of each round, rolling along the surface of the ground. The vapors, being heavier than air, sink to the lowest level of the land, even pouring down openings.

Countermeasures (Sensitive). With a successful DC 12 Wisdom (Perception) check, a creature can spot the sensitivity of the floor. A successful DC 16 Dexterity check using thieves' tools disables the trap, but a check with a total of 5 or less triggers the trap.

Manticore Statue

Mechanical trap (level 9-12, moderate, harm)

A hideous, lifelike statue of a manticore fills this chamber. Inside the statue's mouth is a small button, just at the back of the tongue.

Trigger (Move Lever/Press Button). Pressing the button triggers the trap.

Effect (Dart). A barrage of 6 darts shoot from the creature's tail toward the triggering creature. The creature must make a DC 12 Dexterity saving throw, taking 7 (3d4) piercing damage and 7 (3d4) poison damage on a failed save, or half as much of both on a successful one.

Countermeasures (Difficult). The button is easy to spot, but with a successful DC 12 Wisdom (Perception) check a creature can find some darts scattered around the base of the statue. A successful DC 12 Intelligence (Investigation) check reveals the hidden mechanisms in the statue, and allows a creature to attempt a DC 12 Dexterity check while using thieves' tools to disable the trap.

Pilfering Pincushion

Mechanical trap (level 9-12, moderate, harm)

The floor and ceiling around an object in the room is densely perforated with small holes. Moving the object activates tension cable, releasing needle-sharp spikes from above and below.

Trigger (Pick Up Object). Lifting the object triggers the trap.

Effect (Spikes). Spikes shoot up from the holes in the floor around the object as well as down from holes in the ceiling. Each creature within 10 feet of the object must make a DC 12 Dexterity saving throw, taking 21 (6d6) piercing damage on a failed save, or half as much on a successful one.

Countermeasures (Sensitive). A creature can spot the tension cable with a successful DC 12 Wisdom (Perception) check, and a successful DC 12 Dexterity check using thieves' tools disables the trap. If the Dexterity check totals 5 or lower, the trap is triggered.

Rogue's Bane

Mechanical trap (level 9-12, moderate)

A poorly disguised tripwire is easily detected, but it hides the real trap that is set to go off if the decoy is tampered with.

Trigger (False Trigger). Disarming or attempting to disarm the false trigger sets off the real trap.

Effect (Random). Randomly select a mechanical trap of the same or lower lethality and use its effect

Countermeasures (Difficult). A successful DC 12 Wisdom (Perception) check reveals the false trigger. A successful DC 12 Intelligence (Investigation) check reveals its true nature. A successful DC 12 Dexterity check using thieves' tools disables the real trap.

Scrap Room

Hybrid trap (level 9-12, moderate, harm)

The room ahead is filled with scrap metal: piles of pewter plates, dozens of hollow steel poles leaned up against the walls, and dented cages piled up high. The walls are dotted with inch-wide holes, and a *rune of detection* is inscribed on one wall.

Trigger (Musical/Auditory). Creatures moving through the area must avoid making loud noises, such as knocking over a pile of junk. When a creature moves through the area or takes an action within it must succeed on a DC 12 Dexterity (Stealth) check or trigger the trap.

Effect (Elemental Blast). Each creature must make a DC 12 Dexterity saving throw, taking 21 (6d6) lightning damage on a failed save, or half as much on a successful one.

Countermeasures. A creature can find the rune with *detect magic* or a successful DC 12 Wisdom (Perception) check. Once found, a creature can disable the rune with *dispel magic* or a successful DC 12 Intelligence (Arcana) check.

Spirit Skull

Magic trap (level 9-12, moderate, harm)

A desk is strewn with papers and parchment, and resting atop the mess is a blood-red crystal skull. A *glyph of warding (spirit guardians)* is inscribed on the skull.

Trigger (Look Into). When a creature looks into the skull, the glyph activates.

Effect (Spell Effect). When activated, the glyph casts *spirit guardians*. A sudden swirl fiendish spirits materialize around the triggering creature. The glyph doesn't specify any creatures to be unaffected by this spell.

The guardians affect an area in a 15 foot radius around the triggering creature. In that area, other creatures' speed is halved and when a creature enters the area for the first time on a turn or starts its turn there, it must make a DC 12 Wisdom saving throw. On a failed save, the creature takes 13 (3d8) necrotic damage. On a successful save, the creature takes half as much damage.

Countermeasures. A creature that succeeds on a DC 12 Intelligence (History) check recognizes the skull and understands the trap. The glyph can be found with a DC 12 Intelligence (Investigation) check or with *detect magic*.

Once found, the glyph can be disabled with *dispel magic* or with a successful DC 12 Intelligence (Arcana) check).

Shafted

Mechanical trap (level 9-12, moderate, harm)

Holes an inch or two wide are scattered in a seemingly random array across the walls and ceiling of this room. Housed within are metal rods intended to bludgeon and pin victims. A pressure plate is concealed in the middle of the room.

Trigger (Pressure Plate). A creature that steps on the pressure plate triggers the trap.

Effect (Spears). The trap makes 6 attack rolls with spears against creatures in the area; each spear has a +6 ranged attack bonus and deals 3 (1d6) piercing damage on a hit. If hit by a spear, a creature is restrained by it. Creatures restrained by spears can make DC 12 Constitution (Athletics) checks to free themselves, taking 1 piercing damage if they fail. Other creatures can free those restrained by the spears with a DC 12 Strength (Medicine) check, again dealing 1 damage to the restrained creature if they fail.

Long metal poles, restrained under pressure within the ceiling and walls, eject down vertically or at 45 degree angles in an area up to 40 feet long with the pressure plate being at the center. Any creatures in the affected area must make a DC 16 Dexterity saving throw, taking 21 (6d6) bludgeoning damage on a failed save and be knocked prone. A creature can use its action to make a DC 16 Strength (Athletics) to free itself or another creature pinned by a pole

Countermeasures (Sensitive). A successful DC 12 Wisdom (Perception) check reveals the pressure plate and a successful DC 12 Dexterity check using thieves' tools disables it. A check with a total of 5 or lower sets off the trap.

Level 9-12 Dangerous

These traps are likely to seriously injure (and potentially kill) characters of these levels.

Bewildering Bait

Magic trap (level 9-12, dangerous, hinder)

A seemingly valuable item is inscribed with a *glyph of warding (confusion)*, so as to thwart potential thieves. This is suited to areas with environmental hazards such as falls or spikes.

Trigger (Touch Object). A creature that touches the object triggers the trap.

Effect (Spell Effect). When activated, the glyph casts *confusion*, assaulting and twisting creatures' minds, spawning delusions and provoking uncontrolled action. Each creature in a 10-foot-radius sphere centered on the triggering creature must succeed on a DC 15 Wisdom saving throw or be affected by the spell.

An affected target can't take reactions and must roll a d10 at the start of each of its turns to determine its behavior for that turn.

d10	Behavior
1	The creature uses all its movement to move in a random direction. To determine the direction, roll a d8 and assign a direction to each die face. tThe creature doesn't take an action this turn.
2-6	The creature doesn't move or take actions this turn.
7-8	The creature uses its action to make a melee attack against a randomly determined creature within its reach. If there is no creature within its reach, the creature does nothing this turn.
9-10	The creature can act and move normally.

At the end of each of its turns, an affected creature can make a DC 15 Wisdom saving throw. If it succeeds, this effect ends for that target. This effect also ends if dispelled with *dispel magic* (DC 14, 4th-level spell), or after 1 minute.

Countermeasures. With a successful DC 15 Intelligence (History) check, a creature can discern that the item isn't really valuable at, but a cheap copy. A creature can find the glyph on the item with a successful DC 15 Intelligence (Investigation) check; this doesn't trigger the trap. Using *detect magic* also reveals the glyph.

Once found, the glyph can be dispelled with *dispel magic* or with a successful DC 15 Intelligence (Arcana) check.

Caustic Drop

Mechanical trap (level 9-12, dangerous, harm)

A thin tripwire is stretched across this room or corridor. A basin or container of corrosive liquid is perched on a hidden ledge, ready tip onto a creature that hits the tripwire.

Trigger (Tripwire). A creature that walks through the tripwire triggers the trap.

Effect (Acid/Slime Blast). The vessel tips and douses the triggering creature with acid. The triggering creature and any creatures adjacent to it must make a DC 15 Dexterity saving throw, taking 31 (9d6) acid damage on a failed save, or half as much on a successful one.

Countermeasures. A successful DC 15 Wisdom (Perception) check lets a creature spot the tripwire, and a successful DC 18 Dexterity check using thieves' tools disables it. A Dexterity check that totals 5 or less triggers the trap.

Disappearing Tube

Hybrid trap (level 9-12, dangerous, hinder)

Eight strange metal tubes cross this chamber, covered with condensation. One of the tubes also has a crack, split, or break in its side. The inside of the tube is pitch-black, and covered with a strange mold.

Trigger (Produce Flame). Bringing an open flame or igniting a flame in the tube triggers the trap.

Effect (Invisibility). The mold releases spores that cover the triggering creature; it must succeed on a DC 15 Constitution saving throw or turn invisible for 8 hours. Anything the target is wearing or carrying is invisible as long as it is on the target's person.

A creature can wash the spores off with 10 minutes of solid scrubbing with soap and water.

Countermeasures. A creature that succeeds on a DC 15 Wisdom (Perception) check spots that the moss is reacting to the presence of the flame. A successful DC 15 Intelligence (Nature) check lets a creature figure out the nature of the moss.

Font of Fire

Mechanical trap (level 9-12, dangerous, harm)

A small spout is nestled in the wall, hidden from all but close inspection or keenest perception. When triggered, the spout sprays a gout of flame. A pressure plate is concealed near the spout.

Trigger (Pressure Plate). When a Medium sized creature or larger steps on the pressure plate, the trap activates.

Effect (Elemental Blast). Highly flammable oil blasts forth from a spout on the wall and ignites, creating a 15-foot-cone of fire centered on the triggering creature. All creatures in the area must make a DC 15 Dexterity saving throw, taking 31 (9d6) fire damage on a failed save, or half as much on a successful one.

Countermeasures. A creature that succeeds on a DC 15 Wisdom (Perception) check can spot the pressure plate and the tiny pilot light in the nozzle. With a successful DC 15 Dexterity check using thieves' tools, a creature can disable the trap.

Ice Entice

Magic trap (level 9-12, dangerous, harm)

At the bottom of a pool lies an enticing object, such as a gem, that covers a *glyph of warding (ice storm)*. When a foolhardy soul reaches into the water to recover the object, disturbing the surface of the liquid, a freezing cold rains down on them.

Trigger (Disturb Liquid). When the liquid is disturbed, the trap activates.

Effect (Spell Effect). When activated, the glyph casts *ice storm*; a hail of rock-hard ice pounds to the ground in a 20-foot-radius, 40-foot-high cylinder centered on the triggering. Each creature in the cylinder must make a DC 15 Dexterity saving throw. A creature takes 9 (2d8) bludgeoning damage and 14 (4d6) cold damage on a failed save, or half as much damage on a successful one.

Countermeasures. A creature can spot the glyph without disturbing the water with a successful DC 15 Intelligence (Investigation) check, or with *detect magic*.

Once found, the glyph can be disabled with *dispel magic*; a successful DC 15 Intelligence (Arcana) check would also disable the glyph, but would require disturbing the water.

Magnum Ignis

Magic trap (level 9-12, dangerous, harm)

Cupboards containing a wide variety of objects and curiosities line the walls of this study. One of them is covered with cobwebs as if it hadn't been touched in years. A closer look reveals a single book inside, with a *glyph of warding (wall of fire)* inscribed within.

Trigger (Open/Close Book). Opening the book triggers the trap.

Effect (Wall of Fire). When activated, the glyph casts *wall of fire*, creating a wall of flames on the floor around the triggering creature. The flames form a ringed wall 20 feet in diameter, 20 feet high, and 1 foot thick. The wall is opaque and lasts for 1 minute or until dispelled with *dispel magic* (DC 14).

When the wall appears, each creature within its area must make a DC 15 Dexterity saving throw. On a failed save, a creature takes 22 (5d8) fire damage, or half as much damage on a successful save.

The interior of the wall deals 22 (5d8) fire damage to each creature that ends its turn within 10 feet of that side or inside the wall. A creature takes the same damage when it enters the wall for the first time on a turn or ends its turn there. The other side of the wall deals no damage.

Countermeasures. A creature that succeeds on a DC 15 Wisdom (Perception) check spots a ring of scorch marks in the center of the room, and a successful DC 15 Intelligence (Arcana) check lets a creature deduce the marks are from a *wall of fire* spell.

The glyph can be found with *detect magic*, or with a successful DC 15 Intelligence (Investigation) check. Once found, the glyph can be dispelled with *dispel magic* or with a successful DC 15 Intelligence (Arcana) check. However, to interact with the glyph with an ability check a creature would have to open the book.

Murderous Menagerie

Magic trap (level 9-12, dangerous, harm)

The room or corridor contains weapon racks and various equipment; 8 of the weapons have been enchanted to animate and attack intruders. What constitutes an intruder is up to the trap's designer.

Trigger (Creature Detector). An unauthorized creature (physical characteristics, race, or alignment) that enters the area activates the trap.

Effect (Animate Objects). The enchanted weapons are **8 flying swords**. They attack unauthorized creatures in the area and ignore all other creatures; they will not leave the area. They crumble to dust if reduced to 0 hit points or dispelled. After 1 minute, the weapons return to their resting places and the trap resets.

Countermeasures. A creature that succeeds at a DC 15 Wisdom (Perception) check spots arcane symbols on the enchanted weapons, and a creature that succeeds on a DC 15 Intelligence (Arcana) check understands that the weapons will animate. The enchanted weapons have an aura of transmutation magic.

The weapons can be disabled with a *dispel magic* (DC 14); a spellcaster that succeeds on a DC 15 spellcasting ability check can also disrupt the enchantment, disabling the trap.

No Wizzids Alawd

Magic trap (level 9-12, dangerous, block)

Hanging from the wall in the ramshackle wooden shack is a poorly-made sign painted with black letters that spell out "No Wizzids Alawd." The goblins captured a wizard and forced him to enchant their sign, giving them a steady stream of spellcasting captives.

Trigger (Detect Magic). A creature that casts *detect magic* triggers the trap.

Effect (Teleport). The triggering creature is teleported to a goblin-run prison.

Countermeasures (Difficult). The sign has an aura of conjuration magic when viewed with *detect magic*, although that does set off the trap. With a successful DC 15 Wisdom (Perception) check, a creature can spot some arcane symbols on the sign; with a successful DC 15 Intelligence (Arcana) check, a creature can understand the symbols and knows the danger of the trap.

A spellcaster can disrupt the enchantment on the sign with a successful DC 15 spellcasting ability check; *dispel magic* (DC 14) also disables the trap.

Popping Rot

Magic trap (level 9-12, dangerous, harm)

Puffs of black, rotting dust blow through this room and the withered husks of dead creatures are scattered throughout, including the corridors outside the room. A *glyph of warding (blight)* is inscribed on the room's floor.

Trigger (Creature Detector). When a living creature enters the area, the trap activates.

Effect (Spell Effect). When activated, the glyph casts *blight*; necromantic energy washes over the triggering creature, draining moisture and vitality from it. The target must make a DC 15 Constitution saving throw. The target takes 36 (8d8) necrotic damage on a failed save, or half as much damage on a successful one. This spell has no effect on undead or constructs. If the triggering creature is a plant creature, it makes the saving throw with disadvantage, and the spell deals maximum damage to it.

Countermeasures. The withered remains of a past victim of this trap are easily found at the entrance to the room; a creature that investigates and succeeds on a DC 15 Intelligence (Arcana) check recognizes the effects of the *blight* spell.

The glyph can be found with *detect magic*, or with a successful DC 15 Intelligence (Investigation) check. Once found, the glyph can be dispelled with *dispel magic*, or with a successful DC 15 Intelligence (Arcana) check. However, to use an ability check on the glyph a creature would have to be adjacent to it.

Vile Touch

Mechanical trap (level 9-12, dangerous, harm)

An item has a hidden needle embedded in it, crusted with disease-bearing filth.

Trigger (Touch Object). A creature that touches the object triggers the trap.

Effect (Hidden Needle). The needle attacks the triggering creature with a +8 melee attack bonus. If it hits, the needle infects the creature with a random disease. Roll a d6 and consult the table below to see what disease the needle is infected with.

d6	Disease	Effect
1	Blinding Sickness	Pain grips the creature's mind, and its eyes turn milky white. The creature has disadvantage on Wisdom checks and Wisdom saving throws and is blinded.
2	Filth Fever	A raging fever sweeps through the creature's body. The creature has disadvantage on Strength checks, Strength saving throws, and attack rolls that use Strength.
3	Flesh Rot	The creature's flesh decays. The creature has disadvantage on Charisma checks and vulnerability to all damage.
4	Mindfire	The creature's mind becomes feverish. The creature has disadvantage on Intelligence checks and Intelligence saving throws, and the creature behaves as if under the effects of the confusion spell during combat.
5	Seizure	The creature is overcome with shaking. The creature has disadvantage on Dexterity checks, Dexterity saving throws, and attack rolls that use Dexterity.
6	Slimy Doom	The creature begins to bleed uncontrollably. The creature has disadvantage on Constitution checks and Constitution saving throws. In addition, whenever the creature takes damage, it is stunned until the end of its next turn

At the end of each of the infected creature's turns, it must make a DC 15 Constitution saving throw. After failing three of these saving throws, the disease's effects last for 7 days, and the creature stops making these saves. After succeeding on three of these saving throws, the creature recovers from the disease.

These are natural diseases; any effect that removes a disease or otherwise ameliorates a disease's effects apply to them.

Countermeasures. With a successful DC 15 Wisdom (Perception) check, a creature can spot the needle; with a successful DC 15 Intelligence (Nature) check, a creature can identify the diseased filth on it.

Dousing the object with alcohol removes the disease, and a successful DC 15 Dexterity check using thieves' tools lets a creature remove the needle without exposing themselves to the disease.

Level 9-12 Perilous

These traps may kill characters of these levels, and will definitely injure them severely.

Bathe the Tiger

Magic trap (level 9-12, perilous, block)

In the center of this area is a circular basin with the squat idol of a crouching tiger inside. The tiger is stained a variety of muted colors. Jugs, decanters, and containers of various liquids such as water, alcohol, oil, and milk are arrayed around the room.

Trigger (Offering). A creature that tries to leave the room without bathing the tiger idol in liquid triggers the trap.

Effect (Restraint). A creature that triggers the trap must succeed on a DC 17 Wisdom saving throw or be paralyzed for 8 hours by bands of magical force. A paralyzed creature can make another DC 17 Wisdom saving throw at the end of each hour; on a success, this effect ends for that creature. *Dispel magic* (DC 15) or *lesser restoration* can also end this effect for a single creature.

Countermeasures. With a successful DC 17 Intelligence (Religion) check, a creature understands the trap and knows to pour a liquid on the tiger before leaving. *Detect magic* reveals an aura of enchantment magic around the statue.

A spellcaster can disrupt the enchantment on the statue with a successful DC 17 Intelligence (Arcana) check; the statue can also be dispelled with *dispel magic* (DC 15).

Crystal Light

Magic trap (level 9-12, perilous, harm)

A crystal hovers in the center of this room, shedding light in a 30-foot sphere. If a non-good creature enters the light, they are seared by a burning rebuke.

Trigger (Creature Detector). A non-good creature that approaches within 30 feet of the crystal triggers the trap.

Effect (Elemental Blast). The crystal fires a beam of searing light at triggering creatures. It makes a ranged attack with a +10 bonus, dealing 66 (12d10) radiant damage if it hits.

Countermeasures. A creature that succeeds on a DC 17 Intelligence (History or Religion) check recognizes the crystal and understands the trap. *Detect magic* reveals an aura of evocation magic around the crystal.

A spellcaster can disrupt the enchantment on the crystal with a successful DC 17 spellcasting ability check; *dispel magic* (DC 15) also disables the trap.

Cube of Encaging

Mechanical trap (level 9-12, perilous, block)

The exit from this chamber is blocked by a metal cube, 4 feet on a side. The sides of the cube look like panels that could be opened, though they seem to be bolted shut. Each side has a circular groove on it.

Trigger (Weight Sensitive Surface). Pressing against the cube to move it triggers the trap; it can be triggered up to six times (once for each side of the cube). Triggering a side from a distance allows a character to push the cube without being trapped.

Effect (Cage). The triggering creature must succeed on a DC 17 Dexterity saving throw or be restrained by a metal hemisphere that closes around the creature from the cube. A creature outside the metal hemisphere can retract it with a successful DC 17 Dexterity check using thieves' tools, or a creature can burst out with a successful DC 17 Strength check.

Countermeasures. A successful DC 17 Wisdom (Perception) check reveals the mechanisms hidden in the cube, and a successful DC 17 Dexterity check while using thieves' tools disables them.

The Forest Walks

Mechanical trap (level 9-12, perilous, harm)

Strange pictures are painted on the walls of this wooden temple with thick, gritty paint. They appear to show a forest coming to life and crushing humans beneath their root-like feet. A sodden mound of twigs and leaves occupies one corner — a **shambling mound** in disguise.

Trigger (Draw Weapon). If a weapon is unsheathed within the temple or if a weapon is drawn in the area, the shambling mound rises and attacks.

Effect (Release Creatures). The shambling mound is dedicated to preserving peace in the temple and only attacks the triggering creature. If that creature sheathes their weapon, the shambling mound returns to the corner and settles down.

Countermeasures. A creature that succeeds on a DC 17 Intelligence (Nature) check recognizes the mound as a plant creature, and a creature that succeeds on a DC 17 Wisdom (Insight) check understands that the paintings are probably an admonition against violence in the vicinity.

Invisible Barricade

Magic trap (level 9-12, perilous, block)

Faded and moth-eaten paintings line this portrait gallery. The only painting that has retained its lustre is that of a stern-looking woman clothed in furs and wearing a crown of steel barbs. A *glyph of warding (wall of force)* is concealed in the painting's frame.

Trigger (Pass Area). A creature passing in front of the painting triggers the trap.

Effect (Spell Effect). When activated, the glyph casts *wall of force*. An invisible wall of force springs into existence extending from the painting to the far wall as a horizontal barrier. The wall is 1/4 inch thick and lasts for 10 minutes. If the wall cuts through a creature's space when it appears, the creature is pushed to a random side of the wall.

Nothing can physically pass through the wall. It is immune to all damage and can't be dispelled by *dispel magic*. A *disintegrate* spell destroys the wall instantly, however. The wall also extends into the Ethereal Plane, blocking ethereal travel through the wall.

Countermeasures. A creature that succeeds on a DC 17 Intelligence (History) check recognizes the painting and understands the trap. With a successful DC 17 Intelligence (Investigation) check, or with *detect magic*, a creature can find the glyph without triggering the trap.

Once found, the glyph can be disabled with *dispel magic* or a successful DC 17 Intelligence (Arcana) check.

Mirrored Flame

Hybrid trap (level 9-12, perilous, harm)

Half of this space is shrouded in non-magical darkness. A lantern hangs from a pole on a sturdy chain near the entrance; a *rune of detection* is inscribed on the lantern, hidden in the decorations.

Trigger (Activate Light Fixture). Lighting the lantern triggers the trap.

Effect (Bolts). When activated, the rune triggers a hail of crossbow bolts from weapons hidden in the shadowed side of the room. All creatures within 15 feet of the lantern must make a DC 17 Dexterity saving throw, taking 42 (12d6) piercing damage on a failure, or half as much on a success.

Countermeasures. A creature can find the rune with a successful DC 17 Wisdom (Perception) check or with *detect magic*. Once found, a creature can disable the rune with *dispel magic* or with a successful DC 17 Intelligence (Arcana) check.

Model Disaster

Hybrid trap (level 9-12, perilous, harm)

A miniature model of a room is on display in this chamber. The diorama seems eerily similar to the room it is inside; a *rune of detection* is hidden in the designs of the model.

Trigger (Interact with Bait). Moving parts of the replica room trigger the trap.

Effect (Crushing Ceiling/Walls). The walls of the room begin to close in, moving until the meet in the middle. The walls move at a rate of 1 foot per round at the end of the initiative order. Once the surface reaches a creature's space, they take 1d10 bludgeoning damage. If the surface is still moving on the next turn, the creature is restrained and takes 2d10 bludgeoning damage. A third round spent being crushed inflicts 4d10 bludgeoning damage. The walls retract after three rounds.

Countermeasures (Difficult). A creature that succeeds on a DC 17 Wisdom (Perception) check can find the rune in the model and with a successful DC 17 Intelligence (Investigation) check, a creature can deduce the nature of the trap. *Detect magic* can also reveal the rune.

Once found and understood, the rune can be dispelled with *dispel magic* or disabled with a successful DC 17 Intelligence (Arcana) check.

The Old Needle in Lock

Mechanical trap (level 9-12, perilous, harm)

The lock of the door is covered with silver filigree and tiny crystals.

Trigger (Attempt to Pick Lock). A creature that attempts to pick the lock triggers the trap.

Effect (Needle). A sharp needle pierces the target, dealing no damage but delivering a poison. The target must make a successful DC 17 Constitution saving throw, taking 66 (12d10) poison damage on a failed save, or half as much on a successful one.

Countermeasures (Difficult). A creature examining the lock can discover the needle with a successful DC 17 Wisdom (Perception) check and understands how it works with a successful DC 17 Intelligence (Investigation) check.

Once found and understood, a creature can disable the trap with a successful DC 17 Dexterity check using thieves' tools. This also unlocks the door.

A Riveting Read

Magic trap (level 9-12, perilous, hinder)

A book or tablet lies open in this room, pages dense with text. Somewhere in the text are the words "Stay here, do not move or speak", written in Common or a local language.

Trigger (Read Text). A creature that reads the phrase out loud triggers the trap.

Effect (Suggestion). The triggering creature must make a DC 17 Wisdom saving throw. On a failed save, the creature stays where it is and doesn't move or speak for 8 hours. Creatures that can't be charmed are immune to this effect.

The creature has an aura of enchantment magic when viewed with *detect magic*. Casting *dispel magic* (DC 15), or *remove curse* on the creature ends the effect.

Countermeasures. A creature that succeeds on a DC 20 Intelligence (Arcana) check can spot some hidden sigils and symbols worked into the other parts of the text, alerting them to the enchanted nature of the writing. When viewed with *detect magic*, the text has an aura of enchantment magic.

A spellcaster that succeeds on a DC 17 spellcasting ability check can disrupt the enchantment on the text, or the enchantment can be dispelled with *dispel magic* (DC 15).

Rolling Stop

Hybrid trap (level 9-12, perilous, block)

Walking deeper into the area, a large hallway with an arched ceiling slopes upward; a *rune of detection* is inscribed in the ceiling. If a creature exits the dungeon through this same hallway with a particular item in their possession, a gigantic boulder crashes through the ceiling at the upper end, barreling toward the exit, smashing all in its path. Once it reaches the bottom of the hallway, that exit is now blocked.

Trigger (Pass Area). A creature carrying a particular item across the hallway's upper entrance threshold triggers the trap.

Effect (Rolling Boulder). When the trap is activated, the rune releases a massive boulder; all creatures present roll initiative as the sphere is released. The sphere rolls initiative with a +8 bonus. On its turn, it moves 60 feet in a straight line. The sphere can move through creatures' spaces, and creatures can move through its space, treating it as difficult terrain.

Whenever the sphere enters a creature's space or a creature enters its space while it's rolling, that creature must succeed on a Dexterity saving throw or take 21 (6d6) bludgeoning damage and be knocked prone. The sphere stops when it hits a wall or similar barrier. It can't go around corners.

As an action, a creature within 5 feet of the sphere can attempt to slow it down with a DC 17 Strength check. On a successful check, the sphere's speed is reduced by 15 feet. If the sphere's speed drops to 0, it stops moving and is no longer a threat.

Countermeasures. A creature that succeeds on a DC 17 Wisdom (Perception) check can spot the rune; *detect magic* also reveals the rune.

If a creature can get up to it, they can disable the rune with a successful DC 17 Intelligence (Arcana) check. *Dispel magic* can also disable the rune.

Level 9-12 Deadly

These traps will almost certainly kill characters of these levels.

Back to the Cradle

Magic trap (level 9-12, deadly, hinder)

A statue, made from iron and spider silk, stands in the rear of the room; it depicts a repulsive human-spider hybrid. Around the room are cradles made of spiderweb and rotting canvas. Flickering candles illuminate reliefs of bowing figures on the walls of this room.

Trigger (Insult Idol). Creatures that don't prostrate themselves before the statue trigger the trap.

Effect (Aging). A creature that triggers the trap must make a DC 20 Constitution saving throw; on a failure, a wave of black energy washes over the creature and reduces its age by 16 (3d10) years. Creatures cannot be reduced below 1 year old in this way. This aging can be reversed with *greater restoration* or more powerful magic, such as *wish*.

Countermeasures. A creature that succeeds on a DC 20 Intelligence (Religion) check recognizes the statue and understands the trap. When viewed with *detect magic*, the statue has an aura of necromancy magic.

A spellcaster can disrupt the enchantment on the statue with a successful DC 20 spellcasting ability check; the trap can also be disabled with *dispel magic* (DC 16).

Blazing Ring

Mechanical trap (level 9-12, deadly, harm)

A 1-foot thick ring of decorative stonework surrounds a 25-foot diameter circle area in the center of the room. The ceiling directly above the ring is blackened with soot. In the 5-foot square at the circle's center is something intriguing.

Trigger (Weight Sensitive Floor). When a Small or larger creature steps onto a space adjacent to the 5-foot square at the center of the area within the ring, they activate a pressure plate. Parts of the stonework slide away, revealing spouts which pour flaming oil onto the floor from the ring's inner edge.

Effect (Wall of Fire). The flaming oil creates a ringed wall of flames 25 feet in diameter, 20 feet high, and 1 foot thick. The wall is opaque and lasts for 1 minute. When the wall appears, each creature within its area must make a DC 17 Dexterity saving throw. On a failed save, a creature takes 52 (8d6) fire damage, or half as much damage on a successful save.

The side of the wall facing inwards deals the trap's fire damage to each creature that ends its turn within 10 feet of that side or inside the wall. A creature takes the same damage when it enters the wall for the first time on a turn or ends its turn there. The other side of the wall deals no damage.

A creature that is adjacent to the wall can make a DC 17 Constitution check using thieves' tools to end this effect.

Countermeasures. A successful DC 17 Wisdom (Perception) check reveals the pressure plate, and a successful DC 17 Dexterity check while using thieves' tools disables it.

Burning Barricade

Mechanical trap (level 9-12, deadly, block)

A stone slab etched with an enormous skull and crossbones blocks the way forward. 20 vials of alchemist's fire are hidden in niches in the upper parts of the area blocked by the slab, waiting to fall when the slab is moved.

Trigger (Remove Barrier). The barricade can be removed easily, but doing so triggers the trap.

Effect (Falling Objects). The vials drop down, smash and then ignite. Any creature adjacent to the slab must succeed on a DC 20 Dexterity saving throw or be doused in alchemist's fire, taking 25 (10d4) fire damage at the start of each of its turns. A creature can end this damage by using its action to make a DC 10 Dexterity check to extinguish the flames.

Countermeasures (Difficult). A creature that succeeds on a DC 20 Wisdom (Perception) check can spot the hidden vials, and with a successful DC 20 Intelligence (Investigation) check they can understand how the trap works.

Once understood, the trap can be disabled with a successful DC 20 Dexterity check using thieves' tools. Finding a way to remove the barricade without being next to it also helps creatures avoid this trap.

Corrosive Pit

Mechanical trap (level 9-12, deadly, harm)

Something corrosive is splattered around the base of an unlocked door. It seems to have eaten into the floor. A hidden mechanism is built into the door, ready to drop creatures into a hidden pit.

Trigger (Open/Close Door). Opening the door triggers the trap.

Effect (Drop Into Acid). The triggering creature must make a DC 20 Dexterity saving throw. On a successful save, the creature is able to grab onto the edge of the pit. On a failed save, the creature falls into the 50-foot deep pit and takes 17 (5d6) bludgeoning damage. The pit is filled with three feet of corrosive acid. A creature that enters the acid for the first time or starts its turn in it takes 16 (3d10) acid damage.

Any non-magical weapon or armor that is made of metal that a character is wearing or holding that touches the acid begins to corrode. At the start of each turn in the pit, the following occurs: A weapon takes a permanent and cumulative -1 penalty to damage rolls. If its penalty drops to -5, the weapon is destroyed. Non-magical ammunition made of metal that touches the acid is destroyed after dealing damage. Armor or shields take a permanent and cumulative -1 penalty to the AC it offers. Armor reduced to an AC of 10 or a shield that drops to a +0 bonus is destroyed.

Countermeasures (Difficult). A creature that succeeds on a DC 20 Wisdom (Perception) check spots the trapdoor in front of the door, and with a successful DC 20 Intelligence (Investigation) check they can understand the trap.

Once understood, the trap can be disabled with a successful DC 20 Dexterity check using thieves' tools.

Enchanted Armory

Magic trap (level 9-12, deadly, block)

Polished blades, enamelled suits of armor, and decorated shields fill the racks that line the walls of this armory. A *glyph of warding (blade barrier)* is inscribed on the chamber's floor.

Trigger (Creature Detector). A good creature that approaches within 15 feet of the glyph triggers the trap.

Effect (Spell Effect). When activated, the glyph casts *blade barrier*, creating a wall of whirling, razor-sharp blades made of magical energy. The glyph creates a ringed wall 60 feet in diameter, 20 feet high, and 5 feet thick, centered on the triggering creature. The wall provides three-quarters cover to creatures behind it, and its space is difficult terrain. The wall lasts for 10 minutes or until dispelled with *dispel magic* (DC 16).

When a creature enters the wall's area for the first time on a turn or starts its turn there, the creature must make a DC 20 Dexterity saving throw. On a failed save, the creature takes 33 (6d10) slashing damage. On a successful save, the creature takes half as much damage.

Countermeasures. With a successful DC 20 Intelligence (Arcana) check, a creature can sense a lingering trace of magic on the armor and weapons around the room.

The glyph can be found with a successful DC 20 Intelligence (Investigation) check or with *detect magic*. Once found, it can be disabled with a successful DC 20 Intelligence (Arcana) check, or with *dispel magic*.

Lightning Breath

Hybrid trap (level 9-12, deadly, harm)

The corridor is empty save for a pair of statues that depict many-legged, serpent-like creatures with tooth-filled maws: behirs. A thin tripwire stretches between the statues.

Trigger (Tripwire). A creature that walks between the behir statues snaps the tripwire, triggering the trap.

Effect (Spell Effect). A bolt of lightning arcs from the statues towards the triggering creature. Three bolts then leap from that creature to as many as three other random creatures, each of which must be within 30 feet of the first creature. A creature can be targeted by only one of the bolts.

A creature targeted by a bolt must make a DC 20 Dexterity saving throw. The creature takes 45 (10d8) lightning damage on a failed save, or half as much damage on a successful one.

Countermeasures. A creature can spot the tripwire with a successful DC 20 Wisdom (Perception) check, and the trap can be disabled with a successful DC 20 Dexterity check using thieves' tools.

When viewed with *detect magic*, the statues have an aura of evocation magic. Casting *dispel magic* (DC 16) on the statues disables the trap. The status can also be destroyed (AC 17, 20 hit points, immunity to poison and psychic damage), which disables the trap as well.

Scything Blades

Mechanical trap (level 9-12, deadly, harm)

A pressure plate is concealed in the floor of this corridor, waiting to release massive, heavy, crescent-shaped blades to slice through a 15-foot cube, centered on the pressure plate.

Trigger (Pressure Plate). Stepping on the pressure plate triggers this trap.

Effect (Scything Blades). All creatures in the area of the blades must make a DC 20 Dexterity saving throw, taking 52 (15d6) slashing damage on a failed save, or half as much on a successful one. On a failed save a creature is also restrained as they are pinned against the opposite wall by the blades.

A creature restrained by the blades can free themselves with a successful DC 20 Constitution (Athletics) check or another creature can free them with a successful DC 20 Strength (Medicine) check.

Countermeasures (Sensitive). A creature can find the pressure plate with a successful DC 20 Wisdom (Perception) check; it can be disabled with a successful DC 20 Dexterity check using thieves' tools. If the total of the Dexterity check is 10 or less, the trap activates.

Shockingly Secure

Hybrid trap (level 9-12, deadly, harm)

A door or chest is secured with a lock that requires a specific key. If a creature attempts to tamper with the lock in any way, lightning leaps from the hole of the lock to the creature.

Trigger (Attempt to Pick Lock). A creature attempting to pick or tamper with the lock triggers the trap.

Effect (Spell Effect). A bolt of lightning arcs from the lock towards the triggering creature. Three bolts then leap from that creature to as many as three other random creatures, each of which must be within 30 feet of the first creature. A creature can be targeted by only one of the bolts.

A creature targeted by a bolt must make a DC 20 Dexterity saving throw. The creature takes 45 (10d8) lightning damage on a failed save, or half as much damage on a successful one.

Countermeasures. WIth a successful DC 20 Wisdom (Perception) check, a creature can spot some odd-looking elements inside the lock. Once spotted, a creature that succeeds on a DC 20 Intelligence (Arcana) check understands the trap.

The lock has an aura of evocation magic when viewed with *detect magic*. Casting *dispel magic* (DC 16) on the lock disables the trap. A spellcaster that succeeds on a DC 16 spellcasting ability check can also disrupt the enchantment on the lock.

Sinister Skulls

Mechanical trap (level 9-12, deadly, harm)

The bones and skulls of a wide range of humanoids litter the floor of this chamber, most with soot stains and scorch marks. A **wraith** lies in wait, awakening at the slightest disturbance.

Trigger (Musical/Auditory). A creature that makes too much noise triggers the trap.

Effect (Release Creatures). When roused, the wraith rises up from the piles of bones and attacks, focusing first on the triggering creature. The wraith will not leave the area.

Countermeasures. Creatures that move through the area or take actions in it must succeed on a DC 20 Dexterity (Stealth) check, otherwise the trap activates.

Small Folk Only

Hybrid trap (level 9-12, deadly, hinder)

A small, circular door approximately three feet across is set into the wall or natural environment. The path to it seems well travelled; little footprints can be seen leading to and from it. In front of the door is a hidden pressure plate.

Trigger (Weight Sensitive Surface). If a Small or smaller creature steps on the pressure plate the door opens. A Medium or larger creature stepping on the plate triggers the trap.

Effect (Blindness). All creatures within 15 feet of the door must succeed a DC 20 Constitution saving throw or go blind for 1 day. A creature can repeat the saving throw at the end of every hour, ending the effect for themselves if they succeed. The effect also ends if dispelled with *dispel magic* (DC 16), *heal*, *lesser restoration*, or similar magic.

Countermeasures. The door has an aura of necromancy magic when viewed with *detect magic*. A creature can spot the pressure plate with a successful DC 20 Wisdom (Perception) check; a successful DC 20 Dexterity check using thieves' tools disables the trap.

Level 13-16 Traps

Venturing on from our previous unsettling situation, we arrived at a locked door in a corridor. Its walls were covered in graven faces with yawning, hungry mouths. By now, we knew that sticking around any place like this was likely not the best idea, so we did what we could to make haste. Our wizard, sharp as ever, discovered a mechanism nestled in one of the open mouths and determined that this must open the uncooperative exit.

Working with delicate devices is one of my many diverse abilities, so I stepped up to the contraption and set to work. Because nothing in the world can ever go smoothly, or perhaps because I am beset by a curse which has doomed me to wind up in places that want me dead, something started happening; something that was certainly not the door unlocking.

The floor started shaking, and split in two! It began edging ever-wider as the barbarian stood astride the gap (I find this mildly funny, considering his position in the first hallway was almost the exact opposite of this). To make matters worse, the open mouths (except for the one I was working on) started belching down cascading lava-flows.

Our cleric did his best to shield us from a nearby lavafall, as our wizard took to the air, and our ranger clung to the barbarian's back for dear life. And then there was, of course, myself, whose hands were most certainly rock-steady and not shaking at all at the thought of falling into a gaping chasm before being excruciatingly boiled alive in molten earth.

And then, after an eternity of hand-sweat-producing moments, I felt something and heard every rogue's favorite sound in the world: a satisfying click. The lava-drooling faces ceased their salivation, the floor gap which was threatening to split our barbarian up the middle retracted, and the door to go deeper into the temple was now open.

We went through the door, even if at this point it may well have been against our better judgement...

The traps in this chapter are designed to challenge characters who are levels 13-16 and are grouped by their lethality. Any of these traps can be dropped right into a dungeon or similar adventure and shouldn't require any preparation. For more information on customizing traps, go to **Chapter 8: Designing Traps**, or for a completely random and unexpected trap, go to **Chapter 9: Random Trap Generator**.

Level 13-16 Traps Table

Roll a d100 on the table below to choose a random trap appropriate for 13-16 characters, or select a desired lethality and roll a d10.

	d100	d10	Trap	Page
Setback	1-2	1	Chain the Aggressor	58
	3-4	2	Here's the Magic	58
	5-6	3	Kraken's Wrath	58
	7-8	4	Mirroring	58
	9-10	5	Poison Pot	58
	11-12	6	Slimed	59
	13-14	7	Tap Nap	59
	15-16	8	Touching Transformation	59
	17-18	9	Trapdoor Pitfall, Greater	59
	19-20	10	Turret Salvo	60
Moderate	21-22	1	Burning Combination	60
	23-24	2	Chains of Integrity	60
	25-26	3	Chandelier Drop	60
	27-28	4	Floor Inferno	61
	29-30	5	Hiding Horn	61
	31-32	6	Pacification Panel	61
	33-34	7	Pincushion	62
	35-36	8	Rogue's Bane, Greater	62
	37-38	9	Silver Serpent	62
	39-40	10	Vinesnare	62
Dangerous	41-42	1	Backstabber	63
	43-44	2	Blazing Barrier	63
	45-46	3	Disrespected Deity	63
	47-48	4	Generosity	63
	49-50	5	Impaling Tale	64
	51-52	6	Punji Pick	64
	53-54	7	Spider Architects	64
	55-56	8	Thought Spiral	64
	57-58	9	Up is Down	65
	59-60	10	Voltage Viewer	65
Perilous	61-62	1	Add to the Collection	65
	63-64	2	Clockwork Con-trap-tion	66
	65-66	3	Hanging Hooks	66
	67-68	4	Needletongue	66
	69-70	5	Prismatic Glyph	66
	71-72	6	Sandy Grave	67
	73-74	7	Severe Slumber	67
	75-76	8	Sorcerous Cell	68
	77-78	9	Thin Facade	68
	79-80	10	Trap-a-port	68
Deadly	81-82	1	Blazing Rings, Greater	68
	83-84	2	Blind Leading the Blind	69
	85-86	3	Bolts of Slaying	69
	87-88	4	Corrosive Chains	69
	89-90	5	Hot on the Trail	69
	91-92	6	Lava Lake	69
	93-94	7	Manners Maketh Man	70
	95-96	8	Pass of Gas	70
	97-98	9	Snake Pit	70
	99-100	10	Unstable Ground	70

Level 13-16 Setback

These traps should present a minor inconvenience to characters of this level range.

Chain the Aggressor

Magic trap (level 13-16, setback, block)

The walls of the dungeon are painted with crude depictions of rope, chain, and leather bindings.

Trigger (Unconsciousness). A creature that makes another creature fall unconscious triggers the trap.

Effect (Restraint). The triggering creature and up to 2 others in the room must make a DC 10 Wisdom saving throw or be paralyzed for 10 minutes, held by chains of magic force. At the end of each of its turns, a paralyzed creature can make another Wisdom saving throw. On a success, the effect ends on that creature. This effect also ends for all creatures if dispelled with *dispel magic* (DC 14).

Countermeasures. If a creature investigates the paintings and succeeds on a DC 10 Wisdom (Insight) or a DC 10 Intelligence (Arcana) check they can deduce the nature of the trap. The room also has an aura of enchantment magic when viewed with *detect magic.*

A spellcaster can disrupt the enchantment on this room with a successful DC 10 spellcasting ability check; casting *dispel magic* (DC 14) on the room also disables the trap.

Here's the Magic

Magic trap (level 13-16, setback)

A *glyph of warding (magic missile)* is inscribed on the wall, ready to detect the casting of spells.

Trigger (Cast Spell). A creature that casts a spell within 40 feet of the glyph triggers the trap.

Effect (Spell Effect). The glyph casts *magic missile* as a 4th-level spell. Six glowing darts of magical energy hit the triggering creature; each dart deals 1d4 + 1 force damage.

Countermeasures. With a successful DC 10 Intelligence (History) check, a creature can remember some detail about this room or area, and is aware of the trap.

The glyph can be found with *detect magic*, or with a successful DC 10 Intelligence (Investigation) check. Once found, it can be disabled with a successful DC 10 Intelligence (Arcana) check or with *dispel magic*.

Kraken's Wrath

Mechanical trap (level 13-16, setback, harm)

Fixed half-way up the wall of the chamber is a circular stone door, shaped to resemble the face of a kraken. The door is locked by an internal mechanism inside the kraken's mouth.

Trigger (Use Wrong Key). Using the wrong key for the circular door triggers the trap.

Effect (Elemental Blast). A surging jet of water shoots forth from the lock. The triggering creature must succeed on a DC 10 Dexterity saving throw or take 22 (4d10) bludgeoning damage and be knocked back 15 feet.

Countermeasures. A creature that succeeds on a DC 10 Wisdom (Perception) check can hear the gurgle of water inside the door, and they find the hidden mechanism inside the keyhole. With a successful DC 10 Dexterity check using thieves' tools, a creature can disable the trap.

Mirroring

Mechanical trap (level 13-16, setback, harm)

Hanging on the wall of this chamber is a beautifully constructed mirror, partially covered by a stained linen throw. The mirror can swing out on hidden hinges to reveal a small niche behind it.

Trigger (Look Into). A creature that sees its reflection in the mirror triggers the trap.

Effect (Release Creatures). A **doppelganger** lurks behind the mirror. When a creature looks into the mirror, the doppelganger uses its Read Thoughts action. Since it can now see the triggering creature in the mirror, the doppelganger can change its form and deceive the creatures' companions.

Countermeasures. A creature that succeeds on a DC 10 Wisdom (Perception) check can spot the hinges around the mirror without looking in the mirror. There is nothing keeping the mirror closed.

Poison Pot

Mechanical trap (level 13-16, setback, harm)

Dug into the floor of the chamber are ten cylindrical compartments, each of which has a metal cap. Most of the caps appear locked in place, save one which is slightly askew.

Trigger (Remove Barrier). Removing the unlocked cap triggers the trap.

Effect (Darts). A dart fires from the bottom of the compartment straight up. The trap makes one ranged attack against the triggering creature with a +5 bonus, dealing 2 (1d4) piercing damage if it hits. A creature that suffers the piercing damage must make a DC 10 Constitution saving throw, taking 21 (6d6) poison damage and becoming poisoned on a failed save, or half as much damage on a successful one.

Countermeasures. A creature that succeeds on a DC 10 Wisdom (Perception) check can spot a mechanism attached to the cap, and with a successful DC 10 Intelligence (Investigation) check they understand the trap.

Once understood, a successful DC 10 Dexterity check using thieves' tools disables the trap

Slimed

Mechanical trap (level 13-16, setback, hinder)

A rope dangles in an enticing place, seemingly meant to reveal something or open a door. The rope is attached to a vessel high above. When it's pulled, the rope goes slack and the vessel falls.

Trigger (Pull Chain/Rope). A creature that pulls on the rope triggers the trap.

Effect (Falling Object). A ceramic vessel containing several gallons of a slimey acidic substance comes crashing to the floor, spreading the slime in all directions. All creatures within a 10-foot sphere centered on the triggering creature must make a DC 10 Dexterity saving throw, taking 14 (4d6) acid damage on a failed save, or half as much on a successful one.

Countermeasures. A creature that succeeds on a DC 10 Wisdom (Perception) check can spot the vessel attached to the rope. With a successful DC 10 Intelligence (Investigation) check, a creature can deduce that the rope leads nowhere and can just be avoided.

Tap Nap

Hybrid trap (level 13-16, setback)

Various ornate carvings and symbols adorn panels on the wall of this room. One panel has been inscribed with a *glyph of warding (sleep)*, hidden among the arcane writing.

Trigger (Tap/Prod). A creature that taps, prods, knocks on, pushes, pulls, or disturbs a panel in any way triggers the trap.

Effect (Spell Effect). The glyph casts *sleep* as a 4th-level spell, sending creatures into a magical slumber. The spell can affect 49 (11d8) hit points of creatures. Creatures within 20 feet of a point next to the triggering creature are affected in ascending order of their current hit points (ignoring unconscious creatures).

Starting with the creature that has the lowest current hit points, each creature affected by this spell falls unconscious for 1 minute, the sleeper takes damage, or someone uses an action to shake or slap the sleeper awake. Subtract each creature's hit points from the total before moving on to the creature with the next lowest hit points. A creature's hit points must be equal to or less than the remaining total for that creature to be affected.

Undead and creatures immune to being charmed aren't affected by this spell.

Countermeasures. With a successful DC 10 Intelligence (Investigation) check, a creature can find the glyph without setting off the trap.

Once found, the glyph can be disabled with a successful DC 10 Intelligence (Arcana) check, or with *dispel magic*.

Touching Transformation

Magic trap (level 13-16, setback, hinder)

An important object sits on a pedestal or lies in a chest. The object is enchanted to lignify (turn to wood) anyone who touches it.

Trigger (Touch Object). A creature that touches the object triggers the trap.

Effect (Petrification). The triggering creature must make a DC 10 Constitution saving throw. On a failed save, creatures are restrained as their flesh begins to harden. On a successful save, the creature isn't affected. A creature restrained by this effect must make a DC 10 Constitution saving throw at the end of each of its turns. If it successfully saves against this effect three times, the effect ends for that creature. If it fails its save three times, it is turned into an inanimate wooden doll and petrified. The successes and failures don't need to be consecutive; keep track of both until the creature collects three of a kind.

This effect lasts for 10 minutes or until dispelled, either with *dispel magic* (DC 14) or *greater restoration*. If a creature is physically broken while petrified, it suffers from similar deformities if it reverts to its original state.

Countermeasures. A creature that succeeds on a DC 10 Intelligence (History) check recognizes the object and understands the danger of the trap. The object has an aura of transmutation when viewed with *detect magic*.

A spellcaster can disrupt the enchantment on the object with a successful DC 10 spellcasting ability check; *dispel magic* (DC 14) also disables the trap.

Trapdoor Pitfall, Greater

Mechanical trap (level 13-16, setback, harm)

A 60-foot deep vertical shaft is hidden under a trapdoor disguised to look like the rest of the floor. The trapdoor covers a 5-foot square space and has a pressure plate embedded in it.

Trigger (Pressure Plate). A creature that steps on the trapdoor activates the pressure plate, and the trap door swings open.

Effect (Drop Into Empty Pit). The triggering creature must make a DC 10 Dexterity saving throw. On a success the creature is able to grab onto the edge of the pit. On a failure, the creature falls into the pit and takes 21 (6d6) bludgeoning damage.

Countermeasures. With a successful DC 10 Wisdom (Perception) check, a creature can find the pressure plate and trapdoor. A successful DC 10 Dexterity check using thieves' tools disables the trap.

Turret Salvo

Mechanical trap (level 13-16, setback, harm)

Passing through this area requires raising a well-constructed steel gate using a crank. The gate is bordered on both sides by small, round, openings.

Trigger (Turn Wheel/Crank). Turning the crank triggers the trap.

Effect (Bolts). An array of crossbows hidden inside the turrets fires toward the crank. The trap makes four attacks against the triggering creature with a +5 bonus to the rolls, dealing 5 (1d10) piercing damage on a hit.

Countermeasures. A creature that succeeds on a DC 10 Wisdom (Perception) check can spot the bolts hidden inside the openings. With a successful DC 10 Intelligence (Investigation) check, a creature understands the trap.

Once understood, a successful DC 10 Dexterity check using thieves' tools disables the trap.

Level 13-16 Moderate

These traps will probably harm characters of this level.

Burning Combination

Hybrid trap (level 13-16, moderate, harm)

On the floor of this circular room are four pedestals and in the center is a wooden crate containing four items; a set of manacles, an iron shovel, an oil lamp, and a glass prism. The only other exit from the chamber is a locked portcullis. A *rune of detection* is worked into the floor of the room.

Trigger (Wrong Combination). If the objects are placed in the correct order (manacles in the north, shovel to the east, lamp to the south, prism to the west), the portcullis opens. Otherwise, the trap activates.

Effect (Falling Objects). Burning coals fall from the ceiling around the pedestals. Each creature within 10 feet of a pedestal must make a DC 12 Dexterity saving throw. On a failure, a creature takes 14 (4d6) bludgeoning damage and 14 (4d6) fire damage. On a success, a creature takes half the bludgeoning damage, and none of the fire damage.

Countermeasures. Clues to the correct order for the items are scattered around the room as part of the decorations; a creature that succeeds on a DC 12 Wisdom (Insight) check can deduce the proper sequence.

The rune can be found with a DC 12 Wisdom (Perception) check or with *detect magic.* Once found, the rune can be disabled with *dispel magic* or a successful DC 12 Intelligence (Arcana) check.

The portcullis is firmly locked down; only a successful DC 20 Dexterity check using thieves' tools will release it.

Chains of Integrity

Mechanical trap (level 13-16, moderate, block)

A golden staff, capped with a ruby orb, stands in a metal frame in this room. The staff looks incredibly valuable and it is placed on a dais with a spiraling pattern of tiles atop it.

Trigger (Pick Up/Shift Object). Extracting the staff from the stand triggers the trap.

Effect (Net). The trap releases a net of chains onto all creatures within 10 feet of the staff who must make DC 12 Dexterity saving throws. A creature that fails is trapped under the net and restrained, and creatures that succeed avoid the net. The links of the chains glow with celestial light, and any creature that starts its turn restrained by the net takes 22 (4d10) radiant damage.

A creature restrained by the net can use its action to make a DC 12 Strength check, freeing itself or another creature within its reach on a success. On a failure, the creature takes 11 (2d10) radiant damage

The net has AC 10 and 20 hit points. Dealing 5 slashing damage to the net (AC 10) destroys a 5-foot-square section of it, freeing any creature trapped in that section.

Countermeasures. A creature that succeeds on a DC 12 Wisdom (Perception) check spots the mechanisms attached to the stand; with a successful DC 12 Dexterity check using thieves' tools, a creature can disable the trap.

A creature can attempt to replace the staff with something of equal weight. To attempt this, a creature makes a DC 12 Intelligence (Perception) check to estimate the weight of the staff, then a DC 12 Dexterity (Sleight of Hand) check to make the switch; failure on either check triggers the trap.

Chandelier Drop

Hybrid trap (level 13-16, moderate, block)

This room is decorated in a highly gothic fashion, featuring a large, vicious-looking steel chandelier covered in barbs and spikes. The chandelier is not suspended from the ceiling but from chains connected to the walls.

Trigger (Pass Area). A creature that passes directly beneath the chandelier steps on a pressure plate, opening a trapdoor.

Effect (Teleporting Drop). The 10-foot square trapdoor opens, revealing a 20-foot deep pit with a portal at the bottom. An identical portal appears on the ceiling, the chandelier in between.

Creatures on the trapdoor when it opens must succeed on a DC 12 Dexterity saving throw or fall into the pit. A creature who falls into the pit passes through the bottom portal, out the ceiling portal, through the chandelier, and into the pit again, looping through the portals each round. Each time a creature falls through the chandelier they take 3 (1d6) slashing damage. This damage increases by 3 (1d6) for each time a creature has passed through the chandelier (1d6 the first time, 2d6 the second, 3d6, the third, etc...).

A creature can attempt to stop their loop by grabbing onto the chandelier with a successful DC 12 Dexterity saving throw.

Countermeasures. A creature can spot the pressure plate with a successful DC 12 Wisdom (Perception) check; it can be disabled with a successful DC 12 Dexterity check using thieves' tools. The portals can each be dispelled with *dispel magic* (DC 15).

Floor Inferno

Mechanical trap (level 13-16, moderate, harm)

A section of the floor is littered with pressure plates. A creature that steps on one of them will set off a grid of flaming spires that shoot up from the floor.

Trigger (Pressure Plate). A creature that steps on a pressure plate triggers the trap.

Effect (Fire Blast). Several spouts of flame suddenly erupt from the floor in a 10-foot-by-10-foot square centered on the trigger pressure plate. All creatures in the area must make a DC 12 Dexterity saving throw, taking 28 (8d6) fire damage on a failed save or half as much on a successful one.

Countermeasures. With a successful DC 12 Wisdom (Perception) check, a creature can find the pressure plates. A successful DC 12 Dexterity check using thieves' tools disables a single pressure plate, but a check with a total of 5 or lower triggers the trap.

Hiding Horn

Magic trap (level 13-16, moderate, hinder)

The mouthpiece to a large horn extends out from the wall of this room. When blown, the horn curses its user with invisibility.

Trigger (Musical/Auditory). A creature that blows the horn triggers the trap.

Effect (Invisibility). The creature blowing the horn must make a DC 12 Constitution saving throw or become invisible for 8 hours or until dispelled (*dispel magic* DC 16). Anything the creature is wearing or carrying is invisible as long as it is on the target's person.

Countermeasures. The horn has an aura of illusion magic when viewed with *detect magic.* A creature that succeeds on a DC 12 Intelligence (History) check recognizes the writings and etchings on the horn and understands the danger of the trap.

A spellcaster can disrupt the enchantment on the horn with a successful DC 12 spellcasting ability check; *dispel magic* (DC 16) also disables the trap.

Pacification Panel

Magic trap (level 13-16, moderate, block)

A *glyph of warding (wall of force)* prevents creatures wielding weapons from proceeding. Any creature that draws a weapon or carries a drawn weapon into the enchanted area will trigger a *wall of force* to block their way forward or their way back, or both.

Trigger (Unsheathe Weapon). A creature that draws a weapon in the area or enters the area with a weapon drawn triggers the trap.

Effect (Spell Effect). When activated, the glyph casts *wall of force*, creating an invisible vertical barrier that blocks passage forward. The wall is 1/4 inch thick and lasts for 10 minutes. If the wall cuts through a creature's space when it appears, the creature is pushed to a random side of the wall (your choice which side).

Countermeasures. The glyph can be found with a successful DC 12 Intelligence (Investigation) check. Once found, it can be disabled with *dispel magic* or with a successful DC 12 Intelligence (Arcana) check.

Pincushion

Mechanical trap (level 13-16, moderate, hinder)

A door or chest is closed and secured with a combination lock. The lock consists of three dials, each of which has runic symbols. The correct combination unlocks the lock, the wrong combination is perilous.

Trigger (Wrong Combination). A creature that enters the wrong combination triggers the trap.

Effect (Needle). A poison needle springs out from the lock mechanism. The triggering creature must make a DC 12 Constitution saving throw. On a failure, the creature takes 21 (6d6) poison damage and is poisoned for 10 minutes. While poisoned in this way, the creature is paralyzed. On a success, the creature takes half the poison damage and isn't poisoned.

Countermeasures. A creature can recognize the lock and remember its combination with a successful DC 12 Intelligence (History) check, and a successful DC 12 Intelligence (Investigation) check lets a creature spot the hidden needle.

Once found, the needle mechanism can be disarmed with a successful DC 12 Dexterity check using thieves' tools.

Rogue's Bane, Greater

Mechanical trap (level 13-16, moderate)

A poorly disguised tripwire is easily detected, but it hides the real trap that is set to go off if the decoy is tampered with.

Trigger (False Trigger). Disarming or attempting to disarm the false trigger sets off the real trap.

Effect (Random). Randomly select a mechanical trap of the same or lower lethality and use its effect.

Countermeasures (Difficult). A successful DC 12 Wisdom (Perception) check reveals the false trigger. A successful DC 12 Intelligence (Investigation) check reveals its true nature. A successful DC 12 Dexterity check using thieves' tools disables the real trap.

Silver Serpent

Magic trap (level 13-16, moderate, hinder)

A jade statuette carved to resemble a hissing serpent rests on an altar. Its eyes are made from silver spheres, and silver coins are strewn on the ground before the statuette.

Trigger (Insult Idol). Failure to place a silver coin at the statuette's base before leaving the room triggers the trap.

Effect (Petrification). The triggering creature must make a DC 12 Constitution saving throw. On a failed save, the creature is restrained as their flesh begins to harden. On a successful save, the creature isn't affected. A creature restrained by this effect must make a DC 12 Constitution saving throw at the end of each of its turns. If it successfully saves against this effect three times, the effect ends for that creature. If it fails its save three times, it is turned into a statue made of silver. The successes and failures don't need to be consecutive; keep track of both until the creature collects three of a kind.

This effect lasts for 8 hours, or until dispelled, either with *dispel magic* or *greater restoration*. If a creature is physically broken while petrified, it suffers from similar deformities if it reverts to its original state.

Countermeasures. The statuette has an aura of transmutation magic when viewed with *detect magic*. With a successful DC 12 Intelligence (Religion) check, a creature recognizes the statue and understands the trap.

With a successful DC 12 spellcasting ability check, a spellcaster can disrupt the enchantment on the statue. Casting *dispel magic* (DC 16) on the statue also disables the trap.

Vinesnare

Mechanical trap (level 13-16, moderate, block)

The grove of giant oaks is dappled by sunlight. In the centre of the clearing, surrounded by a circle of stones and dozens of red-capped toadstools, is a heavily scratched wooden trapdoor.

Trigger (Open/Close Object). Opening the trapdoor triggers the trap.

Effect (Snare). A thorned vine attached to a mechanical arm whips around the triggering creature. The triggering creature must succeed on a DC 12 Dexterity saving throw or take 33 (6d10) slashing damage and be restrained until it is freed. The vine has AC 11, 10 hit points, resistance to bludgeoning damage, and vulnerability to fire and slashing damage.

At the beginning of each of its turns, a creature restrained by the snare takes an additional 11 (2d10) slashing damage. A creature restrained by the snare can free themselves with a successful DC 12 Strength (Athletics) check, or they can be free by another creature that succeeds on a DC 12 Strength (Medicine) check.

Countermeasures. A successful DC 12 Wisdom (Perception) check reveals the snare and a successful DC 12 Dexterity check using thieves' tools disables the trap.

Level 13-16 Dangerous

These traps are likely to seriously injure (and potentially kill) characters of these levels.

Backstabber

Mechanical trap (level 13-16, dangerous, harm)

This wooden cabinet has a built-in lock, surrounded by an ornately etched plate of silver. The cabinet itself seems to have been stabbed in multiple places, though none of the marks are deep enough to penetrate the wood.

Trigger (Attempt to Pick Lock). A creature that attempts to pick the lock triggers the trap.

Effect (Spears). A bank of spears shoots out from the wall opposite the cabinet. The triggering creature must make a DC 15 Dexterity saving throw, taking 66 (12d10) piercing damage on a failed save, or half as much on a successful one.

Countermeasures. With a successful DC 15 Wisdom (Perception) check, a creature can spot the mechanisms in the lock; a successful DC 15 Dexterity check using thieves' tools disables the trap.

Blazing Barrier

Magic trap (level 13-16, dangerous, block)

Frozen piles of ash are scattered across the floor of this ice cavern. Dark symbols of a demonic cult are carved into the wall. To those who can understand them, the symbols make it clear that going further into the cave complex requires the sacrifice of a living, thinking creature.

Trigger (Mortal Sacrifice). If a sentient creature is not killed before entering the chamber beyond this one, the trap is triggered.

Effect (Wall of Fire). When activated, the trap creates a wall of fire up to 60 feet long, 20 feet high, and 1 foot thick. The wall is opaque and blocks further entry into the caves.

When the wall appears, each creature within its area must make a DC 15 Dexterity saving throw. On a failed save, a creature takes 22 (5d8) fire damage, or half as much damage on a successful save.

The side of the wall facing into this room deals 22 (5d8) fire damage to each creature that ends its turn within 10 feet of that side or inside the wall. A creature takes the same damage when it enters the wall for the first time on a turn or ends its turn there. The other side of the wall deals no damage.

The wall lasts for 8 hours or until dispelled with *dispel magic* (DC 14).

Countermeasures. A successful DC 15 Intelligence (History or Religion) check reveals the intent of the symbols on the walls, and the room has an aura of evocation magic when viewed with *detect magic*.

A spellcaster can disrupt the enchantment on the room with a successful DC 15 spellcasting ability check; *dispel magic* (DC 14) also disables the trap. Providing a sacrifice disables this trap for 24 hours.

Disrespected Deity

Hybrid trap (level 13-16, dangerous, harm)

In the chamber there sits a stone statue atop a tall pedestal. The statue's right hand is extended and on it rests a silver bowl. The idol must be presented an offering to assure safe passage to the next chamber. Those who fail to appease the idol will be punished.

Trigger. A creature that doesn't present the idol with satisfactory offering triggers the trap.

Effect. One or more creatures are released from one or more cages embedded in the walls of the chamber. The released creature(s) should be thematically and challenge rating appropriate.

Countermeasures. The *detect magic* spell causes an aura to illuminate the idol. A successful DC 15 Intelligence (Arcana) check once it is discovered reveals the nature of the trigger.

Generosity

Magic trap (level 13-16, dangerous, block)

Dappled light filters through an enormous, sealed tank of water that takes up half of the empty room. A statue stands outside the tank with an outstretched hand, and a matching statue but with clenched fists is inside the tank.

Trigger (Offering). If a creature walks past the open-handed statue without placing a gold coin into it, they trigger the trap.

Effect (Swap). The target must succeed on a DC 15 Charisma saving throw or instantly switch places with the clenched-fist statue. If they cannot breathe water, they must hold their breath and may start to suffocate. The glass tank has AC 15, 100 hit points, immunity to slashing, poison, and psychic damage, and vulnerability to piercing and bludgeoning damage.

Giving a coin to the open-handed statue swaps the statue and creature again, but dispelling or disrupting the enchantment doesn't.

Countermeasures. A successful DC 15 Intelligence (Religion) check lets a creature recognize the statue and understand the trap. With *detect magic*, the statues have an aura of conjuration magic.

A spellcaster can disrupt the enchantment on the statues with a successful DC 15 spellcasting ability check. Casting *dispel magic* (DC 16) on the statues also disables the trap.

Impaling Tale

Mechanical trap (level 13-16, dangerous, harm)

A closed book's cover is connected to a mechanism restraining spears in a nearby surface. Opening the book without disarming the connection will release the spears.

Trigger (Open/Close Object). A creature that opens the book triggers the trap.

Effect (Spears). Spears drop from a nearby surface, thrusting into the 5-foot spaces adjacent to the book. A creature in the threatened area must make a DC 15 Dexterity saving throw, taking 66 (12d10) piercing damage on a failed save or half as much on a successful one.

Countermeasures. A successful DC 15 Wisdom (Perception) check reveals the holes in the ceiling hiding the spears. A successful DC 15 Dexterity check using thieves' tools disables the trap.

Punji Pick

Mechanical trap (level 13-16, dangerous, harm)

The door ahead is closed and locked, but it can be picked with a successful DC 20 Dexterity check using thieves' tools. However, a failed attempt releases a trap door that drops the target into a spiked pit.

Trigger (Fail to Pick Lock). A creature that attempts to pick the lock and fails triggers the trap.

Effect (Drop Into Spiked Pit). The floor drops out from under the triggering creature, which must make a DC 15 Dexterity saving throw. On a successful save, the creature is able to grab onto the edge of the spiked pit. On a failed save, the creature falls into the spiked pit and takes 17 (5d6) bludgeoning damage and 49 (14d6) piercing damage.

Countermeasures (Difficult). With a successful DC 15 Wisdom (Perception) check, a creature can spot the mechanisms inside the lock but doesn't know exactly what they do. A successful DC 15 Intelligence (Investigation) check lets a creature understand the trap.

With a successful DC 15 Dexterity check using thieves' tools, a creature can disable the trap.

Spider Architects

Mechanical trap (level 13-16, dangerous, harm)

The chamber ahead is filled with darkness and a soft pattering, like pieces of plaster or stone falling to the floor, echoes throughout. Skittering around the place are hundreds of tiny spiders, their webs marking every surface.

Trigger (Produce Flame). The ceiling is held up by a thin, flammable spider web. Bringing a flame beneath the web causes it to burn away and trigger the trap.

Effect (Crushing Ceiling/Walls). The ceiling moves at a rate of 1 foot per round at the end of the initiative order. Once the surface reaches a creature's space, they take 1d10 bludgeoning damage. If the surface is still moving on the next turn, the creature is restrained and takes 2d10 bludgeoning damage. A third round spent being crushed inflicts 4d10 bludgeoning damage, the fourth and every round thereafter inflicts 10d10 bludgeoning damage. After 7 rounds, the ceiling reaches the floor and then retracts.

Countermeasures. A successful DC 15 Wisdom (Perception) check reveals the spider webs and with a successful DC 15 Intelligence (Nature) check, a creature knows that burning away the webs triggers the trap.

A creature that climbs up the wall disables the trap with a successful DC 15 Dexterity check using thieves' tools.

Thought Spiral

Magic trap (level 13-16, dangerous, hinder)

The stairwell ahead is painted with bright colours in confusing, hypnotic patterns that make it unclear when one step ends and another begins.

Trigger (Fail to Speak Password). A creature that enters the stairwell without uttering the word 'reveal' triggers the trap.

Effect (Amnesia). A hazy fog fills the triggering creature's mind and it must make a DC 15 Wisdom saving throw. On a failure, the creature forgets the previous 1d10 days; these memories form in the magical paint on the staircase. The memories return after 8 hours; *greater restoration* or similar magic also restores the lost memories.

Countermeasures. The patterns in the stairwell can be seen from outside it, and with a successful DC 15 Intelligence (Arcana) check a creature realizes the nature of the trap. *Detect magic* reveals an aura of enchantment magic around the stairwell.

A spellcaster can disrupt the enchantment with a successful DC 15 spellcasting ability check; *dispel magic* (DC 16) also disables the trap.

Up is Down

Magic trap (level 13-16, dangerous, block)

This chamber's vaulted ceiling is 120-feet high, and is marked by archways and alcoves. Blocking your exit from the cathedral-like room is a portcullis, beside which is a hefty iron lever. A *glyph of warding (reverse gravity)* is inscribed on the lever.

Trigger (Move Lever/Press Button). Pulling the lever triggers the trap and also raises the portcullis.

Effect (Spell Effect). When activated, the glyph casts *reverse gravity*. All creatures and objects in a 50-foot radius, 100-foot high cylinder centered on the triggering creature that aren't somehow anchored to the ground fall upward and reach the top of the area. A creature can make a DC 15 Dexterity saving throw to grab onto a fixed object it can reach, thus avoiding the fall.

After 1 minute, or if dispelled with *dispel magic* (DC 17), affected objects and creatures fall back down, taking 55 (10d6) bludgeoning damage.

Countermeasures. A creature can spot the glyph with a successful DC 15 Intelligence (Investigation) check, or with *detect magic*. Once found, the glyph can be disabled with a successful DC 15 Intelligence (Arcana) check or with *dispel magic*.

Voltage Viewer

Magic trap (level 13-16, dangerous, harm)

A crystal ball hovers in this room, glowing and pulsing due to the raging lightning storm captured inside.

Trigger (Look Into). A creature within 10 feet of the crystal ball that looks into it triggers the trap.

Effect (Elemental Blast). A stroke of lightning forming a line 100 feet long and 5 feet wide blasts out from the crystal, aimed at the triggering creature. Each creature in the line must make a DC 15 Dexterity saving throw. A creature takes 35 (11d6) lightning damage on a failed save, or half as much damage on a successful one.

The lightning ignites flammable objects in the area that aren't being worn or carried.

Countermeasures. With a successful DC 15 Wisdom (Perception) check, a creature spots blasts and scorch marks on the walls of this room. A creature that succeeds on a DC 15 Intelligence (Arcana) check can understand the nature of the trap without triggering it. If viewed with *detect magic*, the crystal has an aura of evocation magic.

A spellcaster can disrupt the enchantment on the crystal with a successful DC 15 spellcasting ability check; casting *dispel magic* (DC 16) on the crystal also disables the trap. Either way, the lightning storm dissipates harmlessly with a loud crack of thunder.

Level 13-16 Perilous

These traps may kill characters of these levels, and will definitely injure them severely.

Add to the Collection

Hybrid trap (level 13-16, perilous, hinder)

The room is filled with beautiful sculptures of beasts, standing on ornate stands and plinths. Each has a unique design, and must have been the pinnacle of the artists' career. A thin, transparent wire stretches between two of the plinths.

Trigger (Tripwire). A creature that snaps the wire triggers the trap.

Effect (Transmutation). When activated, a burst of purple energy washes over the triggering creature, transforming it into a random beast unless they succeed on a DC 17 Wisdom saving throw. The trap has no effect on a shapechanger or a creature with 0 hit points.

The transformation lasts 8 hours or until dispelled; the transformation also ends if the creature drops to 0 hit points or dies. The new form can be any beast whose challenge rating is equal to or less than the creature's. The creature's game statistics, including mental ability scores, are replaced by the statistics of the chosen beast. It retains its alignment and personality.

The creature assumes the hit points of its new form. When it reverts to its normal form, the creature returns to the number of hit points it had before it transformed. If it reverts as a result of dropping to 0 hit points, any excess damage carries over to its normal form. As long as the excess damage doesn't reduce the creature's normal form to 0 hit points, it isn't knocked unconscious.

The creature is limited in the actions it can perform by the nature of its new form, and it can't speak, cast spells, or take any other action that requires hands or speech.

The creature's gear melds into the new form; it can't activate, use, wield, or otherwise benefit from any of its equipment.

Countermeasures. A successful DC 17 Wisdom (Perception) check lets a creature spot the tripwire, and with a successful DC 17 Dexterity check using thieves' tools a creature can disable the trap.

The plinths with the tripwire each have an aura of transmutation magic when viewed with *detect magic*. A spellcaster can disrupt the enchantment on the plinths with a successful DC 17 spellcasting ability check; *dispel magic* (DC 14) also disables the trap.

Clockwork Con-trap-tion

Mechanical trap (level 13-16, perilous, block)

A complex clockwork mechanism takes up the majority of this workshop. It whirrs and buzzes like a living insect, spinning and gyrating in place. In front of the mechanism is a panel of buttons and levers.

Trigger (Move Lever/Press Button). Most of the buttons and levers control the workings of the machine. One of the buttons is false: pressing it triggers the trap.

Effect (Barrier). A 5-foot tall, 10-foot wide barrier of whirling blades shoots up from the floor 5 feet behind the control panel, trapping creatures there. A creature that approaches or starts its turn within 5 feet of the barrier must make a DC 17 Dexterity saving throw, taking 28 (8d6) slashing damage on a failed save, or half as much on a successful one.

Countermeasures. A successful DC 17 Wisdom (Perception) check lets a creature spot the top of the bladed wall, flush with the ceiling. A successful DC 17 Intelligence (Investigation) check reveals the false button, and allows a creature to attempt a DC 17 Dexterity check while using thieves' tools to disable the trap.

Hanging Hooks

Mechanical trap (level 13-16, perilous, harm)

On the ceiling of this chamber are nasty barbs that look like meat or fish hooks. The walls and floor are splattered with blood, and the entire place is dimly lit by a single brazier. A metal door with a grated window marks the exit.

Trigger (Tension Cable). A taut cable is fixed between the metal door and the floor. Opening the door triggers the trap.

Effect (Spring Floor). All creatures in the room are flung up into the ceiling and must make a DC 17 Dexterity check. On a failure, the creature takes 28 (8d6) piercing damage and becomes grappled by the hooks on the ceiling (escape DC 17). On a success, the creature takes half the damage and isn't grappled.

A creature that fails their ability check to escape from the hooks takes an additional 28 (8d6) piercing damage.

Countermeasures. With a successful DC 17 Wisdom (Perception) check, a creature can spot the tension cable; it can be disabled with a successful DC 17 Dexterity check using thieves' tools.

Needletongue

Mechanical trap (level 13-16, perilous, harm)

A bizarre skull etched with runes sits in pride of place in the cabinet. It seems vaguely humanoid, but there's something strange about it. The edges of the eye-sockets are encrusted with cut glass, and there is clearly something in the skull's closed mouth.

Trigger (Interact with Bait). Opening the skull's mouth triggers the trap.

Effect (Needle). A poisoned needle in the skull's mouth pierces the creature that opened the skull. That creature must make a DC 17 Constitution saving throw. On a failed save, the target takes 22 (4d10) poison damage and 22 (4d10) necrotic damage and is poisoned. While poisoned in this way, the creature must make another DC 17 Constitution saving throw every hour or take an additional 11 (2d10) necrotic damage. The creature is no longer poisoned after 4 hours or once they succeed on 2 Constitution saving throws to resist the additional damage.

Countermeasures. A creature can spot the hidden needle with a successful DC 17 Intelligence (Investigation) check; with a successful DC 17 Dexterity (Sleight of Hand) check a creature can open the skull without triggering the trap.

The trap can be disabled with a successful DC 17 Dexterity check using thieves' tools.

Prismatic Glyph

Magic trap (level 13-16, perilous, harm)

Thick, black tar stains the tapestry hanging on the wall, concealing a hidden door. The masterpiece of thread work has been ruined by the tar, which is formed into a *glyph of warding (prismatic spray).*

Trigger (Creature Detector). A good creature that approaches within 5 feet of the tapestry triggers the trap.

Effect (Spell Effect). When activated the glyph casts *prismatic spray.* Eight multicolored rays of light flash from the glyph. Each ray is a different color and has a different power and purpose. Each creature in a 60-foot cone must make a DC 17 Dexterity saving throw. For each target, roll a d8 to determine which color ray affects it.

1. **Red:** The target takes 35 (10d6) fire damage on a failed save, or half as much damage on a successful one.
2. **Orange:** The target takes 35 (10d6) acid damage on a failed save, or half as much damage on a successful one.
3. **Yellow:** The target takes 35 (10d6) lightning damage on a failed save, or half as much damage on a successful one.
4. **Green:** The target takes 35 (10d6) poison damage on a failed save, or half as much damage on a successful one.
5. **Blue:** The target takes 35 (10d6) cold damage on a failed save, or half as much damage on a successful one.
6. **Indigo:** On a failed save, the target is restrained. It must then make a DC 17 Constitution saving throw at the end of each of its turns. If it successfully saves three times, the spell ends. If it fails its save three times, it permanently turns to stone and is subjected to the petrified condition. The successes and failures don't need to be consecutive; keep track of both until the target collects three of a kind.

7. **Violet:** On a failed save, the target is blinded. It must then make a DC 17 Wisdom saving throw at the start of your next turn. A successful save ends the blindness. If it fails that save, the creature is transported to another plane of existence of the GM's choosing and is no longer blinded. (Typically, a creature that is on a plane that isn't its home plane is banished home, while other creatures are usually cast into the Astral or Ethereal planes.)
8. **Special:** The target is struck by two rays. Roll twice more, rerolling any 8.

Countermeasures. The glyph can be found with *detect magic* or a successful DC 17 Intelligence (Investigation) check. Once found, it can be disabled with a successful DC 17 Intelligence (Arcana) check or with *dispel magic.*

Sandy Grave

Mechanical trap (level 13-16, perilous, block)

This sandstone tomb is filled with decrepit statues of old kings and queens. Steps lead up to a towering gold statue of a jackal-headed goddess-queen. A pressure plate is hidden on the final step.

Trigger (Pressure Plate). Stepping on the pressure plate triggers the trap.

Effect (Falling Sand). The statue's mouth opens and sand begins to pour into the tomb. Creatures in the area must make successful DC 17 Dexterity saving throws at the beginning of their turns to stay atop the sand. The save DC increases by 2 at the end of each round.

A creature that fails one saving throw is buried up to their knees and restrained. On their next saving throw, if the creature succeeds they dig themselves out and are no longer restrained; if they fail they are buried waist-deep and remain restrained.

A creature buried waist-deep must make a DC 17 Strength saving throw at the beginning of their turn; if they succeed they dig themselves free of the sand and if they fail they are buried to the neck and immobilized. On their next turn, the creature is completely buried and starts suffocating.

As an action, a creature can dig out another creature with a successful DC 17 Strength (Athletics) check against the current save DC of the trap. Spells like *freedom of movement* or movement modes like burrow can also allow creatures to freely move through the sand.

Countermeasures. A creature can find the pressure plate with a successful DC 17 Wisdom (Perception) check; it can be disabled with a successful DC 17 Dexterity check using thieves' tools.

Severe Slumber

Magic trap (level 13-16, perilous, subdue)

An important or significant object has been enchanted to put creatures that remove it from its resting place into a deep sleep.

Trigger (Remove Object). A creature that removes the object from its current location triggers the trap.

Effect (Sleep). The enchantment can affect 76 (17d8) hit points of creatures. Creatures within 20 feet of the enchanted object are affected in ascending order of their current hit points (ignoring unconscious creatures). Starting with the creature that has the lowest current hit points, each creature affected falls unconscious for 8 hours, or until the sleeper takes damage, or someone uses an action to shake or slap the sleeper awake. Subtract each creature's hit points from the total before moving on to the creature with the next lowest hit points. A creature's hit points must be equal to or less than the remaining total for that creature to be affected.

Undead and creatures immune to being charmed aren't affected by this spell.

Countermeasures. A creature that succeeds on a DC 17 Intelligence (History) check recognizes the object and knows about the trap. The object has an aura of enchantment magic when viewed with *detect magic.*

A spellcaster can disrupt the enchantment on the object with a successful DC 17 spellcasting ability check; *dispel magic* (DC17) can also disable the trap.

Sorcerous Cell

Magic trap (level 13-16, perilous, subdue)

A *glyph of warding (forcecage)* is written on the wall, floor, or ceiling. When a creature gets too close the glyph activates.

Trigger (Creature Detector). A creature that gets within 5 feet of the glyph triggers the trap.

Effect (Spell Effect). When activated, the glyph casts *forcecage*. An immobile, invisible, cube-shaped cage composed of magical force springs into existence around the triggering creature. The prison is 20 feet on a side and is made from 1/2-inch diameter bars spaced 1/2 inch apart.

Any creature that is completely inside the cage's area when it comes into being is trapped. Creatures only partially within the area, or those too large to fit inside the area, are pushed away from the center of the area until they are completely outside the area.

A creature inside the cage can't leave it by non-magical means. If the creature tries to use teleportation or interplanar travel to leave the cage, it must first make a DC 12 Charisma saving throw. On a success, the creature can use that magic to exit the cage. On a failure, the creature can't exit the cage and wastes the use of the spell or effect. The cage also extends into the Ethereal Plane, blocking ethereal travel.

This spell can't be dispelled by *dispel magic* and it lasts for 1 hour.

Countermeasures. The glyph can be found with *detect magic* or with a successful DC 12 Intelligence (Investigation) check. Once found, the glyph can be disabled with *dispel magic* or with a successful DC 12 Intelligence (Arcana) check. However, to use an ability check on the glyph a creature would have to be close enough to trigger it.

Thin Facade

Hybrid trap (level 13-16, perilous, harm)

A long, straight, narrow corridor allows passage only to those who know the password. A *rune of detection* is inscribed on the wall of the corridor.

Trigger (Fail to Speak Password). A creature that passes the halfway point of the corridor without speaking the password triggers the trap.

Effect (Crushing Ceiling/Walls). The walls move at a rate of 1 foot per round at the end of the initiative order. Once the surface reaches a creature's space, they take 1d10 bludgeoning damage. If the surface is still moving on the next turn, the creature is restrained and takes 2d10 bludgeoning damage. A third round spent being crushed inflicts 4d10 bludgeoning damage, and the walls then retract.

Countermeasures. With a successful DC 17 Intelligence (History) check, a creature can recall useful information about the trap, including the password; the rune can be found with a successful DC 17 Wisdom (Perception) check.

Once found, the rune can be disabled with a successful DC 17 Intelligence (Arcana) check or with *dispel magic*.

Trap-a-port

Magic trap (level 13-16, perilous, subdue)

A 5-foot radius circular portal is set into the floor of this room, covered by an illusory rug or carpet.

Trigger (Creature Detector). A creature that steps onto the portal triggers the trap.

Effect (Teleport). The triggering creature must make a DC 17 Dexterity saving throw. On a successful save, the creature is able to grab onto the edge of the portal. On a failed save, the creature is teleported to another location.

Countermeasures. The rug has an aura of illusion magic when viewed with *detect magic*, and another aura of conjuration magic outlines the portal. A creature that interacts with the rug can make a DC 17 Wisdom saving throw; on a success, the creature realizes the illusion.

Once discovered, the portal can be disabled with *dispel magic* (DC 17); a spellcaster that succeeds on a DC 17 spellcasting ability check can also disrupt the enchantment.

Level 13-16 Deadly

These traps will almost certainly kill characters of these levels.

Blazing Ring, Greater

Mechanical trap (level 13-16, deadly, harm)

A 1-foot thick ring of decorative stonework surrounds a 25-foot diameter circle area in the center of the room. The ceiling directly above the ring is blackened with soot. In the 5-foot square at the circle's center is something intriguing.

Trigger (Weight Sensitive Floor). When a Small or larger creature steps onto a space adjacent to the 5-foot square at the center of the area within the ring, they activate a pressure plate. Parts of the stonework slide away, revealing spouts which pour flaming oil onto the floor from the ring's inner edge.

Effect (Wall of Fire). The flaming oil creates a ringed wall of flames 25 feet in diameter, 20 feet high, and 1 foot thick. The wall is opaque and lasts for 1 minute. When the wall appears, each creature within its area must make a DC 20 Dexterity saving throw. On a failed save, a creature takes 70 (20d6) fire damage, or half as much damage on a successful save.

The side of the wall facing inwards deals the trap's fire damage to each creature that ends its turn within 10 feet of that side or inside the wall. A creature takes the same damage when it enters the wall for the first time on a turn or ends its turn there. The other side of the wall deals no damage.

A creature that is adjacent to the wall can make a DC 20 Constitution check using thieves' tools to end this effect.

Countermeasures. A successful DC 20 Wisdom (Perception) check reveals the pressure plate, and a successful DC 20 Dexterity check while using thieves' tools disables it.

Blind Leading the Blind

Magic trap (level 13-16, deadly, hinder)

A *glyph of warding* is etched into the floor of the chamber. A creature that creates an open flame in the chamber or brings an open flame into the area suffers the consequences.

Trigger (Produce Flame). The presence of an open flame in the area triggers the trap.

Effect (Blindness). All creatures in the chamber must make a DC 20 Constitution saving throw. On a failed save the creature is magically blinded. This is a curse.

Countermeasures. The *detect magic* spell causes an aura to illuminate the area. A successful DC 20 Intelligence (Arcana) check once it is discovered reveals the nature of the trigger. Casting *dispel magic* at 8th level or higher on the area will disable the trap.

Bolts of Slaying

Hybrid trap (level 13-16, deadly, harm)

The only way to leave the caverns is up a sheer cliff face, with only scattered handholds. At the bottom of the cliff are dozens of boulders, two of which have a *rune of detection* inscribed on them. Enchanted ballistas are hidden in these boulders.

Trigger (Bring Object). Approaching the cliff face with any magic item or non-magical contraption that allows a creature to fly or glide triggers the trap.

Effect (Bolts). Hidden inside two of the boulders are *+3 ballistas* loaded with *bolts of humanoid slaying*. A creature that triggers the trap is targeted with two ranged attacks from these ballistas, each of which have a +15 bonus, and deal 19 (3d10 + 3) piercing damage on a hit. If the target hit is a humanoid, it must succeed on a DC 17 Constitution saving throw, taking an extra 33 (6d10) piercing damage on a failed save, or half as much on a successful one.

Countermeasures. A creature can spot the rune and the hidden crossbows with a successful DC 20 Wisdom (Perception) check, or with *detect magic*.

Once found, the rune can be disabled with a successful DC 20 Intelligence (Arcana) check or *dispel magic*.

Corrosive Chains

Mechanical trap (level 13-16, deadly, block)

The iron chest is battered and dented all over, but is still locked fast. It is the only feature in this deep, dank cavern.

Trigger (Fail to Pick Lock). A creature that tries and fails to pick the lock triggers the trap.

Effect (Snare). The triggering creature must succeed on a DC 20 Dexterity saving throw or be restrained by a chain covered in acid that shoots from the lock. A creature restrained by the chain takes 55 (10d10) bludgeoning damage and 55 (10d10) acid damage. The restrained creature can free themselves with a successful DC 20 Strength (Athletics) check.

Countermeasures. A successful DC 20 Wisdom (Perception) check while examining the lock reveals the trigger. A successful DC 20 Intelligence (Investigation) check reveals the snare, and allows a creature to attempt a DC 20 Dexterity check while using thieves' tools to disable the trap.

Hot on the Trail

Hybrid trap (level 13-16, deadly, harm)

The walls of the chamber have spouts every few feet that fire a blast of flame in a large cone. A *rune of detection* is inscribed on the chamber walls, waiting to detect the presence of a creature of particular physical characteristics, race, or alignment.

Trigger (Creature Detector). When a creature that meets the specified criteria gets within 5 feet of the rune, the trap activates.

Effect (Elemental Blast). Fire erupts from several spouts around the room. Each creature in the chamber must make a DC 20 Dexterity saving throw, taking 87 (25d6) fire damage on a failed save, or half as much on a successful one.

Countermeasures. The rune can be found with *detect magic*, or with a successful DC 20 Wisdom (Perception) check. Once found, the rune can be disabled with a successful DC 20 Intelligence (Arcana) check or with *dispel magic*.

Lava Lake

Magic trap (level 13-16, deadly, block)

High above a lake of lava, resting upon an inaccessible pinnacle of rock, is a statue of a dwarven warrior, armed with a pickaxe and shield. A shrine to dwarven deities of the forge is on ground level.

Trigger (No Command Word). Using a wand, rod, ring, orb, or similar item that requires a command word within the shrine activates the trigger.

Effect (Swap). A triggering creature must succeed on a DC 20 Charisma save, or instantly switch places with the statue. The statue animates as a **clay golem** and attacks all non-dwarfs in the shrine. The golem will not leave the shrine, and if reduced to 0 hit points it crumbles to dust.

If a creature falls from the pinnacle into the lava they take 35 (10d6) bludgeoning damage from the fall, and 99 (18d10) fire damage from the lava. They take the fire damage again at the end of their turn if they remain submerged.

Countermeasures. A creature that succeeds on a DC 20 Intelligence (Religion) check realizes the triggering conditions for the trap. The shrine has an aura of conjuration magic when viewed with *detect magic*.

A spellcaster can disrupt the enchantment on the shrine with a successful DC 20 spellcasting ability check; *dispel magic* (DC 17) also disables the trap.

Manners Maketh Man

Magic trap (level 13-16, deadly, block)

In this room is a statue of a dignified, regal woman holding a golden quill in one hand, and a diamond shaped shield in the other.

Trigger (Insult Idol). A creature that is libellous, scandalous, or rude in the statue's presence triggers the trap.

Effect (Wall of Force). An immobile, invisible, cube-shaped prison composed of magical force springs into existence around the triggering creature. The prison is 10 feet on a side, creating a solid barrier that prevents any matter from passing through it and blocking any spells cast into or out from the area.

Any creature that is completely inside the cage's area when the trap is activated is trapped. Creatures only partially within the area, or those too large to fit inside the area, are pushed away from the center of the area until they are completely outside the area.

A creature inside the cage can't leave it by non-magical means. If the creature tries to use teleportation or interplanar travel to leave the cage, it must first make a DC 20 Charisma saving throw. On a success, the creature can use that magic to exit the cage. On a failure, the creature can't exit the cage and wastes the use of the spell or effect. The cage also extends into the Ethereal Plane, blocking ethereal travel.

The prison can't be dispelled by *dispel magic*; it fades away after 1 day. Apologising to the statue with a successful DC 20 Charisma (Religion) check dispels the prison.

Countermeasures. A creature that succeeds on a DC 20 Intelligence (Religion) check recognizes the statue and understands the trap. The statue has an aura of evocation magic when viewed with *detect magic*.

A spellcaster can disrupt the enchantment on the statue with a successful DC 20 spellcasting ability check; *dispel magic* (DC 17) also disables the trap.

Pass or Gas

Hybrid trap (level 13-16, deadly, harm)

When a creature enters this room, a magical mouth (as per the *magic mouth* spell) appears on the wall asking for a password. This question could take the form of a simple request or a riddle and should be something that pertains to the surrounding area. A *rune of detection* is inscribed on the wall opposite the mouth.

Trigger (Command Word). Not speaking the password triggers the trap.

Effect (Poison Gas). When activated, the rune releases valves that create a 20-foot-radius sphere of poisonous, yellow-green fog centered on the middle of the room. The fog spreads around corners. It lasts 10 minutes or until strong wind disperses the fog. Its area is heavily obscured.

When a creature enters the fog's area for the first time on a turn or starts its turn there, that creature must make a DC 20 Constitution saving throw. The creature takes 36 (8d8) poison damage on a failed save, or half as much damage on a successful one.

Countermeasures. A creature that succeeds on a DC 20 Intelligence (History) or Wisdom (Insight) check can recall stories of this trap or deduce what the password might be.

The rune can be found with a successful DC 20 Wisdom (Perception) check. Once found, it can be disabled with a successful DC 20 Intelligence (Arcana) check or *dispel magic*.

Snake Pit

Mechanical trap (level 13-16, deadly, harm)

The floor in this room is painted with an optical illusion which makes it look like a pit of snakes.

Trigger (Weight Sensitive Surface). A Medium or larger creature that steps on the floor triggers the trap.

Effect (Drop Into Lair). The triggering creature must succeed on a DC 20 Dexterity saving throw or fall 100 feet into a pit which opens beneath them like a trapdoor, taking 35 (10d6) bludgeoning damage. At the bottom of the pit are 5 **swarms of poisonous snakes**.

Countermeasures. A successful DC 20 Wisdom (Perception) check reveals the trigger, and a successful DC 20 Dexterity check while using thieves' tools disables the trigger.

Unstable Ground

Hybrid trap (level 13-16, deadly)

A large chamber has a floor covered in strange runes and symbols, including a *rune of detection*. Casting within the chamber activates the rune, which collapses the floor. Creatures within the chamber fall fifty feet into a pit filled with 25-foot deep water.

Trigger (Cast Spell). Casting a spell in the chamber triggers the trap.

Effect (Drop). The floor of the chamber falls away, starting at the center and moving out toward the walls. Each creature in the room must make a DC 20 Dexterity saving throw. On a success, the creature is able to grab onto the edge of the pit. On a failure, the creature falls into the pit below. Creatures close to the center of the chamber have disadvantage on their saving throw, while creatures close to the walls have advantage.

The pit is 50 feet deep and half-filled with water; climbing out of it requires a successful DC 20 Strength (Athletics) check. After each hour in the pit, a creature must succeed on a DC 20 Constitution saving throw or begin suffocating.

Countermeasures. The rune can be found with a successful DC 20 Wisdom (Perception) check, and with a successful DC 20 Intelligence (History) check a creature can recall some details and bits of lore about this trap.

Once found, the rune can be disabled with a successful DC 20 Intelligence (Arcana) check.

Detect magic can be used to find the rune, and *dispel magic* can disable it, but casting either spell inside the room triggers the trap.

Level 17-20 Traps

We arrived in a great chamber, a vaulted ceiling soaring high overhead. Massive statues stood along the walls, hands raised as if saluting our valiant and unflinching resolve to get to this point. Perhaps this temple was built with so many traps as a sort of trial, a test of mettle and fortitude, if you will. This would certainly make sense, for there, unguarded and awaiting us, was the artifact.

As a group we all proceeded forward, intent on experiencing this long-awaited moment together. We stood around the artifact and took it (I won't say who actually took it, that's for me to know). We waited a moment, sure that something terrible was about to happen, but nothing did. We looked at one another, hesitantly smiled, then quickly devolved into laughter, cheers, hugs, and rejoicing in our accomplishment. We walked out of the room, and out of that awful temple for good.

... At least, that's what I'd hoped would happen. Oh, there were cheers and much rejoicing and all that, but as soon as we started to walk away, everything gave way in an almighty lurch. We saw the massive granite statues sway ominously as streams of dust cascaded down from the ceiling high above. Cracks raced along the walls and up into the ceiling itself as the whole place started coming down.

Dazzling beams of sunlight streamed through as huge chunks of the ceiling broke free and slammed down around us. We darted left and right, avoiding them as best we could. There was a low groaning sound from above, which made our wizard say something I'll not repeat here. One of the towering statues was falling straight toward us. While most of us reflexively screamed and futilely tried to brace for what was coming, our wizard stood tall, stretching out an arm as if mocking the gigantic carving.

As she screamed in defiance, a shimmering orb of force bloomed around us just as the incalculable tons of stone slammed into it. The world was filled with nothing but dust, grit, and the sound of rattling stone. I opened my eyes and saw my companions doing the same. We weren't' smears on the ground! We were alive! As the dust settled, we looked around at the wreckage, and those sunbeams sliced through the gloom as a final, divine reward for our work.

It was finally time to go home.

The traps in this chapter are designed to challenge characters who are levels 17-20 and are grouped by their lethality. Any of these traps can be dropped right into a dungeon or similar adventure and shouldn't require any preparation. For more information on customizing traps, go to **Chapter 8: Designing Traps**, or for a completely random and unexpected trap, go to **Chapter 9: Random Trap Generator**.

Level 17-20 Traps Table

Roll a d100 on the table below to choose a random trap appropriate for 17-20 characters, or select a desired lethality and roll a d10.

	d100	d10	Trap	Page
Setback	1-2	1	Authorization Required	73
	3-4	2	Barfing Book	73
	5-6	3	Burning Bright	73
	7-8	4	Cost of Vision	74
	9-10	5	Font of Flame	74
	11-12	6	Silencing Spikes	74
	13-14	7	Snapping Jaws	74
	15-16	8	Stewards of the Axe	75
	17-18	9	Swinging Spike-Hammer	75
	19-20	10	Trapdoor Pitfall, Treacherous	75
Moderate	21-22	1	Blinding Knowledge	75
	23-24	2	Bronze Blockade	76
	25-26	3	Corrosive Bath	76
	27-28	4	Crushing Chest	76
	29-30	5	Crystal Clear	76
	31-32	6	Dozing Deterioration	77
	33-34	7	Path of Light	77
	35-36	8	Picked Wrong	77
	37-38	9	Rogue's Bane, Treacherous	77
	39-40	10	Swift Imprisonment	78
Dangerous	41-42	1	Acid Lock	78
	43-44	2	Doom Dome	78
	45-46	3	Futile Blade	79
	47-48	4	Froggy Floor	79
	49-50	5	Join Me	79
	51-52	6	Poisoned Path	79
	53-54	7	Run For Your Life	80
	55-56	8	Seal of Embers	80
	57-58	9	Sticky Situation	80
	59-60	10	Violence Cage	80
Perilous	61-62	1	Acidic Ceiling	81
	63-64	2	Arresting Vanity	81
	65-66	3	Dead Men May Grow Tails	81
	67-68	4	Magic Trunk	82
	69-70	5	Searing Spikes	82
	71-72	6	Shocking Exit	82
	73-74	7	Skull Scree	82
	75-76	8	Sweet-Sounding Stench	83
	77-78	9	The Thin Veil	83
	79-80	10	Timber!	84
Deadly	81-82	1	Anti-Wizard Alarm	84
	83-84	2	Blazing Rings, Treacherous	84
	85-86	3	Best Left Alone	84
	87-88	4	Cool Off	85
	89-90	5	Log Ride	85
	91-92	6	Pooling Puddle Problem	85
	93-94	7	Snicker Snack	85
	95-96	8	Telestairs	86
	97-98	9	Unworthy	86
	99-100	10	Wake the Dragon	86

Level 17-20 Setback

These traps should present a minor inconvenience to characters of this level range.

Authorization Required

Magic trap (level 17-20, setback, subdue)

A door or archway is enchanted to allow only certain creatures to pass freely. Any who do not match the qualifications attempting to pass are teleported elsewhere, usually somewhere they would rather not be.

Trigger (Creature Detector). The trap is keyed to certain criteria of creatures, including physical characteristics, race, type, and alignment. If a creature meeting the requirements for safe passage passes the threshold, the trap is deactivated for 1 minute. If a creature that doesn't meet the requirements passes through the archway, the trap activates.

Effect (Teleport). The triggering creature is instantly transported to another location within the dungeon or structure containing the trap.

Countermeasures. The archway has an aura of conjuration magic when viewed with *detect magic*. A creature that succeeds on a DC 10 Intelligence (Arcana) check can spot and decipher a series of sigils or runes along the outside of the archway or door, and understands the trap.

A spellcaster can disrupt the enchantment with a successful DC 10 spellcasting ability check; *dispel magic* (DC 15) also disables the trap.

Barfing Book

Hybrid trap (level 17-20, setback, hinder)

A book of putrid secrets sits atop a plinth or pedestal, covered in pulsing boils and pustules, waiting to be read. Above the book, a hidden nozzle waits to disgorge a gout of vile slime and sludge; a *rune of detection* waits to activate the nozzle.

Trigger (Open/Close Object). A creature that opens the book triggers the trap.

Effect (Acid/Slime Blast). A blast of putrid smelling slime covers the triggering creature, who must make a DC 10 Dexterity saving throw. On a success, the creature avoids the slime. On a failure, the creature must make a DC 11 Constitution saving throw or contract sewer plague from the foul slime.

It takes 1d4 days for sewer plague's symptoms to manifest in an infected creature. Symptoms include fatigue and cramps. The infected creature suffers one level of exhaustion, and it regains only half the normal number of hit points from spending Hit Dice and no hit points from finishing a long rest.

At the end of each long rest, an infected creature must make a DC 11 Constitution saving throw. On a failed save, the character gains one level of exhaustion. On a successful save, the character's exhaustion level decreases by one level. If a successful saving throw reduces the infected creature's level of exhaustion below 1, the creature recovers from the disease.

Countermeasures. The rune and hidden nozzle can be spotted with a successful DC 10 Wisdom (Perception) check. Once found, the rune can be disabled with a successful DC 10 Intelligence (Arcana) check, or with *dispel magic*.

Burning Bright

Mechanical trap (level 17-20, setback, harm)

Multiple shadowed alcoves line the walls of this shrine. Beside the door on a small plinth is a gleaming silver lantern. Flammable oil is held in place by a thin wax coating on the inside upper surface of the lantern.

Trigger (Activate Light Fixture). Lighting the lantern triggers the trap.

Effect (Acid/Slime Blast). Sticky, flammable oil pours forth from the lamp, setting the triggering creature on fire. The triggering creature must succeed on a DC 10 Dexterity saving throw or be covered in flaming oil and take 11 (2d10) fire damage at the start of each of its turns. A creature can end this damage by using its action to make a DC 10 Dexterity check to extinguish the flames and scrape off the oil.

Countermeasures. A creature that succeeds on a DC 10 Wisdom (Perception) check can spot the hidden oil, and with a successful DC 10 Intelligence (Nature) check a creature understands the danger of the trap.

The oil can be easily scraped out of the lantern, or washed out with alcohol or another solvent.

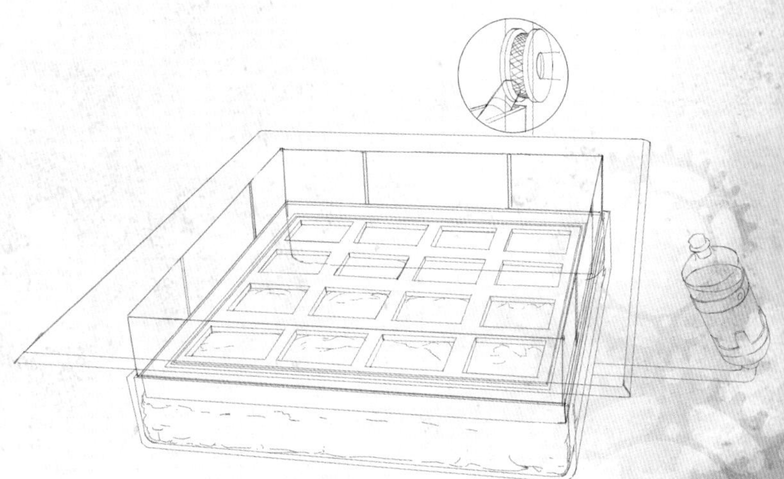

Cost of Vision

Magic trap (level 17-20, setback, hinder)

A gate with an offering bowl blocks the way to a treacherous, labyrinthine path. To open the gate, a creature must place an offering in the bowl representing something that would distract it from a righteous course. If the offering is accepted, the gate allows the creature passage. Any creature who gives an unsatisfactory offering or attempts to sneak through is magically blinded.

Trigger (Offering). A creature that places an unsatisfactory offering in the bowl triggers the trap.

Effect (Blindness). A triggering creature must make a DC 10 Constitution saving throw or be magically blinded for 1 day. The creature can make another DC 10 Constitution saving throw at the end of every hour, ending the effect on a success.

A creature blinded by the trap can have their sight restored with *dispel magic* (DC 17), *remove curse* or *lesser restoration.*

Countermeasures. Pictographs and carvings around the gate provide clues to the nature of the trap; a creature that succeeds on a DC 10 Intelligence (Religion) check can deduce the required offering.

The bowl has an aura of necromancy magic when viewed with *detect magic*. A spellcaster can disrupt the enchantment on it with a successful DC 10 spellcasting ability check, or with *dispel magic*.

Font of Flame

Magic trap (level 17-20, setback, harm)

A locked door bars farther passage. To the right of the door is a small stone font engraved with a flame motif, filled with water. At the bottom of the font is a key, and a hidden *glyph of warding (burning hands)*.

Trigger (Disturb Liquid). A creature that sticks their hand into the water or otherwise disturbs the font triggers the trap. Creatures can remove the key without causing ripples by succeeding on a DC 10 Dexterity (Sleight of Hand) check.

Effect (Spell Effect). A thin sheet of blue flames shoots forth from the font. Each creature in a 15-foot cone centered on the triggering creature must make a DC 10 Dexterity saving throw. A creature takes 17 (5d6) fire damage on a failed save, or half as much damage on a successful one.

The fire ignites any flammable objects in the area that aren't being worn or carried.

Countermeasures. The glyph can be found with a successful DC 10 Intelligence (Investigation) check or with *detect magic*. Once found, the glyph can be disabled with a successful DC 10 Intelligence (Arcana) check or with *dispel magic*.

Silencing Spikes

Hybrid trap (level 17-20, setback, harm)

This 5-foot wide corridor is covered with a fine layer of dust, concealing a *rune of detection.*

Trigger (Musical/Auditory). Any sound triggers the trap. A creature that moves or performs actions in the trapped area must succeed on a DC 10 Dexterity (Stealth) check to avoid triggering the trap.

Effect (Spikes). When activated, the rune activates a mechanism that causes spikes to extend from the walls. Each creature in the corridor must make a DC 10 Dexterity check, taking 17 (5d6) piercing damage on a failed save, or half as much on a successful one.

Countermeasures. With a successful DC 10 Wisdom (Perception) check, a creature can find the hidden holes for the spikes and the rune. The rune can also be found with *detect magic*. With a successful DC 10 Intelligence (Investigation) check, a creature can understand how the trap operates.

A creature can disable the trap with a successful DC 10 Intelligence (Arcana) check to disrupt the rune, or a successful DC 10 Dexterity check using thieves' tools to disable the spikes. *Dispel magic* cast on the rune also disables the trap, and *silence* can negate the trigger entirely.

Snapping Jaws

Hybrid trap (level 17-20, setback, block)

Strange writing is scrawled on the wall, including a *rune of detection*. The writing is spread over 5 feet, and there is a large concealed hole in the wall beneath it.

Trigger (Produce Light/Darkness). Bringing a light source within 5 feet of the writing triggers the trap.

Effect (Snare). A pair of steel jaws launches from the concealed hole in the wall. The jaws make an attack roll against the triggering creature with a +5 bonus to the roll, dealing 16 (3d10) piercing damage on a hit. This attack cannot gain advantage or disadvantage. A target hit by the jaws is restrained until it is freed.

A successful DC 10 Strength (Athletics) check or Dexterity check using thieves' tools makes the jaws release. Failure on either check deals 11 (2d10) piercing damage to the trapped creature.

Countermeasures. A successful DC 10 Wisdom (Perception) check reveals the rune; once found it can be dispelled with *dispel magic* or with a successful DC 10 Intelligence (Arcana) check.

Stewards of the Axe

Magic trap (level 17-20, moderate, harm)

At the far end of this chamber is an anvil, glowing with a throbbing, red heat. Stuck in the anvil is a rune-engraved battleaxe. Lying around the anvil are 4 dwarf corpses in various states of death and decay.

Trigger (Draw Weapon). Pulling the battleaxe from the anvil triggers the trap. It can only be removed by a dwarf.

Effect (Reanimate Creatures). The 4 dead dwarves rise as **wights** and attack all other creatures in the room, focusing on the triggering creature. If the creature that pulled the battleaxe from the anvil drops it or dies, the axe magically reappears in the anvil. The wights fade into nothingness if reduced to 0 hit points, or if dispelled with *dispel magic* (DC 18). They do not leave the room and, if not killed, return to dormancy after 24 hours.

Countermeasures. With a successful DC 12 Intelligence (History or Religion) check, a creature can identify the anvil and understands the trap. A dwarf has advantage on this check. If viewed with *detect magic*, the anvil has an aura of necromancy magic.

A spellcaster can disrupt the enchantment on the anvil with a successful DC 12 spellcasting ability check, or with *dispel magic*.

Swinging Spike-Hammer

Mechanical trap (level 17-20, setback, harm)

A heavy door blocks the way forward; a spring-loaded arm is attached to the ceiling on the other side. A long, sharp metal rod is affixed perpendicular to the arm. The arm is set to release when the door opens.

Trigger (Open Door). A creature that opens the door triggers the trap.

Effect (Swinging Object). A large spike affixed to a spring-loaded arm swings down and attacks the creature standing in the doorway. The spike makes a melee attack roll against the triggering creature with a +5 bonus, dealing 27 (5d10) piercing damage if it hits. This attack cannot gain advantage or disadvantage.

Countermeasures (Difficult). A creature that succeeds on a DC 10 Wisdom (Perception) check can spot some of the mechanisms by opening the door a crack, but it takes a successful DC 10 Intelligence (Investigation) check to understand the trap.

Once understood, a creature can disable the trap with a successful DC 10 Dexterity check using thieves' tools.

Trapdoor Pitfall, Treacherous

Mechanical trap (level 17-20, setback, harm)

A hidden trapdoor opens on to an 80-foot deep vertical shaft. The trapdoor covers a 5-foot square space and has a pressure plate embedded in it.

Trigger (Pressure Plate). A creature that steps on the trapdoor activates the pressure plate, causing the trap door to swing open.

Effect (Drop Into Empty Pit). The triggering creature must make a DC 10 Dexterity saving throw. On a success, the creature is able to grab onto the edge of the pit. On a failure, the creature falls into the pit and takes 28 (8d6) bludgeoning damage.

Countermeasures. With a successful DC 10 Wisdom (Perception) check a creature can spot the pressure plate; it can be disabled with a successful DC 10 Dexterity check using thieves' tools.

Level 17-20 Moderate

These traps will probably harm characters of this level.

Blinding Knowledge

Magic trap (level 17-20, moderate, hinder)

There is a single book left on the shelf in this room. It has a gilded spine covered with a spiralling, graceful motif; a *glyph of warding (blindness/deafness)* is hidden in the book.

Trigger (Open/Close Book). Opening the tome triggers the trap.

Effect (Spell Effect). When activated, the glyph casts *blindness/deafness* as an 8th level spell. The glyph targets the triggering creature and up to 7 other creatures, who all must make a DC 12 Constitution saving throw. If a creature fails, they are blinded for 1 minute. At the end of each of their turns, a blinded creature can make a DC 12 Constitution saving throw. On a success, the spell ends for that creature.

Countermeasures. A creature that succeeds on a DC 12 Intelligence (Arcana or History) check recognizes the book as a rare or unique tome, one that might be trapped in some way. Casting *detect magic* reveals an aura of abjuration magic around the tome, and *dispel magic* disables the trap.

Bronze Blockade

Magic trap (level 17-20, moderate, harm)

A large clay statue stands blocking passage to an important area; a word is written on its forehead in an obscure language. If a creature approaches the statue and doesn't speak the password, the statue animates and attacks.

Trigger (Fail to Speak Password). A creature that gets within 20 feet of the statue and fails to speak the password within 1 round triggers the trap.

Effect (Release Creatures). The statue is a **clay golem** that attacks the triggering creature and its companions. However, its primary purpose is preventing creatures from getting to the area it guards. The golem will not leave the room.

Once roused, the golem will remain active for 24 hours, or until a creature says the password. If reduced to 0 hit points, it crumbles to dust.

Countermeasures. The statue can be identified as a golem with a successful DC 12 Intelligence (Arcana) check. A creature that speaks the obscure language written on the golem can deduce the password; a successful DC 12 Intelligence (History) check can also provide clues about the golem.

Corrosive Bath

Mechanical trap (level 17-20, moderate, harm)

At the center of the chamber is a gold statue sitting on a sturdy stone pedestal. A tension cable is affixed to the bottom of the statue and runs down through a hole through the center of the pedestal.

Trigger (Pick Up Object). A creature that picks up the statue triggers the trap.

Effect (Drop Into Pit). The floor surrounding the pedestal suddenly drops away, revealing a pit filled with acid. Each creature standing next to the pedestal must succeed on a DC 12 Dexterity saving throw or fall into the pit. A creature that starts its turn in the acid takes 7 (2d6) acid damage per round.

At your discretion, the acid can damage weapons, armor, and other items. Any non-magical ammunition the creature is carrying is destroyed, and any non-magical weapons and armor the creature is carrying takes a permanent and cumulative -1 penalty to damage rolls or AC for each round of contact with the acid. If its penalty drops to -5, the weapon or armor is destroyed.

Countermeasures (Difficult). A successful DC 12 Wisdom (Perception) check reveals the trap door, and with a successful DC 12 Intelligence (Investigation) check made while examining the statue reveals the trigger. A DC 12 Dexterity check made with thieves' tools disables the trap.

Crushing Chest

Mechanical trap (level 17-20, moderate, harm)

Scrape marks line the walls of this chamber. A treasure chest banded with iron rests in a slight depression in the center. A hidden mechanism is worked into the base of the chest.

Trigger (Open/Close Chest). Opening the chest triggers the trap.

Effect (Crushing Ceiling/Walls). When activated, the walls of the room begin to move in towards the center, moving at a rate of 1 foot per round at the end of the initiative order. Once the surface reaches a creature's space, they take 1d10 bludgeoning damage. If the surface is still moving on the next turn, the creature is restrained and takes 2d10 bludgeoning damage. A third round spent being crushed inflicts 4d10 bludgeoning damage, the fourth and every round thereafter inflicts 10d10 bludgeoning damage until the surface retracts. Once the walls meet in the middle of the room, they retract.

Countermeasures (Difficult). A successful DC 12 Wisdom (Perception) check reveals the hidden mechanism in the chest. A successful DC 12 Intelligence (Investigation) check reveals the nature of the trigger, and allows a creature to attempt a DC 12 Dexterity check while using thieves' tools to disable the trap.

Crystal Clear

Magic trap (level 17-20, moderate, hinder)

A glowing pillar casts blindingly bright light throughout this room. An altar is just barely visible on the other side of the pillar.

Trigger (Step Into Light/Darkness). Blocking the light falling upon the altar triggers the trap.

Effect (Petrification). Any creature within 30 feet of the altar when there is no light falling on it must succeed on a DC 12 Constitution saving throw if their body is made of flesh. On a failed save, it is restrained as its flesh begins to turn to crystal. On a successful save, the creature isn't affected.

A creature restrained by this effect must make another DC 12 Constitution saving throw at the end of each of its turns. If it successfully saves against this effect three times, it ends. If it fails its saves three times, it is turned to crystal and subjected to the petrified condition. The successes and failures don't need to be consecutive; keep track of both until the target collects three of a kind.

If the creature is physically broken while petrified, it suffers from similar deformities if it reverts to its original state.

Countermeasures. A successful DC 12 Intelligence (Religion or Arcana) check lets a creature recognize this crystal and understand the trap. The crystal has an aura of transmutation magic when viewed with *detect magic*. Casting *dispel magic* (DC 16) on the crystal disables the trap, and spells like *daylight* or *darkness* can also provide ways to bypass the crystal.

Dozing Deterioration

Magic trap (level 17-20, moderate, hinder)

The walls and floors of this chamber are padded with feather-filled cushions. Hanging from the ceiling on a chain is a silver censer.

Trigger (Unconsciousness). If a creature falls unconscious in the room the censer begins to emit magical smoke.

Effect (Aging). The smoke wraps around unconscious creatures, who must on a DC 12 Constitution saving throw or be magically aged/de-aged 1d10 years. If the roll is even, creatures are made older; if the roll is odd, they are made younger. This effect can be undone with *greater restoration*, but only if it is cast within 24 hours of being aged.

Countermeasures. A creature that succeeds on a DC 12 Intelligence (Arcana or History) check recognizes the censer and understands the trap. The censer has an aura of necromancy magic if viewed with *detect magic*. A spellcaster can disrupt the enchantment on the censer with a successful DC 12 Intelligence (Arcana) check; *dispel magic* (DC 18) cast on the censer also disables the trap.

Path of Light

Hybrid trap (level 17-20, moderate, harm)

Outside the entrance to this pitch black room or hall is a small shrine with unlit ceremonial candles, each with an inscription that reads (possibly in a foreign language) "walk safely in the light." Anyone entering the room without one of these lit candles is quickly plunged into a pit beneath the floor. Darkvision does not penetrate the magical darkness within the room.

Trigger (Produce Light/Darkness). A creature standing in the chamber for more than 1 round (6 seconds) without holding one of the lit ceremonial candles triggers the trap.

Effect (Drop Into Spiked Pit). The 5-foot area of floor directly beneath the triggering creature falls way, revealing a 40-foot-deep spiked pit. The triggering creature must succeed on a DC 12 Dexterity saving throw or fall into the pit and take 14 (4d6) bludgeoning damage and 21 (6d6) piercing damage.

Countermeasures. The room and the candles have an aura of evocation magic when viewed with *detect magic*. A creature that succeeds on a DC 12 Wisdom (Insight) check can deduce the nature of the trap and knows to use the candles to grant safe passage.

A spellcaster can disrupt the enchantment on the room with a successful DC 12 spellcasting ability check; *dispel magic* (DC 17) cast on the room also disables the trap.

Picked Wrong

Mechanical trap (level 17-20, moderate, harm)

A locked door blocks the way. The lock can be easily overcome with the key or a skilled burglar using thieves' tools, but an unskilled burglar is in for a surprise.

Trigger (Fail to Pick Lock). A creature that attempts to pick the lock and fails triggers the trap.

Effect (Drop Into Pit). The floor in front of the door suddenly drops away, revealing a 50-foot deep pit. The triggering creature must succeed on a DC 12 Dexterity saving throw or falls into the pit, taking 52 (15d6) bludgeoning damage.

Countermeasures (Difficult). A successful DC 12 Wisdom (Perception) check reveals the break away floor. A successful DC 212 Intelligence (Investigation) check made on the lock reveals the trigger; once found, a creature that makes a successful DC 12 Dexterity check using thieves' tools disables the trap.

Rogue's Bane, Treacherous

Mechanical trap (level 17-20, moderate)

A poorly disguised tripwire is easily detected, but it hides the real trap that is set to go off if the decoy is tampered with.

Trigger (False Trigger). Disarming or attempting to disarm the false trigger sets off the real trap.

Effect (Random). Randomly select a mechanical trap of the same or lower lethality and use its effect.

Countermeasures (Difficult). A successful DC 12 Wisdom (Perception) check reveals the false trigger, and a successful DC 12 Intelligence (Investigation) check reveals its true nature. A successful DC 12 Dexterity check using thieves' tools disables the real trap.

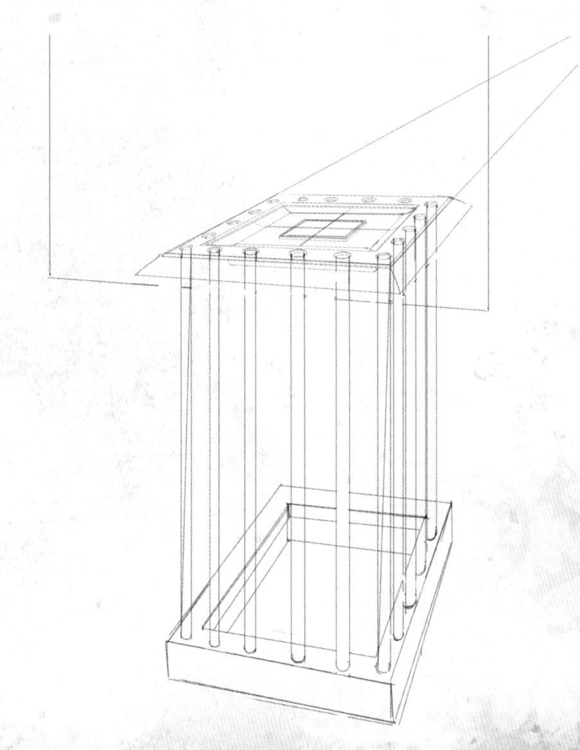

Swift Imprisonment

Magic trap (level 17-20, moderate, block)

The walls of this dark shrine are covered with tapestries depicting mortals engaging in deals with devils, infernal beings emerging from the hells, and angels being brought low by devilish armies. A *glyph of warding (forcecage)* is hidden in the design of one of the tapestries.

Trigger (Mortal Sacrifice). If an evil creature dies in the area, or the corpse of an evil creature enters the area, the trap is triggered.

Effect (Spell Effect). The glyph casts *forcecage*. An immobile, invisible, cube-shaped prison composed of magical force springs into existence around the triggering creature. The prison is a box 10 feet on a side, creating a solid barrier that prevents any matter from passing through it and blocking any spells cast into or out from the area.

Any creature that is completely inside the cage's area is trapped. Creatures only partially within the area, or those too large to fit inside the area, are pushed away from the center of the area until they are completely outside the area.

A creature inside the cage can't leave it by non-magical means. If the creature tries to use teleportation or interplanar travel to leave the cage, it must first make a DC 12 Charisma saving throw. On a success, the creature can use that magic to exit the cage. On a failure, the creature can't exit the cage and wastes the use of the spell or effect. The cage also extends into the Ethereal Plane, blocking ethereal travel.

This spell can't be dispelled by *dispel magic*; it fades away after 1 hour.

Countermeasures. The glyph can be found with a successful DC 12 Intelligence (Investigation) check or with *detect magic*. Once found, the glyph can be disabled with a successful DC 12 Intelligence (Arcana) check or with *dispel magic*.

Level 17-20 Dangerous

These traps are likely to seriously injure (and potentially kill) characters of these levels.

Acid Lock

Mechanical trap (level 17-20, dangerous, harm)

This sturdy adamantine door has an incredibly intricate locking mechanism made of burnished metal. Although dented in places, the door looks incredibly sturdy.

Trigger (Use Wrong Key). Using the wrong key for the lock triggers the trap.

Effect (Acid Blast). Acid blasts out from the lock over the triggering creature. The creature must make a DC 15 Constitution saving throw, taking 82 (15d10) acid damage on a failed save, or half as much on a successful one.

Countermeasures. A successful DC 15 Wisdom (Perception) check reveals the trigger, and a successful DC 15 Dexterity check using thieves' tools disables the trap.

Doom Dome

Magic trap (level 17-20, dangerous, subdue)

A *glyph of warding (forcecage)* is hidden in this chamber, ready to detect the presence of a particular item. Once that item is brought into the chamber a cage of force traps the creature carrying the item.

Trigger (Bring Item). A creature that brings the item into the chamber triggers the trap.

Effect (Spell Effect). The glyph casts *forcecage*. An immobile, invisible, cube-shaped prison composed of magical force springs into existence around the triggering creature. The prison is a cage 20 feet on a side and is made from 1/2-inch diameter bars spaced 1/2 inch apart. It creates a solid barrier that prevents any matter from passing through it and blocking any spells cast into or out from the area.

Any creature that is completely inside the cage's area is trapped. Creatures only partially within the area, or those too large to fit inside the area, are pushed away from the center of the area until they are completely outside the area.

A creature inside the cage can't leave it by non-magical means. If the creature tries to use teleportation or interplanar travel to leave the cage, it must first make a DC 15 Charisma saving throw. On a success, the creature can use that magic to exit the cage. On a failure, the creature can't exit the cage and wastes the use of the spell or effect. The cage also extends into the Ethereal Plane, blocking ethereal travel.

This spell can't be dispelled by *dispel magic*; it fades away after 1 hour.

Countermeasures. The glyph can be found with *detect magic* or with a successful DC 15 Intelligence (Investigation) check. Once discovered, the glyph can be disabled with a successful DC 15 Intelligence (Arcana) check, or with *dispel magic*.

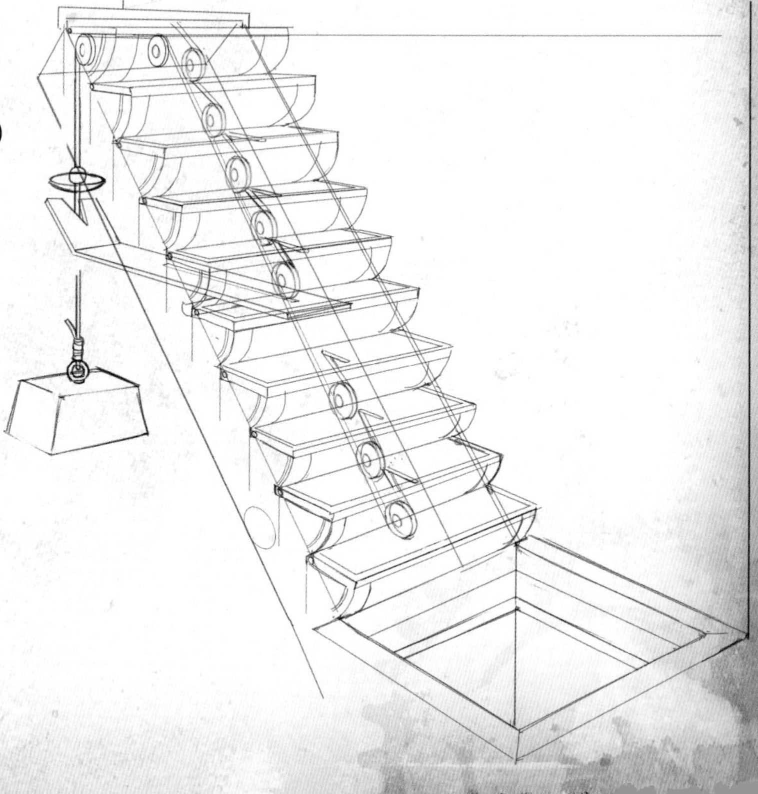

Futile Blade

Magic trap (level 17-20, dangerous, harm)

Resting atop a stand made of twisted iron is a vicious-looking sword forged from adamantine. It seems to hum with power.

Trigger (Spill Blood). A creature removing the sword from the stand must succeed on a DC 15 Dexterity saving throw or take 1 point of slashing damage as they nick themselves on the blade. Spilling blood with the sword in this way triggers the trap.

Effect (Summon Creatures). The spilled blood becomes the red, pinpoint eyes of **3 wraiths**. The wraiths attack all other creatures in the room, focusing on the triggering creature or whoever is holding the sword. They do not leave the room.

The wraiths fade into nothingness if reduced to 0 hit points. They fade back into the walls of the room if the sword is replaced on the stand or after 24 hours.

At your discretion, the sword can be a magic item, or just an adamantine weapon.

Countermeasures. With a successful DC 15 Intelligence (Arcana or History) check, a creature can recognize the sword and knows about the dangers of the trap. With *detect magic*, the stand for the sword has an aura of necromancy magic (if the sword is a magic item, it also has an aura).

A spellcaster can disrupt the enchantment on the stand with a successful DC 15 spellcasting ability check; *dispel magic* cast on the stand also disables the trap.

Froggy Floor

Magic trap (level 17-20, dangerous, hinder)

The floor of this chamber has a beautiful mosaic of a frog, with a *glyph of warding (true polymorph)* hidden in the design.

Trigger (Creature Detector). A character that walks across the mosaic triggers the trap.

Effect (Spell Effect). The glyph casts *polymorph* on the triggering creature, which must succeed on a DC 15 Wisdom saving throw or be transformed into a **frog**. The spell has no effect on a shapechanger or a creature with 0 hit points.

The transformation lasts for 1 hour, or until the target drops to 0 hit points or dies. The target's game statistics, including mental ability scores, are replaced by the statistics of a frog. It retains its alignment and personality.

The target assumes the hit points of a frog. When it reverts to its normal form, the creature returns to the number of hit points it had before it transformed. If it reverts as a result of dropping to 0 hit points, any excess damage carries over to its normal form. As long as the excess damage doesn't reduce the creature's normal form to 0 hit points, it isn't knocked unconscious.

The creature is limited in the actions it can perform by the nature of its new form, and it can't speak, cast spells, or take any other action that requires hands or speech.

The target's gear melds into the new form. The creature can't activate, use, wield, or otherwise benefit from any of its equipment.

Countermeasures. The glyph can be found without triggering it with a successful DC 15 Intelligence (Investigation) check, or with *detect magic*. A creature can disable the glyph *dispel magic* or with a successful DC 15 Intelligence (Arcana) check.

Join Me

Hybrid trap (level 17-20, dangerous, harm)

A corpse covered in blackened armor lies on the floor of the chamber, covering up a *rune of detection*. A vat filled with necrotising fluid is positioned to fall over a creature by the corpse.

Trigger (Interact with Bait). Interacting with the corpse triggers the trap. A successful DC 15 Dexterity (Sleight of Hand) check allows a creature to interact with the bait without activating the trigger.

Effect (Falling/Tipping Vessel). The rune tips the vat onto the triggering creature, who must make a DC 15 Dexterity saving throw, taking 82 (15d10) necrotic damage, or half as much on a success.

Countermeasures. A successful DC 15 Wisdom (Perception) check lets a creature spot the vat and the hidden rune. One found, a creature can disable the rune with a successful DC 15 Intelligence (Arcana) check or with *dispel magic*.

Poisoned Path

Mechanical trap (level 17-20, dangerous, harm)

A 5-foot-wide walkway formed of stone archways spans a chasm. On either side of the walkway is an enormous drop into lightless depths. A creature that falls from the walkway drops 500 feet to the bottom of the chasm, taking 70 (20d6) bludgeoning damage.

Trigger (Pressure Plate). Stepping on the pressure plate in the middle of the walkway triggers the trap.

Effect (Needle). A hard, razor-sharp needle coated with a weakening poison spears up from the center of the pressure plate into the triggering creature's foot. The needle pierces armor that isn't magical. The triggering creature must succeed on a DC 15 Constitution saving throw or become poisoned. A creature poisoned in this way becomes incredibly weak and must succeed on a DC 15 Dexterity saving throw to avoid falling from the walkway.

Countermeasures (Sensitive). A successful DC 15 Wisdom (Perception) check reveals the pressure plate and hidden needle. A successful DC 15 Dexterity check using thieves' tools disables the trap, but a roll that totals 10 or less triggers the trap.

Run For Your Life

Mechanical trap (level 17-20, dangerous, harm)

This 5-foot-wide corridor has a lever at the entrance; a closed gate or door lies at the other end. When the lever is pulled, the barrier opens and the walls begin contracting. Once the walls meet, the door closes and the lever and wall return to their original positions.

Trigger (Pull Lever). A creature that pulls the lever to open the barrier triggers the trap.

Effect (Crushing Ceiling/Walls). The barrier opens and the walls of the corridor begin contracting at a rate of 1 foot at the end of each round. Once the surface reaches a creature's space, they take 1d10 bludgeoning damage. If the surface is still moving on the next turn, the creature is restrained and takes 2d10 bludgeoning damage. A third round spent being crushed inflicts 4d10 bludgeoning damage. On the fourth round, the barriers meet in the middle of the corridor and retract.

Countermeasures. A successful DC 15 Wisdom (Perception) check reveals scrape marks on the floor, indicative of the crushing walls. When examining the lever, a creature that succeeds on a DC 15 Intelligence (Investigation) check spots how the hidden mechanisms work and understands the trap. Once understood, a creature that succeeds on a DC 15 Dexterity check using thieves' tools can disable the trap.

Seal of Embers

Magic trap (level 17-20, dangerous, harm)

A beautifully crafted seal is inlayed into a 5-foot-by-5-foot section of the floor. The seal was originally intended to have some arcane or religious significance, but now it has been perverted by a *glyph of warding (fireball)*.

Trigger (Cast Spell). A creature that casts a spell while standing on the seal triggers the trap.

Effect (Spell Effect). The glyph casts *fireball* as a 9th level spell. A bright streak flashes from the glyph to a point next to the triggering creature and then blossoms with a low roar into an explosion of flame. Each creature in a 20-foot-radius sphere centered on that point must make a DC 15 Dexterity saving throw. A target takes 49 (14d6) fire damage on a failed save, or half as much damage on a successful one.

The fire spreads around corners. It ignites flammable objects in the area that aren't being worn or carried.

Countermeasures. The glyph can be found with a successful DC 15 Intelligence (Investigation) check, or with *detect magic*. Once discovered, the glyph can be disrupted with a successful DC 15 Intelligence (Arcana) check, or with *dispel magic*.

A creature that succeeds on a DC 15 Intelligence (Arcana or Religion) check understands the original purpose of the seal and knows that casting *hallow* on it will also disable the trap.

Sticky Situation

Mechanical trap (level 17-20, dangerous)

A rather average lock seals a door or container and hides a devious parting gift. A tiny sealed vial containing a strong adhesive is hidden within the lock, and breaks open when the lock is picked.

Trigger (Pick Lock). The lock can be picked with a successful DC 10 Dexterity check using thieves' tools. However, a creature that succeeds at picking the lock triggers the trap.

Effect (Acid/Slime Blast). The triggering creature must succeed on a DC 15 Dexterity saving throw or have their hands covered in sticky adhesive. While covered in adhesive, the creature automatically fails any ability checks using Dexterity.

The adhesive can be washed off with 10 minutes of vigorous scrubbing with soap and water, or with a 1 minute soak in a gallon of alcohol.

Countermeasures. A creature that succeeds on a DC 15 Wisdom (Perception) check can spot the hidden vial, and with a successful DC 15 Intelligence (Investigation) check a creature understands the danger of the trap. Once understood, a successful DC 15 Dexterity check using thieves' tools disables the trap.

Violence Cage

Magic trap (level 17-20, dangerous, block)

Intense heat fills this room, radiating from the open trenches filled with lava. Weapon racks line the walls, obscuring a *glyph of warding (forcecage)*. A creature that spends 1 hour in this room must make a DC 15 Constitution saving throw or gain 1 level of exhaustion.

Trigger (Mortal Sacrifice). If a creature is killed by any means other than fire damage, the trap is triggered.

Effect (Spell Effect). The glyph casts *forcecage*; an immobile, invisible, cube-shaped prison composed of magical force springs into existence around the triggering creature. The prison is a solid box, 10 feet on a side, creating a solid barrier that prevents any matter from passing through it and blocking any spells cast into or out from the area.

Any creature that is completely inside the cage's area when it forms is trapped. Creatures only partially within the area, or those too large to fit inside the area, are pushed away from the center of the area until they are completely outside the area.

A creature inside the cage can't leave it by non-magical means. If the creature tries to use teleportation or interplanar travel to leave the cage, it must first make a DC 15 Charisma saving throw. On a success, the creature can use that magic to exit the cage. On a failure, the creature can't exit the cage and wastes the use of the spell or effect. The cage also extends into the Ethereal Plane, blocking ethereal travel.

The wall can't be dispelled by *dispel magic* and it lasts for 1 hour.

Countermeasures. The glyph can be found with a successful DC 15 Intelligence (Investigation) check, or with *detect magic*. Once found, the glyph can be disabled with *dispel magic* or with a successful DC 15 Intelligence (Arcana) check.

Level 17-20 Perilous

These traps may kill characters of these levels, and will definitely injure them severely.

Acidic Ceiling

Mechanical trap (level 17-20, perilous, harm)

The ceiling of this room is covered with a thick layer of slime. The door leading out has been barricaded by a pile of crates and barrels, and the floor or the room is a springy material, carefully balanced by the barricade.

Trigger (Pick Up/Shift Object). Shifting the barricade triggers the trap.

Effect (Spring Floor). Creatures that move the barricade are flung straight up into the ceiling. Those creatures must make a DC 17 Constitution saving throw, taking 63 (18d6) acid damage on a failed save or half as much damage on a successful one. Additionally, the creature takes 3 (1d6) bludgeoning damage from hitting the ceiling, and 3 (1d6) bludgeoning damage from hitting the floor again.

Countermeasures. With a successful DC 17 Wisdom (Perception) check, a creature understands how the spring floor works and can spot the acid on the ceiling. By succeeding on a DC 17 Dexterity check using thieves' tools, a creature can wedge bits of planking into the spring floor, disabling the trap.

Arresting Vanity

Magic trap (level 17-20, perilous, Harm)

A mirror in the chamber is covered by a sheet or curtain. Removing the cover and looking into the mirror may prove deadly due to the *glyph of warding (flesh to stone)* worked into the mirror's frame.

Trigger (Look Into). A creature that looks into the mirror at their own reflection triggers the trap.

Effect (Petrification). The glyph casts *flesh to stone*, targeting the triggering creature. If the target's body is made of flesh, the creature must make a DC17 Constitution saving throw. On a failed save, it is restrained as its flesh begins to harden. On a successful save, the creature isn't affected.

A creature restrained by this spell must make another DC 17 Constitution saving throw at the end of each of its turns. If it successfully saves against this spell three times, the spell ends. If it fails its saves three times, it is turned to stone and subjected to the petrified condition. The successes and failures don't need to be consecutive; keep track of both until the target collects three of a kind.

If the creature is physically broken while petrified, it suffers from similar deformities if it reverts to its original state.

The creature can be restored with *greater restoration* or more powerful magic.

Countermeasures. The glyph can be found with *detect magic* or with a DC 17 Intelligence (Investigation) check. Once discovered, a creature can disrupt the glyph with a successful DC 17 Intelligence (Arcana) check or with *dispel magic*.

Dead Men May Grow Tails

Magic trap (level 17-20, perilous)

A humanoid corpse lies on the floor, clutching an important or valuable item in its dead hands. Retrieving the item will most certainly disturb the body, triggering the trap.

Trigger (Interact with Bait). A creature that disturbs the corpse triggers the trap.

Effect (Summon Creature). The corpse suddenly writhes and convulses, transforming into a **nalfeshnee** (or some other creature of CR 13 or below that is more appropriate to the area) and attacking all creatures in the area. The demon vanishes in a puff of brimstone if reduced to 0 hit points. It will not leave the area, and it becomes a humanoid corpse again after 24 hours.

Countermeasures. With a successful DC 17 Dexterity (Sleight of Hand) check, a creature can retrieve the item without triggering the trap.

When viewed with *detect magic* the corpse has an aura of conjuration magic. With a successful DC 17 Intelligence (Arcana) check, a creature can spot claw marks and traces of hellfire around the corpse, indicative of its demonic transformation.

A spellcaster can disrupt the enchantment on the corpse with a successful DC 17 spellcasting ability check; *dispel magic* (DC 17) also disables the trap.

Magic Trunk

Magic trap (level 17-20, perilous, block)

This large iron trunk looks impenetrable, though the lock is battered and loose.

Trigger (Bring Object). A creature that brings thieves' tools within 5 feet of the chest triggers the trap. The trap doesn't trigger if the tools are in a pouch or pack, only if the tools are out and in the creature's hand.

Effect (Swap). The triggering creature must succeed on a DC 17 Charisma save or instantly switch places with a straw mannequin inside the trunk. The trunk is locked and can be picked open with a DC 17 Dexterity check using thieves' tools. However, a creature attempting to pick the lock from inside the trunk has disadvantage on this check.

Countermeasures (Difficult). A creature that succeeds on a DC 17 Wisdom (Perception) check can spot a few arcane sigils and symbols engraved on the chest. With a successful DC 17 Intelligence (Arcana) check, a creature understands the teleportation effect inscribed by the sigils. The chest also has an aura of conjuration magic when viewed with *detect magic*.

A spellcaster can disrupt the enchantment on the chest with a successful DC 17 spellcasting ability check; *dispel magic* (DC 17) also disables the trap.

Searing Spikes

Mechanical trap (level 17-20, perilous, harm)

Barring entry to the next area is an adamantine door decorated with etchings of flaming serpents. The door seems to give off some heat of its own, though not enough to burn.

Trigger (Open/Close Door). Opening the door triggers the trap.

Effect (Swinging Object). A mechanical arm studded with fiery adamantine spikes swings down from the roof in the next room. The spikes make a melee attack against the triggering creature with a +10 bonus, dealing 88 (16d10) piercing damage and 22 (4d10) fire damage on a hit. This attack cannot gain advantage or disadvantage.

Countermeasures (Difficult). A successful DC 17 Wisdom (Perception) check reveals the hidden mechanism on the door. A successful DC 17 Intelligence (Investigation) check reveals the nature of the trigger, and allows a creature to disable the trap with a successful DC 17 Dexterity check using thieves' tools.

Shocking Exit

Magic trap (17-20, perilous, harm)

The exit from this room is plated with steel that is burnished into jagged, purple patterns. Stamped into these patterns are unusual runes, masking a *glyph of warding (chain lightning)*.

Trigger (Remove Object). Taking any valuable objects from the room triggers the trap.

Effect (Elemental Blast). The glyph casts *chain lightning*, creating a bolt of lightning that arcs toward the triggering creature. Six bolts then leap from that target to as many as six other targets, each of which must be within 30 feet of the first target. A target can be a creature or an object and can be targeted by only one of the bolts.

A target must make a DC 17 Dexterity saving throw. The target takes 45 (10d8) lightning damage on a failed save, or half as much damage on a successful one.

Countermeasures. The glyph can be found with a successful DC 17 Intelligence (Investigation) check, or with *detect magic*. Once found, it can be disrupted with *dispel magic* or a successful DC 17 Intelligence (Arcana) check.

Skull Scree

Mechanical trap (level 17-20, perilous, harm)

The way forward has narrowed down to a perilous, 1-foot-wide ledge. Creatures moving along the ledge risk must succeed on a DC 17 Dexterity saving throw or fall 30 feet to the ground below, taking 10 (3d6) bludgeoning damage. A creature can move at half speed to automatically succeed on the saving throw.

Trigger (Pressure Plate). Part way along the ledge is a pressure plate built into the wall. A Small or larger creature who passes by the plate without noticing it leans on the plate, triggering the trap.

Effect (Falling Objects). A concealed compartment in the wall above the ledge opens to disgorge a barrage of humanoid skulls. The triggering creature must succeed on a DC 17 Dexterity saving throw or take 99 (18d10) bludgeoning damage. They must also make a saving throw to avoid falling from the ledge, as described above.

Countermeasures (Sensitive). A successful DC 17 Wisdom (Perception) check reveals the pressure plate, and a successful DC 17 Dexterity check while using thieves' tools disables the trap. However, a check that totals 10 or less triggers the trap.

Sweet-sounding Stench

Magic trap (17-20, perilous, hinder)

The chamber is filled with musical instruments such as lutes, flutes, and drums resting in various stands or holders. All the instruments appear at least slightly used. On the far side of the chamber is a door with a frame of wood bearing carvings of clouds and wind.

Trigger (Musical/Auditory). A creature that walks through the door doesn't need to be playing the instrument, but if no woodwind is being played in the room when a creature walks through the carved door the trap triggers.

Effect (Acid/Slime Blast). An eruption of terrible smelling slime sprays from the door onto the triggering creature. The target must succeed on a DC 17 Constitution saving throw or become poisoned for 10 minutes. While poisoned in this way, the target must repeat the saving throw at the start of each of its turns. On a failure, the target is incapacitated for 1 round as it gags and retches. Dousing the creature with a gallon of oil or alcohol removes the slime.

Countermeasures. A successful DC 17 Intelligence (Arcana or Performance) check allows a creature to interpret the meaning of the carvings on the wall and understand the trap. When viewed with *detect magic*, the door has an aura of abjuration magic.

A spellcaster can disrupt the enchantment with a successful DC 17 spellcasting ability check; *dispel magic* (DC 17) also disables the trap.

The Thin Veil

Magic trap (level 17-20, perilous)

The air in this area is thick with static electricity and the smell of ozone, like the approach of a thunderstorm. This is all indicative of a place infused with wild magic.

Trigger (Cast Spell). A creature that casts a spell in the area triggers the trap.

Effect (Wild Magic). The triggering creature is hit with a surge of magical feedback. Roll 1d6 + 2 times on the table below.

d10	Effect
1	Heavy rain falls in a 60-foot radius centered on a target creature. The area becomes lightly obscured. The rain follows the creature until they are out of the trap's range.
2	An animal appears in the unoccupied space nearest the target. The animal acts as it normally would. Roll a d100 to determine which animal appears. On a 01-25, a **rhinoceros** appears; on a 26-50, an **elephant** appears; and on a 51-100, a **rat** appears.
3	A cloud of 600 oversized butterflies fills a 30-foot radius centered on the target. The area becomes heavily obscured. The butterflies follows the creature until they are out of the trap's range.
4	Grass grows on the ground in a 60-foot radius centered on the target. If grass is already there, it grows to ten times its normal size and remains overgrown for 1 minute.
5	An object of the DM 's choice disappears into the Ethereal Plane. The object must be neither wrong nor carried, within range of the trap, and no larger than 10 feet in any dimension.
6	Leaves grow from the target. Unless they are picked off, the leaves turn brown and fall off after 24 hours.
7	The trap attacks the target with a large gem worth 1d4 x 10 gp.
8	A burst of colorful shimmering light extends from the target in a 30-foot radius. The target and each creature in the area that can see must succeed on a Constitution saving throw or become blinded for 1 minute. A creature can repeat the saving throw at the end of each of its turns, ending the effect on itself on a success.
9	The target's skin turns bright blue for 1d10 days.
10	The target's size is halved in all dimensions, and its weight is reduced to one-eighth of normal. This reduction decreases its size by one category—from Medium to Small, for example. The target also has disadvantage on Strength checks and Strength saving throws and its weapons also shrink to match its new size. While these weapons are reduced, the target's attacks with them deal 1d4 less damage (this can't reduce the damage below 1). This effect ends if dispelled with *dispel magic* (3rd level spell) or *remove curse*, or after 1 minute.

Countermeasures. A creature that succeeds on a DC 17 Intelligence (Arcana) check understands the nature of the trap. *Detect magic* or a similar effect can also reveal the trap, but might set it off as well.

Timber!

Mechanical trap (level 17-20, perilous,subdue)

After triggering a tripwire in the corridor, 2-foot-diameter horizontal logs roll out of the ceiling. Channels in the walls guide the logs as they slam down in front and behind the area around the tripwire, trapping those near the tripwire between two floor-to-ceiling log walls.

Trigger (Tripwire). A creature that walks through the tripwire triggers the trap.

Effect (Cage). Thick timbers hidden in the ceiling of the corridor drop into channels in the walls in front of and behind the tripwire, creating a 20-foot-long-by-10-foot-wide wooden cage within the corridor. A creature in the path of the falling logs must make a DC 17 Dexterity saving throw, taking 70 (20d6) bludgeoning damage, or half as much on a success. Each log has an AC of 5, 50 HP, immunity to piercing damage, and vulnerability to fire damage.

Countermeasures. A successful DC 17 Wisdom (Perception) check the channels in the walls that the logs fall into. The tripwire can be found with a successful DC 15 Intelligence (Investigation) check, and disabled with a successful DC 20 Dexterity check using thieves' tools.

Level 17-20 Deadly

These traps will almost certainly kill characters of these levels.

Anti-wizard Alarm

Magic trap (level 17-20, deadly, alarm)

A 1-foot thick ring of decorated stonework surrounds a 25-foot diameter circle area in the center of the room. The ceiling directly above the ring has a *glyph of warding (dispel magic)*.

Trigger (Cast Spell). Casting a spell within the ring of stonework triggers the trap.

Effect (Dispel Magic). The glyph casts *dispel magic* as a 9th-level spell, targeting the triggering creature. Any spell of 9th level or lower on the creature ends. The glyph also releases an audible chime that rings out through the area, audible up to 60 feet away

Countermeasures. A successful DC 20 Intelligence (Investigation) check reveals the glyph. Once found, it can be dispelled with *dispel magic*, or disabled with a successful DC 20 Intelligence (Arcana) check.

Blazing Ring, Treacherous

Mechanical trap (level 17-20, deadly, harm)

A 1-foot thick ring of decorative stonework surrounds a 25-foot diameter circle area in the center of the room. The ceiling directly above the ring is blackened with soot. In the 5-foot square at the circle's center is something intriguing.

Trigger (Weight Sensitive Floor). When a Small or larger creature steps onto a space adjacent to the 5-foot square at the center of the area within the ring, they activate a pressure plate. Parts of the stonework slide away, revealing spouts which pour flaming oil onto the floor from the ring's inner edge.

Effect (Wall of Fire). The flaming oil creates a ringed wall of flames 25 feet in diameter, 20 feet high, and 1 foot thick. The wall is opaque and lasts for 1 minute. When the wall appears, each creature within its area must make a DC 20 Dexterity saving throw. On a failed save, a creature takes 87 (25d6) fire damage, or half as much damage on a successful save.

The side of the wall facing inwards deals the trap's fire damage to each creature that ends its turn within 10 feet of that side or inside the wall. A creature takes the same damage when it enters the wall for the first time on a turn or ends its turn there. The other side of the wall deals no damage.

A creature that is adjacent to the wall that succeeds on a DC 20 Constitution check using thieves' tools ends this effect.

Countermeasures. A successful DC 20 Wisdom (Perception) check reveals the pressure plate, and a successful DC 20 Dexterity check while using thieves' tools disables it.

Best Left Alone

Hybrid trap (level 17-20, deadly, hinder)

An altar is adorned with fascinating relics, including a jeweled skull resting under a dome of glass. The cover is enchanted to contain the skull's curse.

Trigger (Pick Up/Shift Object). A creature that removes the glass dome that covers the skull triggers the trap.

Effect (Exhaustion). All living creatures within 60 feet of the jeweled skull must succeed on a DC 20 Constitution saving throw at the beginning of their turns or gain 1 level of exhaustion. The skull has no effect on constructs or undead. Covering the skull with the dome ends this effect.

Countermeasures. With a successful DC 20 Intelligence (History or Religion) check, a creature recognizes the skull and understands the danger it poses. When viewed with *detect magic*, the glass dome has an aura of abjuration magic, while the skull has an aura of necromancy magic.

A spellcaster can disrupt the enchantment with a successful DC 20 Intelligence (Arcana) check; *dispel magic* (DC 20) also disables the trap.

Cool Off

Mechanical trap (level 17-20, deadly, block)

As well as the more conventional exits from this room, a section of one of the wood-panelled walls appears to be made of plaster rather than bricks.

Trigger (Break Object). Breaking the fake wall triggers the trap.

Effect (Cage). Bars shoot up from the floor around the broken section of wall in a 10-foot ring, creating a floor-to-ceiling cage. Any creatures caught in the area when the trap is triggered must succeed on a DC 20 Dexterity saving throw or become trapped in the cage.

The bars are made of adamantine and enchanted and slowly begin to cool down to a freezing temperature. Any creature that starts their turn within 5 feet of the cage takes 11 (2d10) cold damage. This damage increases by 2d10 each round.

Breaking the cage requires a successful DC 20 Strength check. With a successful DC 20 Dexterity check, a creature can make the bars retract.

Countermeasures (Difficult). A successful DC 20 Wisdom (Perception) check reveals the hidden mechanisms in the fake wall and floor. A creature that succeeds on a DC 20 Intelligence check with mason's tools can also spot the falseness of the wall.

Once discovered, a successful DC 20 Intelligence (Investigation) check reveals the nature of the trigger, and allows a creature to disable the trap with a successful DC 20 Dexterity check using thieves' tools.

Log Ride

Mechanical trap (level 17-20, deadly, harm)

A 50-foot-deep, 15-foot-wide chasm lies ahead. A pressure plate at the edge of the chasm activates a swinging log designed to knock any creatures in its path into the chasm. However, clever creatures may use the swinging log to cross.

Trigger (Pressure Plate). A creature that steps on the pressure plate triggers the trap.

Effect (Swinging Object). A massive log attached to the ceiling swings toward the edge of the chasm. All creatures within 15 feet of the edge of the chasm must make a DC 20 Dexterity saving throw. A creature that fails takes 70 (20d6) bludgeoning damage and falls into the chasm, taking an additional 17 (5d6) bludgeoning damage. On a success, a creature takes 35 (10d6) bludgeoning damage and is launched to the other side of the chasm.

Countermeasures (Sensitive). A successful DC 20 Wisdom (Perception) check reveals the pressure plate and a successful DC 15 Wisdom (Perception) check reveals the log. The trap can be disabled with a successful DC 20 Dexterity check using thieves' tools, but a result of 10 or lower triggers the trap.

Pooling Puddle Problem

Hybrid trap (level 17-20, deadly, harm)

The passageway ends at a small area with an old well, water steadily dripping into it from above. The well is overflowing; excess water is running onto the floor and into puddles down the passageway. A tripwire is strung across the puddle farthest from the well.

Trigger (Tripwire). A creature that breaks the tripwire alerts the lurking elementals.

Effect (Release Creatures). The well is home to **2 water elementals** who erupt from the well and attack all other creatures. If reduced to 0 hit points, the elementals collapse into small puddles. They will not leave the area and return to dormancy after 24 hours.

Countermeasures. A successful DC 20 Intelligence (Arcana or Nature) check or Wisdom (Survival) check reveals clues that the water coming from the well is behaving strangely, indicative of an elemental.

Snicker Snack

Hybrid trap (level 17-20, deadly, harm)

A magnificent marble archway stands in the center of this otherwise empty room. Looking through the archway reveals a forest that cannot otherwise be seen beyond it. A *rune of detection* is worked into the design on the keystone of the arch.

Trigger (Pass Threshold). Passing through the archway triggers the trap.

Effect (Swinging Object). When activated, the rune releases a *greatsword of sharpness* that slashes at the triggering creature. The sword makes a melee attack with a +12 bonus, dealing 100 (20d6 + 30) magic slashing damage if it hits. If the sword rolls a 20 on the attack roll, the triggering creature takes an extra 14 (4d6) slashing damage. The sword then rolls another d20. If it rolls a 20, it lops off one of the target's limbs, with the effect of such loss determined by the GM. If the creature has no limb to sever, the sword lops off a portion of its body instead.

Countermeasures. The rune can be found with a successful DC 20 Wisdom (Perception) check or with *detect magic*. Once found, it can be disabled with a successful DC 20 Intelligence (Arcana) check; *dispel magic* also disables the trap.

Telestairs

Magic trap (level 17-20, deadly, block)

A formidable spiral staircase is strewn with bones and scraps of armor. Written in blood on the bottom step is a passage from a demonic text, written in Infernal.

Trigger (Creature Detector). Any non-undead that uses the stairs triggers the trap.

Effect (Teleport). The triggering creature must succeed on a DC 20 Charisma saving throw or be teleported somewhere else in the dungeon or area, usually a prison of some kind.

Countermeasures. A creature that succeeds on a DC 20 Intelligence (Religion) check recognizes the text and understands the nature of the trap. When viewed with *detect magic*, the stairs have an aura of conjuration magic.

A spellcaster can disrupt the enchantment on the stairs with a successful DC 20 Intelligence (Arcana) check; *dispel magic* (DC 19) also disables the trap.

Unworthy

Mechanical trap (level 17-20, deadly, block)

Portraits of undead nobles or royalty hang on the walls, each resting in immaculate white frames of fused bone. One portrait is covered by a red velvet curtain and attached to it is a twisted black rope.

Trigger (Pull Rope/Chain). Pulling the rope triggers the trap.

Effect (Drop Into Monster Lair). The floor below the portrait swings open, revealing a 10-foot wide hole and a drop of 20 feet. A creature standing above the trapdoor must succeed on a DC 20 Dexterity saving throw or fall, taking 70 (20d6) bludgeoning damage.

At the bottom of the pit is a 30-foot square chamber. Inside it is a **stone golem**, carved to resemble a minotaur skeleton. The golem attacks any creature that falls into the pit.

Countermeasures. A successful DC 20 Wisdom (Perception) check reveals the trapdoor, and a successful DC 20 Dexterity check using thieves' tools disables the trap.

Wake The Dragon

Magic trap (level 17-20, deadly, harm)

Within this large chamber is a massive stone statue of a dragon. A sealed door blocks the way forward, and various passages of music are written on the walls of the chamber. Playing the correct musical notes opens the door; playing the wrong notes awakens the dragon.

Trigger (Auditory/Musical). A creature can make a DC 20 Charisma (Performance) check to identify the various bits of music on the wall and play one. On a success, the door opens; a failure triggers the trap.

Effect (Release Creatures). The statue animates, becoming a **young black dragon** that attacks all other creatures in the area. If reduced to 0 hit points, the dragon crumbles to dust. It will not leave the area, and after 24 hours it returns to stone.

Countermeasures. A creature that succeeds on successful DC 20 Intelligence (History or Performance) check knows about the dragon statue and understands the trap. The statue has an aura of abjuration magic when viewed with *detect magic*.

A spellcaster can disrupt the enchantment on the statue with a successful DC 20 spellcasting ability check; *dispel magic* (DC 19) also disables the trap.

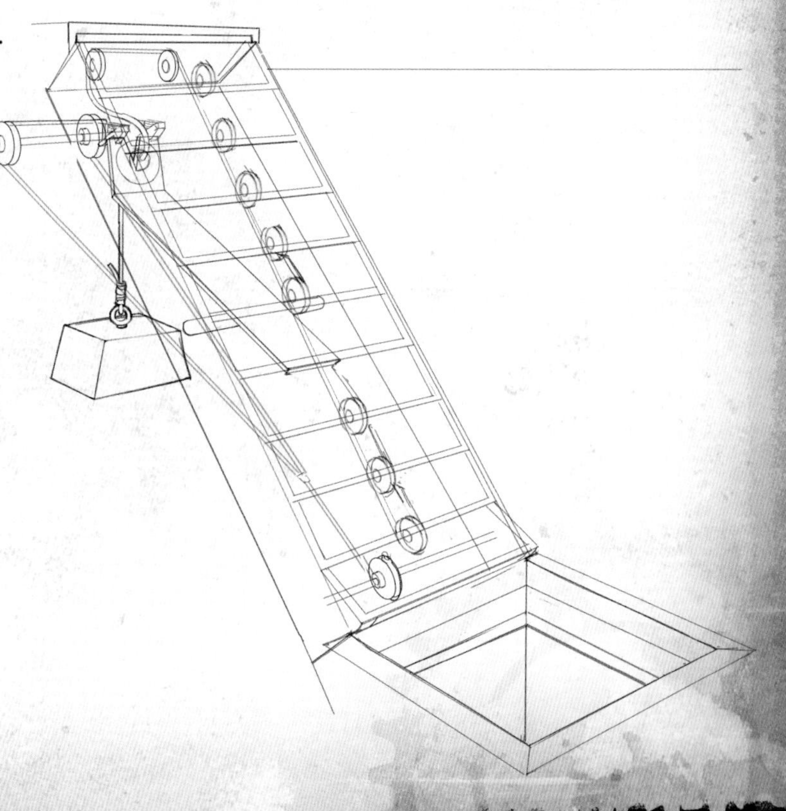

Complex Traps

A complex trap has multiple triggers, or a trigger with multiple inputs (such as levers or buttons), and multiple effects, or an effect with stages. Most of the time, complex traps do reset once they have gone through all their effects or stages.

Like a simple trap, a complex trap is meant to harm, hinder, or impose some negative situation on it's targets. However, a simple trap usually has only one trigger and one effect and, in general, simple traps don't reset once they are triggered.

Complex traps and puzzles can often be mistaken for each other. Both tend to have moving parts (metaphorically or literally), both can be mentally trying, and both can have similar components. The main difference is the purpose of the obstacle. In many cases, a complex trap challenges the *character*, while a puzzle challenges the *player*.

Minor Adjustments. If you're fond of a trap in this chapter, you can always adjust it to provide the right level of challenge for the characters in your campaign. Chapter 9: Designing Traps has tables for things like ability check DC's, damage, and other variables for a trap based. Find what best suits your needs and use that instead of the statistics given in this chapter.

Reading a Complex Trap

A complex trap is a dynamic threat, with more elements than a simple trap. However, a complex trap's type, level range, lethality, purpose, trigger, and countermeasures all work the same as they do for simple traps.

Initiative. A complex trap takes turns like a creature, and this part of the description tells you when the trap acts during the round. A complex trap always acts after a creature that has the same initiative count.

Active Elements. When a trap acts, it produces specific effects as detailed here.

Dynamic Elements. Some complex traps have threats that increase in severity over time. Usually, these elements happen at the end of the trap's turns or in response to a creature's actions.

Constant Elements. A complex trap can damage or affect creatures even when not taking its turn. These elements usually happen to creatures that end their turn in certain areas.

Complex Traps Table

Roll a d100 on the table below to choose a random complex trap, or select a desired level and roll a d10.

	d100	d10	Trap	Page
Level 1-4	1-4	1-2	Stair Slide	88
	5-8	3-4	Wall Blade	89
	9-12	5-6	A Short Drag	89
	13-16	7-8	Hauntedwood Bowl	90
	17-20	9-10	Drenching Pit	90
Level 5-8	21-24	1-2	Stab in the Dark	91
	25-28	3-4	The Hourglass	91
	29-32	5-6	Passageway Piercing	92
	33-36	7-8	Fire Down Below	92
	37-40	9-10	Gassy Gargoyles	93
Level 9-12	41-44	1-2	Trapdoor Floor	94
	45-48	3-4	The Tenderizer	94
	49-52	5-6	Slip-n-Slide	95
	53-56	7-8	Perilous Prisms	96
	57-60	9-10	Flooding Chamber	96
Level 13-16	61-64	1-2	Rats in a Maze	97
	65-68	3-4	Crazy Kitchen	97
	69-72	5-6	Aspect of the Kraken	98
	73-76	7-8	What a Drag	99
	77-80	9-10	Chargrilled	100
Level 17-20	81-84	1-2	Flammable Fluid	100
	85-88	3-4	Necessary Weevil	101
	89-92	5-6	Storm's Run	102
	93-96	7-8	Free Falling	102
	97-100	9-10	Melting Pot	103

Stair Slide

Mechanical trap (level 1-4, setback, harm)

A 200-foot long, 10-foot wide staircase leads up from one floor to the next. 120 feet from the bottom of the stairs is a pressure plate that turns the stairs into a slide. Creatures on the stairs slide down and into the path of bolts fired from holes in the walls. Once they reach the bottom of the stairs, they are deposited into a pit.

Trigger (Weight Sensitive Surface). Two or more Medium or larger creatures standing on the steps past the 120-foot mark triggers the trap.

Initiative. The trap acts on initiative 20 and 10.

Active Elements. The Stair Slide is primarily a ramp depositing creatures in the pit at its bottom, but also has bolts that fire at creatures along the 120 feet from the trigger area to the trapdoor.

- **Stairs to Slide (Initiative 20).** This element activates only once, the first time the trap acts. The stairs fold down, turning into a slide that is difficult terrain. Each creature on any portion of the stairs must succeed on a DC 10 Dexterity saving throw or fall prone.
- **Open the Pit (Initiative 20).** This element activates only once, the first time the trap acts. A trap door at the bottom landing of the stairs opens, revealing a 10-foot deep pit.
- **Hidden Bolts (Initiative 10).** Bolts fire out from holes in the walls in the 120 feet between the trigger area and the trapdoor, making one attack against each creature in the area: +5 attack bonus; 2 (1d4) piercing damage on a hit.

Dynamic Elements. A creature that starts its turn on the slide moves 30 feet down it, towards the pit. The distance the creature moves increases by 30 feet each time it starts its turn on the slide.

Constant Elements. Creatures are subjected to a shower of crossbow bolts while on the slide and drop into the pit when they hit the bottom.

- **Hail of Bolts.** Any creature that ends its turn in the Hidden Bolts' area is targeted by a ranged attack: +5 attack bonus; taking 2 (1d4) piercing damage on a hit.
- **Into the Pit.** A creature that reaches the bottom of the slide while prone or moving faster than their base speed must succeed on a DC 10 Dexterity saving throw or fall into the pit, taking 3 (1d6) bludgeoning damage and landing prone.

Countermeasures. Creatures can avoid activating the Stair Slide and deal with these elements in a number of ways.

Trigger. A creature can spot the weight sensitive stairs that trigger the trap with a successful DC 10 Wisdom (Perception) check. Once found, the trigger can be disabled with a successful DC 10 Dexterity check using thieves' tools.

Stairs to Slide. A creature can try to make the slide revert back to stairs with a successful DC 10 Dexterity check using thieves' tools.

Open the Pit. A creature can climb out of the pit with a successful DC 10 Strength (Athletics) check. The trap doors can be closed with a successful DC 10 Strength check; the doors lock together. A creature that fails this check falls into the pit.

Hidden Bolts. Creatures who succeed on a DC 10 Wisdom (Perception) check find the holes in a 5-foot section of wall from which the bolts fire. They can then plug these holes with cloth or something similar as an action. Plugging the holes prevents the bolts from firing in that area.

Wall Blade

Mechanical trap (level 1-4, moderate, harm)

The 10-foot wide corridor has flagstones along it, one of which is a pressure plate. When a creature steps on the plate, a curved blade pops out from the wall and slices targets within range. It continues to slash out, blocking the corridor.

Trigger. A Small or larger creature stepping on the pressure plate triggers the trap

Initiative. The trap acts on initiative 20.

Active Elements. A scything blade emerges from a hidden panel in the wall and attacks.

Scything Blade (Initiative 20). Creatures in a 10-foot line in front of the blade must make a DC 12 Dexterity saving throw, taking 2 (1d4) slashing damage on a failed save, or half as much on a successful one.

Dynamic Elements. The blade becomes more dangerous the longer the trap remains active.

Blade Accelerates. The blade moves with increasing speed. Each time the trap acts, Scything Blade's damage increases by 2 (1d4) to a maximum of 10 (4d4).

Constant Elements. The Scything Blade slashes creatures in front of it.

Scything Blade. Any creature that ends its turn in a 10-foot line in front of the blade must make a DC 12 Dexterity saving throw, taking the blade's current damage, or half as much on a success.

Countermeasures. The trap's trigger and active element can be thwarted by particular countermeasures.

Pressure Plate (Sensitive). A successful DC 12 Wisdom (Perception) check reveals the pressure plate, and a successful DC 12 Dexterity check while using thieves' tools disables it, preventing the trap from activating. However, if the Dexterity check totals 5 or less the trap activates.

Scything Blade. Characters can smash the blade, damage its components, or discern how to avoid it.

Intelligence (Investigation), DC 12. As an action, a creature that can see the blade can attempt an Intelligence (Investigation) check. A successful check means that the creature has learned how to anticipate the blade's movement, giving them advantage on the next Dexterity saving throw made by the creature to avoid the blade while they aren't incapacitated.

Attack. A creature in the area can ready an attack to strike at the blade as it passes by. The creature has disadvantage on its next Dexterity saving throw made to avoid the blade. The creature then attacks. The blade has AC 15, 15 hit points, and immunity to poison and psychic damage.

Dexterity check using thieves' tools, DC 12. Creatures can use thieves' tools in the blade's area to foil its mechanism. A successful check stops the blade from activating.

A Short Drag

Mechanical trap (level 1-4, dangerous, harm)

A section of floor contains a locked trap door, sensitive to tapping, prodding, or investigating If triggered, the doors open and a grasping vine that snares the triggering creature. The snare pulls the creature through the trap doors and into a nest of **stirges**.

Trigger (Tap/Prod). Applying pressure to the locked trap door via tapping or prodding triggers the trap. Creatures can investigate the trapdoor without activating the trigger by succeeding at a DC 15 Dexterity (Sleight of Hand) check

Initiative. The trap acts on initiative 20.

Active Elements. A Short Drag consists of a trapdoor that swings open, a snare that drags the triggering creature down a slope into a chamber, and a nest of **4 stirges**.

Trap Door Opens (Initiative 20). This element activates only once, the first time the trap acts.The trap door unlocks and swings open, locking into place. A creature standing on the trap door must succeed on a DC 15 Dexterity saving throw or slide down a 30-foot long ramp, taking 3 (1d6) bludgeoning damage and landing prone in the chamber beneath.

Grasping Vine (Initiative 20). A vine whips out from the trap door toward the triggering creature. It must succeed on a DC 15 Dexterity saving throw or take 3 (1d6) bludgeoning damage and be restrained until it is freed.

Dynamic Elements. A creature that ends its turn while restrained by the vine is pulled 30 feet down a slope into the chamber with the stirges. The vine then releases them.

Constant Elements. The chamber is home to **4 stirges** who attack creatures dragged in by the vine. The stirges do not leave the chamber on their own.

Countermeasures. The trap's trigger and the snare can be thwarted by particular countermeasures.

Trigger. A successful DC 15 Wisdom (Perception) check reveals the sensitivity of the trapdoor; it can be disabled with a successful DC 15 Dexterity check using thieves' tools. A success on this check also unlocks the trapdoor

Grasping Vine. A successful DC 15 Strength (Athletics) check allows a creature snared by the vine to escape. The snare can also be cut; it has AC 15, 15 hit points, immunity to poison and psychic damage, and vulnerability to fire damage.

Hauntedwood Bowl

Hybrid trap (level 1-4, perilous, harm)

This 200-foot long, sloping corridor is filled with crushed skeletons and has a locked door at its lowest end. Above the door, spelled out in a mosaic, is a simple riddle. Answering the riddle makes the skeletons reanimate; a giant skull then falls from the ceiling and starts to roll toward the door.

Trigger. Uttering the answer to the riddle while in the corridor triggers the trap.

Initiative. The trap acts on initiative 20 and 10.

Active Elements. Hauntedwood Bowl reanimates the skeletons, then drops a giant skull into the corridor which rolls toward the bottom.

Reanimate Creatures (Initiative 20). **3 skeletons** animate and attack living creatures in the corridor. The trap cannot animate more than 12 skeletons at a time. If it would animate more than 12, the oldest 3 crumble to dust.

Rolling Skull (Initiative 10). The first time this element activates, a massive skull drops from a trap door in the ceiling and starts to roll down the corridor at a speed of 50 feet a round. On subsequent activations, the skull moves another 50 feet down the corridor.

Skeletons (Initiative 10). The animated skeletons move and attack living creatures in the corridor.

Constant Elements. The massive skull barreling down the corridor threatens to crush everything in its path.

Giant Skull. Each creature in the skull's path must make a DC 17 Dexterity saving throw. On a failure, a creature takes 10 (3d6) bludgeoning damage and is knocked prone. On a success, a creature takes half as much damage and isn't knocked prone. Objects that block the skull, such as a conjured wall, take maximum damage from the impact.

Countermeasures. The trap's trigger and active elements can be thwarted by particular countermeasures.

Trigger. A creature that succeeds on a DC 17 Intelligence (Investigation) check or DC 17 Wisdom (Insight) check can deduce or intuit the trigger word. A successful DC 17 Wisdom (Perception) check lets a creature notice the hidden trapdoor in the ceiling. The corridor has an aura of necromancy magic when viewed with *detect magic*; the mosaic has an *rune of detection* hidden in its design.

Reanimate Creatures. The door at the end of the corridor can be opened with a successful DC 17 Strength check, or a successful DC 17 Dexterity check using thieves' tools. Once the door is open, the trap stops animating skeletons.

Rolling Skull. If the skull hits a barrier without destroying it, it stops. Once the skull hits the door at the lowest end of the corridor it smashes into smithereens. If it rolls out of the corridor, it crumbles to dust.

Drenching Pit

Complex trap (level 1-4, deadly, harm)

Hidden in the floor is a trapdoor that drops creatures into a pit that quickly becomes a watery grave.

Trigger. When two or more Medium sized creatures stand on the trapdoor the trap triggers.

Initiative. The trap acts on Initiative 20 and 10.

Active Elements. The Drenching Pit consists of a locked trapdoor and a pit that slowly fills with water.

Trapdoor (Initiative 20). This element activates only once, when the trap first acts. A 10-foot by 10-foot trapdoor is set into the floor and held closed by a heavy spring. Once triggered, the trapdoor opens and drops creatures into the pit below. The door then lifts back into place and rods slide into it, bolting the door in place.

The pit beneath the door is 20 feet deep. A creature standing on it when the trap triggers must make a DC 20 Dexterity saving throw. On a success, the creature is able to grab onto the edge of the pit. Otherwise, the creature falls into the pit and takes 7 (2d6) bludgeoning damage.

Flooding Water (Initiative 10). Water fills the pit at a rate of 5 feet per round.

Constant Elements. The pit slowly fills with water, making attempts to escape more difficult.

Treading Water. After 2 rounds, the water is at chest height for Small creatures, and any ability checks made to disable the trap have disadvantage. Attack rolls to break the spouts or trapdoor are unaffected.

After 3 rounds, creatures start to tread water. A creature treading water can keep it's head clear for a number of minutes equal to 1+its Constitution score. After that time, the creature starts must hold their breath or drown.

After 4 rounds, the water in the pit is deep enough that ability checks made to disable the trap have disadvantage. An attack roll made by a creature that doesn't have a swimming speed (either natural or granted by magic) has disadvantage unless the weapon is a dagger, javelin, shortsword, spear, or trident.

Countermeasures. Creatures can deal with the trap's elements in multiple ways.

Trapdoor. The trapdoor can be found before it opens. Once it shuts, it can be attacked or unlocked.

Detect. A successful DC 20 Wisdom (Perception) check reveals the trapdoor and a successful DC 20 Dexterity check using thieves' tools disables the trap.

Attack. A creature can attack the trapdoor, hopefully breaking it open before their companions drown. The trapdoor has an AC of 15, 50 (5d10) hit points, immunity to piercing, poison, and psychic damage, and vulnerability to fire damage.

Unlock. The trapdoor can be unlocked with a successful DC 20 Dexterity check using thieves' tools.

Spouts. Water flows into the pit from 4 spouts. Once all 4 have been closed in some way, water ceases filling the pit.

Attack. If a creature is adjacent to a spout, they can destroy it with a melee attack. The spouts all have an AC of 19, 5 (2d4) hit points, immunity to poison and psychic damage, and vulnerability to bludgeoning damage.

Plug. If a creature can reach a spout, they can wedge an object or some cloth into it. Any spell that deals cold damage can freeze a spout closed.

Stab in the Dark

Hybrid trap (level 5-8, setback, harm)

This low-ceilinged chamber is warded by a magical charm that triggers a trap when creatures talk inside. When triggered, creatures within the chamber are blinded by a flash of light from a lantern in the middle of the ceiling, while spears stab down repeatedly.

Trigger. Talking in this chamber triggers the trap.

Initiative. The trap acts on Initiative 20 and 10.

Active Elements. Stab in the Dark attempts to magically blind the creatures within and stab them with repeating spears.

Blindness (Initiative 20). All creatures within the chamber must succeed on a DC 10 Constitution saving throw or become blinded. A blinded creature can repeat the saving throw at the end of its turn, ending the effect on itself on a success. A creature who succeeds on the saving throw is immune to the magical blindness for 1 minute.

Spears (Initiative 10). Spears stab down from hidden holes in the ceiling of the chamber. Each creature in the chamber must make a DC 10 Dexterity saving throw, taking 3 (1d6) piercing damage on a failure, or half damage as much on a success.

Constant Elements. The Stabbing Spears affect each creature that ends its turn in the chamber.

Spears. Any creature that ends its turn in the chamber must make a DC 10 Dexterity saving throw, taking 3 (1d6) piercing damage on a failure, or half damage as much on a success.

Countermeasures. The trigger and Active Elements of the trap can be thwarted by particular countermeasures.

Trigger. The lantern on the room's ceiling has an aura of abjuration and necromancy magic when viewed with *detect magic*. A creature that succeeds on a DC 10 Intelligence (Investigation) check while examining the lantern can find some strange sigils on it, and with a successful DC 10 Intelligence (Arcana) check they understand the trap.

A spellcaster can disrupt the enchantment on the lamp with *dispel magic* or with a successful DC 10 spellcasting ability check.

Spears. The easiest way to avoid the spears is to drop prone, as they are not long enough to reach the floor of the chamber. Alternatively, a character can ready an action to snap the spears when they stab down. The creature makes its Dexterity saving throw against the spears with disadvantage. After they have taken damage, they can snap the spear with a successful DC 10 Strength check. This makes one 5-foot square of the room safe from the Spears element.

The Hourglass

Hybrid trap (level 5-8, moderate, hinder)

This trap is set in a conical chamber; an inverted cone filled with sand is hidden by a sliding plate in the ceiling. The plate has a skull-like sigil inscribed on it. If a creature spills blood in the chamber, the sliding plate withdraws, connecting the two chambers and allowing sand to pour into the lower chamber. The doors lock shut, preventing escape, and the sand is cursed to age any creature buried within it.

Trigger. The spilling of blood within the chamber triggers the trap.

Initiative. The trap acts on Initiative 20 and 10.

Active Elements. The Hourglass locks the doors and cursed sand begins to pour into the chamber.

Locked Doors (Initiative 20). This effect activates only once, the first time the trap acts. The exits and entrances to this room slam together and lock shut.

Falling Sand (Initiative 10). A sliding plate in the ceiling withdraws and sand begins to pour into the room through a 5-foot wide hole. Creatures in the area must make successful Dexterity saving throws at the beginning of their turns to stay atop the sand. The DC starts at 12 and increases by 2 at the end of each round.

A creature that fails one saving throw is buried up to their knees and restrained. On their next saving throw, if the creature succeeds they dig themselves out and are no longer restrained; if they fail they are buried waist-deep and remain restrained.

A creature buried waist-deep must make a Strength saving throw at the beginning of their turn, using the current save DC of the trap. If they succeed they dig themselves free of the sand and if they fail they are buried to the neck and immobilized. On their next turn, the creature is completely buried and starts suffocating.

As an action, a creature can dig out another creature with a successful Strength (Athletics) check against the current save DC of the trap. Spells like *freedom of movement* or movement modes like burrow can also allow creatures to freely move through the sand.

Dynamic Elements. The Falling Sand becomes harder and harder to avoid over time.

Avalanche of Grains. Each time the Falling Sand activates, the DC of the saving throws made to avoid becoming buried or dig creatures out increases by 2. The DC for ability checks to unlock or push open the locked doors also increases in this way.

Constant Elements. The Falling Sand is cursed to age any creature that ends its turn buried within it.

Sands of Time. A creature that ends its turn immobilized by the Falling Sand must succeed on a DC 12 Wisdom saving throw or be aged by 1d10 years.

Countermeasures. The trigger and active elements of the trap can be thwarted by particular countermeasures.

Trigger. A creature can spot the gaps around the sliding plate with a successful DC 12 Wisdom (Perception) check. The skull sigil has an aura of abjuration magic when viewed with *detect magic* and a creature that succeeds on a DC 12 Intelligence (Religion) check understands the nature of the trap. The sigil can be disabled with *dispel magic* or a successful DC 12 spellcasting ability check made by a spellcaster.

Open the Doors. The doors' lock has been enhanced with *arcane lock*, which can be found with *detect magic*. As an action, a creature can pick the lock on the doors with a successful DC 12 Dexterity check using thieves' tools. The doors can be pushed open as an action with a successful DC 12 Strength check.

Block the Sand. Characters who can reach the ceiling of the chamber can stop the Falling Sand in the following ways:

Slide the Plate. A creature that succeeds on a DC 12 Intelligence (Investigation) check finds a way to unlock the plate, making it slide back and separate the two chambers.

Replace the Plate. A creature can block the hole in the chamber's ceiling by replacing the plate. As an action, a creature within 5 feet of the hole can block the hole until the start of their next turn with a shield or similar object by succeeding on a DC 12 Strength check. Any conjured barrier that covers the hole also stops the Falling Sand.

Passageway Piercing

Mechanical trap (level 5-8, dangerous, harm)

This trap is triggered by a tripwire set half-way down the corridor. A repeating ballista hidden in the wall at the end of a 5-foot wide, 100-foot long corridor fires upon creatures that trigger the trap, while a barrier drops to block the exit.

Trigger. Tripping the wire triggers the trap.

Initiative. The trap acts on initiative 20, 10, and 5.

Active Elements. The Passageway Piercing fires ballista bolts down the corridor and drops a wooden barrier across its exit.

Barrier (Initiative 20). This element only activates one, the first time the trap acts. A 1-foot thick wooden barrier drops down from the ceiling 10 feet in front of the corridor's exit. A creature within 5 feet of the barrier can make a DC 15 Dexterity saving throw. On a success, the creature can choose which side of the barrier they end up on; on a failure, they must remain where they are.

Bolts (Initiative 10 and 5). A concealed ballista fires down the hallway. The first creature in the corridor is targeted by an attack: +8 attack bonus; 16 (3d10) piercing damage on a hit.

Countermeasures. The trigger and active elements of the trap can be thwarted by particular countermeasures.

Trigger (Sensitive). A successful DC 15 Wisdom (Perception) check reveals the tripwire, and a successful DC 15 Dexterity check using thieves' tools disables the trap.

Barrier. A successful DC 15 Strength check is enough to lift the barrier high enough for a Medium or smaller creature to crawl beneath. The barrier can also be destroyed; it has AC 15, 50 hit points, immunity to poison and psychic damage, and vulnerability to fire damage.

Bolts. A creature within 5 feet of the concealed ballista can disable it after 3 rounds of successful ability checks.

- **Round 1:** As an action, the creature can locate the concealed ballista with a successful DC 15 Intelligence (Investigation) check.
- **Round 2:** As an action, the creature can break away the concealing plaster with a successful DC 15 Strength check.
- **Round 3:** As an action, the creature can disable the ballista with a successful DC 15 Dexterity check using thieves' tools.

Fire Down Below

Mechanical trap (level 5-8, perilous, harm)

A trapdoor on the floor of the chamber hides a 20-foot-deep pit, at the bottom of which are jets of fire.

Trigger. A creature that steps on the trapdoor activates the pressure plate, making it swing open.

Initiative. The trap acts on initiative 20 and 10.

Active Elements. Fire Down Below includes a drop and jets of fire.

Drop (Initiative 20). This element activates only once, the first time the trap acts. The triggering creature must make a DC 17 Dexterity saving throw. On a success, the creature is able to grab onto the edge of the pit. On a failure, the creature falls into the pit and takes 7 (2d6) bludgeoning damage.

Flames (Initiative 10). Each creature in the pit must make a DC 17 Dexterity saving throw. A creature takes 14 (4d6) fire damage on a failure, or half as much on a success.

Constant Elements. The constant flames turn the pit into an oven.

Heat Exhaustion. A creature that ends its turn in the pit must succeed on a DC 17 Constitution saving throw or gain 1 level of exhaustion. Creatures wearing medium or heavy armor, or who are clad in heavy clothing, have disadvantage on this saving throw. Creatures with resistance or immunity to fire damage automatically succeed on this saving throw, as do creatures normally adjusted to hot climates.

Countermeasures. A successful DC 17 Wisdom (Perception) check reveals the pressure plate and a successful DC 17 Dexterity check using thieves' tools disables the trap.

Gassy Gargoyles

Hybrid trap (level 5-8, deadly, harm)

There are four gargoyles in the corners of the chamber. The trap activates when flame is brought into the area; causes magical bonds of flame erupt and grapple creatures, dealing damage to them. In addition, poison gas spouts from the mouths of the gargoyles; once the gas reaches a certain potency, it ignites.

Trigger (Produce Flame). Bringing a flame into the chamber triggers the trap.

Initiative. The trap acts on initiative 20 and 10.

Active Elements. The trap consists of magical restraints made from flames, and poison gas which fills the room from pipes in the mouths of the gargoyles.

Fiery Restraint (Initiative 20). This effect activates only once, the first time the trap acts. Each target within 30 feet of the triggering flame must succeed on a DC 20 Wisdom saving throw or become restrained and take 10 (3d6) fire damage. A creature holding the triggering flame makes the save with disadvantage.

Locked Doors (Initiative 20). This effect activates only once, the first time the trap acts. The exits and entrances to this room slam shut and are locked in place by magic.

Poison Gas (Initiative 10). Poison gas floods the room. Each creature inside must make a DC 20 Constitution saving throw, taking 5 (1d10) poison damage on a failed save, or half as much on a successful one.

Dynamic Elements. The longer the poison gas remains in the room, the more lethal it becomes. After it hits a certain concentration, it ignites.

Increased Potency. The damage from the Poison Gas element increases by 5 (1d10) each round after it activates, to a maximum of 22 (4d10). Once the gas reaches its maximum damage, the gas ignites the next time it activates. Each creature in the chamber must succeed on a DC 20 Dexterity saving throw, taking 35 (10d6) fire damage on a failed save, or half as much on a successful one.

Constant Elements. The Fiery Restraint affects each creature that ends its turn restrained.

Fiery Restraint. A creature that ends its turn restrained by the Fiery Restraint takes 10 (3d6) fire damage.

Countermeasures. The traps trigger and active elements can be thwarted by particular countermeasures.

Trigger. A successful DC 20 Wisdom (Perception) check reveals a *rune of detection* on the ceiling that reacts to the presence of the flame. The rune can also be found with *detect magic*, which also reveals an aura of evocation magic around the gargoyle statues. A successful DC 20 Intelligence (Arcana) check or *dispel magic* disables the trap.

Fiery Restraint. A restrained creature can be freed with a successful DC 20 Strength check, which deals 10 (3d6) damage to the creature attempting the check. Casting *dispel magic* upon the flame dispels each restraint, and deals no damage to the caster.

Open the Doors. The doors' lock has been enhanced with *arcane lock*, which can be found with *detect magic*. As an action, a creature can pick the lock on the doors with a successful DC 30 Dexterity check using thieves' tools. The doors can be pushed open as an action with a successful DC 30 Strength check.

Poison Gas. The gas can be disabled by blocking the flow from the gargoyle's mouths, but heavily damaging a statue leaves the gas vents open. When all four gargoyles are blocked up or disabled, the trap deactivates.

Attack. Reducing a gargoyle to 0 hit points (AC 17; 20 hit points; resistance to fire, piercing, and slashing damage; immunity to poison and psychic damage), or making a successful DC 20 Strength check to break one increases the Poison Gas damage by 5 (1d10).

Dexterity check using thieves' tools, DC 20. A creature can use thieves' tools to disable the gas in one of the gargoyles, reducing the Poison Gas damage by 5 (1d10).

Strength check, DC 15. A creature can block up the gargoyle with a cloak or similar object, reducing the Poison Gas damage by 5 (1d10). Once a character succeeds on the check, someone must remain within 5 feet of the gargoyle to keep it blocked up.

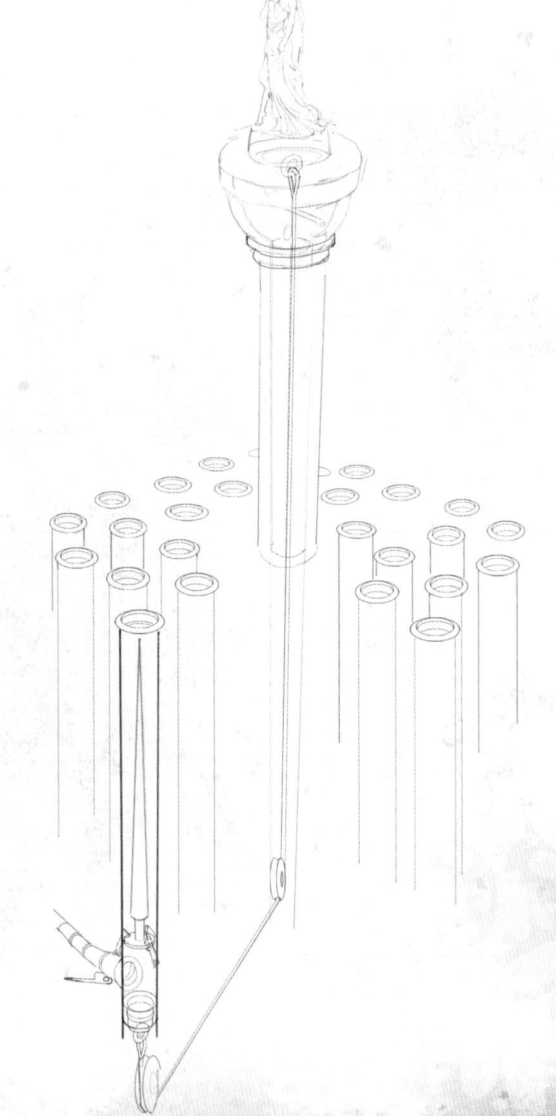

Trapdoor Floor

Hybrid trap (level 9-12, setback, harm)

In the centre of the chamber is a pool of water, glistening with radiant light. A creature that touches the water triggers the trap; the floor of the chamber opens like a trap door, dropping creatures onto spikes. The opening then locks closed and the spikes slowly rises, trapping creatures between the ceiling and the spikes.

Trigger (Disturb Liquid). Upsetting the surface of the liquid triggers the trap.

Initiative. The trap acts on initiative 20, 15, and 10.

Active Elements. The Trapdoor Floor consists of a trapoor, a drop onto spikes, and then a floor that slowly grinds upwards, crushing creatures on the spikes.

Drop (Initiative 20). This effect activates only once, the first time the trap is triggered. Each creature touching the floor falls as the floor gives way. A creature within 5 feet of a solid surface, such as the walls of the chamber or the pool, can grab the edge with a successful DC 10 Dexterity saving throw. A creature that falls takes 7 (2d6) bludgeoning damage from the 20-foot drop, plus an additional 3 (1d6) piercing damage from the spiked surface they fall onto.

Lock (Initiative 15). This effect activates only once, the first time the trap is triggered. The floor swings back into position and locks. A creature hanging on to the edge of the pit can drop down into the pit, taking the damage as described above, before the floor locks shut with a successful DC 10 Dexterity (Athletics) check, otherwise they end up on top of the floor.

Impaling Spikes (Initiative 10). The impaling spikes move at a rate of 1 foot per round. They keep moving until the spikes touch the ceiling of the pit, at which point they retract. When the spikes enter a creature's space, it must make a DC 10 Dexterity saving throw. If the creature fails they take 10 (3d6) piercing damage, or half as much on a success. A creature that fails the Dexterity saving throw is restrained by being impaled on the spikes.

A creature impaled by spikes can free themselves with a successful DC 10 Constitution (Athletics) check but not until there is room equivalent to their size available in front of the spikes. Another creature can free an impaled creature with a successful DC 10 Strength (Medicine) check, as long as there is room. Once the spikes reach the ceiling they retract and return to their starting point, releasing any impaled creatures.

Constant Elements. The Impaling Spikes damage any creatures impaled on them.

Spiked Surface. A creature that ends its turn restrained by the Impaling Spikes takes 3 (1d6) piercing damage.

Countermeasures. The trigger and active elements of the trap can be thwarted by particular countermeasures.

Trigger. With a successful DC 10 Wisdom (Perception) check, a creature can find a *rune of detection* at the bottom of the pool; *detect magic* also reveals the rune. A successful DC 10 Intelligence (Arcana) check or *dispel magic* cast on the rune disables the trap.

Lock. As an action, a creature can find the locking mechanism on the door by succeeding on a DC 10 Wisdom (Perception) check. With another action, and a successful DC 10 Intelligence (Investigation) check, a creature can figure out how to make the door unlock and retract. The locking mechanism is at the top of the pit, so a creature can, as an action, disable it with a successful DC 10 Dexterity check using thieves' tools as long as they are adjacent to it. Unlocking the floor ends the trap.

Impaling Spikes. A creature can stop the spikes from moving by jamming something into the gap between the surface and the walls of the pit with a successful DC 10 Strength check. Once all four sides of the surface have been jammed, the surface stops moving.

The Tenderizer

Mechanical trap (level 9-12, moderate, harm)

Each 5-foot square of the chamber has a large stone pillar hanging above it. These pillars smash down when the pressure plate in the centre of the room is triggered. Additionally, the chamber slowly heats up like an oven as four vents on the walls pump in hot air.

Trigger (Pressure Plate). Applying 20 pounds or more of pressure to the pressure plate triggers the trap.

Initiative. The trap acts on initiative 20 and 10.

Active Elements. The Tenderizer makes pillars to smash down onto creatures within the chamber, and blasts of fire shoot out from the walls.

Crushing Pillars (Initiative 20). Each creature in the chamber must make a DC 12 Dexterity saving throw. On a failed save, a creature takes 10 (3d6) bludgeoning damage and is knocked prone. On a successful save, a creature takes half damage and isn't knocked prone.

Fire Blast (Initiative 10). Each creature in the chamber must succeed on a DC 12 Constitution saving throw, taking 5 (1d10) fire damage on a failed save, or half as much on a successful one.

Dynamic Elements. The Fire Blast becomes more dangerous the longer the trap remains active.

It's Getting Hot in Here. After it activates, the Fire Blast increases in heat; its damage increases by 5 (1d10) to a maximum of 22 (5d10). While its damage is 10 (2d10) or greater, it acts on initiative count 20 and 10.

Constant Elements. The Fire Blast affects each creature that ends its turn in the chamber.

Fire Blast. Any creature that ends its turn within the chamber must make a saving throw against the Fire Blast effect.

Countermeasures. The trigger and active elements of the trap can be thwarted by particular countermeasures.

Trigger (Sensitive). A successful DC 12 Wisdom (Perception) check reveals the pressure plate, and a successful DC 12 Dexterity check using thieves' tools disables the trap.

Crushing Pillars. There are several ways to combat the pillars.

Intelligence (Investigation), DC 12. As an action, a creature that can see the Crushing Pillars and succeeds on an Intelligence (Investigation) check learns how to anticipate the pillars' movement, giving them advantage on the next Dexterity saving throw made to avoid the pillars while the creature isn't incapacitated.

Strength, DC 12. A creature in the chamber can ready an action to brace against a Crushing Pillar when it smashes down. The creature has disadvantage on its next Dexterity saving throw to avoid the pillar. The creature then makes a Strength check. On a success, the pillar becomes jammed, preventing it from smashing down on that 5-foot square again until the trap is reset.

Fire Blast. The vents blasting heat can be disabled by blocking them up. A successful DC 12 Dexterity check using thieves' tools, or a successful DC 12 Strength check made to block up the vent with a cloak or similar object, decreases the fire damage by 5 (1d10). Once a creature succeeds on the check, they or another creature must remain next to the vent to keep it blocked up. When all four vents are blocked in this manner, the trap deactivates.

Slip-N-Slide

Mechanical trap (level 9-12, dangerous, block)

The trap is in a 130-foot long, 10-foot wide corridor. A wall of pipes spans the corridor 90 feet along its length. A creature that breaks the pipes to get past them releases a blast of water that pushes creatures back into a swinging mallet. Beyond the pipes is a doorway exiting the corridor.

SUGGESTION

This trap begs the question "why would there be pipes going straight through the middle of the hallway?" There are many possible answers to this question. The dungeon denizens might be small or otherwise able to fit through or around the pipes. Perhaps the hallway isn't used often, or the pipes fell into their current position due to failed structural supports.

Trigger. Breaking the pipes triggers the trap. There is no room for a Small or larger creature to squeeze through the pipes, but a creature can see through them via small gaps. This might allow a creature to teleport past the pipes with a spell; a creature could also transform into a Tiny animal to get through the pipes.

Initiative. The trap acts on initiative 20 and 10.

Active Elements. Slip-N-Slide unleashes a torrent of water to blast from the broken pipes, and a swinging mallet sweeps through the corridor.

Water Blast (Initiative 20). A 60-foot long, 10-foot wide line of water bursts from the pipes. The first creature hit by the water must succeed on a DC 15 Dexterity saving throw or take 3 (1d6) bludgeoning damage and be pushed 30 feet away from the broken pipes. The torrent counts as difficult terrain when walking into the flow.

Swinging Object - Forward (Initiative 20). An enormous mallet swings forward in an arc that goes through the 50-foot long area beyond the first 20 feet of the corridor. Creatures in the area must make a DC 15 Dexterity saving throw. On a failed save, a creature takes 11 (2d10) bludgeoning damage, is pushed 10 feet toward the pipes, and falls prone. On a successful save, a creature takes half the damage and isn't pushed or knocked prone.

Swinging Object - Backwards (Initiative 10). The mallet swings backwards, in the same arc as detailed above. Creatures in the area must make a DC 15 Dexterity saving throw. On a failed save, a creature takes 11 (2d10) bludgeoning damage, is pushed 10 feet away from the pipes, and falls prone. On a successful save, a creature takes half the damage and isn't pushed or knocked prone.

Constant Elements. The blast of water from the pipes pushes creatures away each round.

Water Blast. Any creature that ends its turn within the 60-foot long, 10-foot wide line extending from the broken pipes must make a saving throw against the Water Blast effect.

Countermeasures. The trigger and active effects of the trap can be thwarted by particular countermeasures.

Trigger (Difficult). A successful DC 15 Wisdom (Perception) check reveals several small cranks and wheels on the pipes. A successful DC 15 Intelligence (Investigation) check reveals that turning these will stop the flow of water into the pipes, and allows a creature to attempt a DC 15 Dexterity check while using thieves' tools to disable the trap.

Water Blast. Once activated, the Water Blast can be turned off with the same process as described for the Trigger.

Swinging Object. A creature can use its action to anticipate the swinging of the mallet. They have advantage on their next Dexterity saving throw made to avoid the Swinging Object from either direction.

Open the Door. Once they are broken, a creature can move past the pipes with a successful DC 15 Dexterity (Acrobatics) check. The door out of the corridor is 40 feet away from the broken pipes, and it can be opened as an action with a successful DC 15 Strength check. Opening the door ends the trap.

Perilous Prisms

Hybrid trap (level 9-12, perilous, harm)

Glittering crystals float in each of the four corners of this room, which only has one doorway leading into and out of it. In the center of the room is a shrine, atop which rests a relic. Taking the relic from the shrine activates the trap; the doors lock, and the crystals fire bolts of radiance at the creature holding the relic.

Trigger (Pick Up/Shift Object). Picking up the relic triggers the trap.

Initiative. The trap acts on initiative 20 and 15.

Active Elements. Perilous Prisms locks the door, and the prisms spin rapidly and fire blasts of light at the creature with the relic.

Locked Doors (Initiative 20). This effect activates only once, the first time the trap is triggered. The door leading out of this room slams shut and is locked in place by magic.

Bolts of Light (Initiative 15). The 4 floating crystals each move up to 30 feet on their turn to get in range of the creature holding the relic. If they cannot,they target the closest creature instead. The crystals cast *guiding bolt* as a 5th-level spell: +10 attack bonus, 28 (8d6) radiant damage on a hit, attack rolls against the creature hit by the bolt have advantage until the crystals' next turn.

Dynamic Elements. Tampering with the crystals in any way makes them emit a burst of radiance.

Blinding Radiance. Every time a crystal is dispelled, or each time an attack hits the crystals, they give off a blinding flash of radiance. Each creature within 30 feet of the targeted crystal must succeed on a DC 17 Constitution saving throw or become blinded until the end of their next turn.

Countermeasures. The trigger and active elements of the trap can be thwarted by particular countermeasures.

Trigger. A creature that succeeds on a DC 17 Intelligence (Religion) check recognizes the relic and knows the danger of the trap. A successful DC 17 Wisdom (Perception) check reveals a weight sensitive plate on the shrine beneath the relic; a successful DC 17 Dexterity check using thieves' tools disables the trap.

To bypass the trigger, a creature can attempt to replace the relic with something of equal weight. The creature must make a successful DC 17 Intelligence (Perception) check to accurately estimate the weight of the relic and a successful DC 17 Dexterity (Sleight of Hand) check to switch the objects. Failure on either roll activates the trap.

Open the Doors. The doors' lock has been enhanced with *arcane lock*, which can be found with *detect magic*. As an action, a creature can pick the lock on the doors with a successful DC 27 Dexterity check using thieves' tools. The doors can be pushed open as an action with a successful DC 27 Strength check. Unlocking the door ends the trap.

Crystals. The crystals have an aura of evocation magic when viewed with *detect magic*. Creatures can smash the crystals or attempt to dispel them.

Attack. Reducing a crystal to 0 hit points destroys it. Each crystal has AC 17; 30 hit points; resistance to radiant damage; and immunity to poison and psychic damage.

Dispel. The enchantment surrounding the crystals can be dispelled with *dispel magic* (DC 15), or with a successful DC 17 spellcasting ability made by a spellcaster.

Flooding Chamber

Mechanical trap (level 9-12, deadly, harm)

In the center of this 25-foot square chamber is a large crank; painted lines around the crank point to a door leading further into the dungeon. Turning the crank makes a square barrier drop from the ceiling, blocking the exits. This 15-foot enclosed area then begins to fill with water from the grated floor. A creature that attempts to damage the barriers is electrified.

Trigger (Turn Wheel/Crank). Turning the crank triggers the trap.

Initiative. The trap acts on initiative 20 and 10.

Active Elements. The Flooding Chamber drops barriers, enclosing creatures in the central 15-foot square of the room, and fills this space with water from below.

Iron Cage (Initiative 20). A 15-foot square cage drops down from the ceiling. A creature within 5 feet of the falling barrier can attempt a DC 20 Dexterity saving throw; a creature that succeeds can choose which side they end up on when the barrier falls. Creatures that fail this saving throw are trapped in the cage.

Flooding Water (Initiative 10). Water begins to fill the enclosed 15-foot cube in the center of the chamber at a rate of 5 feet per round.

Dynamic Elements. The metal cage is studded with crystals that explode with lightning when shattered.

Electrified Cage. Each attack roll that hits the cage makes it emit a pulse of lightning. The attacking creature, and each creature touching the water within the cage , must make a DC 20 Constitution saving throw, taking 27 (5d10) lightning damage on a failed save, or half as much on a successful one.

Constant Elements. The cage slowly fills with water, making attempts to escape more difficult.

Treading Water. After 2 rounds, the water is at chest height for Small creatures, and any ability checks made to disable the trap have disadvantage. Attack rolls to break the cage are unaffected.

After 3 rounds, the water reaches the top of the cage; creatures within must hold their breath or drown. Ability checks made to disable the trap have disadvantage. An attack roll made by a creature that doesn't have a swimming speed (either natural or granted by magic) has disadvantage unless the weapon is a dagger, javelin, shortsword, spear, or trident.

Countermeasures. The trigger and some active elements of the trap can be thwarted by particular countermeasures.

Trigger (Difficult). A successful DC 20 Wisdom (Perception) check reveals the hidden mechanisms connected to the crank. A successful DC 20 Intelligence (Investigation) check reveals the nature of the trigger, and allows a creature to disable it with a successful DC 20 Dexterity check using thieves' tools.

Iron Cage. Reducing a 5-foot square section of the cage to 0 hit points destroys it, allowing the water to pour out into the chamber harmlessly. Each 5-foot square section of the cage has AC 20; 50 hit points; resistance to bludgeoning and slashing damage; and immunity to lightning, poison and psychic damage.

Rats in a Maze

Magic trap (level 13-16, setback, block)

This trap is set in a large chamber with a rune-inscribed door. When creatures enter the chamber, multiple *walls of force* appear, turning the chamber into a maze. Then, shards of metal debris fall into the chamber through portals in the ceiling.

Trigger. Moving through the door and into the chamber triggers the trap.

Initiative. The trap acts on initiative 20 and 10.

Active Elements. Rats in a Maze summons several walls of invisible force and drops debris from portals in the ceiling.

Walls of Force (Initiative 20). This element only activates once, the first time the trap acts. Invisible walls of force spring into existence, turning the chamber into a winding maze. Each wall is made of 10-foot-by-10-foot panels and is 1/4 inch thick. If a wall cuts through a creature's space when it appears, the creature is pushed to a random side of the wall.

Falling Objects (Initiative 10). Portals open above the maze and disgorge shards of metal into the chamber. Each creature in the chamber must make a DC 10 Dexterity saving throw, taking 3 (1d6) slashing damage on a failed save, or half as much on a successful one.

Dynamic Elements. The amount of metal coming from the portals increases every round.

Additional Debris. After it activates, the damage from Falling Objects increases by 3 (1d6) to a maximum of 14 (4d6). While its damage is 7 (2d6) or greater, it acts on initiative count 20 and 10. There are portals above every 5-foot square of the room's floor, but only some of them open up at a time, depending on how much damage this effect deals.

Constant Elements. The Falling Objects affects any creature that ends its turn in the chamber.

Falling Objects. Any creature that ends its turn in the chamber must make a saving throw against the Falling Objects effect.

Countermeasures. The trigger and active elements of the trap can be thwarted by particular countermeasures.

Trigger. A creature that succeeds on a DC 10 Intelligence (Arcana) check can recognize and interpret the runes on the door, revealing the danger of the trap. The runes also have an aura of evocation magic when viewed with *detect magic*. The runes can be disabled with *dispel magic* (DC 14) or with a successful DC 10 spellcasting ability check made by a spellcaster.

Navigating the Maze. A creature can deduce the path of the maze as an action with a successful DC 10 Wisdom (Survival) check. This allows a creature to progress through the maze, which fills the room. Once a creature successfully completes the maze, by either reaching the center or the way out of the room, the trap ends.

Removing the Walls. The walls can be found with *detect magic*; a creature that runs into a wall can figure out what it is with a successful DC 10 Intelligence (Arcana) check. Nothing can physically pass through the walls of force. They are immune to all damage and can't be dispelled by *dispel magic*. A *disintegrate* spell destroys a wall instantly, however. The wall also extends into the Ethereal Plane, blocking ethereal travel through the wall.

Closing the Portals. A 5-foot square portal can be closed by casting *dispel magic* on it. This prevents debris from falling in the 5-foot square portal beneath it.

Crazy Kitchen

Hybrid trap (level 13-16, moderate, harm)

This trap takes place in a chamber filled with artisan tools, such as cook's tools, smith's tools, or mason's tools. When a creature breaks the tripwire, a magical gas pours forth from a vat, putting creatures in the chamber to sleep. The tools then animate and attack the creatures in the room.

Trigger (Tripwire). Breaking the tripwire triggers the trap.

Initiative. The trap acts on initiative 20 and 10.

Active Elements. A vat in the chamber produces a magic sleep-inducing gas. The tools scattered around the chamber animate and attack creatures within.

Sleep Gas (Initiative 20). Each creature in the chamber must succeed on a DC 12 Constitution saving throw or fall asleep for 1 minute. Creatures put to sleep in this way remain unconscious until the effect ends, the sleeper takes damage, or someone uses an action to shake or slap the sleeper awake. Undead, constructs, and creatures that don't need to sleep aren't affected by this effect.

A creature that succeeds on the saving throw is immune to the Sleep Gas for 1 hour.

Animated Objects (Initiative 10). The tools around the room animate and attack creatures that are not unconscious. The trap animates 4 objects, and each object makes one attack against a random target: +6 attack bonus, 7 (2d6) slashing damage on a hit.

Dynamic Elements. More tools animate the longer the trap remains active.

More the Merrier. After their turn, the number of Animated Objects increases by four. There can be no more than 12 animated tools at any one time.

Constant Elements. A creature that ends its turn in the sleep-inducing gas is affected by it, unless they are immune to it.

Sleep Gas. Each creature that ends its turn in the chamber must make a saving throw against the Sleep Gas, unless they are immune or already unconscious.

Countermeasures. The trigger and active elements of the trap can be thwarted by particular countermeasures.

Trigger (Sensitive). A successful DC12 Wisdom (Perception) check reveals the tripwire, and a successful DC 12 Dexterity check using thieves' tools disables the trap.

Sleep Gas. The vat producing the sleep-inducing gas can be deactivated by a creature within 5 feet of it. As an action, the creature can locate magic runes on the vat with a successful DC 15 Intelligence (Investigation) check. The creature can then dispel those runes with *dispel magic* (DC 15); as an action, a creature can also disrupt the runes with a successful DC 12 Intelligence (Arcana) check. Once the vat has been deactivated, the trap ends.

Animated Objects. Each object can be destroyed by attacking it (AC 12; 12 hit points; immunity to poison and psychic damage) or by casting *dispel magic* on it. Characters can take the Dodge action to give the objects disadvantage on attack rolls against them.

Aspect of the Kraken

Magic trap (level 13-16, dangerous, harm)

In the center of this chamber is a plinth with a kraken statuette atop it. When a weapon is drawn in the chamber, the statuette creates an illusory kraken that induces fear in nearby creatures. Additionally, the illusory tentacles attack, dealing psychic damage to creatures they hit. Creatures can leave through the door they entered, or search for a secret door which allows them to progress.

Trigger (Draw Weapon). Drawing a weapon or bringing an unsheathed weapon into the chamber triggers the trap.

Initiative. The trap acts on initiative 20 and 10.

Active Elements. The Aspect of the Kraken creates an illusory kraken that scares creatures and attacks them with phantasmal tentacles.

Kraken Fear (Initiative 20). An illusion of a manifests around the statuette. All creatures within 30 feet of the statuette must succeed on a DC 15 Wisdom saving throw or become frightened. A creature frightened this way must take the Dash action and move away from the statuette area by the safest available route on each of its turns, unless there is nowhere to move.

If the creature ends its turn in a location where it doesn't have line of sight to the illusory kraken, the creature can make a DC 15 Wisdom saving throw. On a successful save, this effect ends for that creature.

Once a creature succeeds on their Wisdom saving throw to resist the Kraken Fear, they are immune to it for 1 hour.

Illusory Tentacles (Initiative 10). The illusory kraken has eight tentacles. Each tentacle makes an attack against a random creature holding a weapon within 30 feet of the statuette: +8 attack bonus, 11 (2d10) psychic damage on a hit.

Dynamic Elements. Tampering with the kraken idol increases the trap's power.

Kraken Idol. Each successful ability check made to disable the statuette increases the damage of the Illusory Tentacles by 5 (1d10) and increases the DC of the Wisdom saving throw to resist the Kraken Fear by 1.

Constant Elements. The Kraken Fear and Illusory Tentacles affect each creature that ends its turn within 30 feet of the kraken idol

Kraken Fear. Any creature that ends its turn within 30 feet of the kraken idol must make a saving throw against the Kraken Fear, unless they are immune.

Illusory Tentacles. Any creature that ends its turn within 30 feet of the kraken idol is targeted by an attack: +8 attack bonus; 5 (1d10) psychic damage on a hit.

Countermeasures. The trigger and active elements of the trap can be thwarted by particular countermeasures. Additionally, creatures can escape the trap by locating a secret door.

Trigger. A creature that succeeds on a DC 15 Intelligence (Religion) check recognizes the kraken statuette and understands the danger of the trap. The statuette also has an aura of illusion magic when viewed with *detect magic*. A spellcaster can disrupt the enchantment on the statuette with a successful DC 15 spellcasting ability check; *dispel magic* DC (DC 16) also disables the trap. This can be done before or after the trap activates.

Kraken Ilusion. Once activated, the illusory kraken can be dispelled with *dispel magic* (DC 16). A creature that succeeds on a DC 15 Intelligence (Investigation) check recognizes that the kraken is an illusion. Once a creature knows the kraken isn't real, it is immune to Kraken Fear and resistance to the psychic damage from the Illusory Tentacles.

Secret Door. If creatures can locate and unlock a secret door, they can escape the chamber. To locate the door, a creature must succeed on a DC 15 Wisdom (Perception) check. Once the door has been found, it can be unlocked with a successful DC 15 Dexterity check using thieves' tools.

What A Drag

Mechanical trap (level 13-16, perilous, harm)

This trap is set in a 140-foot long corridor, which has a pressure plate by the entrance. Applying weight to the pressure plate triggers it, and a chain snare catches the triggering creature around the ankle. The snare then drags the creature through a series of effects triggered by the initial pressure plate.

Trigger (Pressure Plate). Applying 20 pounds or more of pressure to the pressure plate triggers the trap.

Initiative. The trap acts on initiative 20, 15, and 10.

Active Elements. What A Drag snares the triggering creature in the first 5 feet of the trap. It then drags them through the corridor ahead, which fires poison darts in the next 60-foot long area, and scything blades which swing across the corridor in the next 60-foot long area. There is a 10-foot gap between the poison darts and the scything blades

Chain Snare (Initiative 20). This element activates only once, the first time the trap acts. A chain snare catches around the triggering creature's ankle. The target must succeed on a DC 17 Dexterity saving throw or become restrained by the snare until freed.

Poison Darts (Initiative 15). Darts fire across the corridor in the 60-foot long area past the first 10 feet. The darts make one attack roll against each creature in the area with a +10 bonus to the attack roll. A creature hit by a dart must make a DC 17 Constitution saving throw. The creature takes 33 (6d10) poison damage and becomes poisoned on a failed save, or takes half the damage and isn't poisoned on a successful one.

Scything Blades (Initiative 10). Scything blades swing across the corridor in the 60-foot long area past the first 70 feet. Each creature in that area must succeed on a DC 17 Dexterity saving throw, taking 33 (6d10) slashing damage on a failed save, or half as much on a successful one.

Constant Elements. The Chain Snare drags creatures down the corridor, and the Darts and Scything Blades affect any creature that ends its turn in an area affected by these elements.

Chain Snare. The snare drags any creature restrained by it 60 feet down the corridor.

Poison Darts. Any creature that ends its turn in the 60-foot long area past the first 10 feet of the corridor is targeted by the Poison Darts element.

Scything Blades. Any creature that ends its turn in the 60-foot long area past the first 70 feet of the corridor must make a saving throw against the Scything Blades element.

Countermeasures. The trigger and active elements of the trap can each be thwarted by particular countermeasures.

Trigger (Sensitive). A successful DC 17 Wisdom (Perception) check reveals the pressure plate, and a successful DC 17 Dexterity check while using thieves' tools disables the trigger. Disabling the trigger, either before or after the trap activates, disables the trap.

Chain Snare. As an action, a creature can be free themselves from the snare or a creature restrained by the snare with a successful DC 18 Strength check. The snare can also be destroyed: it has AC 18; 20 hit points; resistance to bludgeoning and slashing damage; and immunity to poison and psychic damage.

Poison Darts. The darts can be disabled by closing the holes through which they fire. First, a creature must succeed on a DC 17 Wisdom (Perception) check to uncover the holes. A creature can then stuff cloth or some other material in the holes as an action.

Scything Blades. Characters can smash the blades, damage their components, or discern how to avoid them. The blades are disabled if the Dexterity saving throw DC made to avoid them is reduced below 10. Ways to do that are described below.

Intelligence (Investigation), DC 17. As an action, a creature that can see the blades can attempt an Intelligence (Investigation) check. A successful check means that the creature has learned how to anticipate the blades' movement, giving them advantage on the next Dexterity saving throw made by the creature to avoid the blades while they aren't incapacitated.

Attack. A creature in the area can ready an attack to strike at a blade as it passes by. The creature has disadvantage on its next Dexterity saving throw made to avoid the blades. The creature then attacks. Each blade has AC 15; 15 hit points; and immunity to poison and psychic damage. Destroying a blade reduces the Scything Blades saving throw DC by 2.

Dexterity check using thieves' tools, DC 17. Creatures can use thieves' tools in the blade's area to foil its mechanism. A successful check reduces the Scything Blades saving throw DC by 2.

Chargrilled

Magic trap (level 13-16, deadly, harm)

A beautiful treasure stands in a display case. Opening the display case and touching the treasure triggers the trap.

Trigger (Touch Object). Opening the case and touching the treasure triggers the trap.

Initiative. The trap acts on initiative 20 and 15.

Active Elements. Chargrilled releases a magic adhesive, sticking the treasure and the triggering creature to the display case. A wall of fire appears around the creature and case, and fire blasts them from the ceiling.

Magic Adhesive (Initiative 20). This element activates only once, the first time the trap acts. A magic adhesive pours forth from the treasure, sticking itself and the triggering creature to the display case. The triggering creature must succeed on a DC 20 Dexterity saving throw or be restrained until the adhesive is removed.

Ring of Flame (Initiative 20). This element activates only once, the first time the trap acts. A wall of fire surrounds the triggering creature and display case. The ringed wall is opaque, 20 feet in diameter, 20 feet high, and 1 foot thick. When the wall appears, each creature within its area must make a DC 20 Dexterity saving throw. On a failed save, a creature takes 56 (16d6) fire damage, or half as much damage on a successful save.

Fire Blast (Initiative 15). A blast of flame shoots from the ceiling onto the display case. A creature within 10 feet of the display case must make a DC 20 Dexterity saving throw, taking 88 (16d10) fire damage on a failed save, or half as much on a successful one.

Dynamic Elements. The Ring of Flame and Fire Blast become more dangerous the longer the trap remains active.

Burning Brighter. After it activates, the damage dealt by Ring of Flame increases by 3 (1d6), to a maximum of 70 (20d6).

And Brighter. After it activates, the damage dealt by Fire Blast increases by 5 (1d10), to a maximum of 110 (20d10).

Constant Elements. The Ring of Flame affects each creature that ends its turn inside it or passes through it.

Ring of Flame. The ringed wall of fire deals the damage from Ring of Flame to each creature that ends its turn inside ir or passes through it. The other side of the wall deals no damage.

Countermeasures. The trigger and active elements of the trap can each be thwarted by particular countermeasures.

Trigger. A creature that succeeds on a DC 20 Intelligence (History) check recognizes the trapped object and understands the danger it brings. The object also has an aura of abjuration and evocation magic when viewed with *detect magic*.

A spellcaster can disrupt the enchantment on the object with a successful DC 20 spellcasting ability check; *dispel magic* (DC 18) also disables the trap. Disrupting or dispelling the enchantment deactivates the trap once activated.

Magic Adhesive. A creature that succeeds on a DC 20 Intelligence (Arcana or Nature) check can identify the adhesive. Once identified, the adhesive can be removed with a successful DC 20 Intelligence (Sleight of Hand) check, or with *dispel magic*. Removing the adhesive deactivates the trap.

Ring of Flame. The Ring of Flame can be extinguished with *dispel magic* (DC 18).

Fire Blast. The Fire Blast is emanating from an arcane glyph in the ceiling, which can be spotted with a successful DC 20 Wisdom (Perception) check. It can be disrupted with *dispel magic* (DC 18).

Flammable Fluid

Hybrid trap (level 17-20, setback, harm)

In the center of this chamber is a hidden *rune of detection*. Walking over the rune triggers the trap; greasy oil covers the floor, spikes shoot up, and a blast of fire ignites the room.

Trigger (Creature Detector). Walking over the rune triggers the trap.

Initiative. The trap acts on initiative 20 and 15.

Active Elements. Flammable Fluid makes grease pour into the chamber, spikes erupt from the floor, and releases a blast of flame.

Oil Slick (Initiative 20). Grease spills out from holes that open along the base of the chamber's walls. The chamber floor becomes difficult terrain, and each creature in the chamber must succeed on a DC 10 Dexterity saving throw or fall prone.

Spikes (Initiative 20). This element activates only once, the first time the trap acts. Spikes erupt from the floor of the chamber. Each creature standing on the chamber floor must make a DC 10 Dexterity saving, throw taking 7 (2d6) piercing damage on a failed save, or half as much on a successful one.

Fire Blast (Initiative 15). This element activates only once, the first time the trap acts. A blast of flame erupts from a nozzle hidden in the ceiling, damaging nearby creatures and igniting the oil-covered floor. Each creature within 15 feet of the *rune of detection* must succeed on a DC 10 Dexterity saving throw, taking 10 (3d6) fire damage on a failed save, or half as much on a successful one.

Dynamic Elements. Oil continues to pour into the chamber, and the fire gets hotter and hotter, becoming more dangerous the longer the trap remains active.

Grease Pump. After it activates, the DC for the saving throw to avoid falling prone due to the Oil Slick element increases by 2.

Fan the Flames. After it activates, the damage dealt by Fire Blast increases by 3 (1d6), to a maximum of 17 (5d6).

Constant Elements. The active elements of the trap affect each creature that ends its turn in the chamber.

Oil Slick. A creature that ends its turn standing on the chamber floor must make a saving throw against the Oil Slick element, at its current DC.

Spikes. A creature that ends its turn standing on the chamber floor takes 7 (2d6) piercing damage from the Spikes.

Fire Blast. Any creature that ends its turn standing on the flaming oil must make a saving throw against the Fire Blast element, at its current DC.

Countermeasures. The trigger and active elements can be thwarted by particular countermeasures.

Trigger. A successful DC 10 Wisdom (Perception) check or *detect magic* reveals the *rune of detection*. Once found, it can be disrupted with a successful DC 10 Intelligence (Arcana) check or casting *dispel magic* on the rune. Once the trigger is disabled, the trap deactivates.

Fire Blast. Any spell or other effect that generates a large quantity of ice, water, or a blast of cold prevents creatures from taking damage from the Fire Blast during the round the effect happens.

Necessary Weevil

Hybrid trap (level 17-20, moderate, harm)

An ornate chandelier hangs from the ceiling of this circular chamber. Any creature that passes directly beneath the chandelier triggers the trap. The doors lock, and spiked chains extend from the chandelier, which begins to spin rapidly. Finally, a beam of magical energy shoots down directly beneath the chandelier. Any creature that enters this beam is transformed into a beetle.

Trigger (Creature Detector). Walking directly beneath the chandelier triggers the trap.

Initiative. The trap acts on initiative 20 and 10.

Active Elements. Necessary Weevil first locks the doors. Chains then extend from the chandelier which starts to spin, and a beam of transmutation magic shoots down from beneath the chandelier.

Locked Doors (Initiative 20). This effect activates only once, the first time the trap acts. The exits and entrances to this room slam shut and are locked in place by magic. Tiny creatures can crawl beneath the door frames.

Flailing Chains (Initiative 20). Chains extend from the chandelier, and it begins to spin rapidly. Each creature within 10 feet of the chamber walls must make a DC 12 Dexterity saving throw, taking 17 (5d6) slashing damage on a failed save, or half as much damage on a successful one. Tiny creatures are unaffected.

Transmutation (Initiative 10). This effect activates only once, the first time the trap acts. A beam of transmutation magic energy shoots down from the chandelier. Each creature in the 5-foot square beneath the chandelier must succeed on a DC 12 Wisdom saving throw or be transformed into a beetle (use the statistics for a **frog** statistics) for 1 hour. This effect ends if dispelled (*dispel magic* DC 18), or if the creature drops to 0 hit points or dies, and it doesn't work on a shapechanger or a creature with 0 hit points.

A transformed creature's game statistics, including mental ability scores, are replaced by the statistics of the beast it transforms into. It retains its alignment and personality. The creature assumes the hit points of its new form. When it reverts to its normal form, the creature returns to the number of hit points it had before it transformed. If it reverts as a result of dropping to 0 hit points, any excess damage carries over to its normal form. As long as the excess damage doesn't reduce the creature's normal form to 0 hit points, it isn't knocked unconscious.

A transformed creature is limited in the actions it can perform by the nature of its new form, and it can't speak, cast spells, or take any other action that requires hands or speech. The creature's gear melds into the new form. It can't activate, use, wield, or otherwise benefit from any of its equipment.

Dynamic Elements. The chandelier spins ever faster, becoming more dangerous the longer the trap remains active.

Increased Speed. After it activates, the damage from the Flailing Chains increases by 10 (3d6). While its damage is 35 (10d6) or greater, it acts on initiative 20 and 10.

Constant Elements. The Flailing Chains and Transmutation affect each creature that ends its turn in an area affected by these elements.

Flailing Chains. A creature that ends its turn within 10 feet of the chamber walls must make a saving throw against the Flailing Chains effect.

Transmutation. A creature that ends its turn directly beneath the chandelier must make a saving throw against the Transmutation effect.

Countermeasures. The trap's trigger and active elements can each be thwarted by particular countermeasures.

Trigger. The chandelier has an aura of transmutation magic when viewed with *detect magic*, and a creature that gets close enough to it can find arcane symbols on the chandelier with successful DC 12 Wisdom (Perception) check. The chandelier can be disabled with a successful DC 12 Intelligence (Arcana) check, or with *dispel magic* (DC 18). Disabling the chandelier deactivates the trap.

Open the Doors. The doors' lock has been enhanced with *arcane lock*, which can be found with *detect magic*. As an action, a creature can pick the lock on the doors with a successful DC 22 Dexterity check using thieves' tools. The doors can be pushed open as an action with a successful DC 22 Strength check.

Flailing Chains. Characters can pull down the chains, damage the chandelier components, or discern how to avoid the chains. The chains are disabled if the Dexterity saving throw DC made to avoid them is reduced below 5. Ways to do that are described below.

Intelligence (Investigation), DC 12. As an action, a creature that can see the chains can attempt an Intelligence (Investigation) check. A successful check means that the creature has learned how to anticipate the chains' movements, giving them advantage on the next Dexterity saving throw made by the creature to avoid the chains while they aren't incapacitated.

Strength, DC 12. A creature in the area can ready a Strength check to pull down a chain as it passes by. The creature has disadvantage on its next Dexterity saving throw made to avoid the chans. The creature then makes the check. On a success, the chain is destroyed. Destroying a chain reduces the Flailing Chains saving throw DC by 2.

Dexterity check using thieves' tools, DC 12. Creatures can use thieves' tools within 5 feet of the chandelier to foil its mechanism. A successful check reduces the Flailing Chains saving throw DC by 2.

Transmutation. As an action, a spellcaster directly beneath the chandelier can disrupt the beam of transmutation magic with a successful DC 12 spellcasting ability check; *dispel magic* (DC 18) also disables this element.

Storm's Run

Hybrid trap (level 17-20, dangerous, hinder)

The trap is set in a 200-foot long corridor. Stepping on a pressure plate at the start of the corridor releases a bolt of lightning, aimed at the triggering creature, from the far end of the corridor. A thunderous boom echoes throughout the corridor, potentially deafening the creatures.

Trigger. Applying weight to the pressure plate triggers the trap.

Initiative. The trap acts on initiative 20, 15 and 10.

Active Elements. Bolts of lightning shoot down the corridor from the far end. A thunderous boom erupts, knocking back and deafening creatures.

Lightning Bolt (Initiative 20). A stroke of lightning forming a line 100 feet long and 5 feet wide blasts hurtles from the far end of the corridor to the entrance. Each creature in the area must make a DC 15 Dexterity saving throw, taking 35 (10d6) lightning damage on a failed save, or half as much damage on a successful one.

Thunderclap (Initiative 15). A booming thunderclap fills the corridor. Each creature in the corridor takes 17 (5d6) thunder damage and must succeed on a DC 15 Strength saving throw or be pushed 30 feet back toward the corridor's entrance.

Deafening Echoes (Initiative 10). The echoes of the thunderclap resound through the corridor, reaching deafening volumes. Each creature in the corridor that can hear the echoes must succeed on a DC 15 Constitution saving throw or become deafened. A creature remains deafened for 1 minute after they leave the corridor.

Dynamic Elements. The echoing of the thunderclap gets worse with each successive blast.

Bursting Eardrums. After the Deafening Echoes activates, the saving throw DC to resist being deafened increases by 2.

Countermeasures. The trap's trigger can be thwarted by particular countermeasures. The active elements of the trap end when creatures leave the corridor through the door at the far end, which is locked.

Trigger (Sensitive). A successful DC 15 Wisdom (Perception) check reveals the pressure plate, and a successful DC 15 Dexterity check while using thieves' tools disables the trap. Unfortunately, disabling the pressure plate after the trap is active doesn't deactivate it.

Leave the Corridor. Leaving the corridor through the far end deactivates the trap. The door at the far end of the corridor is locked. It can be unlocked over 3 rounds with the following ability checks, each of which takes an action.

- **Round 1.** A successful DC 15 Wisdom (Perception) check to locate the locking mechanism.
- **Round 2.** A successful DC 15 Intelligence (Arcana) check to understand the workings of the lock.
- **Round 3.** A successful DC 15 Dexterity check using thieves' tools to unlock the door.

Free Falling

Complex trap (level 17-20, perilous, harm)

This chamber has an ornate, tiled mosaic on the floor which depicts spiralling portals. Stepping on one of the mosaic portals triggers the trap, which opens real portals below the triggering creature and above it. The trap also conjures a wall of blades between the two portals.

Trigger (Creature Detector). Stepping onto one of the mosaic portals on the floor triggers the trap.

Initiative. The trap acts on initiative 20.

Active Elements. Free Falling opens two linked portals and summons a wall of blades.

Portals (Initiative 20). This effect activates only once, the first time the trap acts. A portal appears directly above and below the triggering creature, 10 feet apart. The portals remain active until dispelled or otherwise deactivated. The triggering creature must succeed on a DC 17 Dexterity saving throw or be trapped in a loop, falling from one portal to the other.

Wall of Blades (Initiative 20). A horizontal wall of whirling, razor-sharp blades made of magical energy appears between the two portals. The wall is 20 feet square and 5 feet thick.

Dynamic Elements. The longer the trap remains active, the more dangerous it becomes.

Terminal Velocity. Each turn the trap remains active, the creature falling through the portals speeds up. Their falling speed is equal to the number of rounds the trap has been active. A creature falls through the Wall of Blades at more and more points in a round depending on their falling speed, as shown in the table below.

Falling Speed	*Enters Wall of Blades on...*
1	Initiative 20
2	Initiative 20 and 10
3	Initiative 20, 15, and 10
4	Initiative 20, 15, 10, and 5
5	Initiative 20, 15, 10, 5, and 0

Constant Elements. The Wall of Blades damages creatures that pass through it.

Wall of Blades. When a creature enters the wall's area for the first time on a turn or starts its turn there, the creature must make a DC 17 Dexterity saving throw. On a failed save, the creature takes 33 (6d10) slashing damage. On a successful save, the creature takes half as much damage.

Countermeasures. The trap's trigger and active elements can be thwarted by particular countermeasures.

Trigger. A creature that succeeds on a DC 17 Intelligence (Arcana) check or recognizes the mosaics and understands the danger they hide. The mosaics also have an aura of conjuration and evocation magic when viewed with *detect magic*.

A spellcaster can disrupt the enchantment on the mosaics with a successful DC 17 spellcasting ability check; *dispel magic* (DC 19) cast on the mosaics also disables the trap.

Portals. Once activated, faint arcane symbols surround each portal. As an action, a creature can examine the runes and successfully disrupt their function with a successful DC 17 Intelligence (Arcana) check, closing one portal. Alternatively, a portal can be closed with *dispel magic* (DC 19). Closing a portal reduces the falling speed of a creature caught between them by 1.

If one of the portals is closed, the other remains open. This means that a creature falling between them slams into the floor, taking bludgeoning damage equal to their falling speed multiplied by 7 (2d6).

Wall of Blades. The whirling blades can be disrupted, attacked, or dispelled. The Wall of Blades vanishes if its damage is reduced to 0 (0d10). Ways to do that are described below.

Spellcasting ability check, DC 17. As an action, a creature that can see the Wall of Blades can attempt a spellcasting ability check to disrupt the magic that sustains it. On a success, the wall's damage is reduced by 5 (1d10).

Attack. A creature within 5 feet of the Wall of Blades can attack it: the wall has AC 17. On a hit, the blade barrier is partially disrupted, and its damage is reduced by 5 (1d10).

Dispel magic, DC 17. A successful casting of *dispel magic* reduces the blade barrier's damage by 11 (2d10).

Melting Pot

Complex trap (level 17-20, deadly, harm)

A creature that brings a spellcasting focus into this chamber triggers the trap. An obsidian monolith in the center of the chamber emits a petrifying aura, and boulders begin flying around the chamber, smashing into creatures. Finally, acid bubbles up from the chamber floor; both the boulders and acid have potentially catastrophic effects for petrified creatures.

Trigger (Bring Object). Bringing a spellcasting focus into the chamber triggers the trap.

Initiative. The trap acts on initiative 20, 15, and 10.

Active Elements. Melting Pot creates an aura of petrification magic, animates boulders that fly in circles around the chamber, and makes acid seep up through the floor.

Aura of Petrification (Initiative 20). A wave of petrification magic sweeps out from the monolith. Each creature within 60 feet of the central monolith must make a DC 20 Constitution saving throw. On a failed save, creatures are restrained as their flesh begins to harden. On a successful save, a creature isn't affected.

Animated Boulders (Initiative 15). Boulders surrounding the monolith animate, and fly around the chamber in circles. Each creature in the chamber must make a DC 20 Dexterity saving throw, taking 17 (5d6) bludgeoning damage on a failed save, or half as much damage on a successful one.

If a petrified creature takes more than 50 damage in a single turn from a boulder, one random limb is smashed to pieces. A creature reduced to 0 hit points by damage from this source is obliterated. An obliterated creature and everything it is wearing or carrying, except magic items, are reduced to a pile of broken stone. The creature can be restored to life only by *true resurrection* or *wish*.

Seeping Acid (Initiative 10). Corrosive acid bubbles up from the chamber floor. Each creature standing on the floor of the chamber must make a DC 20 Constitution saving throw, taking 17 (5d6) acid damage on a failed save, or half as much damage on a successful one.

If a petrified creature is reduced to 0 hit points by damage from the acid, it melts. A melted creature and everything it is wearing, except magic items, are reduced to slurry. The creature can be restored to life only by *true resurrection* or a *wish*.

Dynamic Elements. Each of the trap's active elements becomes more dangerous the longer the trap remains active. The boulders speed up and the acid becomes more corrosive.

Boulders Accelerate. After it activates, the damage from Animated Boulders increases by 7 (2d6), to a maximum of 87 (25d6). While its damage is 35 (10d6) or greater, this element acts on initiative 15 and 10.

Corrosion Concentrates. After its turn, the damage from Seeping Acid increasing by 7 (2d6), to a maximum of 87 (25d6).

Constant Elements. The trap's active elements affect each creature that ends its turn in an area affected by these elements.

Aura of Petrification. A creature restrained by this element must make a DC 20 Constitution saving throw at the end of each of its turns. If it successfully saves against this effect three times, the effect ends for that creature. If it fails its save three times, it is turned into a stone statue and is petrified. The successes and failures don't need to be consecutive; keep track of both until the creature collects three of a kind.

For each affected creature, this effect lasts until dispelled, either with *dispel magic* (DC 19) or *greater restoration*, or when the monolith is destroyed. If a creature is physically broken while petrified, it suffers from similar deformities if it reverts to its original state.

If a creature successfully saves against this element three times, they are immune to it for 1 hour.

Animated Boulders. Any creature that ends its turn within the chamber must make a saving throw against the Animated Boulders effect.

Seeping Acid. Any creature that ends its turn standing on the floor of the chamber must make a saving throw against the Seeping Acid effect.

Countermeasures. The trigger and active elements of the trap can each be thwarted by particular countermeasures.

Trigger (Difficult). A successful DC 20 Intelligence (Arcana) check reveals the negating symbols covering the monolith, alerting a creature to the trap. The monolith has an aura of transmutation magic when viewed with *detect magic*. A successful DC 20 Intelligence (Investigation) check allows a creature to find the right symbols to deface with a successful DC 20 Intelligence (Arcana) check, disabling the trap. A successful *dispel magic* (DC 20) spell cast on the monolith also disables the trap.

Animated Boulders. A creature who takes the Dodge action can make their next saving throw against the Animated Boulders with advantage.

Monolith. The trap can be deactivated only be destroying the monolith, which also restores all creatures it has turned to stone, ending the petrified effect on them. Ways to destroy the monolith are described below.

Attack. A character can attack the monolith. It has AC 20; 250 hit points; resistance to bludgeoning, piercing, and slashing damage from non-magical weapons; and immunity to acid, poison, and psychic damage.

Dispel Magic, DC 19. Casting *dispel magic* on the monolith deals 25 damage to the monolith.

Spellcasting ability check, DC 20. As an action, a spellcaster can disrupt the enchantment on the monolith with a successful DC 20 spellcasting ability check, dealing 25 damage to it.

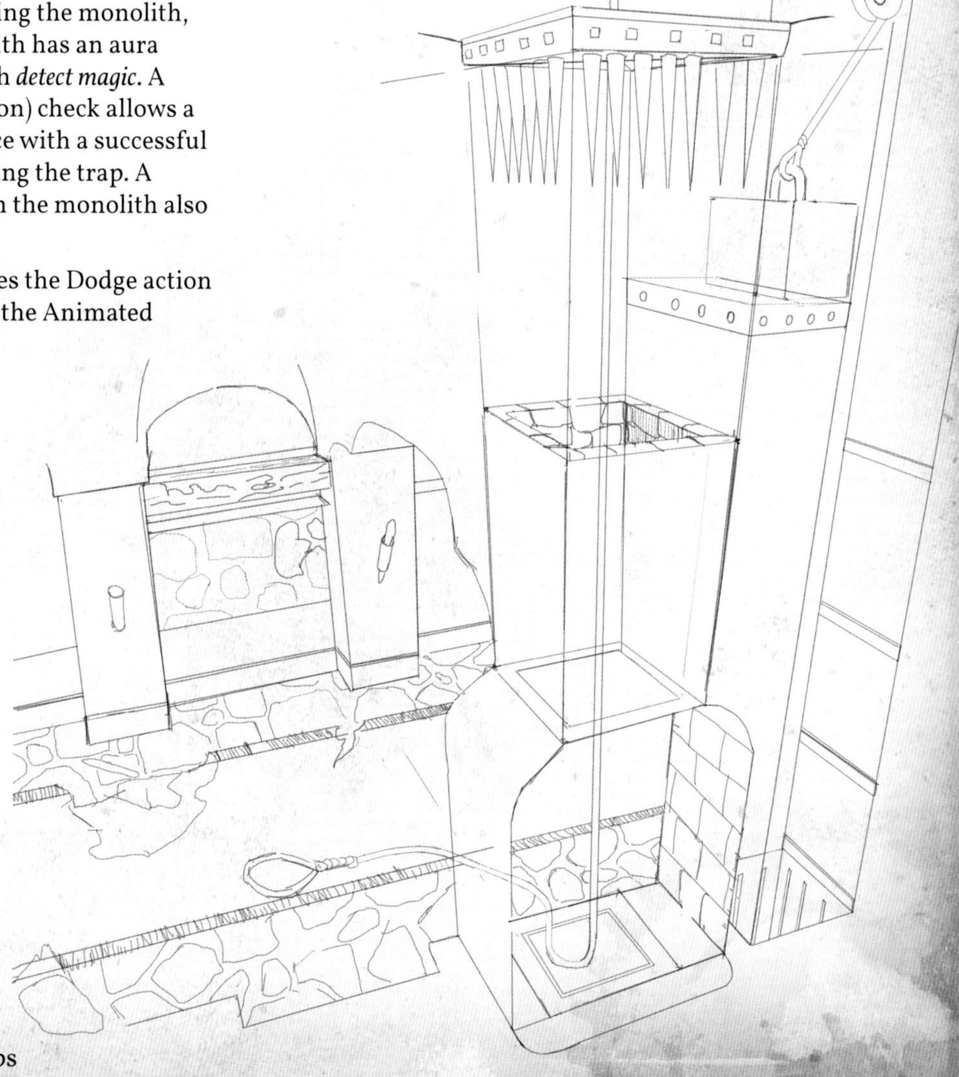

Designing Traps

When designing your traps, consider what your adventure needs. If the dungeon has a particular theme, such as snakes, then perhaps the traps poison their targets or release monstrous snake creatures. If the dungeon has an acid theme then the traps could blast creatures with acid, release oozes, or drop creatures into pools of acid.

Before you start designing your trap, it is important to ask yourself some questions to help give yourself a clear understanding of what you need to accomplish with it. Here are some to get you started:

- Should the trap be complex or simple?
- Who or what is creating this trap?
- How is it powered?
- Why is it needed in this particular spot?
- How do those that live or work in the area get around it?
- What experience do you want the players, not their characters, to have when they reach it?
    - Should this be a quick or lengthy encounter?
    - Will the method for overcoming the trap be readily apparent when they reach the trap, or will they have an opportunity to learn about it beforehand?
- What is the trap mechanically supposed to accomplish?
    - Actually killing characters?
    - Getting characters to use up resources such as spells or abilities prior to a big encounter?
    - Eating up time?
    - Setting the mood or conveying plot details?
    - If the trap takes more resources from the characters than intended, how will things likely go for them once they get through? Will there be an area and/or resources that allow for recovery, or will they simply have to cope with the setback?
    - Could this kill the entire party? If it does, how will you deal with that?

Answering questions like these will help to set you on a firm footing and give you a clear vision of what your trap needs to do and how it needs to do it. It will also help you decide on the trap's severity.

When selecting and implementing traps, think about who is building these traps, how sophisticated they are, and why they were built in the first place. For example, a troop of goblins in the forest are likely to have many nets, snares, and poison darts set up to capture or kill their prey. On the other hand, a group of cultists trying to protect the relics in their deity's temple could have traps designed to blast intruders with elemental magic, fatally wound them with scything blades, or crush them to death with closing walls.

The space a trap occupies matters in terms of how things physically fit together. If a dungeon is built into a hill, but the internal ceiling of the dungeon is just below ground level outside, things that rise up into the ceiling would stick out of the ground above. Creatures walking along would certainly wonder about a large, random-seeming portcullis sticking up out of an otherwise picturesque grassy hillside.

The Purpose of Traps

Traps are obstacles for the characters to overcome. When planning a trap, consider whether or not you want the characters to find it. A trap that the characters are likely to find with ability checks or spells makes them expend resources overcoming the trap, as well as providing an interesting and exciting challenge.

A trap that the characters shouldn't be able to find, usually because the DC to spot it is very high, can provide a nasty surprise. It could serve as a warning that the characters aren't prepared to enter a specific area, or it can be something they stumble into to further the plot of the story you are telling.

However, don't keep a trap hidden or make it extremely hard to find when it would certainly kill one or more of the characters or make it impossible for them to achieve their goal. The characters should have a fair chance to spot a trap that deadly and have a good shot at avoiding its effects. The point of such a trap is not, in fact, to kill anyone or to derail the adventure; it's to confront characters with a life-or-death, win-or-lose challenge that they must overcome. Realizing that everything is on the line has a wonderfully clarifying effect. To paraphrase Winston Churchill, "nothing in life is so exhilarating as being shot at and missed!"

It is always your responsibility as the GM to be prepared for the worst-case scenario when players encounter any traps you use or create. With this thought process as a guide, you can design traps that are not only clever and devious, but that also further the plot and heighten excitement.

Characters Building Traps

At some point, your player characters may wish to build their own traps in your campaign. There are many ways to handle this scenario, and many details to consider.

If a character tries to build a trap in the middle of a game, try to glean from the player what they're hoping the trap will accomplish. Then, consult Chapter 9 and use the Random Trap Generator to determine what trap trigger and effect would best suit their trap. If a player asks about this outside of the game, you may instead choose to explore this chapter with them and design a trap from the ground up together that best suits their character's needs.

Other things to consider for character-created traps may include how long it takes to set up a trap of that type (digging a pit, rigging a hidden weapon, etc.) and what materials are needed to create the trap. It is up to your discretion as a GM to determine how realistic you wish the character's trap creation experience to be.

Simple Traps

A simple trap usually has a single trigger and a single effect, either of which could be magic or mundane. Simple traps do not reset after they've been triggered.

Complex Traps

A complex trap is any that goes beyond having a single trigger and a single effect. It might be a gauntlet of obstacles, a trap that has multiple phases, or a trap that can be triggered by several different things. The intricacies of building complex traps are addressed in Chapter 7.

Complex Triggers

A simple trigger is typically binary, something that is just on or off, such as a switch or button. A multi-stage trigger, however, is one that goes in phases or that has multiple requirements.

One of the scariest real world traps is a carnivorous plant called the venus fly trap. It catches flies and other small insects when they land on its specially evolved leaves. These leaves have many sensitive hair-like protrusions, and the trap only closes when two different hairs are touched within 20 seconds. This helps the plant avoid false triggers.

A locked door with a swinging log hanging behind it, ready to smash any intruders, is a simple trap. But to keep inhabitants of the dungeon from being pulped, the engineer installed it with a multi-stage trigger. If the lock is disabled with thieves' tools, and if the door is then opened, the trap activates. These measures prevent the trap going off when an unintended target unlocks the door with a key and opens it.

Complex Effects

Pairing two or more trap effects can add complexity to the encounter, especially when one effect restrains or confines characters to one area. A trap that restrains creatures with a net makes it much harder for them to run away from a boulder rolling towards them.

Traps as Plot Devices

Traps should be exciting and memorable moments, not frustrating or boring. Avoid situations where characters have no countermeasures against a trap; make them engaging or interesting, not just a way to drain resources. Traps can provide information about the area, take characters to parts of a dungeon, or give clues about the owner or creator of a structure.

Some traps may be detectable, but require characters to have prior knowledge of their existence or some specific piece of information to bypass them or disable them. A successful Intelligence (History, Nature, or Religion) check, depending on the context, can all provide these kinds of clues. The DC for these checks is based on the trap's severity.

For example, if the characters are in a dungeon of some evil antagonist where countless other heroes have lost their lives, there is likely to be some information about the dungeon written down in books. An Intelligence (History) check may be appropriate to reveal clues about possible magical triggers they may find (if anyone got out, able to tell the tale). While exploring the crypt of a long dead and once powerful paladin, searching for an ancient relic, an Intelligence (Religion) check might reveal information about the tomb's defenses.

Even if these checks don't give details about the traps themselves, they may give clues about those who might have set them, or important information that could be creatively applied to the situation.

Traps can provide information even after they've been activated. Finding evidence of triggered traps — such as corpses, burns, rubble, or blood — can let characters know to be wary or that someone else is after the same thing they are.

Level and Lethality

The overall difficulty or threat your trap can pose to characters is a combination of two things: the level of the characters encountering it and the trap's lethality.

Level. A trap's level is expressed as one of five ranges: 1-4, 5-8, 9-12, 13-16, and 17-20. An appropriate trap will be in the range that includes the average level of your characters.

Lethality. Variable statistics for a trap such as attack bonus, damage, ability check and saving throw DC's, and spell level all depend on the trap's lethality. A trap intended to be a **setback** is unlikely to seriously harm characters of the indicated levels, but a **moderate** trap likely will. A **dangerous** trap is likely to seriously injure (and potentially kill) characters of the indicated levels and a **perilous** trap almost definitely will. A **deadly** trap is likely to kill characters of the indicated levels.

Always consider the message that traps of various lethalities and their placement can convey to the players. For example, placing a setback trap near the entrance of the dungeon may help to warn the players that there are probably more traps inside. This should tip them off to beware. Placing a dangerous trap at the entrance, however, could tip them off that they might need more supplies, such as *potions of healing*, or let them know that they aren't of an appropriate level for this area. These are just a few ways that traps can be used to set expectations and tone.

Trap Attacks

Traps attack creatures in one of two ways. If a creature's armor is the main or only thing that could defend against the attack, or if the trap is attacking with a small number of separate weapons, the trap rolls an attack roll against the creature's AC. If a trap would make 6 or more attacks in a single turn, creatures should roll a Dexterity saving throw to avoid damage. A creature takes no damage if they succeed and half damage if they fail.

Trap Damage

Not all traps deal damage, but those that do should be designed as an appropriate challenge. Traps deal damage based on their severity, either to a single target with attack rolls or to multiple targets if they make a group of creatures roll a saving throw. The trap can deal its damage all at once or over several rounds, but the maximum damage it deals shouldn't be more than the value indicated for its severity.

Reference Tables

Below are tables for variable game statistics of traps, such as attack bonus and saving throw DC, based on character level and trap lethality. The values in these tables are guidelines; feel free to adjust them as needed.

Trap Attack Bonus and Save DC

The table below shows appropriate DCs and attack bonuses to use depending on the trap's severity.

	Setback	Moderate	Dangerous	Perilous	Deadly
Attack Bonus	+5	+6	+8	+10	+12
DC	10	12	15	17	20

Single Target Trap Damage

The table below shows recommended average damage amounts based on traps that only target a single creature.

Level	Setback	Moderate	Dangerous	Perilous	Deadly
1-4	5 (1d10)	11 (2d10)	16 (3d10)	22 (4d10)	27 (5d10)
5-8	11 (2d10)	22 (4d10)	33 (6d10)	44 (8d10)	55 (10d10)
9-12	16 (3d10)	33 (6d10)	49 (9d10)	66 (12d10)	82 (15d10)
13-16	22 (4d10)	44 (8d10)	66 (12d10)	88 (16d10)	110 (20d10)
17-20	27 (5d10)	55 (10d10)	82 (15d10)	110 (20d10)	137 (25d10)

Multiple Target Trap Damage

The table below shows recommended average damage amounts for a trap that targets more than one creature.

Level	Setback	Moderate	Dangerous	Perilous	Deadly
1-4	3 (1d6)	7 (2d6)	10 (3d6)	14 (4d6)	17 (5d6)
5-8	7 (2d6)	14 (4d6)	21 (6d6)	28 (8d6)	35 (10d6)
9-12	10 (3d6)	21 (6d6)	31 (9d6)	42 (12d6)	52 (15d6)
13-16	14 (4d6)	28 (8d6)	42 (12d6)	56 (16d6)	70 (20d6)
17-20	17 (5d6)	35 (10d6)	52 (15d6)	70 (20d6)	87 (25d6)

Trap Spell Level

All magic traps have a spell-like effect of some kind. Use the table below to determine the spell level for the trap, which may be important for spells like *dispel magic*.

Level	Setback	Moderate	Dangerous	Perilous	Deadly
1-4	Cantrip	Cantrip	1st	1st	2nd
5-8	1st	2nd	3rd	4th	5th
9-12	2nd	3rd	4th	5th	6th
13-16	4th	5th	6th	7th	8th
17-20	7th	8th	9th	9th+3rd	9th+5th

Trap Creature CR

If a trap releases or summons creatures, use the table below to determine the CR of the creatures and how many the trap can create. This table is just a general guideline; feel free to adjust the trap depending on your needs.

Level	Setback	Moderate	Dangerous	Perilous	Deadly
1-4	Two CR 1/8	Two CR 1/4	Four CR 1/8	Four CR 1/4	Two CR 1/2
5-8	Four CR 1/2	Eight CR 1/4	One CR 2	Two CR 2	One CR 5
9-12	Eight CR 1/4	One CR 2	Two CR 2	One CR 5	One CR 6
13-16	One CR 2	One CR 5	One CR 6	Four CR 2	Two CR 5
17-20	Two CR 5	Two CR 6	Three CR 5	Three CR 6	One CR 7

Trap Duration

Most traps have an instantaneous effect; they deal damage or drop a creature into a pit. But some traps, especially magical ones, have spell effects with a duration. If the duration isn't specified in its description, use the table below to determine the length of the duration, based on character level and severity of the trap.

In most cases, a trap effect with a set duration can be removed with a spell like *dispel magic*, *remove curse*, *lesser restoration*, *greater restoration*, or more powerful magic. An effect with a permanent duration can only be removed with *greater restoration*, or something more powerful like *wish*. Spells that can remove a trap effect with a duration are listed in their descriptions.

Level	Setback	Moderate	Dangerous	Perilous	Deadly
1-4	1 minute	1 minute	1 minute	5 minutes	10 minutes
5-8	1 minute	1 minute	5 minutes	10 minutes	1 hour
9-12	10 minutes	1 hour	8 hours	8 hours	1 day
13-16	10 minutes	8 hours	8 hours	1 day	1 day
17-20	1 day	1 day	permanent	permanent	permanent

Experience Rewards for Traps

Traps do not have a CR, like creatures, but if you feel it is appropriate to award experience for overcoming traps you can use the values in the table below. If awarding experience points for traps would adversely affect the overall pacing or balance of your campaign, don't do it. Maintaining a good flow is far more important than ensuring that every task or challenge the characters overcome has a numerical value.

All suggested rewards presented below, both for simple and complex traps, are for a group, not for each character individually.

Simple Trap Experience Rewards

Level	Setback	Moderate	Dangerous	Perilous	Deadly
1-4	50	75	100	150	200
5-8	550	825	1100	1650	2200
9-12	1200	1800	2400	3600	4800
13-16	2550	3825	5100	7650	10200
17-20	4400	6600	8800	13200	17600

Complex Trap Experience Rewards

Level	Setback	Moderate	Dangerous	Perilous	Deadly
1-4	125	200	250	375	500
5-8	1250	1875	2500	3750	5500
9-12	2750	4125	5500	8000	12000
13-16	5500	8250	11000	17000	25500
17-20	10000	14625	19500	29500	44000

Random Trap Generator

Over time, all GMs develop habits. When we need ideas our favorites come back again and again, until our dungeons and adventures start falling into familiar patterns. Random tables are powerful tools to help break those patterns, because they force us to incorporate elements or combinations that wouldn't spring to mind naturally.

In this chapter, you will find a set of tables for the two crucial parts of a trap: a trigger and an effect. The table doesn't do all of the work for you, but it does generate a concept. You can then flesh out the idea by deciding what the exact details of the trigger and effect are, how they work together, and how they fit into the space where they're found. You can use these tables to generate a trap on the fly, but they function best when you have time to consider all the possibilities and ramifications. Create a few traps in advance so that you have some options for just the right situation.

The table contains 50 unique triggers and 50 unique effects. You can roll a d100 two times, using the first result to determine your trigger, and the second to determine your effect. You can also choose a combination of trigger and effect from the table, or you can choose one half of the trap and roll randomly for the other.

Unlikely Combinations

Generating traps is not without its idiosyncrasies. Every combination of trigger and effect presented in this section can work together, but some may require a little extra thought.

For example, consider a trap with a mundane trigger and a magic effect, such as a pressure plate that teleports the target to another location. The pressure plate could be in a narrow hallway, with a portal disguised as a mirror. When the target approaches to look into the mirror they step on the pressure plate, which catapults them into the portal.

What about a magic trigger paired with a mundane effect? The target draws their weapon in the trap's range, making it cast *produce flame* on a candle hidden in the ceiling. Just above the candle is a thin rope, from which hangs a jug filled with oil. Once the flame burns through the rope the jug falls to the ground, shattering and releasing the oil. The still burning rope tied to the jug ignites the oil and all creatures within a 20 foot radius are set ablaze.

Trigger and Effect Generation Table

Type	d100	d20/10	Trigger	Page	Effect	Page
Mundane	1-2	1	Attempt to Pick Lock	114	Barrier	123
	3-4	2	Break Object	114	Bolts	123
	5-6	3	Fail to Pick Lock	114	Cage	123
	7-8	4	Interact With Bait	114	Crushing Ceiling/Walls	123
	9-10	5	Make Sound	114	Darts	124
	11-12	6	Move Lever/Press Button	114	Drop	124
	13-14	7	Open/Close Door	115	Falling Objects	125
	15-16	8	Open/Close Chest	115	Falling/Tipping Vessel	125
	17-18	9	Open/Close Object	115	Falling Sand	125
	19-20	10	Pick Lock	115	Impaling Spikes	126
	21-22	11	Pick Up/Shift Object	115	Needle	126
	23-24	12	Pressure Plate	115	Net	126
	25-26	13	Produce Flame	115	Release Creatures	126
	27-28	14	Pull Rope/Chain	115	Rolling Boulder	126
	29-30	15	Remove Barrier	115	Scything Blades	127
	31-32	16	Tapping/Prodding	116	Snare	127
	33-34	17	Tension Cable	116	Spears	127
	35-36	18	Tripwire	116	Spikes	127
	37-38	19	Turn Wheel/Crank	116	Spring Floor	127
	39-40	20	Weight Sensitive Surface	116	Swinging Object	127
Ambiguous	41-42	1	Activate Light Fixture	116	Acid/Slime Blast	128
	43-44	2	Disturb Liquid	116	Adhesive	128
	45-46	3	False Trigger	116	Animated Object	128
	47-48	4	Musical/Auditory	117	Blindness	128
	49-50	5	Open/Close Book	117	Deafness	129
	51-52	6	Remove Object	117	Elemental Blast	129
	53-54	7	Step Into Light/Darkness	117	Exhaustion	129
	55-56	8	Touch Object	117	Molten Metal	129
	57-58	9	Use Wrong Key	117	Poison Gas	130
	59-60	10	Wrong Combination	117	Wall of Fire	130
Magic	61-62	1	Activate Rune	118	Aging	130
	63-64	2	Bring Object	118	Amnesia	130
	65-66	3	Cast Spell	118	Bewitchment	131
	67-68	4	Command Word	118	*Dispel Magic*	131
	69-70	5	Corpse	118	Fear	131
	71-72	6	Creature Detector	118	Heat Metal	131
	73-74	7	*Detect Magic*	118	Invisibility	131
	75-76	8	Draw Weapon	119	Petrification	132
	77-78	9	Fail to Speak Password	119	Reanimate Creatures	132
	79-80	10	Insult Idol	119	Restraint	132
	81-82	11	Look Into	119	Seeming	132
	83-84	12	Mortal Sacrifice	119	Sleep	133
	85-86	13	Offering	119	Spell Effect	133
	87-88	14	Pass Area	120	Suggestion	133
	89-90	15	Pass Threshold	120	Summon Creatures	133
	91-92	16	Produce Light/Darkness	120	Swap	133
	93-94	17	Read Writing	120	Teleport	134
	95-96	18	Speak Trigger Word	120	Transmutation	134
	97-98	19	Spill Blood	120	Wall of Force	134
	99-100	20	Unconsciousness	120	Wild Magic	135

Triggers

The best way to be safe from any trap is to notice its trigger and avoid it, which isn't always easy or even possible. No trap should be both impossible to find and impossible to avoid or mitigate. It may, however, be one or the other. If it's easy to find, then it's fair to severely punish creatures who don't find it by making the saving throw difficult or not allowing one at all. If a trap is impossible to find or to bypass, then there should be a way to mitigate or negate the damage entirely.

Always think about triggers in specific, real-world terms, not just dice rolls. You want to be able to describe in detail what characters see or feel as they explore. Consider all the senses. Sight and sound are common descriptors, but smell, taste, and texture can help set the scene as well.

Trigger Types

Trap triggers come in three different forms: mundane, ambiguous, and magic. Each kind of trigger says something about the purpose of the trap and how best to use it.

Mundane Triggers

Mundane triggers are triggers without a magic component. They usually have some sort of mechanical apparatus — like clockwork, gears, or water pressure — but they can also be as simple as a floor tile that breaks away when enough weight is applied.

Ambiguous Triggers

Ambiguous triggers could be mundane, magic, or a combination of both. The Wrong Key trigger, for example, might be a key of the wrong shape or size or it might be the right shape key that hasn't been enchanted properly. One option is mundane while the other is magic.

Magic Triggers

Magic triggers have far fewer limitations. They can be simple or complex, but they often include a hint of mysticism. A glyph that activates when a creature gets close enough is the classic example. There could be a magic trip wire that activates the trap or an *alarm* spell that detects intruders and then activates the trap.

Detecting Triggers

Detecting a trigger of any kind usually requires a Wisdom (Perception) check. Magic triggers can also be found with an Intelligence (Arcana) check, but this doesn't let a creature sense the presence of magic. That's what *detect magic* is for. An Intelligence (Arcana) check represents a creature recognizing some arcane symbols or recalling a piece of lore about an object or area. Once discovered, an Intelligence (Investigation) check can be used to conduct a thorough examination of the trap trigger and deduce how to best to disable it.

There may be times when it may seem more appropriate to use a non-standard check, such as Dexterity (Perception) if something requires a particularly deft touch.

Passive Checks

Always be aware of a creature's passive Perception (10 + the creature's Wisdom/Intelligence modifier + any bonuses, such as proficiency) and compare it to the relevant DCs for any trap they're approaching. If a creature's passive Perception equals or exceeds the DC to detect the trigger, the creature automatically detects it and can try to disable it.

Triggers with the **difficult** trait require an active Intelligence (Investigation) check to understand how they work and how they can be disabled.

Difficult. A trigger with this trait is more complex than usual. Once a creature detects the trigger, they must make a successful Intelligence (Investigation) check to understand how it works. If the check fails, the creature cannot disable the trigger because they do not understand what they have found. A creature can attempt to understand a difficult trap again after completing a long rest.

Disabling Triggers

Identifying a trigger is one thing, but disabling it is another. Mundane triggers usually require a successful Dexterity check using thieves' tools, while disabling magic triggers usually requires a successful Intelligence (Arcana) check or a successful use of *dispel magic*. Ambiguous triggers can require either option.

Most of the time, there's no drawback to failing to disable a trap, but if the trigger has the **sensitive** trait it could be disastrous if the check is particularly low.

Sensitive. Failing to disable a sensitive trigger may result in accidentally setting off the trap. Traps of **setback** and **moderate** lethality are triggered on failed disable checks totaling 5 or less. **Dangerous**, **perilous**, and **deadly** traps are triggered on failed disable checks totaling 10 or less.

Sometimes triggers can be bypassed instead of disabled. Using *silence* to get past a trap triggered by sound bypasses the trap, but it hasn't been disabled. If creatures make sound near that trigger later on, without the protection of the spell, the trap can still activate.

Countermeasure DCs

Refer to the table below when determining the DC for detecting and disabling triggers based on the lethality of the trap.

Lethality	*DC*
Setback	10
Moderate	12
Dangerous	15
Perilous	17
Deadly	20

Trigger Details

Detailed descriptions of each type of trigger are presented below, along with suggestions regarding how the trigger might best be used. Common countermeasures are also provided. By no means are these the only possible options, just the most common.

To make any of these triggers more challenging, you can add the difficult or sensitive trait.

Mundane Triggers

These triggers are primarily mechanical and don't have any magical component. Gears, levers, weights, springs, or other mechanical devices might be involved in the design of the trigger.

Countermeasures. A successful Wisdom (Perception) check reveals a mundane trigger and a successful Dexterity check using thieves' tools disables it. Mundane triggers that operate differently have their countermeasures noted in their descriptions.

Attempt to Pick Lock

The trigger is built into a lock and attempting to pick it triggers the trap. Using a key on the lock will not trigger the trap. This is one of the most common triggers and is a useful deterrent almost anywhere.

Break Object

Breaking an object such as a glass case, crystal vial, or magic gem triggers the trap.

Fail to Pick Lock

Failing an attempt to pick a lock triggers the trap.

Interact With Bait

An object that would pique interest has been placed out in the open and interacting with it triggers the trap. This might be a corpse or object out of its normal place. The object may or may not show evidence of the trap's nature, such as being shot full of darts, or sliced cleanly in half. If the object does have evidence like this it could be intended to deceive potential victims.

Countermeasures. A successful Wisdom (Perception) check reveals the trigger. A successful Dexterity (Sleight of Hand) check allows a creature to interact with the bait without activating the trigger, while a successful Dexterity check made with thieves' tools disables the trigger.

Make Sound

Any sound above a certain level triggers the trap. Creatures must make an effort to be stealthy, and some creatures may not make enough sound to trigger the trap due to flying or other forms of movement.

Countermeasures (Difficult). A successful Wisdom (Perception) check reveals the trigger. Creatures who move or perform actions in the trapped area must make a successful Dexterity (Stealth) check each round to avoid triggering the trap. A successful Intelligence (Investigation) check reveals the nature of the trigger, and allows a creature to attempt a Dexterity check using thieves' tools check to disable it.

Creative characters can use other ways of muffling sound, like casting *silence* on a creature or area, to bypass this trigger.

Move Lever/Press Button

Moving a lever or pressing a button triggers the trap. Depending on the trap, pressing the button or moving the lever again might deactivate the trap once triggered.

WHAT DOES THIS DO?

Multiple levers or buttons quickly turns a simple trap into a complex one. A natural instinct is to test each lever to assess what they all do and how to deal with the trap. Consider ensuring that there are clues in the area of the trap, or make sure characters have a chance to learn about the trap prior to encountering it.

Open/Close Door

Opening or closing a door triggers the trap. Locating these types of triggers is often difficult because the mechanism can be completely hidden on the other side of the door or part of the door itself. Note that this trigger is not something attached to the door; that would be a Tension Cable trigger.

Countermeasures (Difficult). A successful Wisdom (Perception) check reveals the trigger. A successful Intelligence (Investigation) check while examining the door reveals the nature of the trigger, and allows a creature to attempt a Dexterity check using thieves' tools to disable it.

Sawing, burning, or smashing a hole through the door without letting it swing open could bypass this trigger. Using a ranged spell to blow the door off the hinges could also allow creatures to trigger the trap while avoiding its effects.

Open/Close Chest

Opening or closing a chest triggers the trap. Locating this type of trigger is often difficult because the mechanism can be completely hidden within the chest, or part of one or more of the chest's components. Note that this trigger is not something attached to the chest; that would be a Tension Cable trigger.

Open/Close Object

Opening or closing an object may flip a hidden switch, make gears mesh, or act as a mundane trigger in any number of other ways. If an object can be opened or closed — whether with a door, shutter, stopper, or anything else — then it can be trapped. Objects such as a cabinet, a drawer, or book, an oil lamp with a door, or a mechanical eye could all be good candidates for this trigger.

Pick Lock

Picking a lock triggers the trap. This may include attempting to subvert the lock in a way that does not involve using the correct key.

Countermeasures (Difficult). A successful Wisdom (Perception) check lets a creature detect the trigger, and a successful Intelligence (Investigate) check lets it understand the trigger. The trigger can be disabled by successfully picking the lock with a Dexterity check using thieves' tools that exceeds the lock DC by 5 or more.

Pick Up/Shift Object

Picking up or moving an object triggers the trap. The trap could be hidden behind an object or it could be resting on a pressure plate that triggers the trap.

Countermeasures. A successful Wisdom (Perception) check reveals the trigger, and a successful Dexterity check using thieves' tools disables it.

To bypass the trigger, a creature can attempt to replace the object with one of equal weight. The creature must make a successful Intelligence (Perception) check to accurately estimate the weight of the object and a successful Dexterity (Sleight of Hand) check to switch the objects. Failure on either roll activates the trap.

Pressure Plate

Applying weight to the pressure plate triggers the trap. It's possible to avoid the plate by simply jumping over it or putting something across it. The pressure plate could be set into a wall and triggered when someone leans against it or places a steadying hand on it. It could also be at a spot that's hard to search or to avoid, such as on the far side of a 15-foot chasm that creatures are likely to leap across.

Some pressure plates activate only after they have been depressed and then released. Hopefully, a creature that steps onto the plate has companions who can figure out a way to deactivate the trap or negate its effects.

Produce Flame

The presence of flame triggers the trap. Usually this is due to light or heat sensitive mold or fungi in range of the trigger. Bait is important with this kind of trigger. Something such as faint writing etched into the wall of a dark room or cave entices creatures to bring the flame closer.

Countermeasures. A successful Wisdom (Perception) check reveals that a nearby surface is reacting to the presence of the flame. A successful Intelligence (Nature) check disables the trigger.

Pull Rope/Chain

Pulling on a rope, chain, or hanging line of some sort triggers the trap. This could be a rope or chain a creature needs to climb or slide down. It might even be a rope tossed around a rock or other handy projection with the trigger built in.

A rope or chain hanging from an upper level is the perfect opportunity to tie a jug of something nasty to the other end. When pulled, the jug comes down and explodes in tar, fire, poisonous gas, or some other horrible thing.

Countermeasures. A successful Wisdom (Perception) check reveals the trigger, and a successful Dexterity (Sleight of Hand) check disables it.

Remove Barrier

Removal of a barrier triggers the trap. Barriers can be as large as a portcullis or as small as a drain stopper. This trigger could be a stone in the ceiling, wall, or floor that when removed allows water, sand, oil, or some other material into a chamber.

TOO VALUABLE TO LEAVE

The characters find a wondrous crystal orb set onto a pedestal in the middle of the room. It's purpose isn't immediately apparent, but they know it has to be valuable. They don't detect any curse on it so someone picks it up. Within moments, a tube blocked by the orb begins spewing a black, poisonous vapor into the room.

Tapping/Prodding

Applying pressure to a specific spot via tapping or prodding triggers the trap. Rapping on walls or tapping on the floor with a pole are such common methods for finding traps and secret doors that trap builders often take advantage of them.

Countermeasures. A successful Wisdom (Perception) check reveals the trigger. A successful Dexterity (Sleight of Hand) check allows a creature to tap or prod without activating the trigger, while a successful Dexterity check made with thieves' tools disables it.

Tension Cable

A wire, rope, or other line connects an object to the trap. The trap triggers when the tension cable is pulled or goes slack.

Tripwire

A wire, rope, or other line is strung across a high traffic area. Breaking or sufficiently disturbing the line triggers the trap. Often used for traps with external mechanisms, the wire can also be connected to a complicated network of components hidden in a wall or removed area.

Turn Wheel/Crank

Turning a wheel or crank in a certain direction, or turning it to or past a certain point, triggers the trap. A wheel or crank is usually used with opening or closing something, raising or lowering gates, drawbridges, or powering some other mechanical tasks. Accompanying their normal function with a trap trigger turns a seemingly innocuous device into a potentially deadly encounter.

TRAPPED LIKE RATS!

The characters find a heavy portcullis blocking their way. None of them can lift it, but they do find a crank mechanism to raise it. The strongest among them spends several minutes raising the portcullis, then uses a latch built into the crank to lock it. The characters move onward, but a few minutes later they hear a loud thud as the portcullis comes crashing back down. What they didn't realize is that the crank also wound a timed release on the latch and now they are trapped on the other side of the portcullis.

Weight Sensitive Surface

Placing or removing weight on the surface triggers the trap. A weight sensitive surface is a more sensitive version of a pressure plate, and is often used in larger applications. The surface could be a 5-foot by 5-foot square on the floor, or the floor's entire area.

Ambiguous Triggers

These triggers can be magical or not, depending on the situation. A book with a needle hidden in the spine that is on a spring-loaded release is a mundane combination of the Open/Close trigger and a Needle effect.

However, if the book was enchanted to trigger when opened, that would be a magical version of the Open/Close trigger.

Countermeasures

Unless noted otherwise, If a trigger is mundane, a successful Wisdom (Perception) check reveals it, and a successful Dexterity check using thieves' tools disables it.

If a trigger is magic, a successful Wisdom (Perception) check, Intelligence (Arcana) check, or *detect magic* reveals it. A successful Intelligence (Arcana) check or *dispel magic* disables the trigger.

A magic version of an ambiguous trigger is usually the equivalent of a 3rd level abjuration spell for interactions with *detect magic* and *dispel magic*.

Activate Light Fixture

Lighting or dousing a light fixture triggers the trap. A wall sconce with a torch or a lantern is hard for a creature with no darkvision to resist. This could also be an orb with a *continual flame* spell, activated by touch or a command word.

Disturb Liquid

A pool or fountain can be dangerous for any number of reasons: filled with poisonous liquid, the home of a dangerous creature, the trigger for a trap. This trigger can be effective on a pool or basin with gems or valuable items at the bottom. Some trivial amount of disturbance might still be safe; a creature might be able to remove items from the pool as long as they don't make too many ripples.

False Trigger

Some other trigger left out in the open, such as an undisguised pressure plate, can be the perfect bait. Physically or magically interacting with this false trigger is what actually sets off the trap. A creature may get clues to the nature of the true trigger while attempting to disable the false one.

Musical/Auditory

Making a particular sound, or the absence of a sound, triggers the trap. The trigger could be tied entirely to a musical instrument and activated if the object is played in a specific area. Or the trigger could be activated by failing to play the instrument. Other sounds, like speaking or smashing rocks together, could also be triggers.

Countermeasures. If mundane, a successful Wisdom (Perception) check reveals the trigger and a successful Intelligence (History) check gives insight to the required sound. If magic, a successful Wisdom (Perception) check, Intelligence (Arcana) check, or casting *detect magic* reveals the nature of the trigger. A successful Intelligence (Arcana) check or *dispel magic* disables it.

Open/Close Book

Opening or closing a particular book triggers the trap. A creature examining a massive tome on a pedestal or opening a dusty old book they found on a bookshelf can activate this trigger.

Remove Object

Removing a particular object from a certain area triggers the trap. This can be as specific as removing a gem from its ring or as broad as removing a treasure horde from a dungeon.

Step Into Light/Darkness

Moving from light into darkness, darkness into light, breaking a beam of light, casting a shadow onto a particular surface, or standing between a light source and an object triggers the trap.

Countermeasures. If mundane, a successful Wisdom (Perception) check reveals the trigger and a successful Dexterity (Acrobatics or Stealth) check bypasses it. If magical, a successful Wisdom (Perception), Intelligence (Arcana) check, or casting *detect magic* reveals the trigger. A successful Intelligence (Arcana) check or *dispel magic* disables it.

Depending on the nature of the trigger, spells like *daylight* or *darkness* could also serve to disable either a magical or mundane version.

Touch Object

Touching a particular object triggers the trap. There may be parameters that determine who or what may or may not touch the object. These criteria can be as broad or specific as necessary, including race, alignment, gender, spellcasting ability, religious affiliation, or class. Wearing gloves or using something else to touch the object might bypass the trigger instead of disabling it.

Use Wrong Key

Using an incorrect key triggers the trap. Turn the key the wrong way, clockwise instead of counter-clockwise, could also trigger this trap.

Wrong Combination

Combinations can be used for almost anything. They can lock doors or chests, lower bridges, activate portals. Inputs could be nearly anything as well, such as pulling on chains, ropes, levers, pushing buttons, using particular spell components in a certain order, spelling a word backward, or even doing dance steps. The important thing is to consider what correct combination the trap engineer decided on, why they decided on that combination, and why they determined that someone should be seriously penalized for getting it wrong.

In the event that someone who knows the combination is held hostage and forced to enter it, entering the wrong combination might give them the upper hand. If the trap's effect targets the creature entering the combination, the hostage could position themselves in such a way as to avoid the attack, harm their captors and attempt an escape.

COMBO-PUZZLES

When it comes to solving combination puzzles,characters should never be faced with a combination that they could not know by the time they reach it. You could place hints along the way, hide the combination in the room, or use an NPC to tell them the answer cryptically, etc. Just remember that barring progress with a combination that the characters have no way of knowing is frustrating. Arbitrarily pushing buttons or pulling ropes isn't fun, especially if the characters are being punished with traps for each failure.

Magic Triggers

Something that couldn't be achieved by a mechanical process, such as determining when a creature of a specific race enters a room, is probably a magic trigger. Magic triggers are often glyphs or runes of some kind, scribed onto the surface of a wall or object near the trapped area. They can also be crystals, orbs, plants, suits of armor, or something easy to hide in the area. When creating a trap with a magic trigger, it's usually better to have some object or glyph as the trigger since that gives a fixed point for determining range and other parameters of the effect.

Unless otherwise noted, a successful Wisdom (Perception) check or casting *detect magic* reveals a magic trigger. Magic triggers can also be found with an Intelligence (Arcana) check, but this represents a creature recognizing an object or area from their knowledge of magic; it's not a replacement for *detect magic*. A successful Intelligence (Arcana) check or a successful *dispel magic* cast on the trigger disables it.

Detect Magic. Finding magic traps with *detect magic* is usually pretty straightforward, but the spell doesn't reveal the nature of the trigger or what countermeasures might be necessary. *Detect magic* can also be blocked by 1 foot of stone, 1 inch of common metal, a thin sheet of lead, or 3 feet of wood or dirt. In most cases, triggers are abjuration effects.

Dispel Magic. Magic traps of 3rd level or lower are automatically disabled by *detect magic*. For magic triggers of 4th level or higher, the DC required is 10 + the spell's level (or the trigger's spell level equivalent).

The table below shows recommended spell levels for magic traps based on character level and trap lethality. You can use this table to determine the spell level of the trigger for *detect magic* and it's DC for *dispel magic*.

Level	*Setback*	*Moderate*	*Dangerous*	*Perilous*	*Deadly*
1-4	Cantrip	Cantrip	1st	1st	2nd
5-8	1st	2nd	3rd	4th	5th
9-12	2nd	3rd	4th	5th	6th
13-16	4th	5th	6th	7th	8th
17-20	7th	8th	9th	9th	9th

Activate Rune

A *rune of detection* can be activated by simple proximity or it can have more nuanced activation criteria. The rune may be invisible or out in the open. What the rune does may or may not be readily apparent; it may even be beneficial. Whatever effect it has, activating the rune still triggers the trap.

Countermeasures. A *rune of detection* can be found with a successful Wisdom (Perception) check or with *detect magic*. Once found, it can be disabled with *dispel magic* or a successful Intelligence (Arcana) check.

Bring Object

Bringing a specific object or type of object to or past a certain point or area triggers the trap. The object could be something found in the same area as the trap, or something that was brought from further away. This trigger could also be a broad enchantment that triggers if a type of item enters the area such as a weapon, or a set of thieves' tools.

Cast Spell

Casting a spell triggers the trap. The trigger may require a specific spell, or any spell from a specific school of magic, or any spell at all. This type of trigger is especially effective in areas or chambers where creatures are likely to be attacked and will cast spells during combat.

Command Word

Using anything that requires a command word triggers the trap. Creatures can use magic weapons, armor, potions, scrolls, and similar items that don't rely on command words with no risk, unless those items have extra powers that are triggered on command.

Corpse

Bringing a corpse into an area triggers the trap. The trigger might only activate if the corpse is of a creature from a specific race or type.

Creature Detector

A creature of a certain type or with certain qualities entering the detector's range triggers the trap. Such qualities can include type, race, class, alignment, age, or gender. This is especially useful for organizations made up of a particular race and alignment, such as a cult of evil elves. They might set up the trigger to activate if it detects a creature of any other race and alignment.

Detect Magic

The presence of an active *detect magic* spell within a certain area, whether cast in that area or active already, triggers the trap. This is a good trigger to combine with other triggers, especially in an area where *detect magic* would usually see use, like a treasure vault. Note that *detect magic* will reveal this trigger, but it will also set off the trap.

Draw Weapon

Unsheathing a weapon within a specified area triggers the trap. Carrying the specific weapon out and ready for use into the area can also trigger the trap. Drawing the weapon out of an object (anvil, stone, block of wood, etc.) or removing it from being submerged in something could also trigger the trap.

Fail to Speak Password

Failure to speak a certain password within a predetermined amount of time triggers the trap. Another trap trigger such as a pressure plate, tripwire, lever, or button might be rendered safe by uttering a special word or phrase. The trigger could be deactivated only for a short time or only for the person who said the password. The password can be hidden somewhere in the room, revealed by a puzzle, or hinted at in legends or rumors.

Insult Idol

Doing something that would be insulting or distasteful to a deity or otherworldly being while in the presence of an effigy or representation of it triggers the trap. Desecrating an idol or blaspheming against a deity in its shrine might trigger a trap. Ignoring an idol or failing to present an offering may also be considered an insult and trigger the trap.

Countermeasures. A successful Wisdom (Perception) check, Intelligence (Arcana) or (Religion) check, or casting *detect magic* reveals the nature of the trigger. Another successful Intelligence (Arcana) check or a successful *dispel magic* cast on the idol disables it.

Performing specific rites or obeisances can bypass the trap as well.

Look Into

Looking into an object, opening, or material triggers the trap. A magic mirror could trap the viewer or swap them for an evil twin. Looking into a pool of water could cause a creature to become charmed. A creature looking into the eyes of a portrait or the jeweled eyes of a statue could be possessed or charmed. Alternatively, simply seeing the reflection of a rune or glyph in a mirror may be enough to trigger a trap.

Mortal Sacrifice

Killing a creature in a specific area or way triggers the trap. Alternatively, sacrificing the wrong creature, or performing the sacrifice incorrectly, triggers the trap.

Countermeasures. A successful Wisdom (Perception) check, Intelligence (Arcana, History, or Religion) check, or casting *detect magic* reveals the nature of the trigger. Another successful Intelligence (Arcana) check or a successful *dispel magic* cast on the trigger disables it.

THE OL' SWITCHEROO

The wizard was invisible and down to his last spell. After the rest of his companions had been killed and their bodies thrown into the basilisk pit, the cultists resumed the ritual. What the high priest had failed to notice was that his precious snake-tooth dagger was not the genuine article. In the commotion, the wizard had swiped it with mage hand, replacing the real dagger with a simple one enhanced by an illusion. The priest raised the dagger over his head as the ritual reached its climax, then plunged it into the heart of his victim. Suddenly the room began to shake. For a moment the cultists thought they had succeeded in summoning the great serpent from his slumber, but as the ceiling began to collapse, the priest knew that something was terribly wrong. The cultists tried to run, but a massive stone fell and blocked their escape. The wizard dodged boulder after boulder and just as there was nowhere left to go, he cast teleport to make his escape.

Offering

Placing an offering in a vessel triggers the trap. Alternatively, the trigger may be activated if the wrong offering is given, if no offering is given, or if existing offerings are taken from the vessel. Vessels may be plates, vases, wishing wells, fountains, bowls, baskets or any other container capable of receiving items.

Offerings are typically coins, precious metals, gems, magic items or anything of value, though the specifics of what is needed can vary greatly and could certainly be odd, strange, or even humorous. Offerings can also be ephemeral things like a memory or a story instead of physical objects.

Countermeasures. A successful Wisdom (Perception) check or Intelligence (Religion) check reveals the nature of the trigger. A successful *dispel magic* cast on the trigger disables it.

Giving the correct offering or leaving existing offerings as they are bypasses the trap.

Pass Area

Moving into or through an area triggers the trap. This could be triggered by anyone, or only by creatures that meet certain criteria (such as "good-aligned creatures," "elves," or "anyone who *isn't* a goblin").

> **DO NOT PASS THE SEAL**
>
> The characters enter a large room with multiple exits on the near side and a beautifully decorated dragon shrine on the far side. On the floor, in the exact center of the room, is a beautiful mosaic seal of a dragon with ruby eyes and outstretched wings. Referring to his books, the wizard finds a passage about the shrine. "Only the worthy may approach." he reads. Hearing this, the paladin, self-righteous and bombastic, strides forward across the seal to approach the shrine. Suddenly, the entire room begins to shake and rumble. The wizard turns to the fighter, saying "he is not worthy..."

Pass Threshold

Crossing the threshold of a door, entryway, exit, or archway triggers the trap. The trigger could be part of the doorway itself, of just part of the transition from one area to another.

> **THE GUARDS ARE DEAD**
>
> A powerful necromancer has filled his labyrinth with undead minions, and set alarm traps at every major junction. The characters watch the undead minions pass through the main corridor and formulate a plan. Waiting for the most opportune moment, they spring into action, making a break for it through the main corridor. To their dismay they immediately set off a series of bells, chimes, and gongs. Wave after wave of undead minions attack the puzzled group, who had no idea that the necromancer's traps were set to only detect living creatures.

Produce Light/Darkness

Creating light or darkness within a certain area triggers the trap. Magical or non-magical means of creating light or darkness can both trigger the trap.

Read Writing

When a creature reads aloud certain writing it triggers the trap. The writing may be in a book or scroll, carved above a doorway, or etched into the blade of a sword.

Speak Trigger Word

Uttering a particular word or phrase in the area triggers the trap. The trigger word or phrase might be something common that creatures are likely to speak without prompting, or it could be found on a nearby surface in an attempt to trick them into saying it aloud.

A successful Wisdom (Insight) check or Intelligence (Investigation) check reveals any clues in the area or helps creatures to deduce what the trigger word might be.

Spill Blood

The spilling of blood within the area triggers the trap. Alternatively, the enchantment could be placed on a weapon or powerful artifact that the characters will use in combat.

This trigger is especially effective when used in an area where a fight is likely to break out. It also fits as a deterrent if used in a place focused on peace, where the overseers might openly inform guests as to what will happen (or perhaps just that something will happen) if blood is spilled.

Unconsciousness

A creature being unconscious in a particular area triggers the trap. This area can be a single room, a collection of rooms, or an entire dungeon.

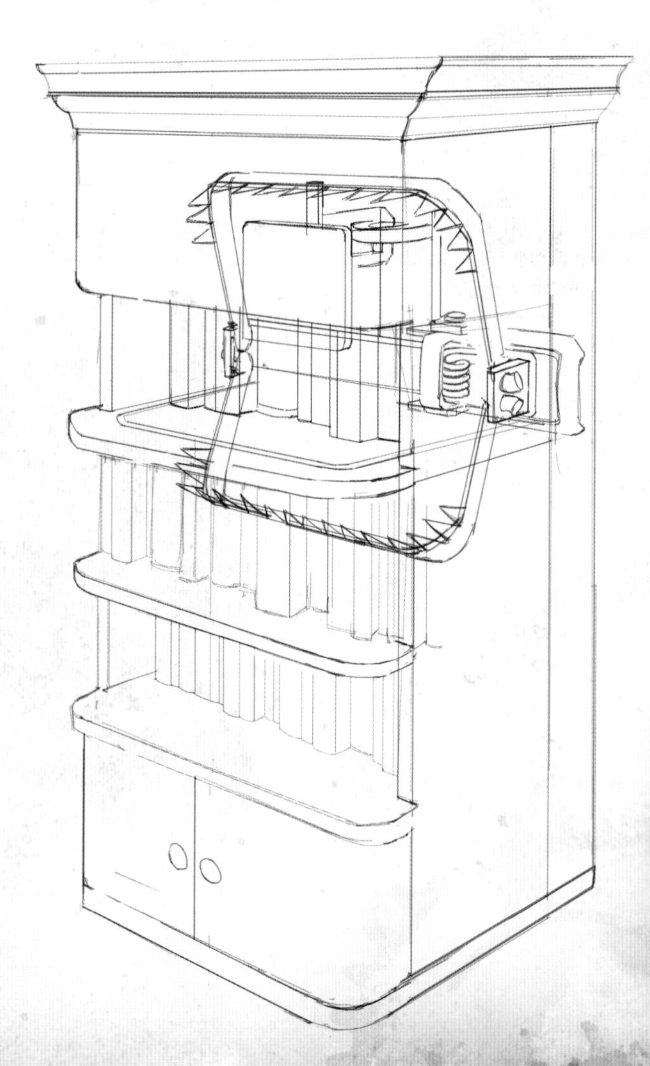

Effects

These are the parts of the trap that eviscerate, immolate, maim, poison, puncture and otherwise really mess up creatures. That is, unless they find ways to avoid them.

Effects can be used in many clever ways. Consider placing an effect so that it targets someone other than the creature who triggered the trap. Whether it's a pit that opens 15 feet behind a pressure plate or a flame jet that engulfs every portion of a room except the 5-foot space containing a chest, shifting the effect away from the trigger provides a nasty surprise and makes some countermeasures less effective or even more dangerous.

Effects can be magic or mundane, depending on what works best for the trap and the nature of the effect. A Ring of Flame effect may be a flammable liquid, or it could be a *wall of flame* spell. A set of spears thrusting out from the passage wall could be as simple as it sounds, or they could be an illusion that deals psychic damage. Always think about the setting and what fits your campaign.

Trap Effect Reference Tables

For trap effects that deal damage, use the tables below to determine the outcome based on character level and trap severity. This damage may be dealt in one round, or it may be dealt over multiple rounds.

Not all traps use a d10 damage die; that's just a baseline average for how much damage the effect should deal. For example, if several darts shoot at a level 10 character, and the trap is dangerous, the attack should deal around 49 damage on average. This means if each dart is dealing 1d4 damage, there will be around 20 darts involved in this one trap.

Trap Attack Bonus and Save DC

Use these values if the trap is making attack rolls against creatures or for any ability checks or saving throws the trap requires.

	Setback	*Moderate*	*Dangerous*	*Perilous*	*Deadly*
Attack Bonus	+5	+6	+8	+10	+12
DC	10	12	15	17	20

Single Target Trap Damage

The table below shows recommended average damage amounts based on traps that only target a single creature.

Level	*Setback*	*Moderate*	*Dangerous*	*Perilous*	*Deadly*
1-4	5 (1d10)	11 (2d10)	16 (3d10)	22 (4d10)	27 (5d10)
5-8	11 (2d10)	22 (4d10)	33 (6d10)	44 (8d10)	55 (10d10)
9-12	16 (3d10)	33 (6d10)	49 (9d10)	66 (12d10)	82 (12d10)
13-16	22 (4d10)	44 (8d10)	66 (12d10)	88 (16d10)	110 (20d10)
17-20	27 (5d10)	55 (10d10)	82 (15d10)	110 (20d10)	137 (25d10)

Multiple Target Trap Damage

The table below shows recommended average damage amounts for a trap that targets more than one creature.

Level	*Setback*	*Moderate*	*Dangerous*	*Perilous*	*Deadly*
1-4	3 (1d6)	7 (2d6)	10 (3d6)	14 (4d6)	17 (5d6)
5-8	7 (2d6)	14 (4d6)	21 (6d6)	28 (8d6)	35 (10d6)
9-12	10 (3d6)	21 (6d6)	31 (9d6)	42 (12d6)	52 (15d6)
13-16	14 (4d6)	28 (8d6)	42 (12d6)	56 (16d6)	70 (20d6)
17-20	17 (5d6)	35 (10d6)	52 (15d6)	70 (20d6)	87 (25d6)

Trap Spell Level

All magic traps have a spell-like effect of some kind. Use the table below to determine the spell level for the trap, which may be important for spells like *dispel magic*.

Level	Setback	Moderate	Dangerous	Perilous	Deadly
1-4	Cantrip	Cantrip	1st	1st	2nd
5-8	1st	2nd	3rd	4th	5th
9-12	2nd	3rd	4th	5th	6th
13-16	4th	5th	6th	7th	8th
17-20	7th	8th	9th	9th + 3rd	9th + 5th

Trap Creature CR

If the effect releases or summons creatures, use the table below to determine the CR of the creatures and how many the trap can create. This table is just a general guideline; feel free to adjust the trap depending on your needs.

Level	Setback	Moderate	Dangerous	Perilous	Deadly
1-4	Two CR 1/8	Two CR 1/4	Four CR 1/8	Four CR 1/4	Two CR 1/2
5-8	Four CR 1/2	Eight CR 1/4	One CR 2	Two CR 2	One CR 5
9-12	Eight CR 1/4	One CR 2	Two CR 2	One CR 5	One CR 6
13-16	One CR 2	One CR 5	One CR 6	Four CR 2	Two CR 5
17-20	Two CR 5	Two CR 6	Three CR 5	Three CR 6	One CR 7

Trap Duration

Most effects have an instantaneous effect; they deal damage or drop a creature into a pit. But some traps, especially magical ones, have spell effects with a duration. If the duration isn't specified in its description, use the table below to determine the length of the duration, based on character level and severity of the trap.

In most cases, a trap effect with a set duration can be removed with a spell like *dispel magic, remove curse, lesser restoration, greater restoration*, or more powerful magic. An effect with a permanent duration can only be removed with *greater restoration*, or something more powerful like *wish*. Spells that can remove a trap effect with a duration are listed in their descriptions.

Level	Setback	Moderate	Dangerous	Perilous	Deadly
1-4	1 minute	1 minute	1 minute	5 minutes	10 minutes
5-8	1 minute	1 minute	5 minutes	10 minutes	1 hour
9-12	10 minutes	1 hour	8 hours	8 hours	1 day
13-16	10 minutes	8 hours	8 hours	1 day	1 day
17-20	1 day	1 day	permanent	permanent	permanent

Effect Details

Detailed descriptions of each type of effect (mundane, ambiguous, and magic) are provided below. Each effect is presented with a description of how it is intended to function and some suggestions for how the effect might best be used. The effect's mechanics are listed, explaining how the trap affects creatures.

Many of these effects refer to creatures within the trap's area or within range of the trap. A trap's specific range or area of effect is up to you, but should be mostly determined by its location and severity. A trap in a 20-foot square room that is only a setback might just target 1 creature or 1 5-foot square; if the trap is perilous it might affect the entire room.

Spell Trap

Some ambiguous effects and most magic effects presented below could be a *symbol* spell or a spell trap version of *glyph of warding*, each of which have specific rules for how its effects resolve. These rules supercede the general rules for trap effects. A trap effect that could be a *glyph of warding* or *symbol* is designated with the **spell trap** trait.

Spell traps have a more fixed severity than other effects, due to the level of the stored spell. A spell trap storing *prismatic spray* is always going to be at least 7th level spell slot, making at minimum a perilous trap for 13th-16th level characters. To allow for more flexibility, we've provided two versions of effects with the spell trap trait; one that is a *glyph of warding (spell trap)* and one that isn't. You can use whichever version best suits your needs.

Mundane Effects

Similar to their trigger counterparts, mundane effects are primarily mechanical or, at the very least, lacking any magical component. Any locomotion is due to machinery, gravity, or naturally generated exertion (such as a goblin riding a bicycle in order to power a rotating pinwheel of death).

Barrier

A barrier can be a portcullis, a stone slab, wooden timbers, or other device designed to block a passageway. A barrier can also be placed cleverly as a way to split up groups of creatures.

Effect. Once triggered, any creatures in the path of the barrier must make a Dexterity saving throw. A creature that fails takes full damage from the trap (usually bludgeoning), or only half damage on a success.

Possible ways to get past the barrier might include a successful Strength (Athletics) check to lift or catch the barrier or a successful Intelligence (Investigation) check to determine how or if it can be dismantled.

Bolts

A hidden crossbow, or an array of crossbows, is set to fire when the trigger is activated. Usually they are carefully hidden behind a wall, on the ceiling, or otherwise hidden out of sight.

Effect. The trap makes one attack roll against a creature in range for each bolt set to fire. The number of bolts should be enough to deal the trap's damage based on its severity, and each bolt deals piercing damage.

Combining this effect with another can produce a trap with flaming bolts that deal additional fire or acid damage.

Cage

A wooden or metal cage drops down onto creatures in the area, or in some cases walls suddenly spring up from the floor. Alternatively, creatures could fall into a locking chest or box.

Effect. Creatures in the area of the trap must succeed on a Dexterity saving throw or be trapped in the cage. If the cage is merely heavy but has no floor, a successful Strength (Athletics) check will lift it.

If the cage is locked, a successful Dexterity check while using thieves' tools will unlock it.

Crushing Ceiling/Walls

The ceiling or walls are designed to slowly crush creatures to death. Once the surfaces reach a creature's space, they start to take damage. This effect can be used in most indoor spaces, such as rooms or corridors, and often includes a barrier to prevent escape.

The trap's speed is variable; at the speed listed below, it takes 1 minute (10 rounds) to move 10 feet. If the ceiling starts at 10 feet up, it will reach most Medium creatures within 5 rounds. If you decide to alter the speed, make sure that the characters have time to attempt to stop or avoid the walls.

This effect also works wondrously in terms of dramatic tension. The walls are a natural countdown, and combining this with descriptions of sounds as the space closes can be incredibly engaging.

Effect. The moving surfaces move at a rate of 1 foot per round at the end of the initiative order. Once the surface reaches a creature's space, they take 1d10 bludgeoning damage. If the surface is still moving on the next turn, the creature is restrained and takes 2d10 bludgeoning damage. A third round spent being crushed inflicts 4d10 bludgeoning damage, the fourth and every round thereafter inflicts 10d10 bludgeoning damage until the surface retracts.

Most traps of this kind are designed to retract once they reach the opposite wall or floor.

Darts

Darts shoot out of the walls, floor, or ceiling at a nearby area. The darts may be smeared with some sort of poison or enchanted in some way.

Effect. Each creature in the trap's area must make a Dexterity saving throw. A creature that fails takes full piercing damage from the trap, or half as much on a succes.

If the darts are poisoned, creatures that fail their Dexterity saving throw must make a Constitution saving throw or be poisoned for 1 minute.

Drop

Creatures drop into a deep pit with sheer sides dug into the ground or floor. The pit could be empty, spiked, filled with water, an entry to lower floor or area, or the lair of a monster.

Effect. Creatures standing over the drop when the trap is triggered must make a Dexterity saving throw. On a successful save, a creature is able to grab onto the edge of the pit. On a failed save, a creature falls into the pit and takes bludgeoning damage from the fall. Climbing out of a pit usually takes a successful Strength (Athletics) check.

Drops are like pastries; they come in many shapes, sizes, and fillings. A big open pit is easy to spot, but stepping on a pressure plate that causes the floor to collapse is hard to avoid. Concealing a pit with a tarp, trapdoor, debris, or magical illusion is also highly effective.

What happens once a creature reaches the bottom of a drop depends on how far they fell. Most drops deal 1d6 bludgeoning damage per 10 feet fallen (maximum 20d6). If creatures fall into water or if they drop into a slanted chute that slows their fall they might take half the damage or reduce the effective fall distance.

Remember that creatures always land prone when they fall, unless they have a way to negate the damage from the fall. That could be from a Strength (Athletics) or Dexterity (Acrobatics) check against the trap effect's DC, although that might not be possible for all drops.

For a drop with more variety, roll a d10 and consult the table below. Except for the Drop Into Teleporter version, these drops can be either magic or mundane. The maximum damage of this drop is determined by the trap's lethality, which also sets the maximum depth of the drop.

d10	Type of Drop	Effect
1	Empty	Creatures take 1d6 bludgeoning damage for every 10 feet they fall.
2	Spiked	Creatures take 1d6 damage for every 10 feet they fall; half of this damage is bludgeoning and half is piercing.
3	Into water	Creatures take 1d6 bludgeoning damage for every 10 feet they fall after the first 20 feet. A creature in the water can keep it's head clear for a number of minutes equal to 1 + its Constitution score. After that time, the creature starts to suffocate.
4	Into lower level	Creatures take 1d6 bludgeoning damage for every 10 feet they fall, or half that damage if the fall ends in a ramp or slide to ease the landing. The creatures are now in a deeper area or a lower floor than they were previously on.
5	Into lair	Creatures take 1d6 bludgeoning damage for every 10 feet they fall, or half that damage if the fall ends in a ramp or slide to ease the landing. The creatures are now in the lair of a monster.
6	Acid	Creatures take 1d6 damage for every 10 feet they fall; half of this damage is bludgeoning and half is acid. For a more challenging drop, the acid can corrode metal. Any nonmagical weapon or armor that is made of metal that a character is wearing or holding that touches the acid begins to corrode. At the start of each turn in the pit, the following occurs: A weapon takes a permanent and cumulative -1 penalty to damage rolls. If its penalty drops to -5, the weapon is destroyed. Nonmagical ammunition made of metal that touches the acid is destroyed after dealing damage. Armour or shields take a permanent and cumulative -1 penalty to the AC it offers. Armour reduced to an AC of 10 or a shield that drops to a +0 bonus is destroyed.
7	Fire	Creatures take 1d6 damage for every 10 feet they fall; half of this damage is bludgeoning and half is fire.
8	Hidden	The trap's trigger gains the difficult trait.
9	Locking	Creatures take 1d6 bludgeoning damage for every 10 feet they fall. After a creature falls into the pit, the cover snaps shut to trap its victim inside. A successful Strength check is necessary to pry the cover open. The cover can also be smashed open. A creature in the pit can also attempt to disable the spring mechanism from the inside with a Dexterity check using thieves' tools, provided that the mechanism is in its reach and the creature can see it.
10	Teleporting	Creatures that fall into the pit are teleported to another location of the trap designer's choosing. Depending on how the trap is arranged, a creature could take damage from a fall when they arrive in the new location.

DOUBLE SURPRISE

The rogue returned from her scouting mission to report that three rooms ahead there was a small group of goblins on guard duty within a large chamber. They shouldn't put up much resistance, so the barbarian ran in swinging, followed by the fighter and the bard, but the rogue and wizard held back to guard the corridor. The barbarian's heroic slaughter was cut short when the first goblin head was sliced clean off and the floor suddenly fell out from under their feet. The three heroes along with the remaining goblins fell thirty feet down into a pit with a dirt floor littered with bones, broken weapons, and shredded armor. The rogue and wizard stood helpless at the doorway, looking down into the pit. A low pitched rumble turned into a roar as their companions regained their footing and prepared for a real fight.

Falling Objects

Objects are positioned in a high place, ready to fall on a creature that triggers the trap. The ceiling or columns holding up the ceiling collapse and send heavy bricks or stone pieces falling to the floor. This effect is especially powerful as part of the final encounter in a dungeon, adding to the drama and tension of the scene.

Effect. Creatures in the area of the trap must make a Dexterity saving throw. A creature that fails takes full bludgeoning damage from the trap, or half as much on a success. Multiple saving throws may be necessary depending on the size of the area and how far creatures must move to get to safety.

Falling/Tipping Vessel

A falling or tipping vessel might be a jug, bowl, or barrel. Inside might be a combustible substance like oil or high-proof alcohol, or something immediately harmful such as burning acid or a poisonous powder.

Effect. The contents of the vessel are emptied onto a creature or into an area. Avoiding a falling object and its contents always requires a successful Dexterity saving throw. Dealing with the vessel's contents depends on the nature of what's inside.

Splashing liquids can reach nearby creatures, who can avoid being splashed with a successful Dexterity saving throw. Fine powders create a cloud which lingers in the area for a time, which can create a lightly or heavily obscured area. If the powder is poisonous, creatures in the area must make a Constitution saving. A creature that fails takes full poison damage from the trap, or half as much on a success.

Small objects such as ball-bearings or caltrops scatter and remain on the ground after hitting their initial target. Ball-bearings usually cover a level, square area that is 10 feet on a side. A creature moving across the covered area must succeed on a DC 10 Dexterity saving throw or fall prone. A creature moving through the area at half speed doesn't need to make the save.

Caltrops usually cover a square area that is 5 feet on a side. Any creature that enters the area must succeed on a DC 15 Dexterity saving throw or stop moving this turn and take 1 piercing damage. Taking this damage reduces the creature's walking speed by 10 feet until the creature regains at least 1 hit point. A creature moving through the area at half speed doesn't need to make the save.

A vessel could be caught to prevent it's contents from spilling. To catch the vessel, a creature (typically the one who triggered the trap) must make a successful Dexterity save and a successful Strength (Athletics) check.

Falling Sand

Sand or gravel pours into a small area. Unless the space is extremely small, or the volume of sand is massive, this trap takes five or more rounds to complete.

Effect. Creatures in the area must make successful Dexterity saving throws at the beginning of their turns to stay atop the sand. The save DC starts at the base DC for the trap's severity and increases by 2 at the end of each round.

A creature that fails one saving throw is buried up to their knees and restrained. On their next saving throw, if the creature succeeds they dig themselves out and are no longer restrained; if they fail they are buried waist-deep and remain restrained.

A creature buried waist-deep must make a Strength saving throw at the beginning of their turn; if they succeed they dig themselves free of the sand and if they fail they are buried to the neck and immobilized. On their next turn, the creature is completely buried and starts suffocating.

As an action, a creature can dig out another creature with a successful Strength (Athletics) check against the current save DC of the trap. Spells like *freedom of movement* or movement modes like burrow can also allow creatures to freely move through the sand.

Impaling Spikes

A surface such as a ceiling or wall is covered in spikes and moves until it reaches another surface, impaling creatures caught in the middle. The trap's speed is variable and the space between the spikes and opposite wall determines the time available for creatures to react to the trap.

The spikes stick 5 feet out from the wall, so remember to give characters time to avoid or stop the spikes. If the space is a 10-foot room, and the spikes occupy 5 feet of that, the characters would start off in immediate danger. If spikes mounted on a ceiling are smooth, when they retract creatures could slide off and take falling damage as normal.

Effect. The impaling spikes move at a rate of 1 foot per round, always at the end of the initiative order. They keep moving until the spikes touch the opposite surface, at which point they retract. When the spikes enter a creature's space, it must make a Dexterity saving throw. If the creature succeeds they take half damage from the trap, otherwise the creature takes the trap's full damage and is restrained by being impaled on the spikes. Spikes generally deal piercing damage but they could be coated with poison or enchanted as well.

A creature impaled by spikes can free themselves with a Constitution (Athletics) check but not until there is room equivalent to their size available in front of the spikes. Another creature can free an impaled creature with a successful Strength (Medicine) check, as long as there is room. Once the spikes reach the opposite surface, they retract and return to their starting point, releasing any impaled creatures.

Needle

Needles are often used in small mechanisms that require the target to have bare hands to manipulate, such as locks or clockwork devices.

Effect. Needles don't do any damage on their own, so they are usually coated in poison, requiring the triggering creature to make a Constitution saving throw. On a failure, the creature takes full poison damage from the trap, or half damage on a success. Needles can be hollow and deliver some other kind of payload, or enchanted to deal fire or ice damage instead of poison.

Net

A net falls on creatures, either from above or shot from a wall. Most nets are made of hemp or silk rope, but some may be made from much tougher materials such as braided rope, chain, or even wire. Nets of rope can carry strong fumes that could knock a creature out if it fails a Constitution saving throw, leaving it waiting and vulnerable.

Effect. The trap releases a net onto creatures in its area, who must make Dexterity saving throws. A creature that fails is trapped under the net and restrained, and creatures that succeed avoid the net. A creature restrained by the net can use its action to make a Strength check, freeing itself or another creature within its reach on a success.

The net has AC 10 and 20 hit points. Dealing 5 slashing damage to the net (AC 10) destroys a 5-foot-square section of it, freeing any creature trapped in that section. If the net has harmful elements worked into it (blades, barbs, etc) a creature takes half damage from the trap on a failed Strength check to free itself, or no damage on a successful one.

Release Creatures

When the trap is triggered, it releases a creature from a cage or from another chamber. Usually this kind of trap releases a vicious beast ready to attack. However, this could release a captive for the characters to slay so the captor doesn't have to. This could be for convenience, or as an insidious trick.

Effect. The trap releases one or more creatures into the area and they act according to their nature and disposition. See the Creatures table above for suggestions on how many creatures the trap can release and what CR they should be.

If the creatures live in the trapped area, they generally won't leave it and just attack intruders. But if the creatures were imprisoned, they might be more focused on escape.

Rolling Boulder

A massive boulder rolls toward creatures in the area, crushing any who don't move fast enough. Where the boulder starts and how fast it moves determines how much time creatures have to outrun the boulder. An effective use of this trap is if the boulder is easy to outrun but another danger lies ahead, like deep chasm. A rolling boulder coming from behind is a good way to force creatures to run blindly into unexplored hallways where more dangers await.

Effect. When the trap is activated, all creatures present roll initiative as the sphere is released. The sphere rolls initiative with a +8 bonus. On its turn, it moves 60 feet in a straight line. The sphere can move through creatures' spaces, and creatures can move through its space, treating it as difficult terrain.

Whenever the sphere enters a creature's space or a creature enters its space while it's rolling, that creature must succeed on a Dexterity saving throw or take bludgeoning damage and be knocked prone. The sphere stops when it hits a wall or similar barrier. It can't go around corners, but smart dungeon builders incorporate gentle, curving turns into nearby passages that allow the sphere to keep moving.

As an action, a creature within 5 feet of the sphere can attempt to slow it down with a DC 20 Strength check. On a successful check, the sphere's speed is reduced by 15 feet. If the sphere's speed drops to 0, it stops moving and is no longer a threat.

Scything Blades

A single curved blade or multiple curved blades are concealed in the walls, floor, or ceiling. When the trigger is activated, the blades swing out to strike creatures.

Effect. Each creature in the area makes a Dexterity saving throw to evade the attack. Creatures take full slashing damage on a failed save, or half as much on a successful one. On a failed save a creature is also restrained as they are pinned against the opposite wall by the blades.

A creature restrained by the blades can free themselves with a Constitution (Athletics) check or another creature can free them with a Strength (Medicine) check.

Snare

A snare can hold a creature in place, hoist a creature into the air, or drag them into harm's way. A snare can be made from various materials such as rope or vine, which can be cut, or it could be a mechanical device like a bear trap.

Effect. The triggering creature must succeed on a Dexterity saving throw or be restrained until it is freed. If the trap is designed to deal damage when activated, it occurs immediately. Snares generally deal either bludgeoning or piercing damage. A successful Strength (Athletics) or a Dexterity check using thieves' tools frees the creature.

Snares can be designed to further damage a struggling victim; a successful Strength (Medicine) or Constitution (Athletics) check lets a creature avoid further damage if they fail an attempt to escape this kind of snare.

Spears

Spears thrust out from the walls, floor, or ceiling at creatures or into a nearby area. A spear head may be barbed to restrain the target. Depending on the level and severity of the trap, there may be multiple spears. Use the appropriate damage and average on a 1d6 roll to determine how many spear attacks to use. For example if the trap is a level 9-12 Setback with an average of 16 damage, and a 1d6 deals an average of 4 damage, divide 16 by 4 to come up with 4 spear attacks.

Effect. The trap makes one attack roll against creatures in the area for every spear that's activated, dealing piercing damage on a hit. If the spears are barbed, a target wearing cloth or leather armor is skewered and restrained on a hit. Creatures restrained by spears can make Constitution (Athletics) checks to free themselves, taking half damage from the trap if they fail. Other creatures can free those restrained by the spears with a Strength (Medicine) check, again dealing half damage to the restrained creature if they fail.

Spikes

This effect covers spikes attached to a fixed surface, which can be almost anything. Possibilities include part of or the entirety of a floor, wall, or ceiling, compartments within stairs, a wooden block, inside a bowl of punch, etc. If a creature could step on it, run into it, be pushed into it, or otherwise come into contact with it, it can be spiked.

Effect. When a creature moves or is shoved into the spikes it must make a Dexterity saving throw. A creature takes full piercing damage on a failed save or half as much on a successful one.

Spring Floor

The spring floor either launches creatures straight up into the ceiling, or into some other effects such as a pit, scything blades, etc.

Effect. A creature in the trap's area must make a Dexterity saving throw or be launched upwards. Creatures that hit a ceiling or object take 1d6 bludgeoning damage for every 10 feet traveled (max 20d6). Creatures that fall back to the ground take 1d6 bludgeoning damage for every 10 feet they fall (max 20d6) and land prone, unless they avoid damage from the fall.

Swinging Object

An object attached to a rigid structure (such as a wooden or metal rod or beam) or flexible line (such as a rope or chain) swings down from above, into the creatures' path. Containers filled with flammable liquid, or poisonous powders, or an object with spikes on it can all be attached to the swinging line.

Effect. The trap makes an attack against one creature it could hit, unless the object is very large and could hit multiple creatures. Usually the object deals bludgeoning damage, but can just as easily be piercing if the object has spikes, or slashing if it is a wide blade.

Ambiguous Effects

Ambiguous effects can vary widely and could be either magical in origin or some sort of natural phenomenon. A pit could be filled with magically sustained fire, or be situated on a geothermal vent. A water blast could be a magically conjured jet of water, or a geyser.

Acid/Slime Blast

Acid or slime in liquid or ooze form sprays onto creatures. Slime could be highly flammable, poisonous, suffocating, or slick.

Effect. The particulars of this effect depend on the acid or slime itself. An acid effect could be an actual ooze creature, like a **black pudding**, or a spray of caustic chemicals.

If the trap sprays a jet of acid, creatures in the trap's area must make a Dexterity saving throw, taking full acid damage from the trap on a failure or half damage on a success.

Slime can be flammable or slippery, making creatures in the area vulnerable to fire damage or have to succeed on a Dexterity saving throw to avoid falling prone. Slime could also deal poison damage; creatures affected by such a trap must make a Dexterity saving throw. They take full poison damage from the trap on a failed save, or half as much on a success.

Creatures that fail a Dexterity saving throw to avoid the slime could start suffocating instead of taking damage, depending on the viscosity of the slime.

Adhesive

When triggered, the trap applies an adhesive to creatures. The adhesive may take the form of a slime that bubbles out of the floor, a layer of glue hidden under a trapdoor, or an ooze that drips from the ceiling. An interesting situation can occur if there is a chance that escape may mean leaving boots, clothes, or other equipment behind, permanently stuck in the fast-acting glue.

Effect. If the trap releases the glue onto creatures, it makes an attack roll to hit them. Otherwise, creatures in the trap's area or creatures that enter the area make Dexterity saving throws. A creature hit by the trap or that fails their saving throw is restrained.

If restrained by the glue, a creature can pull themselves free with a successful Strength (Athletics) check against the traps' DC. One creature can pull another out of the glue with the same check if they are adjacent to each other.

Animated Object

Nearby inanimate objects unexpectedly spring to life, either with a spell like *animate objects* or with elaborate clockwork mechanisms. By default, objects animate with orders to attack anyone they see, but they could be ordered to simply prevent entry within an area, or might not attack a creature bearing a certain token or object.

Other orders for the objects could include removing creatures' gear, herding them in a particular direction, keeping them from leaving an area, serving them food and drink, bathing them, singing an amusing musical number, cutting the supports of a rope bridge, or assembling the pieces of a golem.

Effect. Whether animated with magic or mechanisms, animated objects have game statistics based on their size as per the *animate objects* spell. The object's hit points and damage might be different due to its material; a suit of armor may have more hit points than a piece of furniture. The objects, once animated, immediately execute the order that was set for them.

Objects remain animate for 1 minute or until reduced to 0 hit points. If the objects were animated with magic, a successful *dispel magic* returns the objects to normal.

Blindness

A flash of extremely bright light or a wave of darkness blinds any creatures in the area. This trap is most effective when coupled with an immediate attack by other elements of the trap, hostile creatures, or some other danger that can take advantage of the blindness.

Effect (Spell Trap). Creatures in the trap's area must succeed on a Constitution saving throw or be blinded for a duration set by the trap's lethality. Creatures can attempt another Constitution saving throw at the end of each of their turns if in combat, or at the end of each minute. On a successful save, this effect ends for that creature. You can adjust the interval between saving throws as needed.

If this effect is magical in nature, it can be dispelled with *dispel magic*, or ended with *remove curse* or *lesser restoration*.

This effect can also create darkness that fills a 15-foot-radius sphere around the triggering creature or an object. The darkness spreads around corners. A creature with darkvision can't see through this darkness, and non-magical light can't illuminate it.

The darkness emanates from the triggering creature or object and moves with it. Completely covering an object with an opaque object, such as a bowl or a helm, blocks the darkness. If any of this effect's area overlaps with an area of light created by a spell of 2nd level or lower, the spell that created the light is dispelled.

As a spell trap (2nd level slot), the glyph casts *blindness/deafness* or *darkness* on the triggering creature.

Deafness

All creatures in the area go deaf due to a magic effect or an incredibly loud noise.

Effect (Spell Trap). Creatures in the trap's area must succeed on a Constitution saving throw or be blinded for a duration set by the trap's lethality. Creatures can attempt another Constitution saving throw at the end of each of their turns if in combat, or at the end of each minute. On a successful save, this effect ends for that creature. You can adjust the interval between saving throws as needed.

If this effect is magical in nature, it can be dispelled with *dispel magic*, or ended with *remove curse* or *lesser restoration.*

As a spell trap (2nd level slot), the glyph casts *blindness/deafness* on the triggering creature.

Elemental Blast

A sudden eruption of fire, lightning, cold, thunder, water, or other elemental force hits creatures in the trap's area.

Effect (Spell Trap). This effect can have many variations, depending on the type of energy or element. It can either make an attack roll if it's targeting a small number of creatures, or it can affect an area and creatures must make Dexterity saving throws to avoid it. Some possible options for this effect are presented below:

Acid Blast. A burst of acid strikes the triggering creature. The trap makes a ranged attack and deals acid damage on a hit, and half the acid damage at the end of the creature's next turn. On a miss, the trap splashes the creature with acid for half as much of the initial damage and no damage at the end of its next turn.

Fire Blast. Creatures affected by the trap must make a Dexterity saving throw. They take full fire damage from the trap on a failed save, or half as much on a success. Creatures that fail their saving throw continue to burn, taking 1d4 fire damage at the start of each of their turns. A creature can end this damage by using its action to make a DC 10 Dexterity check to extinguish the flames.

As a spell trap (2nd level slot), the glyph casts *scorching ray*, targeting all three rays at the triggering creature.

Lightning Blast. Creatures affected by the trap must make a Dexterity saving throw. They take full lightning damage from the trap on a failed save, or half as much on a success.

As a spell trap (3rd level slot), the glyph casts *lightning bolt*, aimed at the triggering creature.

Poison Spray. The triggering creature must make a Constitution saving throw, taking full poison damage on a failed save, or half as much on a successful one.

Thunder Blast. Each creature in a 15-foot cube centered on the triggering creature must make a Constitution saving throw. On a failed save, a creature takes full thunder damage and is pushed 10 feet away from the triggering creature. On a successful save, the creature takes half as much damage and isn't pushed.

As a spell trap (1st level slot), the glyph casts *thunderwave*, centered on the triggering creature.

Water Blast. he trap makes an attack roll against a creature it can affect. If it hits, the trap deals bludgeoning damage and the creature must make a Strength saving throw or be pushed 10 feet away from the trap.

Exhaustion

Creatures in the area begin to suffer from exhaustion due to extremes of temperature or a magical enchantment. The longer they linger, the more levels of exhaustion they endure.

Effect. Creatures in the trap's area must succeed on a Constitution saving throw or gain 1 level of exhaustion. Creatures can attempt another Constitution saving throw at the end of each of their turns if in combat, or at the end of each minute. On a successful save, this effect ends for that creature. You can adjust the interval between saving throws as needed.

If this effect is magical in nature, it can be dispelled with *dispel magic*, or ended *greater restoration.*

Molten Metal

Trenches or channels in the area fill with molten metal when the trap is triggered.

Effect. Creatures in the trenches when they are flooded, or creatures that touch the molten metal for the first time, must make a Constitution saving throw. A creature takes full fire damage on a failed save, or half as much damage on a successful one.

Each creature that ends their turn within 5 feet of a trench filled with molten metal must succeed on a Constitution saving throw or gain 1 level of exhaustion. Creatures wearing heavy armor have disadvantage on their saving throw.

Additionally, when a creature enters a flooded trench, it sinks 1d4+1 feet into the metal and is restrained. If a creature is restrained by molten metal at the start of its turn, it sinks another 1d4 feet. If the creature isn't completely submerged in the molten metal, it can escape as an action by succeeding on a Strength check. The DC is 10 plus the number of feet the creature has sunk into the molten metal. A creature that is completely submerged in molten metal can't breathe.

A creature can pull another creature within its reach out of the molten metal by using its action and succeeding on the Strength check. The DC is the same as above, but the creature helping has advantage.

Poison Gas

The trap triggers an expulsion of poisonous gas into the area. Usually, toxic fumes create a thick cloud with a foul smell and greenish hue. However, an alternative (and especially lethal) version of this effect employs colorless, odorless gas.

Detecting this gas requires a Wisdom (Perception) check with disadvantage. Creatures that succeed recognize the subtle signs of danger, such as hearing the hiss of the gas filling the area.

Effect. A 20-foot-radius sphere of poisonous, yellow-green fog erupts from a point next to the triggering creature. The fog spreads around corners. It lasts for 10 minutes or until strong wind disperses the fog, ending the spell. Its area is heavily obscured.

When a creature enters the fog's area for the first time on a turn or starts its turn there, that creature must make a Constitution saving throw. The creature takes full poison damage from the trap on a failed save, or half as much damage on a successful one.

The fog moves 10 feet away from its starting point at the start of each round, rolling along the surface of the ground. The vapors, being heavier than air, sink to the lowest level of the land, even pouring down openings.

Wall of Fire

The trap triggers a wall of fire that prevents creatures from leaving the area. This could be a *wall of fire* spell, or flame jets built into a surface, or a river of magma. As with other effects the keep creatures in one place, this is most effective when the creatures are simultaneously faced with another danger that may be even worse than the flames.

Effect (Spell Trap). The wall can be up to 60 feet long, 20 feet high, and 1 foot thick, or a ringed wall up to 20 feet in diameter, 20 feet high, and 1 foot thick. The wall is opaque and lasts for 1 minute, although it can be dispelled or disabled earlier. When the wall appears, each creature within its area must make a Dexterity saving throw. On a failed save, a creature takes the trap's full fire damage, or half as much damage on a successful save.

One side of the wall, determined by the trap's designer, deals the trap's fire damage to each creature that ends its turn within 10 feet of that side of the wall. A creature takes the same damage when it enters the wall for the first time on a turn or ends its turn there. The other side of the wall deals no damage.

If the wall is mundane, a creature that is adjacent to the wall can make a Constitution check using thieves' tools to end this effect.

As a spell trap (4th level slot), the glyph casts a ringed wall version of *wall of fire*, centered on the triggering creature.

Magic Effects

Traps with magic effects are clearly wondrous in some way. They either initiate spell effects when activated or they are spells such as *glyph of warding* and *symbol* that function as traps.

Not all magic effects need to be explained by a spell that already exists already. Magic can do nearly anything, so you can come up with your own magic effects to best suit your needs. To prevent complications though, try and do this sparingly and make sure that the effect couldn't be duplicated with a spell. If you do create a custom effect, make sure to give it a spell level appropriate to it's severity and school of magic for interactions with spells like *detect magic* and *dispel magic*.

Aging

All creatures in the area are magically aged, either older or younger.

Effect (Spell Trap). Creatures in the area must succeed on a Constitution saving throw or be magically aged 1d10 years. If the roll is even, creatures are made younger; if odd, creatures become older. The magical aging can be undone with *remove curse* or more powerful magic.

As a spell trap (3rd level slot), the glyph casts *bestow curse* on the triggering creature, inflicting the aging described above as the curse.

Amnesia

A hazy fog fills the mind or creatures in the area, blurring or blocking memories.

Effect. Creatures in the trap's area must make a Wisdom saving throw. Those that fail lose a number of days of memory based on the trap's lethality, as shown in the table below.

Lethality	Number of Days Lost
Setback	2 (1d4)
Moderate	3 (1d6)
Dangerous	4 (1d8)
Perilous	5 (1d10)
Deadly	6 (1d12)

A *remove curse* or *greater restoration* spell cast on a creature that lost memories in this way restores that lost time.

Bewitchment

The victim(s) of the bewitchment are beset by generally bad luck.

Effect. The triggering creatures must succeed on a Charisma saving throw or be cursed by bad luck. When a cursed creature enters a new situation or starts a new encounter, roll a d20 and reference the table below.

This poor luck does **not** extend to dice rolls, inflict status effects, confer advantage or disadvantage, or impact combat in any way. It is intended to impact circumstances, such as extra guards or a poor first impression with an important NPC.

d20	*Bad Luck*
1-2	**Catastrophic.** The circumstance is as bad as it could be. Important NPCs are hostile or the city watch is on high alert for some reason. A serious, time-consuming, or difficult impediment crops up.
3-9	**Terrible.** The circumstance is much worse than it might otherwise be. There are a few additional guards, a moderately difficult complication, or an unfriendly NPC.
10-19	**Unfortunate.** The circumstance is slightly worse than it might otherwise be. There's only 1 or two guards, an indifferent NPC, or a complication that's easy to overcome.
20	**Lifted.** The cloud of bad luck lifts and the creature is no longer cursed.

At the end of each day, a bewitched creature can make a DC 15 Charisma saving throw. If it succeeds, this effect ends for that creature. *Remove curse* or more powerful magic can also end the bewitchment.

Dispel Magic

When triggered, the trap dispels magic on creatures in its area. Trap makers often make use of this kind of trap strip intruders of their protective enchantments.

Effect (Spell Trap). The trap targets each creature in its area with *dispel magic*. The trap uses a spell slot of 3rd level or one determined by its severity, whichever is higher. If the has to make a spellcasting ability check to dispel effects of a level higher than it can automatically end, use its attack bonus as its spellcasting ability modifier.

As a spell trap (3rd level slot), the glyph casts *dispel magic* on the triggering creature.

Fear

The trap generates a terrifying force such as a haunting figure, an evil cackle, or a low pitched rumbling growl.

Effect (Spell Trap). All creatures that can sense the terrifying force must succeed on a Wisdom saving throw or become frightened. A creature frightened this way must take the Dash action and move away from the trap's area by the safest available route on each of its turns, unless there is nowhere to move.

If the creature ends its turn in a location where it doesn't have line of sight to the trap's area, the creature can make a Wisdom saving throw. On a successful save, this effect ends for that creature.

This effect ends for all creatures if dispelled or after 1 minute.

As a spell trap (3rd level slot), the glyph casts *fear* on the triggering creature.

Heat Metal

A manufactured metal object, such as a metal weapon or a suit of heavy or medium metal armor, worn or wielded by the triggering creature glows red-hot.

Effect. Any creature in physical contact with the object takes fire damage from the trap, as per its severity. If a creature is holding or wearing the object and takes the damage from it, the creature must succeed on a Constitution saving throw or drop the object if it can. If it doesn't drop the object, it has disadvantage on attack rolls and ability checks until it does so.

This effect lasts for 1 minute or until dispelled with *dispel magic*.

Invisibility

The trap makes some or all objects or creatures in the area invisible. Depending on the specifics of the trap, it could only affect weapons, armor, hats, boots, or all objects.

Effect. The objects targeted by the trap become invisible. If a target object is being worn or carried by a creature, that creature can make a Constitution saving throw. On a successful save, the targeted object doesn't become invisible.

If this effect targets a creature, it must make a Constitution saving throw or become invisible. Anything the creature is wearing or carrying is invisible as long as it is on the target's person.

This effect lasts for a duration determined by its lethality, or until dispelled with *dispel magic*.

Petrification

The trap turns creatures into stone, salt, wood, crystal, or some other solid material.

Effect (Spell Trap). Creatures in the trap's area must make a Constitution saving throw. On a failed save, creatures are restrained as their flesh begins to harden. On a successful save, the creature isn't affected. A creature restrained by this effect must make a Constitution saving throw at the end of each of its turns. If it successfully saves against this effect three times, the effect ends for that creature. If it fails its save three times, it is turned into a statue of some solid material and petrified. The successes and failures don't need to be consecutive; keep track of both until the creature collects three of a kind.

For each affected creature, this effect lasts until dispelled, either with *dispel magic* or *greater restoration*, or after a certain amount of time, depending on the effect's lethality. If a creature is physically broken while petrified, it suffers from similar deformities if it reverts to its original state.

As a spell trap (6th level slot), the glyph casts *flesh to stone* on the triggering creature.

Reanimate Creatures

When the trap is triggered, it reanimates one or more dead creatures in the area to attack, block, or otherwise impede creatures. This effect requires some way to get a regular supply of dead creatures.

Like the Animate Objects effect, the reanimated creatures can be given a general command, such as to guard a particular chamber or corridor. Otherwise, the creatures mindlessly attack any other creatures in the area.

This effect could be used with a Corpse trigger; a body is brought into the area, and then reanimated when the trap goes off.

Effect. This effect turns piles of bones into **skeletons** or the corpses of Medium or Small humanoids into **zombies**. The number of creatures created depends on the trap's lethality, as shown in the Creatures table earlier. If there aren't enough bones or corpses in the trap's area when it triggers, it still makes as many creatures as it can. This effect can create undead of higher CR if it's severity allows.

Creatures reanimated by this effect stay active until reduced to 0 hit points, or until 24 hours pass, at which point they crumble to dust. The reanimated creatures will not leave the trap's area.

Restraint

All creatures in the area are held in place. This can be via an unseen force, or animated ropes or chains. As a simple trap, a deadly version of this effect might just be very difficult to break loose. However, as part of a complex trap, this effect can expose creatures to great danger.

Effect (Spell Trap). All creatures in the trap's area must succeed on a Wisdom saving throw or be paralyzed. At the end of each of its turns, a creature paralyzed by this effect can make another Wisdom saving throw. On a success, this effect ends for that creature.

This effect ends for all creatures if dispelled, either with *dispel magic* or *lesser restoration*, or after a period of time determined by the trap's lethality.

As a spell trap (2nd level slot), the glyph casts *hold person* on the triggering creature.

Seeming

Creatures in the area are cloaked with an illusion, taking on a new appearance determined by the trap creator. This can make other creatures they encounter hostile; intruders into a dwarven vault made to look like orcs will likely be attacked.

Effect. Creatures in the area must succeed on a Charisma saving throw or gain a new, illusory appearance. The illusion disguises physical appearance as well as clothing, armor, weapons, and equipment. It can make each creature seem 1 foot shorter or taller and appear thin, fat, or in between. The illusory appearance has the same basic arrangement of limbs as the target creature. Otherwise, the extent of the illusion is up to the trap designer.

The changes wrought by this effect fail to hold up to physical inspection. For example, if the illusion adds a hat to a creature's outfit, objects pass through the hat, and anyone who touches it would feel nothing or would feel the creature's head and hair. If the illusion makes a creature appear thinner than it is, the hand of someone who reaches out to touch it would bump into it while it was seemingly still in midair.

A creature can use its action to inspect a target creature and make an Intelligence (Investigation) check against the trap DC. If it succeeds, it becomes aware that the target is disguised.

The effect lasts for the duration determined by the trap's lethality, or until dispelled with *dispel magic*.

Sleep

Creatures in the area are magically put to sleep. This effect can be tailored to only affect only certain races, alignments, genders, or other such criterion.

Effect (Spell Trap). All creatures in the trap's area must succeed on a Constitution saving throw or fall asleep. Creatures put to sleep in this way remain unconscious until the effect ends, the sleeper takes damage, or someone uses an action to shake or slap the sleeper awake. Undead, constructs, and creatures that don't need to sleep aren't affected by this effect.

For each affected creature, this effect lasts until ended, either with *dispel magic* or *remove curse*, or until 24 hours pass.

As a spell trap (1st level slot), the glyph casts *sleep,* centered on and including the triggering creature.

Spell Effect

The trap is a *glyph of warding* with a spell stored inside it, or a *symbol*. When the glyph is triggered, the stored spell is cast. A *glyph of warding* can store any spell, except cantrips, that targets a single creature or an area. The trap's severity determines the level of spell that the glyph can store.

This effect can also serve as a catch-all for any generically magical effect that you want to use but doesn't exist in a specific form as a spell or other ability. Magic can do lots of different things and this effect can conform to the needs of your story. However, make sure that if you take this route you consider how the players will interact with the effect. Assign it a spell level and school of magic, and consider ways that creatures can deal with the effect after it happens.

Effect. If the spell has a target, it targets the creature that triggered the glyph. If the spell affects an area, the area is centered on that creature. If the spell summons hostile creatures or creates harmful objects or traps, they appear as close as possible to the intruder and attack it. If the spell requires concentration, it lasts until the end of its full duration.

Suggestion

The trap implants a course of activity (limited to a sentence or two) into the minds of creatures in the area and magically influences them to carry out that idea. The suggestion must be worded in such a manner as to make the course of action sound reasonable. A suggestion that makes a creature stab itself, throw itself onto a spear, immolate itself, or do some other obviously harmful act doesn't take hold in the target creature's mind.

Effect. Target creatures must make a Wisdom saving throw. On a failed save, it pursues the course of action implanted by the trap described to the best of its ability. Creatures that can't be charmed are immune to this effect.

The suggested course of action can continue for the entire duration of the effect, determined by the trap's lethality. If the suggested activity can be completed in a shorter time, the effect ends when the subject finishes what it was asked to do.

Casting *dispel magic* on a creature affected by the trap ends the effect for that creature.

Summon Creatures

When triggered, the trap summons creatures to the area. Creatures summoned this way are usually considered hostile, but do not necessarily need to be. The summoned creatures can be given a general command, such as to guard a particular chamber or corridor. Otherwise, the creatures only act to defend themselves.

Effect (Spell Trap). The number of creatures summoned depends on the trap's lethality, as shown in the Creatures table. Summoned creatures remain until reduced to 0 hit points, or until an amount of time passes, based on the trap's lethality. The summoned creatures will not leave the trap's area.

As a spell trap (variable level slot), the glyph can cast any of the *conjure* spells, such as *conjure animals* or *conjure elemental.*

Swap

The trap makes a creature magically change places with something else in another location. This exchange could be used to transplant a dangerous creature into the midst of the characters. It can also swap a creature with an object in a dangerous area. The trap could even swap things such as minds or personalities.

Effect. A target creature must succeed on a Charisma save, or instantly switch places with something else. Usually, the swap lasts for a duration determined by the trap's lethality. However, if the swap doesn't put creatures in immediate danger it can last for a longer amount of time, or be permanent.

If the swap involves non-physical things like personalities, it can be reversed by ending the effect with *dispel magic* or *remove curse.*

Teleport

When the trap is triggered, it teleports creatures elsewhere. Creatures don't need to be teleported into immediate danger, though that's always a possibility. Just splitting up a group can be problematic enough.

Effect. All creatures in the trap's area must succeed on a Charisma saving throw or be instantly teleported to a location set by the trap's designer.

Transmutation

When the trap is triggered, it unleashes magic which turns one thing into another.

Effect (Spell Trap). All creatures in the trap's area must make a Wisdom saving throw. A creature that fails is transformed into a random beast until the effect ends, they drop to 0 hit points, or they die. This effect doesn't work on a shapechanger or a creature with 0 hit points. Use the table below to determine what beast the creature transforms into.

d100	Beast	d100	Beast
1-2	Ape	51-52	Hawk
3-4	Axe beak	53-54	Hyena
5-6	Baboon	55-56	Jackal
7-8	Badger	57-58	Lion
9-10	Bat	59-60	Lizard
11-12	Black bear	61-62	Mammoth
13-14	Blood hawk	63-64	Mule
15-16	Boar	65-66	Owl
17-18	Brown bear	67-68	Panther
19-20	Camel	69-70	Poisonous snake
21-22	Cat	71-72	Polar bear
23-24	Constrictor snake	73-74	Pony
25-26	Crab	75-76	Rat
27-28	Crocodile	77-78	Raven
29-30	Deer	79-80	Rhinoceros
31-32	Dire wolf	81-82	Riding horse
33-34	Draft horse	83-84	Saber-toothed tiger
35-36	Eagle	85-86	Scorpion
37-38	Elephant	87-88	Spider
39-40	Elk	89-90	Tiger
41-42	Flying snake	91-92	Vulture
43-44	Frog	93-94	Warhorse
45-46	Giant centipede	95-96	Weasel
47-48	Giant fire beetle	97-98	Wolf
49-50	Goat	99-100	Worg

A transformed creature's game statistics, including mental ability scores, are replaced by the statistics of the beast it transforms into. It retains its alignment and personality. The creature assumes the hit points of its new form. When it reverts to its normal form, the creature returns to the number of hit points it had before it transformed. If it reverts as a result of dropping to 0 hit points, any excess damage carries over to its normal form. As long as the excess damage doesn't reduce the creature's normal form to 0 hit points, it isn't knocked unconscious.

A transformed creature is limited in the actions it can perform by the nature of its new form, and it can't speak, cast spells, or take any other action that requires hands or speech. The creature's gear melds into the new form. It can't activate, use, wield, or otherwise benefit from any of its equipment.

At the end of each of its turns, a creature transformed by this effect can make another Wisdom saving throw. On a success, this effect ends for that creature.

This effect ends for all creatures if dispelled, either with *dispel magic* or *remove curse*, or after a certain amount of time, depending on the effect's lethality.

As a spell trap (4th level slot), the glyph casts *polymorph* on the triggering creature. It can also cast *true polymorph*, which requires a 9th-level spell slot.

Wall of Force

An invisible *wall of force* appears in the area, becoming a confusing impediment.

Effect (Spell Trap). The *wall of force* can appear in any orientation set by the trap's designer, as a horizontal or vertical barrier or at an angle. It can be free floating or resting on a solid surface. It can be a hemispherical dome or a sphere with a radius of up to 10 feet, or it can be a flat surface made up of ten 10-foot-by-10-foot panels. Each panel must be contiguous with another panel. In any form, the wall is 1/4 inch thick. If the wall cuts through a creature's space when it appears, the creature is pushed to a random side of the wall.

Nothing can physically pass through the wall. It is immune to all damage and can't be dispelled by *dispel magic*. A *disintegrate* spell destroys the wall instantly, however. The wall also extends into the Ethereal Plane, blocking ethereal travel through the wall.

This effect ends after 24 hours, and the trap automatically resets.

As a spell trap (5th level slot), the glyph casts a hemispherical dome version of *wall of force*, centered on the triggering creature.

Wild Magic

When triggered, a surge of chaotic magic fills the area and makes an unexpected effect occur. This effect is designed to be unpredictable and the possibilities aren't limited to the options in the table below.

Effect. The trap targets a random creature in it's area when triggered, then roll d10 and consult the following table to discover what happens.

d10	Effect
1	Heavy rain falls in a 60-foot radius centered on a target creature. The area becomes lightly obscured. The rain follows the creature until they are out of the trap's range.
2	An animal appears in the unoccupied space nearest the target. The animal acts as it normally would. Roll a d100 to determine which animal appears. On a 01-25, a **rhinoceros** appears; on a 26-50, an **elephant** appears; and on a 51-100, a **rat** appears.
3	A cloud of 600 oversized butterflies fills a 30-foot radius centered on the target. The area becomes heavily obscured. The butterflies follows the creature until they are out of the trap's range.
4	Grass grows on the ground in a 60-foot radius centered on the target. If grass is already there, it grows to ten times its normal size and remains overgrown for 1 minute.
5	An object of the DM 's choice disappears into the Ethereal Plane. The object must be neither worn nor carried, within range of the trap, and no larger than 10 feet in any dimension.
6	Leaves grow from the target. Unless they are picked off, the leaves turn brown and fall off after 24 hours.
7	The trap attacks the target with a large gem worth 1d4 x 10 gp.
8	A burst of colorful shimmering light extends from the target in a 30-foot radius. The target and each creature in the area that can see must succeed on a Constitution saving throw or become blinded for 1 minute. A creature can repeat the saving throw at the end of each of its turns, ending the effect on itself on a success.
9	The target's skin turns bright blue for 1d10 days.
10	The target's size is halved in all dimensions, and its weight is reduced to one-eighth of normal. This reduction decreases its size by one category—from Medium to Small, for example. The target also has disadvantage on Strength checks and Strength saving throws and its weapons also shrink to match its new size. While these weapons are reduced, the target's attacks with them deal 1d4 less damage (this can't reduce the damage below 1). This effect ends if dispelled with *dispel magic* (3rd level spell) or *remove curse*, or after 1 minute.

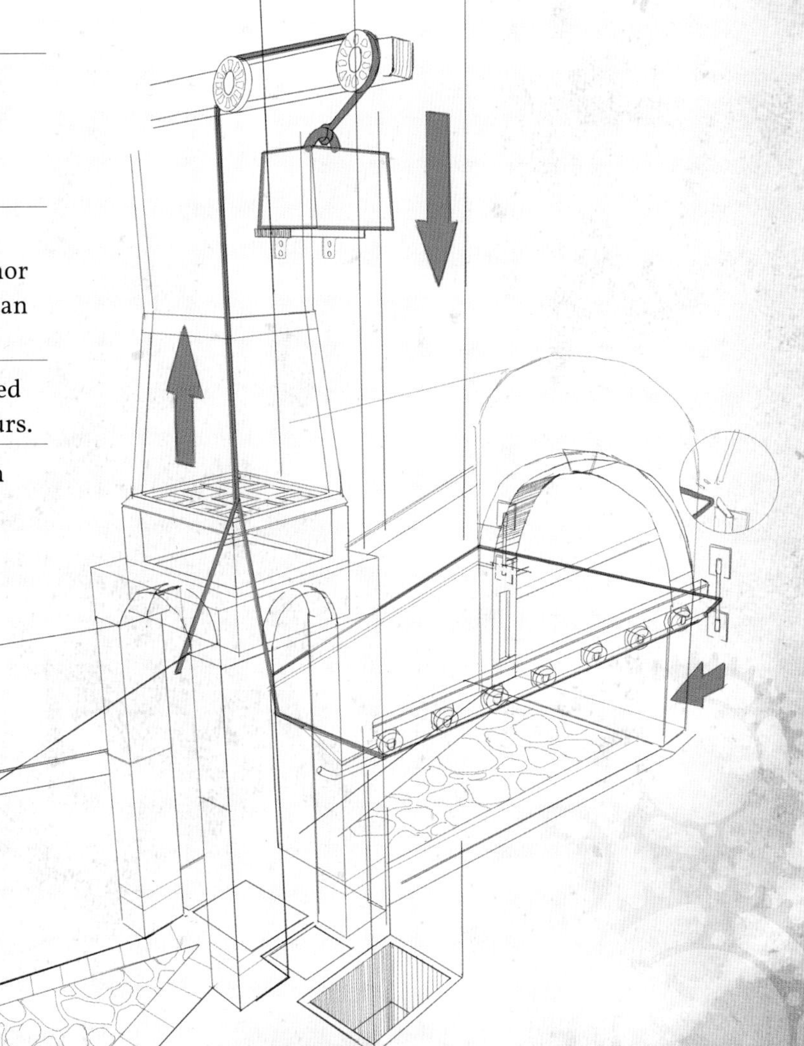

Trap-Centric Dungeons

Dungeons, ruins, crypts, and the like are all renowned for being places that folk in their right minds avoid. One major reason for this is that many of them are fraught with traps. These ingenious, sometimes brutish, devices, contraptions, and bits of magical malpractice are found all over, just waiting for some hapless adventurers to come put them to the test. There are plenty of times where having a monster or ruffian go to work on the characters is a perfectly serviceable course of action. At other times, good help is hard to find, and you want something dependable that can do the job without needing to be paid.

LESS IS MORE

Traps can get stale very quickly and can easily be overused. A trap (especially a simple one) can often be spotted and disabled by one character, leaving the others waiting around. They can also hamstring certain characters who are not well-suited for traps.

Be judicious about which traps you choose and why. Make sure that you consider the capabilities of the characters and provide opportunities for them to shine, both as a group and as individuals. Try to have only one major trap, one combat encounter and one social situation between short rests. This gives most characters a chance to do something meaningful in an encounter between each short rest.

Overusing traps can make the game drag as players are overcome with paranoia, searching and checking every little thing. Traps are more effective and entertaining when they are a surprise.

Traps for Small Spaces

Small spaces are usually less than a 20-by-25-foot room (500 square feet). The dimensions and shapes can vary, but what makes small spaces similar is that they are a room or enclosed space, not a corridor, passageway, or other primarily transitional space.

Small spaces are ideal for effects that are intended to impact the entire group since they ensure that targets are easier to hit. Gas clouds, collapsing floors, and magic glyphs are ideal for small rooms. As a general rule, think about traps that can take advantage of all potential targets being in close proximity.

Fiery Fall

Mechanical trap (13-16, dangerous, harm)

This trap can be set in any small chamber. When too much weight rests on the chamber floor, it gives way. Any creatures in the chamber are dropped down into a pit filled with flaming coals.

Trigger (Weight Sensitive Surface). When 500 or more pounds of pressure are placed on the floor of the chamber, the trap triggers.

Effect (Drop, Fire Jet). Each creature in the chamber must make a DC 15 Dexterity saving throw. On a success, the creature can grab onto the edge of the pit. On a failure, the creature falls into the pit and takes bludgeoning damage. The sides of the pit are sheer, requiring a DC 15 Strength (Athletics) check to climb out.

Each creature that enters the pit for the first time on a turn, or starts its turn there, takes 42 (12d6) fire damage from the burning coals in the bottom.

Countermeasures. A successful DC 15 Wisdom (Perception) check reveals the weight sensitive floor and hidden trapdoors, and a successful DC 15 Dexterity check while using thieves' tools disables the trap.

No Way Out

Mechanical trap (level 1-4, setback, subdue)

This trap is set in the antechamber of any kind of dungeon. The antechamber should have one entrance from outside and one leading further into the dungeon. When creatures enter and use the door that leads further into the dungeon, the entrance door slowly begins to slide shut. Once shut, it is almost impossible to open. To make matters worse, a gas cloud fills the room that could knock creatures unconscious, sealing them within the antechamber.

Trigger (Open/Close Door). A creature that opens the door leading further into the dungeon triggers the trap.

Initiative. The trap acts on initiative count 20.

Active Elements. The exits from the antechamber slowly seals shut.

Sliding Door (Initiative 20). The doors to and from the antechamber grind slowly shut. After 2 rounds, the space between the door and the frame is only big enough for a Small creature. After 3 rounds, the doors are fully closed and they lock shut.

Constant Elements. A cloud of sleep-inducing gas is injected into the chamber through holes in the wall

Gas Cloud. Each creature that ends their turn inside the antechamber must succeed on a DC 10 Constitution saving throw or be knocked unconscious for 1 minute. An unconscious creature wakes up if they take damage or if another creature uses an action to shake them awake.

Countermeasures. Creatures can avoid activating the trap with a successful DC 10 Wisdom (Perception) check. This reveals the hidden mechanisms in the door, as well as the small nozzles for the gas. A successful DC 10 Dexterity check using thieves' tools disables the trap.

Once activated, a creature can stop up the nozzles emitting the Gas Cloud as an action, but they have disadvantage on their Constitution saving throw to resist falling asleep.

Psychic Panic

Magic trap (17-20, deadly, hinder)

This trap should be placed in a room that stores treasure, including a particularly valuable or important object. When a creature looks at the trapped object, it emits a pulse of magic that causes fear and deals psychic damage.

Trigger (Look Into). If a creature looks directly at the trapped object while within 5 feet of it, the trap triggers.

Effect (Spell Effect). Once triggered, the object glows with a pale light, filling a 60-foot-radius sphere with dim light for 10 minutes, after which time the effect ends and the trap resets. Each creature in the sphere when the trap activates is targeted by its effect, as is a creature that enters the sphere for the first time on a turn or ends its turn there.

Each target must succeed on a DC 20 Wisdom saving throw or become frightened by the object. A creature that starts its turn frightened by the object must succeed on a DC 20 Wisdom saving throw or take 49 (9d10) psychic damage. If a frightened creature ends its turn in a location where it doesn't have line of sight to the object, the creature can make a DC 20 Wisdom saving throw. On a successful save, this effect ends for that creature. This effect also ends for a creature if *dispel magic* (DC19) is cast on them.

Countermeasures. A creature that succeeds on a DC 20 Wisdom (Perception) check can find hasty messages scrawled on the walls of the room, as well as scattered bits and bobs left by those running away. The trapped object has an aura of abjuration and illusion magic when viewed with *detect magic.*

A spellcaster can disrupt the enchantment on the trapped object with a successful DC 20 spellcasting ability check; *dispel magic* (DC 19) also disables the trap.

Traps for Large Spaces

Large spaces are usually larger than a 20-by-25-foot room (500 square feet). The dimensions and shapes of these large areas can vary, but, like their smaller brethren, they are often destinations, not transitional areas like hallways.

Large spaces are ideal for effects that can single-out or endanger members of a group. Obstacles that separate the characters from each other – such as runes of chain lightning, falling objects, and summoned monsters – all work well in larger areas. As a general rule, think about things that might require more space to function well. This is especially important if you're considering combining a combat encounter with a trap.

Climactic Traps

Large spaces are usually where something important takes place. Consider placing a trap that leads to a big moment in the campaign. The ceiling of the dungeon collapses, an epic monster is summoned, or the characters are paralyzed so that the main antagonist can deliver their final monologue.

Intriguing Traps

Some trap triggers cover areas, but often they are centered or focused on a specific point within a location. In large areas, the trap engineer can take advantage of room features that draw attention or beg inspection. This can be things such as an item on display, a piece of architecture, or even a sound emanating from an unclear source.

The trap effects can also take advantage of the wide space. In a large area, setting up forty hidden crossbows with enough ammunition to blanket the area in bolts is extremely resource and labor intensive. Perhaps those resources are available, but if it's unlikely the engineer would be able to build something like that, it is wise to consider what other trap effects might be more reasonable for the space.

Falling Debris

Magic trap (level 13-16, perilous, harm)

This trap is set in a chamber containing a treasure chest amongst piles of debris that litter the floor. The chest is secured to the floor by thick chains linked to the handles of the chest. When a creature attempts to pick the lock on the chest, they trigger the trap. A *glyph of warding (reverse gravity)* is hidden in the designs on the chest, causing creatures to fall to the ceiling when activated. The debris scattered across the floor falls upward as well, bombarding the characters.

Trigger (Attempt to Pick Lock). A creature that attempts to pick the chest's lock triggers the trap. Using a key does not trigger the trap.

Effect (Spell Effect). When activated, the glyph casts *reverse gravity*, reversing gravity in a 50-foot-radius, 100-foot high cylinder centered on the chest. All creatures and objects that aren't somehow anchored to the ground in the area fall upward and reach the top of the area when the glyph casts this spell. A creature can make a DC 17 Dexterity saving throw to grab onto a fixed object it can reach, such as the chest, thus avoiding the fall.

If some solid object (such as a ceiling) is encountered in this fall, falling objects and creatures strike it just as they would during a normal downward fall. If an object or creature reaches the top of the area without striking anything, it remains there, oscillating slightly, for the duration.

This reversal of gravity lasts for 1 minute, or until dispelled with *dispel magic* (DC 17). Once gravity is restored, affected objects and creatures fall back down.

The debris scattered across the floor also falls upward toward the ceiling, hitting any creature stuck there by reverse gravity. Each creature on the ceiling must succeed on a DC 17 Dexterity saving throw to avoid taking damage from the objects. Multiple saves may be necessary depending on the size of the area and how far creatures must move to get to safety.

Countermeasures. A creature examining the chest can find the glyph with a successful DC 17 Intelligence (Investigation) check, or with *detect magic*. Once found, it can be disabled with a successful DC 17 Intelligence (Arcana) check; *dispel magic* also disables the glyph.

The chest can be picked open with a successful DC 17 Dexterity check using thieves' tools.

Freezing Fountain

Magic trap (level 13-16, moderate, harm)

In the center of this large circular chamber is a beautiful fountain or pool. Disturbing the water triggers the trap; a barrier of blades springs up around the triggering creature, and the temperature in the chamber drops over the course of several rounds.

Trigger (Disturb Liquid). Any creature that disturbs the water in the fountain triggers the trap.

Initiative. The trap acts on initiative 20.

Active Elements. A wall of blades forms around the fountain or pool, emanating from a glowing ring of arcane symbols.

Blade Barrier (Initiative 20). This element only activates once, the first time the trap is triggered.A ringed wall up to 60 feet in diameter, 20 feet high, and 5 feet thick appears around the fountain or pool. The wall provides three-quarters cover to creatures behind it, and its space is difficult terrain.

When a creature enters the wall's area for the first time on a turn, it must make a DC 12 Dexterity saving throw. On a failure, the creature takes 33 (6d10) slashing damage. On a success, the creature takes half as much damage.

The wall of blades lasts for 10 minutes, or until dispelled with *dispel magic* (DC 16).

Dynamic Elements. The temperature in the chamber drops markedly every round, quickly suffusing the room with a bitter cold.

Ice Cold. The chamber drops to 0 degrees Fahrenheit and decreases by 5 degrees every round.

Constant Elements. Creatures in the chamber must navigate the wall of blades while fighting off the deadly chill.

Bitter Cold. A creature must succeed on a DC 12 Constitution saving throw or gain 1 level of exhaustion for each 1 minute they spend in the room after the trap is triggered. Creatures with resistance or immunity to cold damage automatically succeed on this saving throw, as do creatures with cold weather gear and creatures naturally adapted to cold climates.

Blade Barrier. When a creature ends their turn inside the wall of blades, it must make a DC 12 Dexterity saving throw. On a failure, the creature takes 33 (6d10) slashing damage. On a success, the creature takes half as much damage.

Countermeasures (Sensitive). A creature that succeeds on a DC 12 Wisdom (Perception) check can find the ring of arcane symbols around the fountain, frosted over with unearthly cold. The ring has an aura of evocation magic when viewed with *detect magic*.

With a successful DC 12 Intelligence (Arcana) check, a creature can disrupt the symbols without setting off the trap. However, a check that totals 5 or less triggers the trap. Casting *dispel magic* (DC 16) on the ring also disables the trap.

Streams of Silver

Hybrid trap (level 17-20, deadly, harm)

This trap should be set in a large chamber with multiple 10-foot deep trenches cut into the floor. When creatures pass a certain point in the chamber, scribed with a *rune of detection*, molten metal pours into the trenches. Additionally, a metal barrier erupts from the floor, giving cover for a villain and allowing them to escape.

Trigger (Pass Area). Creatures of a certain type, race, or alignment (determined by the villain), moving past the rune trigger the trap.

Initiative. The trap acts on initiative 20.

Active Elements. Gateways on the far wall open, spewing molten metal that floods the trenches cut into the floor of the chamber. A barrier also rises at the far end of the room.

Adamantine Barrier (Initiative 20). This element only activates once, the first time the trap is triggered. A 10-foot tall adamantine barrier rises from a platform at the far end of the chamber, where a villain might be standing. The barrier has a 1-foot high gap at the eye level of a Medium creature, allowing creatures to see through it. The barrier counts as three-quarters cover for anyone on the platform.

Molten Metal (Initiative 20). Creatures in the trenches when they are flooded, or creatures that touch the molten metal for the first time, must make a DC 20 Constitution saving throw. A creature takes 87 (25d6) fire damage on a failed save, or half as much damage on a successful one.

Additionally, when a creature enters a flooded trench, it sinks 1d4+1 feet into the metal and is restrained.

Constant Elements. The molten metal in the trenches gives off immense heat in a 5-foot area around it; creatures restrained by the metal suffer fire damage.

Metal Trench. Each creature that ends their turn within 5 feet of a trench filled with molten metal must succeed on a DC 20 Constitution saving throw or gain 1 level of exhaustion. Creatures wearing heavy armor have disadvantage on their saving throw.

Sink or Swim. If a creature is restrained by molten metal at the start of its turn, it sinks another 1d4 feet. If the creature isn't completely submerged in the molten metal, it can escape as an action by succeeding on a Strength check. The DC is 10 plus the number of feet the creature has sunk into the molten metal. A creature that is completely submerged in molten metal can't breathe.

A creature can pull another creature within its reach out of the molten metal by using its action and succeeding on the Strength check. The DC is the same as above, but the creature helping has advantage.

Countermeasures. The rune can be found with a successful DC 20 Wisdom (Perception) check, or with *detect magic*. Once found, it can be disabled with *dispel magic* or with a successful DC 20 Intelligence (Arcana) check.

Once activated, a creature adjacent to the barrier can rip it off its moorings with a successful DC 20 Strength check. With a successful DC 20 Dexterity check using thieves' tools, a creature can make the barrier retract.

Traps for Corridors & Passageways

Corridors and passageways are spaces meant to be transitional, leading from one area to another. They are often narrow and are ideal areas for traps due to their linearity. Traps such as hidden crossbows, scything blades, and falling ceilings all benefit from targets with limited mobility. The dungeon engineer is also able to much more easily predict what potential targets will do and where they will go in a passageway than in an open room.

Blocking the Way

Whether by a wall of fire or a 2-ton stone cube, blocking the corridor at one or both ends creates a confined space for the targets of a trap. This may even be used to separate characters from one another.

Projectiles

Crossbows or darts are most effective when placed at the end of the corridor. The target doesn't have much space to dodge out of the way, and if the projectile doesn't hit the target in the front it might hit a target further back.

Blazing Barricade

Mechanical trap (level 5-8, moderate, subdue)

A tripwire stretches across this thin corridor. Breaking the wire triggers the trap and reveals gas vents along the corridor. Ignited by a spark, the gas forms walls of fire to erupt, sealing creatures in the corridor and separating them. The vents are at 15 feet and 40 feet in a 50-foot long corridor.

Trigger (Tripwire). Breaking the tripwire triggers the trap.

Effect (Wall of Fire). Gas vents open and a spark causes them to ignite, creating two walls of flame that block the corridor at 15 and 40 feet. The walls reach from floor to ceiling and are 1 foot thick. They are opaque and last for 1 minute.

When the walls appear, each creature within a wall's area must make a DC 12 Dexterity saving throw. On a failed save, a creature takes 22 (5d8) fire damage, or half as much damage on a successful save.

The side of each wall facing towards the center of the corridor deals 22 (5d8) fire damage to each creature that ends its turn within 10 feet of that side or inside the wall. A creature takes the same damage when it enters the wall for the first time on a turn or ends its turn there. The other side of each wall deals no damage.

Once active, the walls can be deactivated by closing or blocking the gas vents. This requires a successful DC 12 Intelligence (Investigation) check to determine how they might be thwarted, and then either a successful Dc 12 Strength check to block the vents, or a successful DC 12 Dexterity check using thieves' tools to close them.

Countermeasures (Sensitive). A successful Wisdom (Perception) check reveals the tripwire, and a successful Dexterity check using thieves' tools disables the trap. However, a Dexterity check that totals 5 or less triggers the trap.

Pin Cushions

Mechanical trap (level 1-4, dangerous, harm)

If a creature walking through the corridor steps on a hidden pressure plate, they trigger the trap. Darts laced with crawler mucus fire from the doorframe at the far end of the corridor.

Trigger (Pressure Plate). Applying 20 or more pounds of pressure to the pressure plate triggers the trap.

Effect (Darts). Darts shoot from the frame of the door at the far end of the corridor. Each creature in the corridor must make a DC 15 Dexterity saving throw. A creature that fails takes piercing damage and succeed on a DC 13 Constitution saving throw or be poisoned for 1 minute. The poisoned creature is paralyzed. The creature can repeat the saving throw at the end of each of its turns, ending the effect on itself on a success.

A creature that succeeds on its Dexterity saving throw takes half the piercing damage and isn't poisoned.

Countermeasures. A successful DC 15 Wisdom (Perception) check reveals the pressure plate, and a successful DC 15 Dexterity check using thieves' tools disables the trap.

Perplexing Puzzles

Puzzles are often confused with complex traps. However, a trap can be disarmed while a puzzle must be solved. Puzzles are often used as a filter of sorts, preventing those without the right knowledge or who are unworthy from getting access to an item or a place.

Good puzzles challenge the creatures interacting with them in ways other than a trap or a monster. Puzzles can be simple or complex, they may have a single stage or multiple stages with escalating difficulty, and they may have mechanical or magic elements. All of these aspects depend on who made it and what the puzzle is intended to do.

Challenging Players

Puzzles are, by their nature, designed to challenge *players* rather than their characters. They are intended to engage the brains of the players and give them an opportunity to tackle an intellectual exercise. This often means ignoring most of what's on the character sheet and just letting the humans around the table figure out the solution. Ability checks should be used to offer hints when the group is stumped or stalled, but don't use them to simply give away the answer.

Harmful Puzzles

Puzzles may or may not have an element that deals damage, but such an effect should be passive or used as a penalty rather than an integral part or purpose of the puzzle. A floor with safe places to stand marked by runes while all other places have a breakaway floor is a good example of this. If the creature attempting the puzzle makes a mistake, the penalty is a fall into the unknown.

Unexpected Solutions

It can be jarring when a puzzle you introduce, especially a complex one, is bypassed in an unexpected way.

When using puzzles in a freeform, tabletop game it is important to know that sooner or later, players ***will*** solve a puzzle in a way you did not intend. When this happens, do not railroad players into finding *your* solution. Reward your players' ingenuity and enjoy the experience of seeing how *your* players interact with your puzzle.

In situations like these, we have a hard-and-fast rule: a *working* solution is the *correct* solution.

Puzzle-Centric Dungeons

Dungeons don't have to be designed around monsters or traps. Instead, they can be designed around puzzles. Such dungeons focus on problems that need to be solved using player cleverness rather than in-game character prowess.

Theme

Theme is of particular importance when it comes to puzzles, much more so than traps. Sometimes the mere fact that a trap can dish out a desired effect is enough to use it. Puzzles, on the other hand, say something about the dungeon's owner and reinforce the theme of a dungeon. For instance, if a dungeon is the home of a lich who utilizes the undead, it would make sense for puzzles in that dungeon to be themed around death, life, and things tangentially related to those topics. It is very important that the puzzles found in the dungeon fit with its theme.

Puzzle Placement

A puzzle presents a problem that needs solving, and the characters should be able to solve the problem. This means that they must have access to the items, tools, or information required to solve the puzzle. There might be clues available in or around the puzzle, or they could have found some something before reaching the puzzle.

If the characters aren't ready for the puzzle, there needs to be a clear way for them to understand that they should come back later. They should also have some idea of what will indicate when they are ready. It need not be so obvious as "you must be this tall to ride" but there should be clear indications of what they don't have that they will need to solve the puzzle.

In the case of puzzles characters may not be ready for, be sure to provide other paths they can take. These alternatives can lead them to places where they will find what they need to solve the puzzle. If there are no alternate paths, ensure that they can go back the way they came and track down what they need to accomplish the puzzle.

Regarding the physical location of the puzzle, think like the dungeon's owner and ask yourself why they would want a puzzle in a particular spot, instead of a trap or monsters. A puzzle is, in most circumstances, a way to make sure that those who deserve to can proceed, and those who don't are stuck. Avoid placing puzzles in arbitrary places. This will help to make whatever is beyond the puzzle much more rewarding.

Puzzles for Small Spaces

Puzzles that work well for small spaces are those that involve small things. This might involve things like a board game whose pieces need to be moved, or a puzzle box. This should be something where everyone can generally gather around and participate.

Puzzles for Large Spaces

Puzzles that work well for large spaces are those that can utilize different creatures doing different things at the same time. These puzzles make use of space, or situations where multiple creatures need to achieve something that one of them alone couldn't, such as pulling a lever in two different locations.

Puzzles for Corridors and Passages

Puzzles that work well for corridors and passages often make use of distance. This may mean that the components are laid out along the length of the hall, or it may require creatures to travel certain amounts of distance.

Premade Puzzles

Below you will find 30 puzzles that we have designed to be usable in a wide array of environments and situations. We encourage you to use them and modify them as you see fit. Many of them will have optional adjustments or changes that can be made, but they are by no means the *only* changes that can be made. If you think of something else, by all means try it. Experiment and have fun!

1. Walk the Plank

The entrance to the chamber is on level, stable ground, but much of the rest of the room's floor has collapsed, revealing an area below the room. Several planks of wood in various lengths, are laying near the entrance to the chamber.

Scattered around this lower area in a seemingly random pattern are 15 feet high stone pillars which seem to have been intended to support the now-collapsed upper floor. Each column can accommodate one Medium or two Small creatures safely. If the top of a column is occupied by a Medium or two Small creatures and another creature of Small or larger size attempts to move into or through the occupied space, all the creatures must succeed on a DC 10 Dexterity (Acrobatics) check. Creatures that fail fall from the pillar and take 3 (1d6) bludgeoning damage.

Solution. Creatures must use the planks in order to cross the chamber. Of the planks at the entrance, only three are sturdy enough to span a gap between pillars. The sturdy pieces are a 10-foot, 15-foot, and 20-foot piece. The pieces can bridge gaps that are 5 feet less than their total length (ie. a 20-foot plank can bridge a 15-foot gap). With a successful DC 10 Intelligence (Nature) or Intelligence check using woodcarver's tools, a creature can determine if a plank is sturdy or not.

Any configuration of the boards which allows the party to cross to the other side is a correct solution. A creature attempting to cross a rotted or unstable plank will fall once they reach the middle of the plank. If it is adjacent to a pillar when it falls, a creature can catch themselves with a successful DC 10 Dexterity saving throw.

Difficulty. This puzzle is extremely flexible. To increase or decrease the difficulty of the puzzle, the amount of sturdy planks as well as the quantity and spacing of the pillars can be altered. Decoy paths — paths where the available boards would take you most of the way, but ultimately fall just short — also increase the difficulty of this puzzle.

You can add some damaging element, such as spikes or a river of magma, to the lower area as another way to increase the challenge of the puzzle.

Planning. Whether you implement this puzzle using miniatures & terrain or simply using theatre of the mind, it will be important to have a rough idea of pillar locations in advance. Graph paper will allow you to easily mark the distances between different pillars so you can guide your players as they attempt to cross.

2. The Necrodial

A round metal object the size of an amulet hangs from a necklace or chain. On one side, the amulet has four concentric round dials, each inscribed with ten runes; the other side is blank. The amulet is meant to contain a key, gem, note, or other small object.

The dials on the amulet have a handle, ridges, or some other method of rotation. Over the uppermost portion of each dial is a small downward-facing triangle of raised metal to indicate what rune is selected. In the center of the dials is a button with a skull engraved on it.

Solution. Spinning all four dials to the correct rune and then pressing down on the center button makes the amulet come apart in two pieces.

The exact combination of runes necessary to solve this puzzle is up to your discretion. Perhaps these runes are a repeating motif in the hidden annals of a necromancer's study, or perhaps the runes are instead letters that must be combined to spell out a particular 4-letter word.

Zap. Attempting to open the device with the wrong combination of runes could be painful. A surge of lightning, fire, psychic or necrotic damage could hit the holder of the amulet if the combination is incorrect.

3. Revealed in Reflections

Several mirrors are suspended in midair, as if weightless. They can be repositioned or rotated easily; once in place, they remain perfectly still.

Within the area where these mirrors are found are objects, decorations, or doors that are invisible to the naked eye. These features are only visible if viewed through one or more of the mirrors that float in this area.

Solution. Once the mirrors are repositioned, players must find a method of interacting with the exit or retrieving the objects that the mirrors reveal. This could involve interacting with the objects in real life as if they're invisible, or perhaps even stepping *through* the mirror to bring objects back through to the real room. Allow the players' creativity to shine in how these mirrors are used, especially if combat or other nefarious traps and dangers are present.

Shining Shields. Any reflective surface, such as well-shined metal, will do in place of mirrors if you desire. Perhaps even bodies of water could be utilized and positioned in interesting ways!

4. Tears of the Angels

A chamber has one or more exits, but they are all blocked by heavy stone doors. In the center of the chamber is a raised platform with a stone pressure plate. On the pressure plate sit three empty, silver decanters, beautifully adorned with elvish script and filigree. Each one is a different size: large, medium, and small. Upon close inspection, the bottom of the decanters have numbers on them, indicating how many glasses of wine they can hold. The large decanter holds 7 glasses, the medium on holds 5, and the small one holds 3. One of the decanters weighs down a note with the following words:

In the greatest decanter
shall be served wine for friends
Just enough for the four of us
For our fifth has met their end.

If any of the vessels are removed from the pressure plate, the pressure plate rises slightly. A heavy stone door descends from above to cover the entrance into the room, sealing the party inside. The entrance and all exits can now only be opened once the puzzle is solved.

Also in the chamber is a statue of an angel, its head bowed. Tears steadily flow from the corners of its closed eyes, trickling in small rivulets down into a shallow basin held in its hands at waist height. The bowl appears to remain full, but does not overflow.

Solution. The object of the puzzle is to fill the large vessel with four glasses worth of liquid. The most obvious source of liquid to complete this puzzle is the angel's basin, which contains more than enough to attempt the puzzle multiple times. There are many ways to solve the puzzle, but the following is an example of a correct solution:

1. Fill the medium decanter.
2. Pour the contents of the medium decanter into the small decanter until it is full.
3. Pour the remaining contents of the medium decanter (2 glasses of liquid) into the large decanter, and empty the small decanter.
4. Repeat steps 1 and 2, so that another 2 glasses of liquid end up in the medium decanter.
5. Pour the contents of the medium decanter into the large, now bringing the large decanter to contain 4 glasses of liquid.
6. Set the large decanter on the pressure plate.

Once the large vessel is set on the pressure plate and contains exactly 4 glasses worth of liquid, all exits from the chamber open.

No Sweat. Puzzles involving distribution of water and finding exact measurements using less-than-ideal containers are a classic trope, and likely to be something that at least *some* players are familiar with. That makes "Tears of the Angels" a great lower-stress puzzle, or perhaps an introduction to more complex versions of the same puzzle concept in other forms.

5. Descension

On the floor of this chamber are 4 concentric circles. The largest circle is 10 feet in diameter, while the smallest is 5 feet in diameter. The 3 outermost circles each appear to be made of a single piece of metal which, imbedded into the floor. These metal rings each have 12 2-inch-diameter holes evenly spaced around their perimeter, and each hole is marked with a unique rune. Placing a piece of wood, spear shaft, or other such object into a hole allows the connected ring to be rotated without difficulty.

The innermost circle is made of twelve triangular-shaped wedges all pointing inward, similar to a sliced pie. If tapped or prodded the wedges sound solid, and if stuck with a hammer they will chip but not shatter — they are quite strong. A line is burned into the metal plating of one of the innermost triangular wedges. Directly across from this line, on the floor outside of the largest circle, is another line marked or carved into the floor.

Solution. In order to solve this puzzle, the three outer rings must align between the marked lines in the correct order. The runes on the rings could represent months, astrological signs, faces in a card deck, or perhaps letters that spell a 3-letter word, acronym, or a character's initials. The correct orientation of the rings is completely variable depending on what suits your campaign.

When the three metal rings are properly aligned, the segments of the innermost circle begin to descend slowly, each wedge stopping lower than the one previous until a 10-foot deep spiral staircase has formed. This staircase could lead to a lower level, a secret chamber, or a hidden passageway.

Control Rod. For more complexity, rotating the rings could require a specific object. This object could be necessary due to a special locking mechanism that prevents any other object from rotating the ring. To add yet another level of complexity, each ring could require a different object in order to rotate it.

6. Turn Back Time

A sundial sits on a pedestal in a circular room filled with light. Directly across from each hour mark on the sundial is a sconce on the wall. Each sconce features a small lever in an upright position.

Switching a lever down will extinguish the flame for 30 seconds as the lever cranks back upwards. When the lever returns to the upright position, the sconce reignites. Aside from the lever, the sconces have some sort of enchantment that prevents creatures from tampering with the flame or the sconce itself.

The exit to the room is utterly sealed and unable to be opened directly by mundane or magical means. A doorstop sits on the floor nearby.

Solution. Extinguishing all but one of the sconces casts a shadow on the sundial, thus displaying a particular time. When this happens, the room surrounding the sundial changes to reflect the previous state it was once in, at time shown on the dial. One of the hours on the dial reveals a time when the exit was open. The party must use a wedge or heavy object to prop the door open before the torches reset. Characters may also try to escape through the door before it closes without propping it open, which is entirely possible, though that would make a return journey quite challenging.

Turn Back Time. The hours on the sundial could instead be tied to spans of time other than literal minutes and hours. For instance, 1 o'clock on the sundial might instead show the room as it was 100 years ago. In this case, perhaps there is no exit in the present, but 100 years ago, there was a door in one of the walls that now opens when the sundial shows 1 o'clock.

So That's What Happened. Though the main goal of the puzzle is to exit the room, other hours on the sundial can still reveal information that is of interest to the characters. For example, casting a shadow at 3 o'clock could show a merchant finishing a journal entry before being placing the book in a desk. This journal entry could perhaps even contain a message meant specifically for the party by an unknown author.

Aside from the exit door, other objects around the room may rearrange, appear, or disappear according to the shadow cast on the sundial. Feel free to play around with this concept and potentially craft an underlying story as to what occurred at each hour of the sundial.

7. Now You're Thinking with P-... Sand

Characters enter a massive 40-foot wide and 50-foot long room. There is an empty 5-foot square at the entrance and exit of the room, on the far side, but otherwise, the entirety of the ceiling, walls and floor are all covered in churning, gravity-defying sand. Amidst the sand are a number of large, obvious buttons.

If creatures touch any part of the sand, it will begin to suck them in. It takes 1 round for the sand to fully absorb a creature, and 6 seconds for them to reemerge on the ceiling, wall, or floor exactly *opposite* of where they entered. When characters reemerge, they continue to fall in the *direction they were previously sucked into the sand.* This means characters can "fall" vertically or horizontally, even in opposing directions; gravity is relative to each creature depending on the direction they were sucked into the sand.

Solution. The party must find ways to redirect their gravity, reposition themselves, and push or pull each other, while falling in order to hit the buttons, making them light up. You can use a map to show the location of these buttons can be shown or describe them verbally (ex: "There is a red button 20ft high and 40ft across on the left wall.")

Once all buttons are lit, any falling creatures are sucked into the sand a final time before emerging right-side up from the sandy floor. At this point, the exit door unlocks and the sand becomes walkable.

Shifting Sands. Combat in this room would be an absolute nightmare, and is thus highly discouraged. However, if you are a particularly brave (or unstable) GM with an excellent working knowledge of 3D space, or have players that have seen it all, feel free to give it a try!

8. Wicked Patience

This 15-by-15 foot room has a lever on the back wall and on the right wall is a metal door. Evenly spaced along the stone walls are a series of small, numbered, 1-foot-diameter metal hatches that cannot be opened and do not have handles. One of these is above the metal door.

Pulling the lever makes a large, metal door slam down over the entrance to the room, barring creatures from entering or exiting. The hatch above the right door slides open to reveal a countdown timer made of small numbered wooden tiles, automatically flipping as time ticks down.

Once the lever has been pulled, and the door has slammed shut, hatches 1, 2, 4, 6, 7, 9, and 10 open to reveal a series of mundane items within cubby holes. Interacting with an item has the effect shown in the table below:

Hatch Number	Cubby Contents	Result After Interaction
1	A rope hanging from the top of the cubby	When this rope is pulled, hatch #5 opens. If the rope is released, hatch #5 closes.
2	A handle with a leather grip sticks out from the left cubby wall.	Nothing. The grip is mildly comfortable.
3	A chain hanging from the top of the cubby	When the chain is pulled, hatch #8 opens. If the chain is released, hatch #8 closes.
4	A metal crank	Every full rotation of the crank adds 1 second to the timer.
5	2 buttons	Pressing the left button adds 10 seconds to the timer. Pressing the right button adds 20 seconds to the timer.
6	A lever	Pulling the lever down adds 5 seconds to the timer. The lever can not manually be pushed back up.
7	A wooden handle connected to a chain	When the chain is pulled, hatch #3 opens.
8	A 10-digit dial with center button; a small triangle indicates the number selected	Pressing the button adds the amount of seconds selected on the dial to the timer
9	A button	Resets the lever in hatch #6
10	A button	Every 5 seconds the button lights up red. If pressed when unlit, the button does nothing, but if pressed when lit, 5 seconds are added to the timer.

Solution. When the countdown timer reaches 0, both the entrance and exit doors open. The party simply needs to wait. That's it. Nothing else.

An Object Lesson. This puzzle lends itself to certain settings or applications more than others. It could be a teaching tool found in a monastery or church to teach the lesson that "patience is a virtue." Or it could be an intentional test of restraint, meant to find out how long it takes the group to "solve" the room. If it takes them longer than a certain amount of time, perhaps they're refused a prize or are simply met with disappointment from the test-giver. Or the puzzle could be a delaying tactic, allowing something else to catch up to the party, or give someone monitoring the room extra time to react.

One or the Other. The room could be set up so there are 2 exit doors and the timer is between them. If the timer ends in a certain amount of time or less, the left door is opened, and the right remains shut. If the timer takes longer, the left door remains shut and the right door opens. In this situation, the left door is assumed to have something positive waiting.

9. Sea Legs

The floor of this area is one large slab or wooden deck, 40 feet wide and as long as necessary. Down the center of the deck runs a narrow, 5-foot-tall barrier. The entire floor is mounted on a horizontal cylindrical beam or log running directly below the barrier, allowing the floor to tilt.

At the entrance to the room is a 10-foot wide doorway; a 5-foot wide door covers one half, leaving the other half open. Once someone enters through the open half of the doorway, the door slides over, opening the other side and forcing creatures to enter the room on both sides of the barrier. Creatures can then attempt to move across the floor, but run the risk of tipping the floor if they're not careful.

Determine which way the floor tips by following these steps and referencing the diagram below:

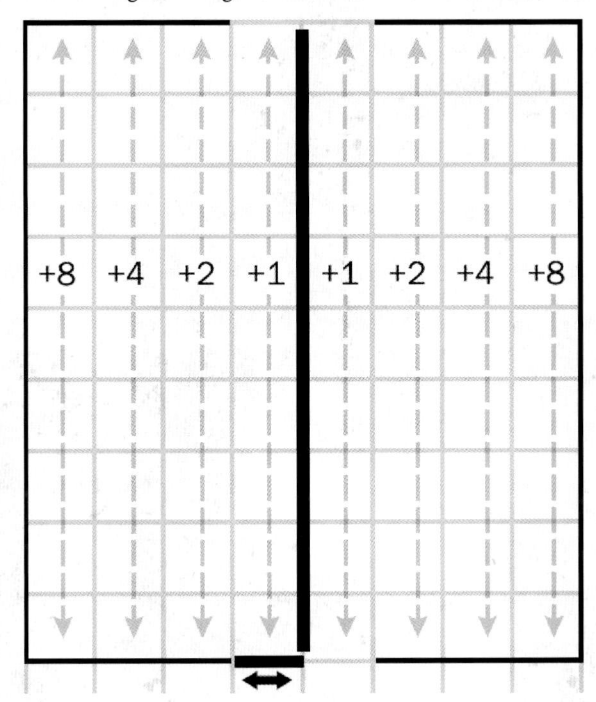

- Everyone rolls initiative. The puzzle always acts last.
- Everyone is allowed a turn as normal to move and take an action. When moving, the entirety of the floor is always considered **difficult terrain**.
- Values are totaled for each side of the barrier. Each "lane" of space to the right or left of the barrier has a value for every 5 feet of distance from the barrier (+1, +2, +4, +8). A creature generates that value for each space they occupy for whatever side of the barrier they're on. This means a Large creature adds +6 to the side they are on (2 spaces in the +1 lane, 2 spaces in the +2 lane).
    - Total the amount for the left side.
    - Total the amount for the right side.
- The room tips in the direction of the side with the larger number.
- Subtract the lower total from the higher total, then add 10. This new number becomes the DC of the Dexterity saving throw that all creatures on the floor must make to hold their ground.
- Any creature that fails the saving throw slides down the tipped floor. If they are on the higher side of the barrier, they slide into it. If they are on the lower side of the barrier, they slide to the edge and must make a second Dexterity saving throw (same DC) or fall over the edge.
- Now that the floor is tilted, the lane values of the higher side of the barrier are reduced to +0, +1, +2, and +4. This represents the difficulty of fighting gravity and reducing the incline. You may skip this value change to simplify the puzzle if desired.
- Repeat the steps as necessary.

Solution. The characters simply need to cross the floor to the exit, hopefully without losing a friend or two to the unknown depths waiting below the tipping floor.

Heads Up. When the floor tips, if someone on the upper portion of the floor fails their Dexterity saving throw by 5 or more, have them bounce, fly, or roll *over* the barrier and wind up on the edge on the opposite side!

Wall Walker. Depending on how steep the floor gets, ability checks using skills like Climbing or Acrobatics might be necessary to prevent slipping or falling. Axes or daggers stabbed into the surface can also keep a creature from sliding. Let your players get creative with their preventative attempts, and allow unorthodox solutions that make sense when they try to save themselves from a slippery demise.

How Long?. The length of the room can have a strong impact on this puzzle's difficulty because it will lengthen the amount of time the characters are on the floor. Keep their speed in mind when choosing your room length. Keep your players' overall patience and sanity in mind as well.

Rolling Around. A combat encounter or the presence of other weighted objects could make this puzzle much more unpredictable. Adjust this puzzle concept however you desire in order to spice things up!

Crunch the Numbers. If you care to be a bit more simulationist, here are some ways in which you can alter the puzzle's numbers:

- -1 from a side's total for each Small creature on that side.
- -2 from a side's total for each Tiny creature on that side.
- When the floor tips and is no longer level, the lower floor's values could change to +2, +4. +8, and +16. Climbing over the barrier to get to the other side will be necessary to adjust the weight.

10. Puzzle Floor

The floor of the room is covered in tiles, and the exit is locked. Except for one, all the tiles are smooth and unremarkable. The unique tile has a rune, letter, or other marking.

When a creature stands on the unique tile, it glows; all adjacent tiles then reveal glowing symbols which were previously hidden. Stepping to an adjacent tile will then reveal the other symbols adjacent to it, and so on.

Solution. Stepping on the tiles in the correct sequence unlocks the exit.

For a puzzle like this, clues are incredibly important. Prior to arriving at this puzzle, introduce knowledge about who rules the dungeon. A journal or written orders that mention important information, a repeated motif, or strange sequences of unknown symbols could hold the solution to this puzzle.

The entire solution to the puzzle could only be learned once different clues (such as separate pages) are found and viewed together. When looking at the clues all at once, it should be clear what they all have in common, be it a word, a name, a sentence, etc. You can even write the solution on a piece of paper, tear the paper into 3-6 pieces, and make each of those pieces into a clue the players must retrieve.

In order to set up this puzzle, you can follow these steps:

1. Determine what your solution will be.
2. Figure out how many tiles that solution would occupy (i.e. the word "love" would occupy 4 tiles if each tile was a letter).
3. On a grid, lay out the path you would like the party to take, placing each letter or symbol of the correct solution on a separate tile.
4. Fill in any remaining empty tiles with other symbols.

Spell It Out. For a more in-depth challenge, each tile of your puzzle floor could contain an entire word as opposed to a single letter or symbol. Perhaps the party came across a journal in which the villain wrote down his greatest life philosophy amongst their other rantings. Stepping on the tiles that spell out this important sentence could be the solution.

If using words, try giving the words adjacent to each glowing tile a sense of cohesion, with at least some of the revealed words making sense in context. For instance, if the starting tile is the word "I," possible words adjacent to it could be "love", "hate", "go", "went", "feel", "think", etc.

Where to Begin. To make this puzzle more difficult, you can remove the starter tile entirely. This makes *all* the tiles blank, forcing the party to experiment and find their starting position.

Are We Done Here? To ensure the engagement of all party members, create a solution with a number of tiles equal to your number of players. Then, the solution to the puzzle could require characters to all be standing on a tile.

Don't Step on That! If you're feeling particularly devilish, stepping on an incorrect tile can erase the characters' progress, forcing them to restart at the beginning.

11. Spin-N-Smash

This 40-foot diameter circular room has an entrance on one end and an exit directly across from it. A thick vertical axle goes from floor to ceiling at the dead center of the room. Affixed horizontally to this axle is a massive boom arm which sweeps a 15-foot diameter circle inside the room; the boom is 10 feet wide and 15 feet long. The party must cross the room across a series of tiles, each of which spin the arm either clockwise or counter-clockwise.

The room is enchanted with an effect similar to *reverse gravity*, but instead of changing the direction of gravity this effect increases its pull. A creature can only move 5 feet on its turn, or 10 feet if the creatures takes the Dash action. This enchantment also prevents flight and levitation of any sort, and makes jumping nearly impossible.

Each traversable tile in the room is marked with a clockwise or counterclockwise arrow in the diagram below. Immediately after a creature steps on a tile (even in the middle of its turn), the boom arm swiftly spins a quarter-turn in the tile's indicated direction.

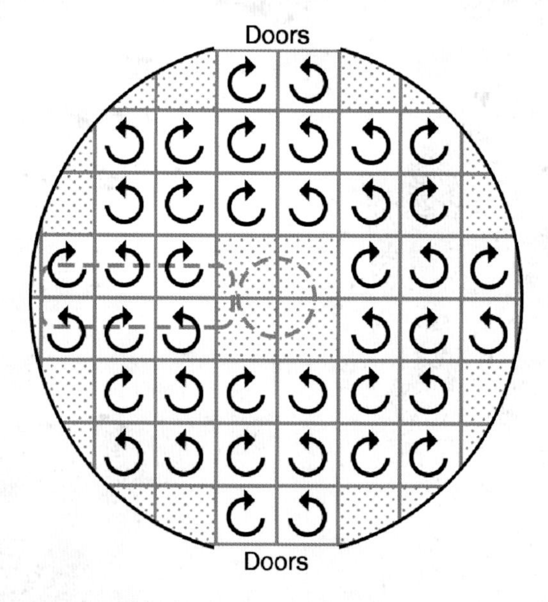

When the boom arm spins, creatures whose space the boom arm would move into or through must make a successful DC 12 Dexterity saving throw. A successful saving throw means the creature was able to avoid being struck. A failed saving throw results in 14 (4d6) bludgeoning damage and the creature is knocked prone.

Being hit with the arm is intended to hurt, but not kill. If a creature dies from this puzzle, it should be because they were battered *over* and *over* and *over* by the boom arm (and, at that point, could anyone *truly* be upset by their fate?)

A Medium sized or larger creature who shares a space with the arm can only do so by squeezing. Creatures can intentionally go prone and lie flat enough to avoid the boom arm, should it swing through. Due to the room's increased gravity, crawling or moving while prone is entirely too difficult to accomplish.

Solution. Players must move through the room to the exit, taking as little damage as possible.

Mix it Up. The clockwise and counterclockwise symbols need not be arranged in the configuration shown. If you think of a different arrangement, feel free to experiment.

What Does This Mean? The symbols on the tiles do not need to so obviously illustrate clockwise and counter-clockwise. There could be hints or a translation of these symbols earlier in the dungeon, or the characters could simply discover what the symbols do through experimentation.

Backwards. Especially devious GMs could add an additional twist: each time a character successfully exits the room, the meaning of the symbols *reverses.* At that point, all counter-clockwise symbols will start rotating the boom arm clockwise, and vice versa. Whether this change is represented by the actual symbols on the tiles, or is simply left to be discovered in flabbergasted horror by your players, is entirely up to you.

12. Three-Bottle Quaff

On a table in this room are 6 potion bottles, each filled with a different liquid and carrying a unique label. The numbers 1-6 are drawn on a nearby surface such as a table, bookshelf, or individual stools. Indentations or clean circles amidst the dusty surface indicate that a bottle is meant to be placed by each number.

Players are also presented with the following riddle, either verbally or in writing:

One's the money,
Two is funny,
Three's a filthy liar!
Four's a pain,
Five's insane,
and Six will soon retire.

Once three potions are consumed,
You may move on (but you may be doomed!)

None of the bottles are numbered, but they do carry labels with unique text. This text is the key to determining a potion's number, which can then be compared to the descriptions in the riddle.

Solution. In order to proceed (either into a secret passage, through a locked door, or past the person presenting the test), the party must consume 3 of the 6 potion bottles in their entirety.

No numbers are written on the potion bottles themselves. However, the true number of each potion can be determined by the number of exclamation points found on each label. Using this information paired with the riddle, the more dangerous potions can hopefully be avoided.

These potions should be presented in a random order. The label and effects of each potion are as follows:

Potion Number	Label	Effect When Consumed
1	"For emergencies!"	The creature heals 2d4+2 hit points.
2	"One drop per audience member!!"	The creature falls prone and laughs uncontrollably for 2 minutes. They are incapacitated during this time.
3	"This one REALLY hurts!!!"	The creature burps loudly. It tastes like coconut. Nothing else happens.
4	"Caution! Do not drink! Contents are poisonous!!"	The creature is poisoned until they finish a long rest.
5	"DriNK?!?! DRink! Tell THE WoRLd of the cOMing APOcaLyPse!!"	The creature is paralyzed for 1 minute. At the end of that minute, the creature takes 2d4 psychic damage after suffering strange antagonistic hallucinations.
6	"Made! While! Drunk! Please! Consume! Wisely!"	The creature gains one level of exhaustion.

13. Too Tall to Ride

Characters open the door to an abandoned laboratory, study, library, or other space containing information or valuable goods. Though the door is normal-sized, the handle to the door is only 1.5 feet from the base.

As soon as a Medium or larger creature opens the door, a loud, high-pitched alarm rings out. Whether this space is in a location where the ringing alarm could wake guards, frighten civilians, or alert nearby monsters is up to your discretion. Shutting the door turns off the ringing if the room is empty. When inside the room with the door closed, the ringing is not loud enough to alert people outside the room.

For those inside the room, the ringing is not loud enough to cause pain, but it is loud enough to drown out all other sources of sound, including speech. While the alarm is sounding, all precious materials in this room (books, ingredients, potions, treasure, etc.) are enclosed behind bars or some type of magical ward until the alarm can be shut off.

Solution. Players must note from your description of the door and room contents that the room's former occupant was exceptionally small. Examples of hints include the door handle's height; the presence of tiny desk, chair, and writing utensils; a small coat hung on a low rack; or the presence of many various ladder sizes to ascend and descend the bookshelves.

If no Medium sized or larger creatures are in the room, the alarm stops ringing, and all previously barred materials in the room become accessible.

It's All Small. This idea can be extended further to multiple rooms, or even an entire building. Remember that crawling creatures move half speed, or one-third speed over difficult terrain.

14. The Gift of a Linguist

A tall wooden door contains etched lines of text written in different languages. Each line of text is preceded by a carved symbol, and followed by a circular lock. Both the text and symbol in each line hint at a task that must be completed to open each lock.

Solution. When a task is successfully fulfilled, the corresponding lock makes an audible click as it opens. It's up to you how many locks must be unlocked to open the door.

It's also up to you to decide what languages each line of text is written in, and what tasks the text demands. At least one line of text should be in Common, since almost all creatures speak this language. Other options include, in order of difficulty:

- **Easy.** Common
- **Moderate.** Dwarven, Elvish
- **Hard.** Celestial, Draconic, Gnomish, Halfling, Infernal, Undercommon
- **Very Hard.** Aarakocra, Abyssal, Aquan, Auran, Deep Speech, Druidic, Giant, Goblin, Gnoll, Ignan, Orc, Primordial, Sylvan, Terran

Each line of text begins with a symbol, to help players guess the tasks if they cannot translate its matching text.

Below are some examples of potential symbols and their paired text:

Symbol	*Translated Text*	*Solution*
A circle with an arrow inside of it, rotating clockwise	"Spin me once round!"	The lock must be rotated once, clockwise.
A set of lockpicking tools	"Pick me!"	The lock must be picked (DC 12 Dexterity check using thieves' tools).
A pair of parted lips with music notes emerging from them	"Sing me a little ditty!"	The lock opens when a song.
A hand, palm facing outward, with a large X across it	"DON'T TOUCH ME!"	Every time the lock is touched, the creature that touched it takes 1d4 lightning damage.
A pair of lips whispering into the ear of a blushing, happy face	"Compliment me!"	The lock opens when complimented.
A pair of lips whispering into the ear of a shocked face	"Tell me a secret!"	Someone must tell a secret about themselves to this lock. It must be true, or the lock won't open.
A heart with a question mark in its center	"Tell me who you love most!"	Someone must tell the lock who they love most. It must be true, or the lock won't open.
A wash cloth surrounded by sparkles	"Clean me!"	The lock is covered and grime and must be cleaned.
A large flame	"Warm me up!"	The lock must be warmed up with a torch flame or a fire spell.

15. Blossoming Connections

A large flower-like design is arrayed on the floor of this room, either carved into the ground or outlined with stones, shrubs, or other natural material. At the center of the flower stands a stone pedestal. The petals of the flower extend from the base of the pedestal, and the petals cross each other like a Venn diagram.

A single white flower somehow thrives on the top of the pedestal. Neatly engraved on the pedestal is the following statement:

Here lies a beautiful pair, whose bond was so strong that they passed on together. From their grave blossomed a beautiful flower: the truest representation of their connection. Even in death their love lives on here, continuing to bless those who present tokens of their own shared bonds.

When a creature steps into the space of a flower petal at any time, that petal glows with a faint light, the color of which is unique to every creature (determined by you). If two creatures occupy the same petal at any time, the glow disappears.

When two creatures stand next to each other in petals that overlap, the overlapping section of petal glows white, and a second pedestal emerges from the floor in the center of the flower.

Solution. Each pair of creatures must present a physical token of their relationship with the creature in the petal beside them. For example, the pair could place a weapon on the pedestal if they bonded while training together. They could also present an important item the two found together, a pair of binoculars to represent their night watches together, or even an inside joke scribbled on a note. Whether the token presented accurately represents that pair's bond is up to your discretion (and the pair to defend, if necessary.)

If the token is deemed worthy, each individual's petal glows brighter, and their shared pedestal descends into the earth. When it reemerges, two flowers lay on or next to their presented token. The flowers are a mix of each individual's color (for example: an orange and yellow swirl, for individuals standing in orange-lit and yellow-lit petals). These flowers will never wilt, but are otherwise non-magical.

I Don't Know Them. If two creatures stand next to each other and are strangers or do not share a bond, the overlapping petal glows gray, and the pedestal does not rise. If two individuals stand next to each other who actively dislike or hate each other, the overlapping petal goes black, and their personal colored lights disappear.

Before the Last Petal Falls. The puzzle as-is provides room for character building and roleplay opportunities; the flower becomes a permanent, physical manifestation of two characters' shared bond. These flowers can become a powerful symbol throughout the game if you let them. Perhaps if the characters' bond strengthens or weakens, the flower can grow brighter or more dim to represent that. Perhaps the flower can become more poignant still if one of the characters represented in its colors passes on.

All for One and One for All. For a more challenging or rewarding experience, you can adjust the number of petals to fit the number of characters in your party. Instead of each individual pedestal lowering with a valid token, all pairs have to find a valid token of their bond before the puzzle is solved. This is more difficult, so perhaps completing the puzzle causes a more powerful magic item to materialize on the central pedestal, or perhaps the pedestal itself descends to reveal a secret room or passageway.

16. The Impossible Boy

The characters enter any empty space, be it a dungeon room or a seemingly abandoned building, with a bright lantern that sits on a stool against one wall. The lantern casts strong shadows around the room. The shadow of a small humanoid figure is projected on one wall, but nothing in the light's path could possibly cast such a shadow.

Once the characters spot the shadowy silhouette, it begins to jump up and down and wave at them, gesturing its arm in a beckoning motion. If they attempt to approach the wall or interact directly with the shadow on the wall, it simply shakes its head and repeats the gesture.

Solution. One of the characters must cast their shadow onto the wall, repositioning the light if necessary. Once their shadow is on the wall, the shadowy figure excitedly beckons them closer, putting its hand by its face. If the character allows their shadow to approach the shadowy figure, they feel a hand on their physical ear as they hear the voice of a young boy. The voice whispers that he needs help retrieving his favorite ball, which is hidden somewhere in the room. You can determine where the ball is and how hard it is to find.

Once they find the ball, the characters give it to the boy by casting its shadow on the wall. When the boy takes it, the ball disappears from the physical hand of the creature presenting it. As a token of thanks, the boy then hands over a gift that materializes in the hand of the presenting creature. This could be anything from a magic item to simply a mote or ball of shadow, the use of which is up to your discretion.

Who is This Boy? Characters may try to learn more about this shadow boy or interact with him in other ways. Feel free to let your imagination run wild as to what history or other capabilities this shadow may have, and what other potential purpose he could have in your world!

17. Predicament in Purgatory

The characters enter a storage room filled with hundreds of uniquely shaped, ash-filled terra cotta urns. Scattered among them, easily noticeable, are 6 empty, clay urns, painted with vibrant colors: green, purple, magenta, orange, red, and blue. The purple, magenta, and red urns have square bases, while the green, orange, and blue urns have round bases. This information should be made clear to the players from the start.

At the far end of the room is a small empty fireplace. In the floor of the hearth are 6 urn-sized indents in an alternating square-circle pattern:

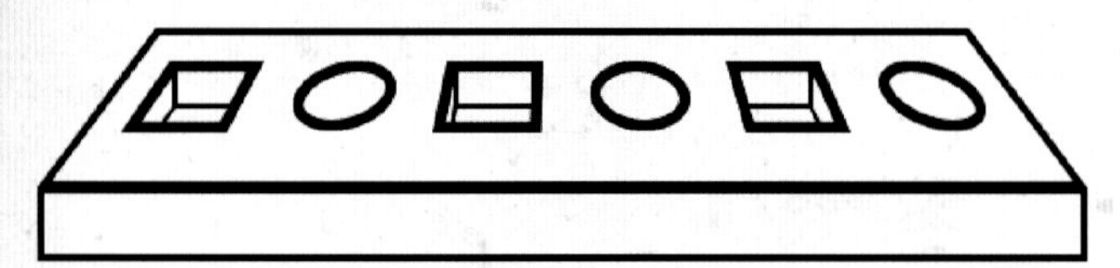

On the mantle over the hearth is a folded piece of parchment with the following message written in elegant calligraphy:

Apple, Pinky, Cherry, Violet, River, and Oz'flob died at the very same instant. The day their spirits arrived at the gates to the afterlife, the line was rather long, and so they were provided chairs to await their turn in Judgement. But these unfortunate spirits were more unfortunate still, for they could not make up their minds on where to sit.

Apple refused to sit beside Cherry, whose breath (even in spirit) was unimaginable in its putrescence.

Pinky and Apple declared that they must sit right beside each other (they are twins, after all).

River and Violet declared that they must be as far apart as possible (ex-lovers are always so picky).

Lastly, Oz'flob declared that she'd love to sit betwixt as much drama as possible (living alone for so long can make you hungry for such gossip).

Some say these spirits are still there today, locked in eternal disagreement, longing for a solution that will finally put their souls to rest.

Solution. Players must correctly arrange the colored urns in the hearth following the proper square-circle pattern in accordance with the logic puzzle. In this puzzle, Apple is the green urn, Pinky is the magenta urn, Cherry is the red urn, Violet is the purple urn, River is the blue urn, and Oz'flob is the orange urn. Using this knowledge, the only correct solution is the following:

1. Purple Urn (Violet, Square Bottom)
2. Green Urn (Apple, Round Bottom)
3. Magenta Urn (Pinky, Square Bottom)
4. Orange Urn (Oz'flob, Round Bottom)
5. Red Urn (Cherry, Square Bottom)
6. Blue Urn (River, Round Bottom)

Only once all urns are correctly placed is the puzzle complete, the once-empty urns now fill with valuable gems, *potions of healing*, or further clues towards something elsewhere in the dungeon. The puzzle could also open a secret door in the fireplace.

18. Aquatic Allies

An empty room or cavern is brightly lit with sconces, and a 10-by-10 foot hole is roughly cut out of the floor. Next to the hole rests a large glass bowl. Underneath the cutout is another room entirely entirely with water, lapping at the edges of the hole. 20 feet below the water's surface, a school of blue, luminescent koi are swimming to and fro. If anyone dives into the water within 10 feet of the fish, they notice that the creatures' luminescence illuminates strange white markings on the walls.

Solution. Characters must catch and bring at least one fish above the surface. If a fish is brought above the surface without being submerged in water, the fish immediately stops glowing and shrivels, lifeless. Once exposed to air, the fish cannot be revived or set aglow again. To keep the fish glowing above water, it must remain submerged, either in the glass bowl or another similar vessel.

When a glowing koi is brought to the walls of the upper room, the markings revealed are too faint to read if the sconces are still lit. Extinguishing all other lights in the room except for one of the glowing koi allows any writing or markings on the walls, floor, and ceiling to be easily visible. These markings can provide clues to another relevant key character or quest, directions to a hidden treasure (perhaps in the pool below), or arrows pointing to specific portions of the room that must be interacted with before revealing a hidden passageway.

Secret Notes. This puzzle is a great way to introduce luminescent koi and invisible writing as a mechanic for further puzzles, or even an entire dungeon. Perhaps the next room requires transporting a koi across a precarious gap without exposing it to air. Perhaps the luminescent koi lets the characters see a safe path drawn on the map of a room filled with hidden traps. Characters could even receive a pot of this invisible ink and a luminescent pendant as treasure that allows them to use this mechanic themselves in the future. The koi fish, so long as it is consistently fed and cared for, could even be kept as a pet!

19. The Arcanic Liftomatic Vertical Transportation Device

A few steps lead up to a sliding door, inside which is a 15-by-15-foot platform. The platform's edge is surrounded by a rail with hinged gates in the center of all its sides but one. If a creature stands on the platform and looks up, they see a vertical lift shaft rising high above them. Other doorways open on the left shaft at certain points high above.

On the rail that does not have a hinged gate is a brass box with 7 wheel-like cylindrical dials set into it. The dials have four pictograms etched into them: a flame, a water droplet, swirling air lines, and a simple dash line. Above each dial is a small brass frame which indicates what pictogram ss selected.

Dangling from a chain beside the console is a battered manual, the contents of which follow:

Arcanic Liftomatic Vertical Transportation Device

- *Do input the elements thee desire upon the brazen tumblers.*
- *Verily, ensureth thou hast input thine elements in the ord'r they shall be made manifest.*
- *Noteth that pow'r inflammatory in singular shall only beareth thee loft no more than ten spans of the standard foot of a human.*
- *Be thee ware that improp'r mixture of elements arcane may causeth unintended or grave consequences.*
- *Thine elements must remain with others of their kind, excepting only when transitioning unto a new set of elements. Once a contiguous group of elements has been created upon the brazen tumblers, further groups will be unable to be created.*
- *Should thee desire to loft thineselves above a height of ten spans of the standard human foot, thou must NOT alternate the elements inflammatory and aqueous repeating, for functioning shall cease.*
- *Elements thee may selecteth:*
  - *Inflammatory - Indicated by flame - Produces fire, heat, necessary for loft fuel.*
  - *Aqueous - Indicated by droplet - Produces moisture, necessary for sustained lift.*
  - *Zephyrous - Indicated by swirling lines - Produces air, lift, necessary for initial propulsion.*
  - *Null - Indicated by a dash.*
- *To propelleth thineselves, thou must combineth the elements in sufficient quantities so as to loft thineselves to the desired destination.*
- *An amount of element aqueous shall be added post entry of element inflammatory. Such is required to formeth pressurized gaseous aqueous, responsible for sustained lifting pow'r.*
- *A single instance of element zephyrous shall be added post entry of element aqueous, no more, no less. Such is required to produceth necessary initial thrust for loft.*
- *If calculated properly, The Liftomatic Vertical Transportation Device shall pause at the peak of its loft for lo 30-seconds before descending with gentility.*
- *Should thee be desirous to stoppeth upon a certain location whilst lofted within the shaft, whether thee be beyond the point thou intended to reacheth, or mayhaps thou calculated wrongly and undershotteth thine loft, pulleth the timed break lever, which shall locketh the platform in place for lo 30-seconds. The break lever may be reset, though if it is not, and additional loft has not been created in the arcanic elemental containment chamber, the Arcanic Liftomatic Vertical Transportation Device shall descend with gentility.*
- *Should thee be desirous of the creation of further loft, thou mayest pull thine timed break lever, set thine brazen tumblers to null, and input the elements thee require and proceedeth per usual directations.*
- ***A Note of Warning Most Dire!*** *Should symbols inflammatory be input in series numbering greater than four, the elemental containment chamber shall be unable to contain the element and the Liftomatic Vertical Transportation Device will be engulfed in truly manifested element inflammatory.*

Solution. The solution to this puzzle is simply to read the manual and make heads or tails of the controls.

To lift themselves 10 feet, the characters must input the following on the tumblers: flame, water, air, null, null, null, and null.

To lift themselves 20 feet, they must input the following: flame, flame, water, water, air, null, null.

To lift themselves 30 feet, they must input the following: flame, flame, flame, water, water, water, air.

Call the Lift. Depending on how accessible you would like this elevator to be, you can create panels at any upper-level door to allow the platform to be called from above so long as the operating procedures are remembered.

Holy Hand Grenade. To enhance the comedic value of the reading of the manual, the reader may read it in their best quavering, pseudo-Shakespearean voice.

20. Ancient Guardian of the Hall

A hallway is almost entirely blocked by a large stone statue, with but a few inches of space to spare on each side. The statue can look like a cross-eyed goblin, a slack-jawed ogre, or anything else exceptionally doofy-looking. When approached, the statue shouts in an equally-doofy voice:

"I AM THE ANCIENT GUARDIAN OF THE HALL. NO ONE GETS PAST, AND NO ONE EVER WILL, BECAUSE I'M A REALLY GREAT GUARDIAN."

Players can investigate the statue further, all while the statue continues on loudly and incessantly about their hall-guarding prowess. Below the statue is a small blackboard plaque with the poorly-written words "Persuns Who Got Pasd" displayed across the top. No names are written below it. The statue will proudly call attention to this plaque as evidence that no one has ever gotten by, because if they had, their name would be on it.

Solution. There are many potential solutions to this puzzle depending on the players' approach. The easiest solution, and the one that is hinted at the most, is for players to simply write their names on the "Persuns Who Got Pasd" plaque with chalk, a pencil, or even carved with a knife. As they do this, the poor dumb statue will be positively gobsmacked, and may even beg or bribe the characters to stop writing their names before they finish. Unfortunately, the statue will have no choice but to let the characters through once they write each of their names on the plaque.

Other potential solutions may involve bribing the statue ("I know of a really great, even BIGGER hall we could bring you to for you to guard!") or possibly lying to the statue ("You've let us through before!" "We created you!"). Much of the fun of this puzzle is interacting with players as this statue, and allowing players' outlandish plans to work on it, seeing as the statue is *delightfully* dumb.

If your players do attack the statue, it has the stats of a large animated object as created by a 5th-level *animate object* spell (HP: 50, AC: 10, Attack: +6 to hit, 2d10 + 2 damage, Movement Speed: 0ft).

21. For Whom the Pyramid Rattles

A pyramid-shaped object roughly the size of a watermelon is in this room. The pyramid is made of a lightweight metal and has no seams or means to open it. A round, metallic-sounding object can be heard and felt rolling around inside the pyramid when it is tilted.

If the characters take the pyramid with them, eventually the ball begins to rattle within the pyramid on its own. How long it takes for the pyramid to start rattling is up to you. This rattling can be heard up to 50 feet away, and is audible even when the object is kept in an extra-dimensional space such as a *bag of holding*. The rattling only stops when the pyramid is held by a creature, who can feel that one of the corners of the pyramid is warm to the touch.

Solution. The pyramid is reacting to the presence of a place it needs to get to, getting warmer or colder as it gets closer or further away. The built-in alarm activates once the pyramid gets within range of the location.

Often, the characters will point the party towards impassable terrain (large gaps, solid walls, etc.) leaving them to determine the best path towards their destination. If the pyramid is tracking an object instead of a location, and that object moves feedback changes to match.

Once the characters reach the location or object (or even creature) the pyramid is tracking, it rattles loudly for a few seconds before falling silent and growing cold once more. The tracked item could be a fragment of a whole object, whose other pieces must be located elsewhere using the pyramid. It could also be a special treasure, or even a person (such as the creator of the object, or a key character in the campaign).

Testing. There is great potential for customization with this puzzle, seeing as it operates around an object that players must learn to utilize. Perhaps your pyramid features a sentient or cursed ball in the center, or perhaps the pyramid is one of a pair that can be used by party members to communicate or track each other across long distances.

Is This Thing On? To increase the difficulty of the puzzle, consider limiting the feedback of the pyramid by making the entirety of it grow warmer or hotter depending on the proximity of the target. You can also limit the temperature feedback of the pyramid to simply "tepid", "warm", or "hot" to remove the sliding scale of heat and further increase difficulty.

Which Way? Add more fun to the object-hunt by presenting your players with gated choices at certain points along their path. For example, perhaps the pyramid points them to a room with two side-by-side doorways. When characters select and enter a doorway, it closes and locks behind them, now committing them to that path (which is either closer or further from their goal). They can investigate the forked paths for clues (footprints, debris, fur stuck in a door hinge, etc.) that may also help them decide which direction to go.

22. Well-Read, Well-Reasoned

Characters find an empty room with nine books laying randomly scattered across the stone floor. Into the floor in large letters is carved the following poem, with a few feet of space between the stanzas:

The space between awaits us,
Red, numbers, stares, and home

A clever placement wakes us,
Boys, embraces, fright, and stone

The magic happens at the end,
Then close your eyes and count to ten...

Solution. The solution to the puzzle is physically arranging the books in order within the spaces between the stanzas. Describe the books and their titles in a random order.

The books which should be laid out from left to right in the space between stanzas one and two are:

1. **Red:** *Crimson Nightmare* by Terrance Black
2. **Numbers:** *Our World As Understood in Mathematics* by Harmony Sikh
3. **Stares:** *Warring Gazes* by Bobson Loveleaf
4. **Home:** *The City Whence She Came* by Tordwynn Aralance

The books which should be laid out from left to right in the space between stanzas two and three are:

5. **Boys:** *Puberty in Young Male Half Orcs: A Study* by Graak Hogthorn
6. **Embraces:** *Hold Me, Hardly* by Elizabet Skylancer
7. **Fright:** *Tales to Tell After Twilight* by Desdemona Reaper
8. **Stone:** *A Miner's Guide to Minerals* by Tokk Orlach

The book that should be placed at the end of the last stanza is:

9. **Magic:** *The Arcane Stairway* (no author)

Once the books are arranged in this order, the entire party must close their eyes and count to ten (per the poem's instructions). During this time, they hear the sound of flipping pages and feel rushing wind on their faces. When they open their eyes, the books have each grown to roughly 5 feet in length and have embedded themselves into a wall to form an ascending staircase. The stairs can then be climbed up through an illusory portion of the ceiling, where a hidden library or other important location can be found.

Speed Read. You should expect that characters will look through the books. We encourage you to prepare or improvise what the contents of the books might be.

23. Uplifting Words

Characters open a seemingly normal door into the middle of a 15-foot square, 60-foot high shaft. On the far wall, across from the entrance, the following proverb is painted:

The hammer does pale when compared to the tongue.
To build and to break, there is no better one.
It is not of matter, but soul that we speak,
So forge with thine words, for the crop ye shall reap.

30 feet up from the proverb is a white door, flush with the ceiling. 30 feet below is a black door, flush with the floor.

Although there are no visible or tangible walking surfaces, characters can enter the room and seemingly walk on thin air. However, they are unable to ascend or descend in the shaft by normal means, such as climbing, jumping, or using magic; each attempt results in the character being yanked back to the invisible "floor" where they first stood.

Solution. Each time a character compliments a fellow party member, that character ascends 10 feet. Each time a character insults a fellow party member, that character descends 10 feet. This means, from the starting middle ground, a character must give 3 compliments (30 feet) to reach the top white door, or 3 insults (30 feet) to reach the bottom black door.

Characters may discover a blessed item behind the white door and a cursed item behind the black door, or perhaps the doors are simply two entrances into the same location, presented simply to reveal the character of those who accessed them.

Have At You! You could take this idea to the extreme by pairing this idea with combat. Perhaps the rules of the shaft only affect the players, requiring them to shout niceties or obscenities at each other mid-battle whilst trying to thwart a flying enemy. Perhaps other speaking or sentient enemies are beholden to the room's rules as well, resulting in further mayhem, and requiring you to hurl insults or compliments as needed too!

24. We Are as Water

This room is a 30-by-30 foot area with a 10-foot-wide ledge of ice on one side, where the characters enter, and a 10-foot-wide ledge of stone, covered in a thick haze of steam. A 10-foot-wide river of water flows between the ledges, running impossibly from a stone wall on one side of the room to a dark stone tunnel on the other. If characters investigate the icy area, steamy area, or water, they find nothing out of the ordinary.

In the center of the river, a rowboat and oars is anchored by a rope tied to a wooden stake in the ice. On the archway above the river tunnel is a plaque engraved in elegant script:

"We are as water, ever in three forms: who we were, who we are, and who we will be."

If characters get in the boat and row through the tunnel, they will emerge from the tunnel into the room they just left; they see and feel nothing behind them but the stone wall. They do, however, see a ghostly vision of their immediate past selves on the ice, replaying from the moment they initially entered the room until they rowed into the tunnel. If any characters stayed behind without getting on the boat, they do not see this vision, but they do see the boat phase through the stone wall. Any subsequent passes through the tunnel reveal the same thing.

Solution. The icy portion of the room represents the characters' past, while the river portion of the room represents the characters' present. If characters enter the steamy portion of the room after traveling through the tunnel, they see another ghostly vision, presumably of their future selves. This vision shows themselves lowering to the floor to lay motionless in a fetal position. After a moment, the vision melts through the stone floor and disappears. If the characters follow this vision's lead and curls into a fetal position on the floor, they too will phase through the floor and into a new area.

In this new area, or as they phase through to this area, characters may have further dream-like visions of their past or future selves, personalized and described at your discretion.

Be Creative. This puzzle presents ample opportunity for adjustment to suit your party's needs. Especially since the players will likely try many things outside of the "correct" solution, you can think of many other ways to reward their creativity with additional visions or discoveries. For example, what if players try to break through the stone wall from which the river mysteriously originates, or they try to travel backwards through it? What if players try to stop or turn around in the middle of the dark river tunnel — would they discover anything?

You don't need answers to every possibility right from the start, but leave yourself open to having fun and being creative with your responses to your players' efforts.

25. "Meta" Magic

Characters find a small diorama in the center of an empty room. The diorama is stuck to the floor, and is an exact replica of the room the characters are currently in, as well as the surrounding dungeon. The diorama even includes strange, miniature figurines that seem to match the character's current positions, and move about as they do.

If a miniature figurine is moved on the board, the character it represents is also moved a proportionate distance in the room. No miniature figurine can be tilted or lifted from the diorama — they may only be slid. In the same vein, if a character jumps vertically or goes prone, their miniature figurine remains unchanged. Miniature figurines cannot be damaged or destroyed.

Creatures can take damage as normal from this movement due to traps or dangers in their path. Creatures that want to prevent this forced movement can make a DC15 Charisma saving throw. If the creature fails, they are moved against their will. If they succeed, they are unmoved, and their connection to the miniature figurine is severed, preventing them from being moved this way again.

Solution. This puzzle concept has an infinite number of applications and solutions depending on the campaign and in-world location of the diorama. The following are potential scenarios and solutions for this puzzle, which can be adjusted or replaced with your own ideas:

- Characters examining the diorama discover a hidden room with no entrance that can't be seen or accessed in real life. Characters must find a way to carve a path in the diorama to make this room accessible; or, similarly, they may find a way to relocate the treasure within this hidden room to a separate accessible location in the dungeon.
- Characters notice a room further into the dungeon with the lurking miniature figurines of sinister creatures. Under the same limitations of the characters' figurines (no lifting, no laying down, cannot be destroyed) players must relocate, restrain, or otherwise clear a path through these creatures in order to advance. This can also be applied to disarming traps and clearing other map obstacles before advancing.
- Characters notice a miniature in their current room of a hostile creature they can't otherwise see or detect. Players must battle this creature, and may use their action to move themselves, allies, or the creature to another location using the diorama. If the creature is sentient and intelligent, it may even try to commandeer the diorama to use against the characters instead.

26. 'Tis the Season

Characters enter a 15-by-15 foot room that is unnaturally brimming with springtime atmosphere. The floor of the room is covered in grass, flowers, and foliage. Sunlight streaks through rain clouds that drift and drizzle from the ceiling, 25 feet above.

In the center of the grassy floor sits a 1-inch square metal box. The box is nearly impossible to break open in its current state, though something can be heard brushing against the inside of it. In the back right corner of the room is a 5-by-5 foot square patch of tilled, unused farming soil. On the far left corner of the room is an unlocked metal door.

Past this initial room are three more nearly identical rooms, each which embody the seasons of summer, autumn, and winter. The summer room is cloudless, bright, hot, and flooded with the scent of summery earth and flowers. The metal box in the summer room is hot to the touch. The autumn room is slightly chilly with crunchier, browning grass, and is filled with a sourceless breeze that wafts through it. This room's metal box shows the beginnings of rust, but is still very difficult to open. The winter room is very cold, coated in a layer of snow that drifts slowly down from the clouds above. The metal box in this room is thoroughly rusted and looks easier to open. Unlike the other rooms, the door at the back of the winter room is locked, has no handle, and sports a deep, half-circle indent in its center, a bit larger than a fist.

Solution. The metal box can be opened in any room, but it's hardest to open in summer and easiest to open in winter. It contains a 6-inch tree sapling, and once the box is opened in one room it is opened in all rooms.

Characters can then plant the seed in the farming soil in the spring room. Nothing happens immediately, but in the winter room there is no a 4-foot tall tree of the same kind as the sapling. Removing this tree and replanting it in the spring room, makes a large, fruit-bearing tree appear in the autumn room. Characters can then take this fruit to the winter room, place it into the circular indent on the door, and the door will open.

What lies beyond the door could be a bounty of mystical fruits and vegetables, or perhaps a portal to another location or plane that is similarly governed by the quick shifting of seasons.

Remembering the Past. The core concept of this room could instead be used to provide interesting opportunities for roleplay with the players. Perhaps key events in your characters' lives occurred in a particular season, creating a ripe atmosphere for flashbacks or plot advancement. It's also possible that the rooms don't culminate in a locked door at all, but simply serve as a physical representation of characters' journey thus far.

27. Short and Sweet

The space is a room of any particular size, but cluttered with things in some degree of disarray. On the wall hangs a large picture frame as tall as a person. The painting inside the frame is flat black.

Notable items found amongst the clutter in are:

- An ant farm
- A journal lying next to the ant farm
- A sack containing a large amount of dried meat.
- A rough and slightly misshapen 3-by-3-foot, 6-foot tall block of sugar under a tarp.
- A small chisel and hammer nearby.
- A small workbench with alchemical tools and a wooden crate of small brown glass bottles labeled "ant repellent, not ale."
- A round, metal shield that looks like it was almost shorn in half by massive jaws.

Solution. An item the characters seek has been hidden inside the ant farm. Any creature stepping through the frame exits a Tiny frame within the ant farm, stepping out onto a small area of stone. The stone is carved with wards which prevent the ants from approaching the frame and escaping. Beyond the stone, is a typical ant farm.

Creatures inside the ant farm appear Tiny to those outside it, but they are their normal size relative to other creatures inside the ant farm. The ants in the farm are highly territorial and attack intruders.

The journal describes the room's owner using the ant farm as a place to store valuables. He discovered that his ants were temperamental, and he tried several things to deal with them including homebrewed ant repellant, dried meat, and sugar.

The ant repellant doesn't work at all. Instead, it enrages any ants in the immediate area until the characters flees.

The ants quickly devour the dried meat, but it does nothing to make them more friendly. The sugar, however, makes ants who eat it friendly towards the characters.

28. Stoned

In the center of the room is a large, simple clay pot surrounded by beautiful colored stones. A creature who picks up a stone is unable to speak, unable to release the stone, and cannot pick up another stone.

Each stone telepathically whispers a particular requirement to the mind of the creature who picks it up, and meeting this requirement allows the creature to drop the stone.

The conditions for each stone are:

- **Red.** You must take 5 hit points of damage while holding the stone, then you may place it in the pot.
- **Orange.** You must place your stone in the shoe of a fellow party member, and place the shoe in the pot.

- **Yellow**. You must get every party member to give you a hug. The stone can then be placed into the pot.
- **Green**. You must have no currency on your person or within your belongings. Once you have no coin in your possession, the stone can then be placed into the pot.
- **Blue**. You must douse any sources of light in the room. The stone may then be placed in the pot.
- **Purple**. Your stone can only be placed into the pot while you are upside-down (feet above your head).
- **Black.** You must make someone kneel on both knees and bow to you. Once someone does, you may put your stone in the pot.
- **White.** Get the rest of your party to leave the room. Once you are alone, you may put your stone in the pot.

Solution. The puzzle is solved once every party member has taken a stone and fulfilled its requirement. This may mean that sealed exits open, treasure is revealed, or clues can be found. Once the puzzle has been solved, the stones placed in the pot magically return to their original locations, and any personal items removed to fulfill the stone's requirements are magically returned.

We All Have to Get Stoned. The puzzle might require that every member of the party take a stone, even those who are not in the room. This might mean some or all of the characters who are in the room need to leave, find the others, and come back with them. Having one hand occupied with a stone may impede a character's ability to use weapons or cast spells.

Where's the Pot? For an even greater challenge, the stones may be found separate from the clay pot, and perhaps even separate from each other.

29. Mean Muggin'

Within the tavern, 3 humanoids sit at a table, one Large, one Medium, and one Small.

The tavernkeep says:

"'Ey, c'mere. You wanna play a bit of a game? See those three? Them's regulars 'n' they order the same thing every night. Here's the game:

"These here are their drinks." He puts three drinks on the bar. *Three of you each grab a drink, and you take the drinks t' them at the same time. They get the right drinks, they won't start no rukus. Give 'em the wrong drinks, and they're like t' fight.*

"They get the right drinks, you get rooms, food and drinks on the house. Any of 'em fights, you pay full price, and buy a round for those three and everyone else in here. Whaddaya say?"

There are three clay mugs on the bar, each with different contents: water, sweet mead, and fire whiskey. The patrons are at their table, sober.

The Large humanoid seems perfectly happy at the moment, but starts a fight if given mead or whiskey.

The Medium humanoid is eating some spicy food, and sweat is beading on his forehead. They want whisky, and get belligerent if given water. Mead makes them start a fight.

The Small humanoid is enjoying some bread with honey smeared on it. They want mead, and get belligerent if given water; whiskey makes them start a fight.

Solution. The Large humanoid gets water, the Medium humanoid gets fire whiskey, and the Small humanoid gets the sweet mead.

30. A Lasting Impression

The characters enter an ancient, dusty room built entirely from roughly-carved sandstone bricks. Each of these bricks has carvings that resemble rudimentary hieroglyphics or early pictographs. The pictographs on certain bricks depict religious rituals, interactions with gods, famous wars, and prophetic stories.

One corner of a wall has crumbled, leaving an empty space where six bricks used to be. Six sandstone bricks lay on the floor beneath the crumbled portion of wall, though they are strangely pristine and have an aura of transmutation magic visible with *detect magic*. The bricks look like they cover an empty space of wall with the words "tell your story" carved roughly into it.

Solution. Using a knife, chisel, or other tool, characters must recreate six of their previous adventures, accomplishments, or memorable encounters on the fallen bricks. They must then place these bricks into the crumbled portion of the wall, filling the hole. The bricks then glow with a soft white light as they become part of the wall.

Across the room, a different section of bricks shifts outwards to reveal a 2-by-2 foot section of stone wall with a strange, stony face carved into it. The face speaks to the characters, thanking them for their stories and rewarding them with a story in return: any single one of the stories they find depicted somewhere else in the room.

After the retelling, the face asks the characters to return someday with more stories, promising to reward them once more with it's knowledge. Finally, the bricks shift back into place, covering the face, and the corner section of bricks crumbles once more, the characters' stories erased from the brick faces.

We Have to Draw? It is highly recommended that you require your players to actually draw their chosen memory or adventure on an index-card-sized piece of paper. Even if you are playing remotely, have players draw their brick face and send a picture of it to you and the gaming crew! The worse the drawing, the better, trust us. You can even get them framed afterwards to have a lifelong memory of your campaign and its wild adventures!

Years and Years. You can provide a more concrete reward for this puzzle. When the characters finish placing their bricks into the wall, the floor starts to shudder, then slowly descends. Describe how the brick walls continue downward as the floor lowers, depicting thousands more stories on the bricks, perhaps ones that grow more dark or sinister as they continue down. Eventually, the characters find themselves in a secret underground tomb or tunnel system long forgotten by time.

Subtle Secrets

Adding depth, mystery, and intrigue to an adventure can be the difference between a good campaign and a great one. Storytelling usually benefits from keeping a bit of information being from the main characters and then revealing that information at the moment that gives the best dramatic effect. This could be something as important as a relationship between the main antagonist and the heroes (such as the villain being one of the hero's blood relatives) or something more mundane, like a secret escape tunnel out of the final chamber of the dungeon.

Characters can learn these secrets by seeking out learned scholars or ancient creatures that might know obscure facts. They can also pour over books, scrolls, and runes on dungeon walls. Dreams, visions, flashbacks, and other magical occurrences can also yield useful information.

Each of these methods requires a different approach. Wisdom and Charisma-based skills such as Insight, Persuasion, and Intimidation are useful when dealing with other creatures. When searching for written secrets, Intelligence-based skills like History and Religion are appropriate. For supernatural occurrences, Wisdom and Intelligence-based skills such as Arcana, Insight, and Investigation are useful, depending on the nature of the occurrence.

Hidden information can be broken down into three categories: story secrets, quest secrets, and environment secrets.

Story Secrets

Story secrets include things having to do with the overarching campaign and the characters' roles within it. The noble who gives the characters their quest to rid the land of vampires is himself a vampire. Two characters find out that they are actually half-siblings and share a psychic connection. The entire planet has a giant dragon slumbering inside of it. These are all secrets that could change the characters or how they relate to the world of your campaign.

The best way to give out these secrets is slowly, as clues to a larger puzzle. Each piece helps to form a clearer picture of the whole secret. Better still, but more challenging, is to leave a trail of clues that lead the characters to the wrong conclusion. Then, when the final clue is in place, the revelation comes as a shock.

Here are some example story secrets to inspire you in your own storytelling:

- The person setting the characters on their journey is actually a blood relative of the antagonist, though they may or may not know it. The closer the relationship, the more impactful the final reveal.
- A powerful noble and several of their colleagues are secretly vampires, lycanthropes, or some other accursed creature. One member of this group wants to eliminate the others to gain power and eliminate the only people who know their horrible secret.
- One of the characters is either vulnerable or immune to the main antagonist's signature ability. The reason for this unique situation might be a magical blessing or curse, a twist of fate, or some other quirk of your campaign's setting.
- The dragon who is thought to guard the treasure died a long time ago, but it's skeletal remains still lurk in its lair.
- The individuals who hired the characters are actually members of a different faction opposed to the one they claim to represent.
- The characters aren't expected to succeed or even survive on their adventure, but instead to act as a distraction while another group accomplishes its goal.

Quest Secrets

Quest secrets pertain to specific tasks within an adventure itself. These could be the location of a map the characters need to begin the next leg of their journey, a secret password to open a chest that contains the artifact they need to proceed, or learning that touching the glowing orb on the pedestal will instantly disintegrate someone who is not the chosen one.

Here are some example quest secrets to inspire you in your own storytelling:

- If they want to release the captive creature from its magical bonds, the characters must replace it with someone else.
- The lock that foiled the characters is enchanted with *arcane lock*, requiring a specific key or a *knock* spell.
- The object at the center of the characters' quest can only be touched by a creature of a particular bloodline, a creature wearing a particular ring, or a creature in possession of a particular enchanted item.
- Over the years, many replicas of the item the characters are searching for have been made. Only the version with a specific maker's mark is the original.
- An unassuming creature, whether ally or adversary, connected to the characters' journey is secretly very powerful and not to be underestimated. This reveal should be sudden and dramatic.
- The antagonist may only be defeated by a specific person, spell, element, item, etc. This could also be a specific location where the antagonist can be defeated such as a particular building, environment, or dimension.

Environmental Secrets

Environmental secrets can be a compartment in a desk, a false wall in an alchemy lab, or a hatch in the floor under the rug. Often these types of secrets are related to a simple or complex trap. Stepping in the wrong place, opening the wrong door, and picking up an object might all trigger a trap.

In many cases, characters stumble over environmental secrets by accident; detecting a faint draft through a crack that reveals a hidden passageway, looking up at the perfect moment to notice a lever on the ceiling, accidentally falling down a pit trap to discover the next level of the dungeon.

Here are some examples of environmental secrets to inspire you in your own storytelling:

- Stepping through a mirror is the only way to reach the next level of the dungeon.
- A secret passageway connects an early section of the dungeon with a deeper area. The hidden doors of the passageway can only be opened from the deeper area.
- A chest has a secret compartment that can be accessed from the inside by pressing on a release mechanism.
- A password or command word for a magical device is written on the back of the tapestry.
- An illusion hides a door or passageway.
- Grooves on the floor, left by a trap, are revealed only when light hits the tiles at a particular angle.

Ridiculous Riddles

Riddles are questions or verbal puzzles that are presented so as to be cryptic or indirect, while still seeking a specific answer. Consider the classic "Riddle of the Sphinx" found in Greek mythology:

What walks on four legs in the morning, two legs in the afternoon, three legs in the evening, and no legs at night?

The answer, as most people know, is "a human," or "people."

The riddle is a test of the ability to avoid overly literal thinking, and to think figuratively. It would be very easy to simply ask "What crawls at the beginning of its life, walks on two legs after that, and later uses a cane, and then dies?" The point is to test the cleverness of the listener.

Guidelines for Riddle Design

Here are some guidelines for creating riddles:

1. It should be solvable.
2. It must provide the necessary information.
3. It should have only one answer
4. Have clues ready.

Now we'll elaborate on these various points.

It should be solvable!

Riddles and brain teasers can either make players feel wonderful and clever, or stupid and frustrated. There is also something about sitting around playing a tabletop RPG, or playing a game with a group, that can turn an otherwise clever individual's brain to mush. Here are some things that can impact one's ability to solve riddles at the table:

- The pressure of other people watching
- Distractions
- Having the input of other individuals or solving as a committee
- If the players must remain "in character" while they try to solve the riddle
- In-game pressure (such as a character's life depending on a correct answer)

Because of these (and, very likely, many other reasons not mentioned here), it is important to remember that you, the GM, ***want*** the players to solve your riddle! If you make it too hard, it is almost inevitable that they will be stuck there all night (or worse, multiple *sessions*). As a general rule, the riddle will always be at least one degree harder for your group than it is for you, if not two. If you think your riddle is hard, expect it to be ***very*** hard for your players. If you think your riddle is easy, expect it to be moderately difficult (which is exactly the range that's generally best to aim for, unless your group is a bunch of hardened riddle-breakers).

It must provide the necessary information

The contents of the riddle must be sufficient to reveal the answer on their own, to a reasonable degree. For instance, with our Sphynxian example, the riddle does not **state** "man" or "a human" (or, in the case of fantasy RPGs, perhaps it would be human*oid*?). However, it is *reasonable* to think that someone is aware of their own species and how the flow of life tends to work. It is knowledge that the subject is guaranteed to have. The riddle just forces them to realize the connection between the abstract clue they were given, and the firm information locked in their own minds.

The answer should be the only one

Good riddles have a way of giving the solver that "Ah HA!" moment, because there should be only one answer. When the solver lands on an idea, they can check it by asking themselves, "Does my idea meet the criteria of the riddle?" If the answer is a firm "yes" for all points of the riddle, that should be the answer.

Having said that, designing riddles can be difficult and, unless you're an expert at it, you might make a riddle that can be answered by something that you didn't expect. If the answer given by the players perfectly fits the criteria of the riddle, it is important to accept it. It will make the players feel extremely clever and the game will keep moving.

Have clues ready

Players *will* get stumped sometimes and it is important to be ready to give clues. This is an excellent opportunity to use ability checks pertaining to what characters know or have encountered before. Make sure that the clue is *just* a clue, and not the entire answer.

Exceptions

Coming up with a riddle can be an amorphous, tricky, and confusing thing to do, even when you have guidelines like these to help. Sometimes the guidelines may even steer you away from where your mind wants to go. If you get inspired and come up with something that doesn't follow the guidelines, but still works, *great!* Even in the examples below, you will find some that may not quite fit what's above, but they are still fun. Follow your inspiration and practice, practice, practice.

General Tips

- Think of things with multiple meanings, such as an object or commonly used word or phrase.
- Use a simple rhyme scheme such as one of the following:
- Every line rhymes (go for similar syllable pacing in the sentences).
- Every other line rhymes (first with third, second with fourth, etc).
- Limerick (five lines; first, second and fifth rhyme, third and fourth rhyme).
- Limit your lines; simpler is better.

Example Riddles

Now that we've broken down the elements of designing a riddle, we've come up with some examples that you are free to use or change as you see fit.

Riddle: With a large appetite, I don't bother to chew. I remain unarmed, yet still fear is my due. I forge my own armor, but throw it out, too.

Answer: A snake

Riddle: I can be tall, but beyond hips never placed. Though empty I rest, trav'ling full's to my taste. To keep me at home is naught but a waste.

Answer: Boots

Riddle: I can be cliche, or rife with banality. I do not have sides, but can have plurality. I can be be turned 'round, but more in mentality.

Answer: A phrase

Riddle: I reach around earth, grasping ever so tight. Once born, I exist for a time out of sight. Though later I reach into firmament's light.

Answer: A tree

Riddle: A thread in the curtain of your soul's window. A bond for the sep'rate, I hold things just so. A message in crimson to mutineers go.

Answer: A lash

Riddle: My glow, it is warm, but for warmth you don't want me. I live and die, but no tear is shed for me. But I'll see you anon, when you resurrect me.

Answer: A candle

Riddle: All walk through me, though many misconstrue me. My meaning is subjective, but I'm always the objective.

Answer: Life

Riddle: I am a master of true transmutation. Once I've been set to work, there's often little cessation. I inspire and drown, bring you up and then down, help you have a great time then get you kicked out of town.

Answer: Alcohol

Riddle: I come from the moon or from the smile of a friend. I also rest in a building, making sure it won't bend.

Answer: A beam

Riddle: I lie inside you, and deep underground. My arms are outstretched, in them treasure is found. My riches crown kings, and bathe battlegrounds.

Answer: A vein

Riddle: I keep an eye open, but yet I am blind. I am sharp as a tack, but I have no mind. Please try not to lose me, for I'm hard to find.

Answer: A needle

Riddle: I have no real strength, so to speak

My appearance does seem rather meek

Though I am thin and flimsy

I've held wit and whimsy

And the wisdom that sages did seek

Answer: Paper

Riddle: Sometimes might I look like a pig

More often I am grand and big

Give me what you've got

If it's worth a little or lot

For aught else I don't give a fig

Answer: A bank

Riddle: When I go to work I get nailed

I get battered and trounced while impaled

When finally off-shift

I'm given a lift

To get hammered and again assailed

Answer: A horseshoe

Riddle: The reason I'm loved is quite clear

I am prized for my excellent ears

But what I haven't told

Is they're ears made of gold

And what they certainly can't do is hear

Answer: Corn

Riddle: On the outside, I seem hard and hairy

If I lurk above, you best be wary

I yield for stone

Or steel alone

I'm also too much for a swallow to carry

Answer: A Coconut

Trapsmith Legends

The trapsmith is a clever, cunning, and devious creator of obstacles and impediments. In this chapter, you will find information on the trapsmith background, as well as three trapsmith NPCs who can accompany an adventuring party on their journeys, for the right price.

Trapsmith Background. The trapsmith is proficient in building and disarming traps, and has the tools and knowledge to do so. This background comes with a unique set of equipment, features, and characteristics, all suited to the dungeon-delving experience.

NPCs & Hirelings. For those facing an especially challenging dungeon — full of scything blades, pitfalls, and fire blasts at every turn — there are folk who make a good living acting as guides through such treacherous places.

Trapsmith

You love traps and you always have. The satisfaction when something comes together *just* right is a feeling you're very familiar with. You have always enjoyed tinkering with things and finding ways to defend your home or place of business with dangerous devices. You understand that traps can be, and often are, harmful but you treat your profession with some degree of ethics, depending on whether or not you consider the potential victims of your traps to be deserving of their fate.

Skill Proficiencies: Perception, plus your choice of one of the following: Arcana, Investigation, Sleight of Hand, or Survival.

Tool Proficiencies: Thieves' tools, trapmaker's tools*

Equipment: A set of tough, rugged clothing, a set of trapmaker's tools*, a small boot knife, string, a wooden hammer, box of 50 1-inch iron nails, a small envelope holding 15 hollow needles, a thimble, a round leather scroll case containing 10 pieces of parchment, 5 small pieces of writing charcoal, a spool of wire, a spool of thin braided rope, a spring, a pulley, and a pouch containing 5 gp.

Feature: Professional Courtesy. When you come into contact with other trap makers with whom you share a language, you can talk shop. When you do this, you have a better chance of building professional rapport. At the GM's discretion, this might shift them away from being hostile, provide you a discount on materials, or they may decide to do you a small favor.

Suggested Characteristics. Being especially perceptive, you're always keeping a keen eye on your surroundings. Even in polite company, you're always looking for the nearest exit. You're rarely surprised since you have likely thought of many different ways a particular situation could go. You may also have some scars from your exploits, which you may or may not wear proudly.

d8	Personality Trait
1	I'm persistent and don't give up easily.
2	It takes a lot to aggravate me but, once I reach that point, I explode like a powder keg.
3	I have a particular aversion to being confined in a space with no exit. My favorite places have no walls and no ceilings.
4	I'm trusting of those who seem genuine and always try to see the best in people.
5	I'm attracted to people with money and power.
6	I'm willing to risk everything for the sake of adventure.
7	I've regaled many a stunned crowd with stories of my adventures.
8	I'm especially sensitive, and resistant to criticism.

d6	Ideal
1	**Practical.** I use my skills to aid those with righteous intent. (Lawful)
2	**Reckless.** We may lose a few people along the way so the rewards better be worth it. (Chaotic)
3	**Supportive.** The coin I make from my skills goes to benefit the needy. (Good)
4	**Selfish.** Me, myself, and I. (Evil)
5	**Assignment.** It doesn't really matter who I'm working for, or to what end, as long as I get paid. (Neutral)
6	**Unpredictable.** People around me never know what I'm going to do next. (Chaotic)

d6	Bond
1	Most of my earnings go to my guild.
2	I'm avoiding a manipulative and dependent family.
3	I regret putting my friend in a dangerous situation, one that led to their death.
4	Folk from far and wide will one day tell tales of my exploits.
5	I go it alone, and I always have.
6	I'm quick to make new friends, but also quick to lose them.

d6	Flaw
1	The desire to see what's beyond the horizon has gotten me in trouble more than once.
2	When I earn money I quickly, and foolishly, spend it.
3	It's every foolhardy adventurer for themselves when the plan goes sideways.
4	I have a loose relationship with the truth and will say whatever I need to if it's advantageous to me.
5	I am cowardly in the face of adversity.
6	I'm cheap and refuse to pay fair prices for goods and services.

d6	Physical Feature
1	I'm missing a digit or two.
2	I have a nasty scar on my face or head.
3	I have a prosthetic appendage.
4	A section of my body has been horribly burned.
5	I have a permanent limp.
6	I don't have any eyebrows, and they never grow back.

*Trapmaker's Tools

This kit includes tools handy for crafting traps, such as lightweight wire-cutters, pliers, various clips, and a pair of thick gloves designed for the handling of sharp objects.

NPCs & Hirelings

Throughout the land, there are folk who are wise when it comes to traps and how to deal with them, and some of them are for hire. Each of these NPCs has a unique skill set which may be useful to an adventuring party.

Compensation. Some trapsmiths require an upfront fee for their services, others may demand a share of the profits; some may demand both. The more potential danger, the more the trapsmith charges.

Alterations. The characters below are designed as by-the-book characters (with the exception of the Trapsmith background and trapmaker's tools). If they are too powerful, or not powerful enough, for your needs, feel free to increase or decrease their level and adjust as necessary.

Berf Barbender

Medium humanoid (hill dwarf), chaotic neutral

Class Cleric 9
Background Trapsmith
Occupation Hireling

Armour Class 16 (leather armor, shield)
Hit Points 66 (9d8 + 18)
Speed 25 ft. (not reduced by heavy armor)

STR	DEX	CON	INT	WIS	CHA
16 (+3)	16 (+3)	12 (+1)	13 (+1)	15 (+2)	8 (-1)

Saving Throws Wis +6, Cha +3
Skills Arcana +5, History +5, Investigation +5, Medicine +6, Nature +6, Perception +6
Tools smith's tools, thieves' tools, trapmaker's tools
Damage Resistances poison
Senses darkvision 60 ft., passive Perception 16
Languages Common, Draconic, Dwarvish, Sylvan

Channel Divinity (2/Short Rest). As an action, Berf can channel divinity (DC 14) to create one of the following effects:

- *Turn Undead.* Each undead that can see or hear Berf must make a Wisdom saving throw. If the creature fails its saving throw, it is turned for 1 minute, or until it takes damage.
  A turned creature must spend its turns trying to move as far away from Berf as it can, and it can't willingly move to a space within 30 feet of him. It also can't take reactions. For its action, it can use only the Dash action, or try to escape from an effect that prevents it from moving. If there's nowhere to move, the creature can use the Dodge action.
  When an undead fails its saving throw against Berf's Turn Undead feature, it is instantly destroyed if its CR is lower than 1.
- *Knowledge of the Ages.* Berf gains proficiency in any skill, or with any tool, for 10 minutes.
- *Read Thoughts.* Berf chooses one creature that he can see within 60 feet of him. That creature must make a Wisdom saving throw. If the creature succeeds on the saving throw, Berf can't use this feature on it again until he finishes a long rest.
  If the creature fails its save, Berf can read its surface thoughts when it is within 60 feet of him. This effect lasts for 1 minute. During that time, Berf can use an action to end this effect and cast the *suggestion* spell on the creature without expending a spell slot. The target automatically fails its saving throw against the spell.

Dwarven Combat Training. Berf has proficiency with battleaxes, handaxes, light hammers, and warhammers.

Dwarven Resilience. Berf has advantage saving throws against poison.

Spellcasting. Berf is a 9th-level spellcaster. His spellcasting ability is Wisdom (spell save DC 14, +6 to hit with spell attacks). Berf has the following cleric spells prepared:

- Cantrips (at will): *guidance, light, mending, thaumaturgy*
- 1st level (4 slots): *bless, command, identify*
- 2nd level (3 slots): *augury, suggestion*
- 3rd level (3 slots): *nondetection, speak with dead*
- 4th level (3 slots): *arcane eye, confusion*
- 5th level (1 slot): *legend lore, scrying*

Stonecunning. Whenever Berf makes an Intelligence (History) check related to the origin of stonework, he is considered proficient in the History skill, and has +9 to his roll.

Actions

Mace. *Melee Weapon Attack:* +7 to hit with, reach 5 ft., one target. *Hit:* 6 (1d6+3) bludgeoning damage, and 4 (1d8) radiant damage.

Light Crossbow. *Ranged Weapon Attack:* +7 to hit, range 80/320 ft., one target. *Hit:* 7 (1d8+3) piercing damage, and 4 (1d8) radiant damage.

Overview

Berf Barbender is an old dwarf cleric with a craggy, grizzled appearance; he wears a long, red waistcoat with big brass buttons. He is knowledgeable about religious artifacts, the locations where they might be stored, and the traps that might protect them. On his back, Berf carries a massive pack filled with all manner of trap detecting and disarming devices. He has the tools and skills to handle just about any type of trap, but even he will admit that he's not a master of any particular type; more of a generalist. Very few people know that he is a cleric; he keeps his holy symbol covered, and only reveals it in the most dire of circumstances.

Personality Traits

Berf is persistent and doesn't give up easily. He nearly starved to death once when he delved into a trap-laden dungeon in search of a lost relic.

Ideals

Berf is a bit reckless at times; a few people may be lost along the way, but the rewards might be worth it.

Bonds

Berf regrets putting his former partner in a dangerous situation, one that led to their death.

Flaws

The desire to see what's beyond the horizon has gotten Berf into trouble more than once.

Roleplaying Berf

Berf says what he thinks and lacks any subtly with his words. He is one of the toughest dwarves you'll ever encounter, with the stamina of someone half his age. He tries to make everyone around him think he doesn't get scared or feel pain but, deep down, even he has a breaking point.

"Don't touch a thing!"

Equipment

A set of tough, rugged clothing, a set of trapmaker's tools*, a small boot knife, string, a wooden hammer, box of 50 1-inch iron nails, a small envelope holding 15 hollow needles, a thimble, a round leather scroll case containing 10 pieces of parchment, 5 small pieces of writing charcoal, a spool of wire, a spool of thin braided rope, a spring, a pulley, and a pouch containing 5 gp.

Izzy Freeleaf

Small humanoid (rock gnome), lawful neutral

Class Wizard 13
Background Trapsmith
Occupation Hireling
Armour Class 11 (*mage armor*)
Hit Points 45 (13d6)
Speed 25 ft.

STR	DEX	CON	INT	WIS	CHA
8 (-1)	13 (+1)	10 (+0)	20 (+5)	17 (+3)	13 (+1)

Saving Throws Int +10, Wis +8
Skills Arcana +10, Insight +8, Investigation +10, Perception +8
Tools thieves' tools, tinker's tools, trapmaker's tools
Senses darkvision 60 ft., passive Perception 18
Languages Common, Gnomish

Arcane Recovery (1/Day). When Izzy finishes a short rest, she can choose expended spell slots to recover. The spell slots can have a combined level that is equal to or less than 7, and none of the slots can be 6th level or higher.

Artificer's Lore. Whenever Izzy makes an Intelligence (History) check related to magic items, alchemical objects, or technological devices, she adds +15 to her roll.

Empowered Evocation. Izzy can add her Intelligence modifier (+5) to one damage roll of any wizard evocation spell she casts.

Gnome Cunning. Izzy has advantage on all Intelligence, Wisdom, and Charisma saving throws against magic.

Potent Cantrip. Izzy's damaging cantrips affect even creatures that avoid the brunt of the effect. When a creature succeeds on a saving throw against her cantrip, the creature takes half the cantrip's damage (if any) but suffers no additional effect from the cantrip.

Sculpt Spell. Izzy can create pockets of relative safety within the effects of her evocation spells. When she casts an evocation spell that affects other creatures that she can see, she can choose a number of them equal to 1 + the spell's level. The chosen creatures automatically succeed on their saving throws against the spell, and they take no damage if they would normally take half damage on a successful save.

Spellcasting. Izzy is a 13th-level spellcaster. Her spellcasting ability is Intelligence (spell save DC 18, +10 to hit with spell attacks). Izzy has the following wizard spells prepared:

- Cantrips (at will): *dancing lights, mage hand, mending, minor illusion, prestidigitation*
- 1st level (4 slots): *detect magic, mage armor, feather fall, floating disk*
- 2nd level (3 slots): *knock, levitate, locate object, shatter*
- 3rd level (3 slots): *dispel magic, gaseous form, lightning bolt*
- 4th level (3 slots): *arcane eye, dimension door, wall of fire*
- 5th level (2 slots): *cone of cold, passwall*
- 6th level (1 slot): *true seeing*
- 7th level (1 slot): *antimagic field*

Tinker. Using her tinker's tools, Izzy can spend 1 hour and 10 gp worth of materials to construct a Tiny clockwork device (AC 5, 1 hp). The device ceases to function after 24 hours (unless she spends 1 hour repairing it to keep the device functioning), or when she uses her action to dismantle it; at that time, she can reclaim the materials used to create it. She can have up to three such devices active at a time. When she creates a device, she chooses one of the following options:

- ***Clockwork Toy.*** This toy is a clockwork animal, monster, or person, such as a frog, mouse, bird, dragon, or soldier. When placed on the ground, the toy moves 5 feet across the ground on each of Izzy's turns in a random direction. It makes noises as appropriate to the creature it represents.
- ***Fire Starter.*** The device produces a miniature flame, which Izzy can use to light a candle, torch, or campfire. Using the device requires her action.
- ***Music Box.*** When opened, this music box plays a single song at a moderate volume. The box stops playing when it reaches the song's end, or when it is closed.

Actions

Dagger. *Melee or Ranged Weapon Attack:* +6 to hit, reach 5 ft. or range 20/60 ft., one target. *Hit:* 3 (1d4 + 1) piercing damage.

Overview

Izzy Freeleaf is a 29-year-old gnome wizard, and an expert when it comes to identifying and overcoming magical traps. She takes great pride in her unique set of skills, as well as her ability to use magic to simply bypass traps in clever ways. She is tall and slender (for a gnome), with a rosy pink complexion and silvery-white hair. She wears fine clothing and rarely gets her hands dirty.

Personality Traits

If Izzy gets dirty (literally or figuratively), then she has done a poor job. Izzy works smart, not hard.

Ideal

Izzy strives for perfection and the best possible outcomes in all aspects of her life.

Bond

Izzy does what she does because she loves the challenge and the feeling of accomplishment it gives her. The money is simply a necessity.

Flaw

When something goes wrong, Izzy immediately tries to assign blame, even if it is with herself. She has a difficult time letting go of failure.

Roleplaying Izzy

Izzy is a somewhat frantic gnome who is obsessive about cleanliness and efficiency. Despite the manner in which she works, her spellcasting and her work with traps is perfect almost every time. She holds herself accountable for any failures, often to her detriment.

"Yes! That's the ticket!"

Weapons, Armor & Items

Component pouch, spellbook (containing all the spells she has prepared, plus the following: *arcane eye*, *arcane lock*, *fabricate*, and *secret chest*), a set of tough, rugged clothing, a set of trapmaker's tools*, a small boot knife, string, a wooden hammer, box of 50 1-inch iron nails, a small envelope holding 15 hollow needles, a thimble, a round leather scroll case containing 10 pieces of parchment, 5 small pieces of writing charcoal, a spool of wire, a spool of thin braided rope, a spring, a pulley, and a pouch containing 5 gp. enhanced dungeoneer's pack

Max Rosewater

Medium humanoid (human), neutral

Class Rogue 5
Background Trapsmith
Occupation Hireling

Armour Class 15 (leather armor)
Hit Points 17 (5d8 - 5)
Speed 30 ft.

STR	DEX	CON	INT	WIS	CHA
11 (+0)	18 (+4)	9 (-1)	15 (+2)	14 (+2)	13 (+1)

Saving Throws Dex +7, Int +5
Skills Acrobatics +7, Deception +4, Investigation +5, Perception +5, Sleight of Hand +7, Stealth +7
Tools thieves' tools, trapmaker's tools
Senses passive Perception 15
Languages Common, Elvish

Cunning Action. Max can take a bonus action on each of his turns to take the Dash, Disengage, or Hide action.

Fast Hands. Max can use the bonus action granted by his Cunning Action to make a Sleight of Hand check, use his thieves' tools to disarm a trap or open a lock, or take the Use an Object action.

Sneak Attack (1/Turn). Max can deal an extra 10 (3d6) damage to one creature he hits with an attack with a finesse or ranged weapon, if he has advantage on the attack roll. He doesn't need advantage on the attack roll if another enemy of the target is within 5 ft. of it, that enemy isn't incapacitated, and he doesn't have disadvantage on the attack roll.

Second-Story Work. Climbing no longer costs Max extra movement and, when he makes a running jump, the distance he covers increases by 4 feet.

Thieves' Cant. During his rogue training, Max learned thieves' cant, a secret mix of dialect, jargon, and code that allows him to hide messages in seemingly normal conversation. Only another creature that knows thieves' cant understands such messages. It takes four times longer to convey such a message than it does to speak the same idea plainly.

In addition, Max understands a set of secret signs and symbols used to convey short, simple messages, such as whether an area is dangerous, in the territory of a thieves' guild, loot is nearby, the people in an area are easy marks, or whether they will provide a safe house for thieves on the run.

Actions

Dagger. *Melee or Ranged Weapon Attack:* +7 to hit, reach 5 ft. or range 20/60 ft., one target. *Hit:* 6 (1d4+4) piercing damage.

Shortsword. *Melee Weapon Attack:* +7 to hit, reach 5 ft., one target. *Hit:* 7 (1d6+4) piercing damage.

Shortbow. *Ranged Weapon Attack:* +7 to hit, 80/320 ft., one target. *Hit:* 7 (1d6+4) piercing damage.

Reactions

Uncanny Dodge. When an attacker that Max can see hits him with an attack, he can use his reaction to halve the attack's damage against him.

Overview

Max Rosewater is a 39-year-old human rogue with a focus on the detection, disarming and circumvention of non-magical traps. He's run into magical traps enough to know to look out for them, but he hasn't quite figured out good ways to deal with them. Though he may seem rough around the edges at first glance, he is actually quite the gentleman and highly respected in low places. He has a wiry build and wears his favorite leather armor which is tattered, but very comfortable.

Personality Traits

Max loves meeting new people and hearing about their lives. He's even got some tales of his own!

Ideal

Max is never too proud for anything. He'll work with anyone, so long as they do their part.

Bond

Max once failed in disarming a trap, which then got the entire team he was with killed. Max barely escaped, and has never fully been able to forgive himself.

Flaw

Max can be overly cautious, and sometimes take too long to do a thing. He gets irritated if he gets rushed.

Roleplaying Max

Max will take on almost any job he's offered. He is a sucker for tall tales and scintillating stories, and has plenty of his own to share. Despite this, he sometimes becomes melancholy while reflecting on his past. A tragedy killed many of his friends, and he holds himself to blame. This makes him extremely cautious while on the job.

"Steady now. Don't rush me..."

Weapons, Armor & Items

A set of tough, rugged clothing, a set of trapmaker's tools*, a small boot knife, string, a wooden hammer, box of 50 1-inch iron nails, a small envelope holding 15 hollow needles, a thimble, a round leather scroll case containing 10 pieces of parchment, 5 small pieces of writing charcoal, a spool of wire, a spool of thin braided rope, a spring, a pulley, and a pouch containing 5 gp.

Legal Appendix

Designation of Product Identity: The following items are hereby designated as Product Identity as provided in section 1(e) of the Open Game License: Any and all material or content that could be claimed as Product Identity pursuant to section 1(e), below, is hereby claimed as product identity, including but not limited to: 1. The name "Nord Games" as well as all logos and identifying marks of Nord Games, LLC, including but not limited to the Nord Games logo as well as the trade dress of Nord Games products; 2. The product name "Game Master's Toolbox," "Treacherous Traps," as well as any and all Nord Games product names referenced in the work; 3. All artwork, illustration, graphic design, maps, and cartography, including any text contained within such artwork, illustration, maps or cartography; 4. The proper names, personality, descriptions and/or motivations of all artifacts, characters, races, countries, geographic locations, plane or planes of existence, gods, deities, events, magic items, organizations and/or groups unique to this book, but not their stat blocks or other game mechanic descriptions (if any), and also excluding any such names when they are included in monster, spell or feat names. 5. Any other content previously designated as Product Identity is hereby designated as Product Identity and is used with permission and/or pursuant to license.

This printing is done under version 1.0a of the Open Game License, below.

OPEN GAME LICENSE Version 1.0a

Notice of Open Game Content: This product contains Open Game Content, as defined in the Open Game License, below. Open Game Content may only be Used under and in terms of the Open Game License.

Designation of Open Game Content: Subject to the Product Identity Designation herein, the following material is designated as Open Game Content. (1) all monster statistics, descriptions of special abilities, and sentences including game mechanics such as die rolls, probabilities, and/or other material required to be open game con-tent as part of the game rules, or previously released as Open Game Content, (2) all portions of spell descriptions that include rules-specific definitions of the effect of the spells, and all material previously released as Open Game Content, (3) all other descriptions of game-rule effects specifying die rolls or other mechanic features of the game, whether in traps, magic items, hazards, or anywhere else in the text, (4) all previously released Open Game Content, material required to be Open Game Content under the terms of the Open Game License, and public domain material anywhere in the text.

1. Definitions: (a)"Contributors" means the copyright and/or trademark owners who have contributed Open Game Content; (b)"Derivative Material" means copyrighted material including derivative works and translations (including into other computer languages), potation, modification, correction, addition, extension, upgrade, improvement, compilation, abridgment or other form in which an existing work may be recast, transformed or adapted; (c) "Distribute" means to reproduce, license, rent, lease, sell, broadcast, publicly display, transmit or otherwise distribute;(d)"Open Game Content" means the game mechanic and includes the methods, procedures, processes and routines to the extent such content does not embody the Product Identity and is an enhancement over the prior art and any additional content clearly identified as Open Game Content by the Contributor, and means any work covered by this License, including translations and derivative works under copyright law, but specifically excludes Product Identity. (e) "Product Identity" means product and product line names, logos and identifying marks including trade dress; artifacts; creatures characters; stories, storylines, plots, thematic elements, dialogue, incidents, language, artwork, symbols, designs, depictions, likenesses, formats, poses, concepts, themes and graphic, photographic and other visual or audio representations; names and descriptions of characters, spells, enchantments, personalities, teams, personas, likenesses and special abilities; places, locations, environments, creatures, equipment, magical or supernatural abilities or effects, logos, symbols, or graphic designs; and any other trademark or registered trademark clearly identified as Product identity by the owner of the Product Identity, and which specifically excludes the Open Game Content; (f) "Trademark" means the logos, names, mark, sign, motto, designs that are used by a Contributor to identify itself or its products or the associated products contributed to the Open Game License by the Contributor (g) "Use", "Used" or "Using" means to use, Distribute, copy, edit, format, modify, translate and otherwise create Derivative Material of Open Game Content. (h) "You" or "Your" means the licensee in terms of this agreement.

2. The License: This License applies to any Open Game Content that contains a notice indicating that the Open Game Content may only be Used under and in terms of this License. You must affix such a notice to any Open Game Content that you Use. No terms may be added to or subtracted from this License except as described by the License itself. No other terms or conditions may be applied to any Open Game Content distributed using this License.

3. Offer and Acceptance: By Using the Open Game Content You indicate Your acceptance of the terms of this License.

4. Grant and Consideration: In consideration for agreeing to use this License, the Contributors grant You a perpetual, worldwide, royalty-free, non-exclusive license with the exact terms of this License to Use, the Open Game Content.

5. Representation of Authority to Contribute: If You are contributing original material as Open Game Content, You represent that Your Contributions are Your original creation and/or You have sufficient rights to grant the rights conveyed by this License.

6. Notice of License Copyright: You must update the COPYRIGHT NOTICE portion of this License to include the exact text of the COPYRIGHT NOTICE of any Open Game Content You are copying, modifying or distributing, and You must add the title, the copyright date, and the copyright holder's name to the COPYRIGHT NOTICE of any original Open Game Content you Distribute.

7. Use of Product Identity: You agree not to Use any Product Identity, including as an indication as to compatibility, except as expressly licensed in another, independent Agreement with the owner of each element of that Product Identity. You agree not to indicate compatibility or co-adaptability with any Trademark or Registered Trademark in conjunction with a work containing Open Game Content except as expressly licensed in another, independent Agreement with the owner of such Trademark or Registered Trademark. The use of any Product Identity in Open Game Content does not constitute a challenge to the ownership of that Product Identity. The owner of any Product Identity used in Open Game Content shall retain all rights, title and interest in and to that Product Identity.

FSC
www.fsc.org
MIX
Paper from
responsible sources
FSC® C016890